Petticoat Spy

To Helen — a much loved
sister-in-law. Wish we could
spend more time with you
With love
Carol
Carol Warburton
'2017'

OTHER BOOKS AND AUDIO BOOKS
BY CAROL WARBURTON

Edge of Night

Before the Dawn

Eyes of a Stranger

Midnight Whispers

The Legend of Shannonderry

Whisper Hollow

Petticoat Spy

A NOVEL

CAROL WARBURTON

Covenant Communications, Inc.

Published by Covenant Communications, Inc.
American Fork, Utah

Printed in the United States of America
First Printing: January 2017

22 21 20 19 18 17   10 9 8 7 6 5 4 3 2 1

ISBN 978-1-52440-111-5

To my grandson, Cody Watterson,
who suggested many years ago that I write a novel
set during the Revolutionary War

Acknowledgments

PETTICOAT SPY WOULD NEVER HAVE come to be without family and friends who asked, "When is your next book coming out?" At last, it's here!

As always, to my fellow writers in the Fortnightly Group—Dorothy Keddington, Ka Hancock, and Lou Ann Anderson—our fortnightly sessions of reading, critiquing, and friendship always keep me on the right track and encourage me to better writing. And, Nancy Hopkins, you make our writing retreats to Oregon brim with warmth, laughter, and wonderful Oregon hazelnut bread.

To Samantha Millburn, editor extraordinaire—your encouragement and belief in me kept the words and pages coming. Thanks for your insightful suggestions and for all you have done to make *Petticoat Spy* a better novel.

And to Stephanie and Michelle at Covenant for your excellent marketing and cover efforts and suggestions.

Chapter One

MAYFIELD, MASSACHUSETTS
February–April 1775

IT WAS BEN, OUR HIRED boy, who put my nerves on edge that February morning, coming to meet me with a finger to his lips as I crossed the back-yard to feed the chickens.

"Look, Miss Abigail," he whispered, his blue eyes large as he pointed to the roof of the house. "Two crows a sittin' on your roof."

I looked up and saw the birds, their black feathers glistening in the winter sun.

Ben stepped closer, his voice still a whisper. "You know what they say 'bout crows: 'Two crows on the thatch . . . soon death lifts the latch.'"

"'Tis but an old saying, Ben, and nothing for you to worry about."

"You think so?" Ben didn't look convinced. "Jacob Warren said he saw two crows sittin' on the Miller's roof the day their baby died."

"The baby had been sick for weeks. I'm sure 'twas only happenstance."

"But Jacob says . . ." Ben's freckled face screwed up with worry. "Jacob says crows have a way a knowin' when death's comin'. 'Tis why I thought to warn you."

Seeing the twelve-year-old boy's concern made me want to pull him close. Fearing to embarrass him, though, I only smiled and held his gaze. "That was very thoughtful, Ben. But 'tis only superstition. We're both too wise to give it any thought, aren't we?"

"Yes'm." Looking like a great weight had been taken off his thin shoulders, Ben shouted and waved his arms at the crows. "Off with you," he cried and grinned when the birds took flight. "There," he said. Still grinning, he set off for the barn, his booted feet trampling the crusted snow, the ends of his dark woolen scarf fluttering.

I pulled my blue hooded cape closer about me to ward off the morning chill. Had it not been for the need to feed the chickens, I'd have stayed in the house where it was warm.

As I poured grain for the chickens, broke ice on the frozen water trough, and gathered eggs, my mind remained on what Ben had said about crows knowing when death was coming. There had been no crows on the roof ten months ago when my twin brother, Jonathan, had died. His death had wounded us all, our sorrow like a fresh gash whose pain still hadn't diminished. Some years before, death had also taken two of my little sisters. Now there was only ten-year-old Bethy and me, her nineteen-year-old sister.

"'Tis only superstition," I told myself, needing the reassurance as much as Ben. But the idea upset me, especially since Father had ridden to Cambridge and Boston almost a week ago and still hadn't returned.

When I finished with the chickens and returned to the kitchen, the heat from the large fireplace rushed like a warm quilt to envelop me. Rather than give in to the enticement to stay inside, I handed the egg basket to Jane, Ben's older sister who helped with the cooking and cleaning, and said I'd be back in a few minutes.

I crossed the snowy yard to the lane that led from our farm to the road into Mayfield. Week-old snow crunched beneath my boots as I walked up the tree-lined lane. Wrapping my red woolen scarf more tightly around my neck, I tried to ignore the cold creeping through my boots and heavy woolen stockings. Something larger than me pulled me at a steady pace along the lane where slender shadows from bare-branched maples laid delicate patterns across the snow. In another month, the snow would be melting, and I consoled myself with the thought as my breath rose in white puffs of vapor around me.

Glittering white beauty stretched in all directions, but Ben's words and my unease about Father made my mood somber. What was keeping him? He'd said he'd be back in three or four days. Today made six.

I didn't expect to see Father riding along the Mayfield road at such an early hour, but when I got there, I stared down the rutted snowy surface that ran in a winding course until it curved around the rise that marked the halfway mark to the village. "Where are you?" I whispered into the crisp air. "What's keeping you?"

Times were uneasy in Massachusetts as we embarked on the new year of 1775. In retaliation for the Sons of Liberty's dumping a shipload of tea into Boston Harbor to protest the tea tax, England's Parliament had passed the hated Intolerable Acts, which, in addition to closing Boston Harbor, had abolished self-government and allowed British troops to be quartered in colonial homes. Although our Continental Congress had sent a letter to England requesting the abolishment of the acts, Parliament and the King had ignored it.

Now voices clamored for the colonists to break with England. Flaring tempers sometimes brought men who'd once been friends to fisticuffs as they debated matters of English sovereignty and Colonial rights in taverns throughout New England.

Although Mayfield was some twenty miles from Boston, talk was heated here as well. Despite cries of treason from Tories and those loyal to the Crown, more than forty Mayfield men and older boys had signed their names on the roster of the Committee of Correspondence, my father among them. They now drilled weekly on the common with the militia. Minutemen, they called themselves—men ready to defend their freedom at a minute's notice.

Boston was a hotbed of Liberty Men bent on revolution, and their leaders—Sam Adams, Paul Revere, and Dr. Warren—were closely watched. Had more riots broken out? Was this why Father was late?

I was about to turn back when I heard the distant sound of hoofbeats. Shading my eyes from the sun, I discerned the outline of a horse and rider coming from the direction of the village.

"Father?" His name slipped from my mouth, for the rider wore a gray cloak like Father's, and the horse was chestnut like his horse, Jumper. Bundled with scarves against the cold and wearing a tri-corn hat, the man's features were difficult to discern. As he drew closer, I realized he wasn't Father, nor was he anyone familiar.

The rider slowed his mount and, turning, doffed his hat as he drew near. "Good day to ye, mistress."

I curtsied, noting that the man's brown hair, rather than powdered, was neatly pulled back and bound by a dark ribbon. He was also younger than I'd first supposed, perhaps in his mid- to late twenties.

His gaze as it traveled over me was admiring. Such was not unusual, for I had known for some years that men, both young and old, found pleasure in looking at me.

"My name is Gideon Whitlock, late from Boston. I was told at Hillam's Tavern where I lodged last night that I can find the home of Charles Carter not too far down this road."

"'Tis but another two miles . . . a white clapboard house set close to the road."

"I'm much obliged." Replacing his hat, he smiled, and his face, which I'd thought neither plain nor handsome, leaned on the side of handsome.

I stepped closer. "Please, sir, has there been new trouble in Boston? My father went there almost a week ago and hasn't yet returned."

Mr. Whitlock's face lost its smile. "There is always trouble in Boston. Who's to say what the rabble-rousers are up to?"

I lifted my chin. "My father is not a rabble-rouser but a man who believes that England lays too heavy a hand on the colonists. He's—"

"One of traitor Sam Adams's Liberty Boys, hey?" he cut in sharply. "Tell your father he'd best stay home where he belongs, not traipse around the county looking for trouble." He urged his horse past me. "Now, if you'll excuse me."

Taken aback, I stared after him in chagrin. Though this Gideon Whitlock claimed to have come from Boston, he obviously lacked the good breeding and manners for which Bostonians were noted. Since he'd asked directions to the home of Mr. Carter, an avowed Tory, he was a Tory as well.

"How rude," I said in a voice loud enough for him to hear. "But what can one expect from a Tory?"

Without slackening his horse's pace, the stranger looked back and doffed his hat a second time, his wide grin making the corners of his eyes crinkle with amusement.

Heat rose to my cheeks, and I turned so he couldn't see it. "Insolent man!" Still fuming, I started back down the lane, consoling myself that at least the arrogant Tory hadn't mentioned any new trouble in Boston. Since Father dearly loved to talk, he was probably spending time with friends in Boston and Cambridge. At least that was what I told myself as I gave the receding figure of Mr. Whitlock a dismissive frown.

Pique sent me down the lane at a brisk pace. Even so, the sight of my home, its windows glinting in the morning sun, made me pause. Despite Reverend Whipple's frequent sermons on the sin of pride, pride was exactly what I felt as I gazed at the two-storied, red-brick house. There were four windows facing east on each floor, with shutters painted a crisp white like the large double door of the entryway.

Our house had been built by Grandfather Stowell some fifty years before, but the farm, with barn and numerous outbuildings, had been in the Stowell family since the late sixteen hundreds. An orchard with over twenty trees sat to the north of the barn, and three hundred acres of fields and pasture stretched all the way to Hobb's Woods. Like Father, Stowell farm was well known in Middlesex County, and though I didn't think myself better than others, I was proud I bore the Stowell name.

"Abigail! Where are you?"

The sound of Mother's voice sent me hurrying to the back of the house, where Ben carried filled milk pails from the barn. Mercy! Had I been gone so long?

Mother stood by the kitchen doorway, a heavy woolen shawl around her shoulders. Her worried face was framed by a white cap and fringes of dark hair. "Where have you been at such an early hour?"

Not wanting her to know of my concern for Father, my answer was evasive. "I thought to walk up the lane."

Mother's look was knowing. "You needn't try to hide your worry. Yesterday I walked up to the road to look for him too."

"There was no sign of him this morning either," I said. "But I did meet a stranger riding from the village."

Mother's brows lifted. "Stranger? What is a stranger doing in Mayfield in the dead of winter?"

"He called himself Gideon Whitlock, and he asked directions to Mr. Carter's farm."

Mother's mouth tightened. "Likely a Tory."

"A rude Tory," I corrected indignantly. "When I asked for news of Boston, he called Sam Adams's followers a bunch of rabble-rousers . . . Father included . . . and said Father should stay home instead of traipsing around looking for trouble."

"Nathan Stowell is not a rabble-rouser." Her voice was as indignant as mine. "There's not a better man in all of Middlesex County."

"In all of Massachusetts, but before I could tell him, he rode away."

"Well, 'tisn't likely you'll ever see him again. Still, it does seem peculiar that someone from Boston should be looking for Charles Carter. I think 'twould be wise to tell your father about it when he returns. He'll know what to make of it." Sighing, she turned back to the house. "How I wish he'd hurry back."

Chapter Two

FATHER RETURNED LATE THAT AFTERNOON, riding Jumper down the lane, hat pulled low and body hunched against the north wind. From the kitchen window, I watched him dismount as Ben rushed out of the barn and led Jumper inside.

"'Tis Father," I cried.

Mother's relief mirrored mine as she pushed her chair away from the table. Bethy hurried and pulled her cloak from the peg by the kitchen door before Mother could say a word. We watched from the opened door, smiling as Bethy threw her arms around Father's waist. He pulled her to him before hurrying her out of the wind and into the house, his eyes alight when he saw Mother and me in the doorway.

"Hurry," Mother said. "The wind is blowing something fierce."

"Snow's on the way," Father predicted as he took off his heavy woolen cloak and unwound the scarves from his neck and lower face. "I've missed you," he told Mother when she took his cloak and hung it on its peg. "I've missed all of you."

I smiled as I took his hat and scarves. "We began to worry when you took so long."

Father moved to the fireplace and spread his large hands to the flames. "I feared 'twould be the case when I learned that the man I went to see in Boston had gone north to Salem on business. I had to wait two days for his return."

Mother gave him a fond look. "And no doubt you filled those extra days talking politics instead of pacing the floor of your room."

Father's broad features creased into a smile. "You know me well, Elizabeth. Better than I know myself." The light from the fire sparked his blond hair with highlights when he bent to move an errant log closer to the flames.

Without being asked, Jane took a cloth and lifted the tankard of cider warming on the hob of the fireplace. "Would ye like some hot cider, Master Stowell?"

Before answering, Father turned to warm his backside. "Thank you, Jane. Such should help drive some of the cold from my bones."

Dropping a quick curtsey, Jane fetched a beaker from the cupboard and poured out a generous amount of steaming cider.

Father wrapped his long fingers around the beaker to let the heat penetrate his hands. Giving a contented sigh, he said, "'Tis nothing better than hot cider, a warm fire, and a man's family gathered around him." His gaze traveled over each of us, even Jane, who was so often in the house that I think she sometimes considered herself one of the family.

Although he smiled, I caught a glimpse of pain in his eyes, as if he remembered that the number of his children had shrunk from five to two.

Father lowered his blue eyes and took a cautious sip of the steaming cider. His blue eyes and blond hair had been bequeathed to me, but my features were delicate, my build slender like Mother's.

"Joseph Lind asked after you and bade me give you his best regards," he said to Mother.

She looked up from cutting a thick slice of bread. "The Linds have always been most cordial," she said. "What of his wife, Caroline? Did you visit with her as well?"

"She is unwell, and I wasn't able to see her."

Mother looked up in concern. "Unwell?"

"That's what Joseph told me."

Though I was fond of the Linds, especially Mistress Lind, whom I affectionately called Aunt Caroline, I was eager for news of political unrest. "What of Boston itself?"

Father frowned. "Like a powder keg needing but a spark to explode into war against England. 'Tisn't just Sam Adams's Liberty Boys who prowl the streets looking to cause trouble. Since the blockade of the harbor, half the men from the wharves are out of work, and Gage's soldiers are everywhere."

Mother frowned and set bread and cheese on a plate.

Taking the cider over to the scrubbed oak table, Father pulled out a chair and sat down.

"How was the provincial congress meeting in Cambridge?" I asked. "Did you get there in time to hear the opening speeches?"

"I did. There was much talk and debate, but in the end, John Hancock and Joseph Warren were named to begin defensive preparations for a state of war."

My heart gave a start, and Mother closed her eyes as if in prayer. "I've prayed for weeks that a solution could be found that didn't include war. Is there no other way, Nathan?"

Father covered her hand with his. "Our spies say General Gage has received correspondence from the King commanding him to put down any sign of rebellion. They mean to make a show of force, and we must be prepared to resist it." He looked long at Mother. "War is inevitable . . . Whether next month or next summer, it will come."

"And not a moment too soon," I said. "What right has Gage and his army to march throughout the countryside and tell us what to do?"

"Abigail!" Mother's voice was indignant. "Have you stopped to think what war will bring? The killing and suffering?"

"If 'tis the price we must pay for freedom, we should do it gladly. If Jonathan were alive, I know he'd say the same. He'd be one of the first to challenge the redcoats. Jon would . . ." Emotion closed my throat and sent me rushing from the kitchen, wiping tears as I climbed the back stairs, aware of the heavy silence I'd left behind. Instead of going to my room, I stopped at Jonathan's bedroom door.

I took a deep breath and girded myself before I slowly turned the knob. The inside shutters were tightly closed. Resolutely crossing the dim room, I opened them. Instead of his room being stripped bare of furnishings, Mother had chosen to leave it as if Jon would at any moment return—chairs by the fireplace, his writing desk, the ewer and basin. Next to his bed was a table with a brace of candles and his favorite book. In the months since his death, I'd only once seen Mother emerge from his room, her face ravaged and red-splotched from crying. I didn't think Father or Bethy had ever opened his door.

Leaving the window, I went to the bedside table and picked up the leather-bound copy of *The Odyssey.* It was my favorite book too. Being so alike, I knew without doubt that had Jonathan been alive today, he would have ridden into any upcoming battles alongside Father and the Mayfield militia.

Fresh tears stung my eyes, and I held his book more closely." Oh, Jon," I whispered. "If only you were still here."

A slight noise made me catch my breath and turn, half expecting to see my brother's apparition blending with the shadows in the corner of the room. Instead I saw Father, his large frame filling the doorway, his face pained like a man who'd received a hard blow to the stomach.

I took a ragged breath and wiped my tears with the palm of my hand. Neither of us spoke, the agony on his face seeming to join hands with the ache in my heart. I watched while his gaze made a painful journey around the room, pausing at long last at the bed where he and Prudence Blood had fought unsuccessfully to save his son's life.

I spoke into the silence, and though my voice still trembled from tears, my shoulders were resolute. "No matter what Mother said, had I been born a man instead of a woman, I would ride with you when you go to challenge Gage's redcoats."

"I know you would. Your courage is like your brother's." He nodded again. "Even so, I thank my Maker every day that you are who you are and that you will stay safely behind with your mother and sister."

Fearing I'd cry again, I strove for lightness. "You thank God for a daughter who sometimes speaks her mind in unladylike fashion?"

Father's lips lifted. "I do. How could I expect otherwise from a young woman of intellect and spirit?"

"Even a daughter who has refused a proposal of marriage and leaves you with a spinster on your hands?" I said, pressing further, whether to put the room's sorrow more firmly into the corners or to draw from Father an acknowledgement that it wasn't just Jonathan he loved.

"Even then," Father answered. "I hope you know I never want you to feel you must marry just to be addressed as Goodwife. William Graff, though from a good family, is too full of himself and lacks brains." Nodding, Father smiled. "I have faith you will find someone who suits you, Abigail, perhaps even someone you will love as dearly as I love your mother." He gave me a long, steady look, one that bespoke his love for his wife as well as for me. Then, letting me know he'd said all he intended to say, he ended with, "Come; your mother has need of you in the kitchen."

Returning his nod, I left Jonathan's room, heard the soft click of the door as Father closed it behind me, and felt his steadying presence as he followed me down the stairs.

★

On weekdays, we supped at the oak table in the kitchen, serving ourselves as dishes of steaming food were passed from person to person. But on the

Sabbath and special days, rather than using our weekday dishes and plain-ware, we ate in the dining room, where the linen cloth Mother had woven as a bride was spread the length of the long table, with delicate blue-patterned china and the Stowell family silver set at each place. Since Father was safely home, Mother deemed it a special occasion.

Jane waited on us, her ginger-colored hair framed by her white cap as she removed our empty soup bowls and replaced them with platters and bowls filled with Mother's donkers, potatoes, parsnips, and boiled pudding. Mother took great pride in her donkers. She'd taught me to make them, but mine never turned out as light and flaky as hers. The fact was, I preferred to spend my time reading or growing herbs and flowers in the kitchen garden.

We made no mention of rebellion or war. Instead, Mother remarked on how well Bethy was doing with her lessons. Bethy's fair cheeks flushed, and Father looked at her with pride before saying he hoped the roan mare wouldn't foal until the weather warmed. "'Tis certain we'll have several inches of snow by morning," he concluded.

Slices of apple pie finished the meal, the crust as light and flaky as that of the donkers. While Jane cleared the table and washed up, we retired to the sitting room for the evening—Mother and I to sew and Bethy to knit.

A fire had been lit an hour before to ward off the cold, and the cheery crackling flames highlighted the rich oak of my chair set close to the fire-place with Mother's. It was my favorite room, one my Grandmother Stowell had papered and furnished with sofas and tables tastefully arranged around the green-papered room. Carved white molding near the ceiling and at chair height around the walls broke up the intense green of the brocaded paper, which, like most things in the colonies, had been imported from England with a heavy duty paid as it had entered a port.

My sewing basket sat on the floor next to my chair. I grabbed the pink skirt I was mending, holding it up to catch the best light from the flick-ering candles. Father went to the mantel and took down his pipe. It was an elaborately carved Dutch pipe given to him some years before by his friend Joseph Lind.

The thought of impending war made me try to imprint the scene of our home on my mind—the warmth of the fire and Mother's head bent over the shirt she sewed for Father, Bethy's dark brows furrowed as she turned the heel on the stocking she knitted, Father leaning to retrieve a coal from the fire. I watched from my chair, my fingers still on my mending as my eyes drank in the sight of those I loved.

Despite our efforts to act otherwise, Father's news had infused the room with tension. The lines around Mother's mouth were more pronounced than they'd been that morning, and Bethy shot furtive glances at Father as if to reassure herself of his solid presence.

The words I spoke to Father seemed to heighten the tension. "I met a man riding along the Mayfield road this morning. He said he was from Boston and asked directions to Charles Carter's farm."

"Indeed," Father said, his attention still taken with finding a coal for his pipe.

I was disappointed at his lack of interest. Still, I persisted. "When I asked for news of Boston and told him you were visiting there, he called you a rabble-rouser, along with Sam Adams and his Liberty Boys."

Father gave an amused chuckle. "I've been called much worse in my day. Since the man asked directions to Carter's farm, he's likely a Tory and can't tell his right foot from his left." He dropped a coal into the bowl of the pipe and drew on it until it glowed enough to please him. Only then did he look at me. "Did he give you his name?"

"He said 'twas Gideon Whitlock, but who's to say if he spoke the truth. He was rude, and I was glad to see the last of him."

Something flicked in Father's blue eyes, a look that made me want to ask if he knew or had heard of the man.

Before I could question him, Mother spoke. "I was quick to tell Abigail that rather than a rabble-rouser there is no better man in all of Middlesex County."

Father gave her a fond smile. "I put far greater store in your good opinion than that of a stranger."

An hour later, Bethy and I climbed the stairs to our bedroom. It was a front-facing room across the wide landing from my parents' room. My father's sister had chosen the patterned blue wallpaper. Twenty years had passed since she'd married and moved away, but thanks to Mother's careful housewifery, the room's blue window coverings and bed hanging were still in good repair.

The entire house glowed from Mother's loving care. The kitchen, dining room, sitting room, and Father's study made up the first floor, while three bedrooms and a schoolroom filled the second.

Tonight, snow-laden wind gusted against the windows, and the resulting chill sent Bethy and me into bed and under the covers in a trice. As I closed my eyes, instead of the scene of our family gathered around the fire in the sitting room, I saw images of Father and the Mayfield's militia riding off to fight General Gage and his vast army of redcoats.

★

Despite the heavy snow on Friday, we attended church on the Sabbath. Ben's older brother, Israel, drove our carriage while his father, Thomas, our hired man, followed in the cart with his wife, Hester, and Ben and Jane. The Boatricks were bundled against the cold, and a metal box filled with coals sat by their feet to help ward off the bite of the morning air. I was grateful for our own foot box that Father would carry into church to warm our feet during the long Sabbath sermon.

Although Mayfield was but a village, it boasted two taverns and two churches, each segregated by the political leaning of those who entered its doors. Hillam's Tavern and the red-brick Anglican Church were frequented by Tories and those loyal to the crown, while Miller's Tavern and the white clapboard Congregationalist Church drew from free thinkers and those of a more rebellious nature.

Our family attended the Congregationalist Church, where Reverend Whipple preached his stirring sermons that oft were as much political as they were against the lusts and sins of men.

Reverend Whipple stood at the door to greet his followers. After exchanging a few words with him, Father escorted Mother into the church to our pew near the middle of the chapel. In not many minutes, the white steeple church was completely filled, and those who came last were forced to stand at the back.

As the clock chimed ten, Reverend Whipple mounted the steps to his lectern and, after invoking the Lord's blessing upon us, began to preach. The goodly man was tall and plain like his church, and the deep hollows in his cheeks gave the impression he spent more time ministering to his flock than eating.

I settled myself into his sermon, the hood of my blue cape draped across my shoulders, my quilted petticoat spread wide to let in as much heat as possible from the warming box.

As was often the case, Reverend Whipple's sermon dealt with pride, a subject that always made me uncomfortable. In addition to the color of my hair, Father had passed on a generous slice of Stowell pride, one I prayed daily to conquer.

Today I wasn't in a penitent mood, and instead of listening to the preaching, I let my mind wander to Father's prediction that war was imminent. I looked over the congregation, counting those who were members of the militia. In the event of war, Reverend Whipple's congregation would be reduced to mostly women and children.

It was some minutes before I realized the reverend had changed the focus of his sermon. Instead of lecturing his followers, he was busily painting an unflattering picture of King George and General Gage, whose actions fair reeked with pride. Since the sin was aimed at someone other than me, I nodded in agreement, as did the majority of the congregation.

Following my nod, I had the uncomfortable sensation that someone was watching me. Since my hair had a tendency to pull loose from its pins, I surreptitiously ran my fingers along the edges of my ruffled cap and found that all was neat and tidy. I had no sooner turned my attention back to the sermon than the sensation came again. Certain it was William Graff, the man whose proposal I'd refused, my mouth tightened. Why did he continue to act as if he were my suitor? Had he no brains?

I lifted my chin and tried to concentrate on the sermon.

"How can a king who's never set foot on our soil think to know our needs better than we?" Reverend Whipple's loud voice thundered. "'Tis pride . . . sheer pride!"

And 'tis prideful for William to think he can gain my favor by staring at me in meeting, I thought indignantly.

I glanced back, intending to give him a quelling look, but rather than meeting his lovesick eyes, I encountered the amused gaze of Gideon Whitlock. I was so taken aback that I gaped and looked longer than was needful.

Heat warmed my cheeks, and I jerked my head back so quickly Bethy looked at me in surprise. Why was Mr. Whitlock still in Mayfield? And what was the prideful man doing in our unpretentious church? My mind was in such a state that I couldn't think of anything except the arrogant Tory. And why that bothered me, I couldn't say.

Tripping through my indignation was the image of his masculine features and the amusement in his eyes as he'd given a tiny nod from his place across the aisle and behind me. I was convinced that if I should be so foolish as to look back again, I would encounter his amusement still. Odious man! Then, as if I had no will, I did exactly that. Darting a look over my shoulder, I again encountered Gideon Whitlock's gaze. Rather than amusement, I read admiration in his green eyes—eyes the very hue of my favorite color!

It took me some time to put my jumbled thoughts back in order and to realize that the man who'd caused the jumble was sitting next to Mr. Carter.

Though I knew he and his family were the only Tories to still attend our church, I was also aware that he'd twice walked out when Reverend Whipple's enthusiasm had caused him to speak critically of the Crown. I wondered why he continued to attend and why he and Gideon Whitlock hadn't walked out today.

A chilling thought shot through my muddled brain. Were the two men gathering evidence of the reverend's seditious words? Had the King's new directive to put an end to all talk and show of rebellion prompted Gideon Whitlock's visit? Just as frightening, were there others in the congregation of like thoughts—others listening to the reverend and not agreeing?

I quickly looked at those sitting around me, looking for signs of disapproval. The sight of nodding heads and expressions warm with approval brought relief.

It seemed an eternity before the sermon ended and we had sung a hymn and prayed. Though I knew only a fool would try to arrest Reverend Whipple with his loyal congregation present, I nonetheless shot a quick glance at Gideon Whitlock as I followed Father from the church. Rather than watching me, his attention was engaged with Mr. Carter's eldest daughter, Sarah. I was also aware of his broad-shouldered frame and that he stood several inches above that of his host. If Mr. Whitlock found Sarah—who had no chin and constantly squinted—attractive, his taste was as lacking as his manners.

A cold wind prevented us from lingering outside the church to talk. Pulling up my lined hood, I quickly walked after my parents, the metal pattens I wore over my slippers to protect them from the snow and ice crunching with each step. Mother sighed with relief when she climbed out of the cold and into the carriage.

"If Reverend Whipple hadn't talked so long, the coals would still be warm in the foot box," Bethy complained. When Mother frowned, she hastily added, "I enjoyed his sermon, especially when he called King George a proud peacock."

As Israel spoke to the horses and the carriage moved away from the church, I said to Father, "I'm surprised Mr. Carter didn't walk out of church like he did a fortnight ago." As I spoke, I saw the Carter family and Mr. Whitlock on their way to their carriage. "Look, Father, 'tis the man I told you about . . . Gideon Whitlock."

Father turned his head to look. Seeming to feel our gaze, Mr. Whitlock paused and lifted his tri-corn hat, his expression solemn instead of amused as his eyes briefly met Father's. His nod and demeanor were those of a perfect Boston gentleman as his gaze shifted to me. His actions surprised me, as did those of Father, who touched his hat and nodded back.

"Do you nod to a Tory?" I exclaimed indignantly.

"I nod to all who are courteous enough to nod to me," Father replied, his words edged with censure.

Fearing a lecture, I quickly apologized. "'Tis not my place to criticize your actions."

"No." Father's reply was firm like the set of his jaw. Though he might have allowed me to be tutored with Jonathan and hadn't pressured me to marry, he didn't take well to having his actions questioned.

I pretended interest in the few homes and shops we passed and didn't speak until I thought it safe. "I'm puzzled why Mr. Carter continues to attend our church when he has twice walked out during the reverend's sermons. Why do you think he still comes?"

"I believe he attends out of gratitude for Reverend Whipple's help some years ago," Father replied. "Despite Mr. Carter's lack of sense in matters of politics, he is not one to easily forget a kindness."

"But what if . . ." I paused to consider my words. "What if General Gage has called on loyal Tories to report any talk of sedition and criticism of the King? What if Mr. Carter brought this Gideon Whitlock to church today so he can report to General Gage what the reverend said?"

The crunch of the carriage wheels rolling and bumping over the rutted snow was the only sound to follow my question.

"Surely not," Mother said after a moment. "Though Charles Carter is a Tory, he is still a good man," She turned to Father. "Is that not so, Mr. Stowell?"

Father nodded. "I can't see him doing such to the man whose words and actions saved Carter's farm from the grasping, dishonest hands of a land speculator."

"But what of Mr. Whitlock, who has no such loyalties? Why didn't he walk out?"

Father shook his head. "That I don't know, nor can I speak for Gideon Whitlock's motives, but I shall certainly keep him in mind now that I've seen him." He took Mother's gloved hand and looked at Bethy and me. "None of you, however, are to give the man any more thought. You are not to worry either. For now, you must learn to take each day as it comes and enjoy it as much as you can."

Despite Father's words, I continued to think about Gideon Whitlock. I wondered about him all through the Sabbath meal, which had been prepared the day before. Had he business to transact with Mr. Carter? Perhaps on the Carters' last visit to Boston, Sarah's mincing ways had beguiled Mr. Whitlock so much that he'd come to court her—Sarah, whose ways had always been a trial to me.

"You're unusually quiet," Father observed as he took a second helping of cold meat.

"I'm but thinking of Reverend Whipple's sermon on pride. 'Tisn't just the King and General Gage who possess it. Gideon Whitlock is guilty of it as well."

"What makes you to think so when you scarcely know him?"

"His manner when he spoke to me on Friday was both arrogant and rude. And I saw—" I stopped, not wanting Father to know I'd been aware of Mr. Whitlock throughout much of the meeting. "I only know I neither like nor trust him," I concluded.

Father's lips trembled as if to suppress a smile. "Then 'tis fortunate Mr. Whitlock only comes to Mayfield to visit, not to reside."

Father took another bite of meat and complimented Mother on her cooking while I set myself to thinking of something less unsettling than Gideon Whitlock.

Chapter Three

On Thursday, as we ate our midday meal, Father said he meant to ride into Mayfield to attend the Committee of Correspondence meeting. "Since the militia is training afterward, 'twill likely be dark before Thomas and Israel and I return."

Having grown used to his trips to the village for meetings and militia drills, Mother nodded. Our hired man, Thomas Boatrick, and his son Israel and over forty other men and older boys attended as well. It galled Ben greatly to be left behind with the women. Truth be told, it galled me that I was left behind too.

"I noticed the sugar bin is almost empty," I said in a casual voice. "If war comes"—just saying the words tightened my stomach—"it might be wise to have extra on hand." I looked innocently at Mother. "Ben and I could follow Father in the cart to buy sugar and be back before dark."

"Since the blockade of the harbor, sugar is growing scarce," Father said. "There might be other things to buy and keep on hand."

Mother thought for a moment. "I'm running low on nutmeg, and we definitely need to buy more tea."

For a second, Father looked thunderstruck. "I trust you are jesting, Goodwife. No tea or goods imported from England are to cross the Stowell threshold."

Mother's eyes twinkled. She did enjoy teasing Father. "My feelings are in agreement with yours, Mr. Stowell. Just the same, I do grow tired of the mint and chamomile we drink in place of good English tea."

Father's expression softened. "I miss my cup of tea too, but chamomile and mint it will be until the King and Parliament cease to tax us without allowing representation or voice in the matter." His mouth turned stubborn like it always did when he spoke of the King. "Sugar and nutmeg are all you need?"

Mother nodded and turned her attention to me. "You must take an extra quilt and the warming box with you."

A short time later, Ben and I climbed into the cart to follow the men up the lane. Israel turned and gave a cheeky wave, clearly pleased that he was old enough to ride with the men. Ben snapped the reins at Dolly and gave me a quick smile. Though he might envy his brother, he was still glad to be going to the village.

The weather had moderated since the Sabbath. Even so, the mushy snow and rutted road made it impossible to keep up with the men.

"After we finish at the store, can we go to the common and watch the militia drill?" Ben asked.

I pretended to ponder the question, for I enjoyed teasing as much as Mother. "Mother asked me to leave a recipe with Goodwife Rawson after we finish at the store and . . ." I paused and looked into Ben's doleful blue eyes. "After that, we shall both stroll over to the common to watch the militia."

Ben grinned. "I shoulda known you was just teasin'. You and Jonathan was—" His voice broke, and he shot me an apologetic look. "Sorry," he whispered. Quickly changing the subject, he said, "By now, the men should be to the village."

"One day you'll be able to go with your father instead of riding in the cart with a woman."

"'Tisn't that, Mistress Abigail, for I like you just fine. It's just . . ."

"I don't like being left behind either. But we can still have a good time."

For the rest of the trip, we hummed and sang, though we lowered our voices when we reached the outskirts of Mayfield so as not to invite censure as we passed the home of elderly Goody Parker.

Since committee meetings ran long, with everyone wanting to express an opinion, there was ample time to buy the sugar and nutmeg—both items smuggled in from the West Indies by enterprising seamen. Goodwife Morris was minding the store while her husband was at the meeting. The heavyset woman slowly measured out the sugar and spice, her movements punctuated by numerous questions. Aware of Ben's restlessness, I sent him on to the common as soon as we left the store.

Once I had delivered the recipe, I set out for the common too, stepping carefully through the slushy snow in my pattens. As I neared the village forge, I became aware of two men arguing loudly.

"I ain't fer lettin' no stranger tell me what I can and can't say 'bout the King and the rascals in Parliament . . . nor say not to drill with the militia," elderly Matthew Giles shouted.

"I don't care if you fought in the seven-year war or in a dozen wars, you're still subject to the King of England," a loud voice retorted.

Looking, I saw Mr. Giles shake his cane at a tall, well-built man. I immediately recognized the proud tilt of his head. My temper rose. How dare the Tory speak like that to a man as brave and sweet as Mr. Giles!

Without thinking, I hurried toward them, my long skirt and cape tangling with my pattens, my indignation rising with each step. Their angry voices drowned out my approach.

"I won't bow to a king who puts a hand in my pocket for taxes while the other shakes a finger at my nose and tells me when to breathe!" Mr. Giles's cane was perilously close to Mr. Whitlock's nose.

"He's your king. You're his subject!" the Tory responded hotly. "Can't you get that through your thick head? He's your king!"

"Only God is my king!" Matthew yelled, swinging his cane.

In a quick movement, Mr. Whitlock snatched the stick from Mr. Giles's hand and made as if to turn it on him.

"Stop!" I cried. "Stop this minute!"

Both men turned in surprise as I moved between them, Gideon Whitlock holding the cane high, Matthew Giles staring at me with a dumfounded expression.

Before either could speak, I turned on the Tory. "What kind of man are you to hit someone half your size?" I demanded.

Though his breathing was quick, Mr. Whitlock's voice was calm. "I had no intention—"

"I saw what happened, and I heard what you said!" Anger rose hot in my chest. "Mr. Giles suffered a serious injury while defending us from the French and Indians, and now you come here . . . a stranger . . . and presume to tell him what he can and cannot do?"

I was vaguely aware that a crowd had gathered, but I paid them no heed. Nor did I wonder how attraction had somehow attached itself to my anger. Instead of my heated words making Mr. Whitlock angry or ashamed, something very like amusement shone in his eyes.

Frustrated, I hurried on. "Furthermore, you should know that—" The weight of a heavy hand on my shoulder brought my angry words to a halt.

"You have said quite enough, Abigail." Father's voice was tight with suppressed anger, and his hand on my shoulder squeezed hard like he wanted to shake me.

"He was going to hit Mr. Giles and—" My anger shrank at the sight of Father's stern expression.

"Mr. Giles is capable of speaking for himself . . . as is Mr. Whitlock," Father said, his blue eyes as cold as his voice. "Find Ben, and go home at once."

I knew better than to argue when Father spoke in that tone. Nonetheless, I took time to look at Mr. Giles to reassure myself he was all right. His weathered face was still flushed with anger and his hat slightly askew, but instead of meeting my eyes, he kept his gaze squarely on his adversary.

I gave Mr. Whitlock a parting look that failed to elicit anything more than the lift of his brows. Father stood at his side, a stern expression on his face. Since Ben was part of the crowd, it didn't take me long to find him.

Though his face was bright with excitement, such wasn't the case with many of the others. Some avoided my gaze, and others, especially the women, looked at me with disapproval.

Shame replaced anger as I realized my actions would be common knowledge by nightfall. *When are you going to learn to guard your tongue and think before you rush in?* It wasn't the first time and probably not the last time I would ask myself that question. *When, Abigail? When?*

As we left the crowd, Ben looked up at me with questions shining in his eyes, but his regard for me was such that he didn't voice them until we were in the cart and had left the village.

"What happened, Mistress Abigail? Folks was saying old Mr. Giles and that man was 'bout to fight."

"A very rude man," I corrected, "who grabbed Mr. Giles's cane and was about to hit him."

Ben's eyes grew large. "Truly?"

"Truly," I repeated; yet as I spoke, I wondered if Mr. Whitlock had only held the stick high so Matthew Giles couldn't reach it. Even so, the Tory shouldn't have goaded him.

"The way you tore into him was somethin'," Ben said in admiration.

Instead of pleasing me, his words only made me feel worse. Had I mistaken Mr. Whitlock's intentions? No matter how many times I tried to put the thought aside, it stayed. "Please, I don't wish to talk about it."

"Yes'm." His voice held disappointment, and I was aware of the questioning glances he gave me on the very long ride home.

"You mad at me or somethin'?" Ben asked when he stopped Dolly at the barn and helped me out of the cart.

"No. I'm only mad at the Tory." *And yourself. Because of your foolish interference, Ben didn't get to watch the militia drill.* "It was Gideon Whitlock's fault," I rationalized, and I entered the house with a scowl instead of a smile on my face.

I dreaded Father's return, knowing that despite my age of nearly twenty years, he would feel it his duty to lecture me on my conduct in the village. Didn't I live under his roof and bear the Stowell name? Weren't the actions of a man's family a reflection on himself? If he couldn't govern those of his own household, how could he be expected to regulate anything else?

Mother questioned me almost at once. "What's wrong, Abby?"

Not wanting to have to explain twice, I shook my head and concentrated on refilling the sugar bin. "If I may, I'd rather wait until Father returns to tell you."

Mother sighed. If the problem involved Father, it was serious. When he entered the kitchen an hour later, Mother's greeting was subdued, and Bethy and I said nothing. Instead, we each dished up our hot soup.

Father usually had much to recount after a trip into Mayfield, but tonight, other than saying grace, he made no attempt at conversation. Following his example, we ate in silence, the clink of plainware on dishes filling the uncomfortable silence at the table. As the minutes passed, I grew more unsettled.

I took a deep breath. "I apologize for my conduct today, Father. But old Mr.—"

He held up his hand. "I don't wish to have my digestion upset by speaking of this now. I will expect you in my study after you've washed the dishes." His tone was even rather than angry, but his clipped delivery said it had taken effort.

"Yes, sir." My reply came as even as his, and I thanked providence that I wasn't a woman easily provoked to tears. Pride saw me through the rest of dinner and washing up.

"Go," Mother finally said. "Get whatever is wrong over and done with so we can return to normal."

I untied my apron and hung it on a peg. Neither Mother nor Bethy spoke again, but I saw concern in their eyes.

My slippers made little noise as I walked to Father's study. My heart beat quickly as I knocked on the closed door.

Father immediately opened it, the act telling me that instead of sitting at his desk, he'd been pacing the floor or staring into the kindled fire.

Neither of us spoke as he crossed the room to his desk.

"Sit down, daughter." He indicated the chair that usually sat next to the fire but was now placed squarely across the desk from him.

I did as he said, my head high, my fingers unclasped and resting lady-like on the folds of my quilted petticoat.

Father studied me for a long moment, his expression solemn and his blue eyes on mine. Time stretched so long, the paneled walls with their shelves of books seemed to fade until there was only Father and me.

"I don't think I need to say that I'm disappointed in your conduct and the scene you caused in the village."

"No, sir." My hands moved uncomfortably in my lap as he continued to hold my gaze.

"I realize that what happened today is partially my fault."

I blinked in surprise, even as I noticed that the lines on his face had deepened in the past weeks.

"I have been too lenient with you . . . allowing you to share in Jonathan's studies and to speak your mind more freely at home than a woman should." His hands shifted on his desk. "I took risk, but I felt it unjust to deny your quick mind the opportunity to learn and grow."

"An act for which I daily thank you and God," I said quickly.

Father acted as if I hadn't spoken. "Had you learned to school your tongue in public, perhaps no great harm would have come of it, but after today—" He shook his head.

"I never meant to cause a scene or embarrass you," I said, "but when I saw Mr. Whitlock bullying Mr. Giles, I couldn't let it go unanswered."

"Did you not stop to think that Matthew Giles might not wish to have you interfere? That he's capable of taking care of himself?"

"I didn't interfere," I protested.

"Didn't you?"

The flush to Father's cheeks told me only tight control kept him from losing his temper. "Did he invite you into the conversation? Did he ask for your help?"

"No . . . but he . . ." The realization of what I'd done made me stop.

"Matthew Giles may be old and crippled, but he doesn't welcome a woman who thinks him so feeble she must come to his defense."

Sickness and shame gathered in my stomach. How I must have hurt the dear man. "I . . . I didn't think," I stammered.

"You didn't take time to think," Father countered. "Your penchant to speak before you think has caused problems in the past but never in public."

Tears threatened, and my mouth trembled. "I thought only to help. I'm truly sorry."

"'Tis to Matthew Giles you owe your apology."

Pride warred with contrition as I nodded. "'Twas the Tory's fault. If he hadn't goaded Mr. Giles—"

"They were arguing politics as men often do," Father interrupted.

"But he grabbed Mr. Giles's cane."

"With the intent to protect himself and calm the situation."

His words struck deep. Hadn't I wondered if such was the case? "How can you be so sure?" I asked.

"I've had more years than you to assess men's actions. Trust me." His expression softened. "And trust that I think only of your welfare when I say you must learn to guard your tongue." Sighing, he rose in a show of dismissal. "Think long on this as you approach your Maker in prayer tonight. God has given you a keen mind, but you must learn to school it."

Instead of joining Mother and Bethy in the sitting room, I slowly climbed the stairs to my bedroom. I hadn't received such a scolding in a long time. *Think, Abigail. You must learn to think before you speak.*

The words followed me into my room and perched on the bed as I undressed. After donning my nightgown, I braided my long blonde hair and knelt by my bed to pray.

Like Jacob in the Bible, I wrestled with the Lord, sometimes trying to justify my actions and words, then contrite and pleading for forgiveness for hurting Matthew Giles.

I missed Bethy's warm body when I finally climbed into bed, missed the sound of her soft breathing on the pillow next to mine. Other than a relentless stream of unpleasant thoughts, chilling cold and darkness were my companions. I tossed and turned until Bethy came upstairs and climbed into bed. Not wanting to talk, I feigned sleep when she twice whispered my name.

It wasn't long until Bethy was asleep, her stillness like a taunt to my wakefulness. After what seemed like hours, I climbed out of bed and put on my lined wrapper and slippers. Going to the window, I quietly opened the shutters.

The front yard was bathed in the glow of a half-moon whose light silhouetted the bare-branched trees into a tracery of delicate lace. Under the trees, the partially melted snow lay in a quilt of irregular black-and-white patterns.

Unbidden peace stole over me, quieting my restless, guilt-ridden thoughts. The sight of a horse tethered to the corner post of the fence jerked me from tranquility. Puzzled, I stared at the horse while my mind searched for a possible explanation. I'd heard the clock in the sitting room chime eleven. Who had come to see Father at such a late hour?

Curiosity sent me creeping down the front stairs. Reaching the bottom step, I saw a slit of light beneath the study door and heard the faint sound of male voices. Who could it be? Was it Thomas Boatrick on some farm matters? But since he and his family lived in the rooms over our laundry house, why would he ride a horse?

Inquisitiveness impelled me out the front door. The cold hit me like a physical force, and had I not been so curious about Father's guest, I would have turned back.

Intending to stay outside for only a minute, I stepped away from the house for a better view of the study. Both windows were shuttered from the inside, but a chink of light escaped through a knothole in the closest one. By standing on tiptoe, I could fit my eye to the knothole and peer inside.

I blinked, then blinked again. Surely not! Yet even as the thought formed, I knew I wasn't mistaken. Gideon Whitlock sat across the desk from Father, the two men in deep conversation.

Too stunned to think rationally, I could only watch and wish they would speak louder. Even a word or two might give a clue to their business, which, judging by their expressions and the closeness of their heads, was serious indeed.

Rather than arguing, they looked like men bound in a common cause, though whether 'twas Tory or patriot, I didn't know. I knew only that I was so shaken I opened the front door, climbed the stairs, and got into bed in a half daze. There, confusion and sickness edged with fear lay in my stomach like a heavy weight no matter which way I turned. "Oh, Father," I whispered into the dark silence. "What is going on?"

Chapter Four

THE MEMORY OF FATHER AND Gideon Whitlock in the study pounced on me the minute I opened my eyes the next morning. The undeniable truth of what I'd seen was etched in dark ink on my mind, leaving me feeling slightly off balance. The sight had also shaken my confidence. Hadn't I misjudged the situation between Mr. Whitlock and Matthew Giles? What if I'd done the same with this?

I wouldn't believe Father was a traitor, but the idea of Gideon Whitlock being anything other than an arrogant Tory didn't set well either. There had to be a reasonable explanation. Unable to fathom it, I was left not knowing what to think.

Part of me wanted to go to Father to tell him what I'd seen, but the thought of adding spying to my list of faults stopped me. Instead, I smiled when I didn't feel like smiling, ate when I had no appetite, and hoped my quietness would be laid to guilt for the scene in the village. How I wished I had only that to trouble me.

When I wasn't thinking about Father and Gideon, I was weighed down with concern for having unwittingly hurt poor Matthew Giles. The next day I asked Ben to hitch the gray mare to the cart so I could go into the village. Sitting tall, I nodded to the few people I saw and was pleased when most nodded back. Even so, I was aware that they stared after me, the incident still on their minds.

Getting out of the cart, I approached the front door of Matthew Giles's small cottage with a basket of eggs on my arm and an apology on my lips. His face was solemn and bore no sign of a smile. Although he accepted the eggs and my plea for forgiveness, I knew it would be some time before things were right between us again.

As I set out for home, I waved to my friend Agnes Wright. Married less than a year, her winter cloak didn't quite hide the roundness of her body. As she returned my wave, I was reminded that most of my friends were now married and that some were mothers with babes. I tried to shut my mind to the fact that unlike my friends, I still lived with my parents and was mistress of nothing except a small plot of snow-covered ground that made up the kitchen garden.

★

The following morning, I awoke with a headache. More than that, my mood was dull and weighed down with bleakness and worry. When a hot cup of chamomile tea failed to ease the throbbing pain, I told Mother I was going to visit Prudence Blood to see if she had something better for headaches.

Mother studied me for a long moment. "You mustn't worry so much about what happened in the village. Life has taught me that unpleasant things happen. They also pass, and in a short time, people find something new to gossip about."

I inwardly flinched when she said gossip, and I wondered what she'd think if I told her that Mr. Giles had accepted my apology with stiffness or that Father had met with a Tory or that one by one my friends were marrying without me.

I knew very well why I suffered the headache and why I saw little in my life to be happy about. Besides needing something to diminish the pain in my head, I badly needed to get away. What better place to go than Prudence Blood's?

A short time later, I set out in the cart for the home of the old woman. It sat at the end of Tipple Road, the walls and roof of the cottage weathered to a shade of gray that closely resembled the drab color of her clothes. A sagging wooden fence outlined a yard given over to plants and flowers and the herbs she used for her healing concoctions. At this time of year, they were still weighed down by melting snow and lay in matted tangles of old leaves.

Years before, pricks of unease had accompanied me on my first visit. Since then, I'd visited the strange little woman so often I gave no credence to rumors of eerie lights emitting from her cottage late at night or talk of the curse she'd cast on Josiah Ryder. To me, she had shown nothing but kindness.

I got down from the cart and unlatched the gate that sagged as badly as the fence. "Mistress Blood," I called. "'Tis Abigail Stowell."

Two cats came around the corner of the cottage. The large tabby walked sedately while the black cat ran ahead to greet me. Mistress Blood wasn't many steps behind them.

Instead of a white cap, the woman's plain face was framed by a worn gray bonnet. Though she didn't smile in greeting, her deep-set eyes sparked with interest. "You have come," she said. "I've known since yesterday you would be here."

"How did you know?"

She pointed down at the black cat. "Ebony told me. He always tells me when you're coming. See how he purrs and circles your skirt? He has wished you here."

I bent to pet him. Although I put great stock in Mistress Blood's knowledge of plants and healing, I took what she said about Ebony with a grain of salt. It wasn't the cat who'd wished me here but a headache and the need for something more to think about than my problems.

When I looked up, Mistress Blood was studying me.

"I see by your eyes that you're not well."

"'Tis a headache, one that chamomile tea can't cure."

"Sometimes a bad headache requires more than chamomile tea." She motioned for me to follow her along a cobbled path still damp from melting snow to the back room of the cottage. It was here where the old woman brewed her tinctures and pounded roots and leaves with a pestle for her physics and salves. Bags of herbs hanging from strings along the wall gave off strong but not unpleasant aromas.

She went without hesitation to one of the bags. "Lady Slipper roots." Laying it on her worktable, she took down another bag. "Valerian roots." She handed me a root from each bag. "When you get home, pound and grind them as I've shown you and put this much"—she cupped her hand to indicate the amount—"into two cups of water and boil for a few minutes. Pour half a cup into half a cup of chamomile tea and drink it. If 'tis more bitter than you like, add a little sugar."

"This will cure a headache?"

"If you do as I say, your headache will be gone." She studied me as she spoke, and after a tiny pause, she added, "If you warm the tea and drink it before you go to bed, it will help you sleep as well."

I lifted my brows. How did she know I hadn't been sleeping well?

"I had only to look at you to know that of late your sleep has been troubled," she said as if I'd spoken my thoughts aloud.

Her kindness brought the sting of tears. "Thank you." I reached into my pocket for a coin to pay her.

"I don't take payment from my friends, Mistress Abigail. Your friendship is all I ask for my services."

"You know you have it."

She nodded. "Just as I have the friendship of your parents."

The aroma of the herbs and Ebony's purr filled a small silence.

"Now," Mistress Blood said like we'd reached the end of a book and were about to begin a new one. "I know 'twas more than a headache and Ebony that brought you here." She paused, and her dark eyes probed mine as if she could see into the depths of my mind. After a moment, she nodded. "'Tis time for me to read your fortune."

A shiver skimmed down my spine. "Fortune?" I echoed.

"But only if you wish it."

When I hesitated, she said, "I do not read a maid's future if 'tis only a whim. My tea leaves speak to me the same as my plants. They talk of many things. Some I whisper to those that believe . . . Some I hold to myself." Again her dark eyes looked long into mine. "Would you care to see what the leaves have to say about your future, Mistress Abigail?"

Still I hesitated, my curiosity warring with the notion that tea leaves prophesied the future and crows on a roof predicted death. Wasn't God in charge of death and the future? More than that, I knew what Reverend Whipple had to say on the reading of tea leaves. "'Tis straight from the devil," he'd said more than once.

Think before you speak. The words clattered in my brain, but what came out was unexpected. "Yes," I answered. "I believe I would."

I followed her into the keeping room where a fire burned low in a stone fireplace. Motioning me to a chair by a much-scrubbed table, she took the kettle warming on the hob and poured steaming water into a cup. I watched as she took a jar from the shelf, measured leaves into the palm of her hand, and poured them into the cup.

Her voice broke the stillness. "'Tis but joe-pye weed, and though its taste is bitter, the leaves are always true. 'Twill take a minute for the leaves to steep."

A shiver of nervousness danced across my shoulders. What if Mistress Blood truly did possess the power to read the future in the dregs of joe-pye weed? Could they also go back and tell me what Father and Mr. Whit-lock had been conversing about?

"'Tis naught to worry about," she went on, her small eyes seeming to read my emotions and thoughts. "Though your future be unseen by you and others, 'tis there just the same and can be read if the time is right." She glanced at the steaming cup on the table. "In a minute, I'll know whether 'tis the right time."

"How can you know if the time is right? And why is one time better than another?" I asked, ever curious.

"If the time isn't right, the leaves will create jumbled dregs that have no meaning." Her brow furrowed. "As for why one time is better?" She shrugged her narrow shoulders. "My mother thought 'twas to do with the alignment of the moon and stars, while Granny Elspeth . . ." Her gaze slid away. "Granny sometimes dabbled in things I don't hold with." Mistress Blood handed me a spoon. "Stir the tea," she instructed.

I stirred the brown, steaming liquid and watched the leaves swirl like an eddy in a rushing stream. What secrets did they hold, or was it but silly superstition?

As she peered at the liquid, her face was intent, her shoulders tight and hunched. Time stretched long as we waited for the leaves to settle.

Mistress Blood's phlegmy voice broke the stillness. "Take only a sip at first. The touch of your lips will name the leaves as your own."

I nervously took a sip of the brown joe-pye tea. It was bitter . . . so bitter I pulled a face.

Mistress Blood watched me closely as I took a second sip, then another. Was the time right? She didn't speak until after I'd forced myself to drink the bitter liquid down to the lees. Only then did she pick up the cup and carry it to the window, where the light was better.

I watched her as closely as she'd watched me, her lips moving as if whispering a chant . . . or was it only what she saw in the leaves? Were they an unfathomable clump, or did they mark the pattern of my future?

I barely stifled a cry when Ebony suddenly jumped up onto my lap and began to purr, his white whiskers silhouetted against the blackness of his fur, his paws kneading the green fabric of my skirt.

As my fingers combed through his long fur, I began to relax. Only then did I realize that his mistress no longer stared into the cup.

Her dark eyes studied me, and she spoke in a voice as solemn as her expression. "They have spoken to me, Mistress Abigail." She paused to ascertain that she had my full attention. "Soon you will have to depend on your wits to save what you hold dear. You will also encounter great danger . . . one that will test both you and the man you love."

"The man I love?" I echoed.

The lines outlining the herb woman's thin lips softened. "The leaves show that you will find great love, Mistress Abigail."

The image of Gideon Whitlock flitted across my mind. Hard as I tried to banish the arrogant Tory's green eyes and amused smile from my mind, they remained.

With an annoyed shrug, I turned my mind to Mistress Blood and the tea leaves. *Love. She said love.* I took a deep breath. "And will there be marriage?"

This time Mistress Blood actually smiled. "That, Mistress Abigail, will be entirely up to you."

Chapter Five

I DIDN'T THINK IT WISE to tell Mother that Mistress Blood had read my future in her tea leaves. Instead, I showed her the lady slipper and valerian roots. "She told me to grind and boil them and make a tea."

I set at once to the task and drank a cup of the somewhat unpleasant tea that night before I went to bed. Just as the little woman had predicted, I awoke the next morning feeling refreshed and with all signs of my headache vanished. As I unwound my hair from its bedtime plait, I wondered if Prudence Blood's prediction about my future would also prove correct.

We were into March now, and on this particularly fine day, Father suggested we visit Mother's brother and his family in Lexington. Normally I would have welcomed the prospect, for I was very fond of both Uncle William and Aunt Martha.

This time the situation was different. The tea leaves had said nothing about Father's meeting with Mr. Whitlock, and though I wouldn't believe Father was a traitor, my mind couldn't accept the fact that Gideon Whitlock might be anything other than a dyed-in-the-wool Tory. With my mind still in a quandary, I didn't look forward to being with Father in the carriage for several hours and acting as if nothing was amiss. I also knew that if I didn't play my part well, I would be plied with endless questions.

Thanks to Mother's tact and ability to steer the conversation to topics that wouldn't upset, we passed the journey in comparative ease. The visit passed pleasantly as well, and it was with reluctance that we set out on our return journey to Mayfield two days later.

Instead of joining in my parents' and Bethy's conversation, I kept my eyes on the passing landscape. The hickory trees along the road were still without leaves, but a suggestion of green tinged the willow branches draped over a tiny stream.

Even so, I was aware that Mother's gaze was often on me. Her dark eyes held concern, and worry furrowed her brow. Though I might fool Father that my aloofness with him was from a guilty conscience, Mother knew me too well to be deceived.

After several miles, conversation lagged, and like me, Father turned his attention to the passing landscape. Suddenly he changed position, his expression intent, his shoulders taut as if ready to spring from the carriage. Opening the window, he leaned his head out of the carriage. "Stop!" he shouted to Israel, who was driving the carriage.

As soon as it stopped, Father sprang out to accost two men walking along the road. I wondered at this, for the men looked to be laborers in search of work, their shabby coats unbuttoned and their knee-length breeches and blue stockings splattered with mud. The closest one nervously fingered the stick with his possessions tied in a kerchief, and the second man looked ready to bolt into the trees.

I put my head out the window and heard Father ask the men their destination.

"Concord," the closest man answered.

"We're gunsmiths and heard there was work there," the other man put in. His eyes darted from Father to Israel sitting atop the carriage.

"I live in Mayfield but five miles from Concord, and I've heard nothing about a need for gunsmiths," Father said. He studied them for a moment. "Where did you hear of this?"

Their answers came as one. "Boston . . . Charles Town."

"'Tis known in both towns," the second man amended.

By now, Bethy and Mother had moved to listen too.

"I would offer you a ride up top with my driver, but I know for a fact that it will do you no good to go to Concord," Father told them. "Your information is incorrect, and you will be wise to return to wherever you came from . . . England to judge from your accents."

Though Father's back was to me, I could picture his narrowed blue eyes and the stern expression on his face. Had I not experienced such a look but a few days before?

The closest man shuffled his feet, and I caught a glimpse of apprehension on the other man's face, but neither one turned to leave.

Father's voice rose, as did his cane. "Have I made myself clear? If you know what's good for you, you'll go back to Boston."

The men exchanged sullen glances and grudgingly turned toward Lexington. Father looked after them for several minutes, his expression grim. Only when he was satisfied they were on their way did he nod to Israel and climb back into the carriage.

"Who were they?" I asked Father.

Instead of answering, he closed the window and settled onto the seat. "I don't know, but they aren't who they pretend to be."

"Could they have been sent by—"

Father held up his hand. "Let's not spoil our outing with unpleasant speculation." To change the subject, he said, "I see you have a new plant to add to your collection." He pointed to the burlap bundle by my feet. "Was that something your aunt gave you?"

Only the memory of the stern lecture he'd given me about thinking before I spoke kept me from asking more questions. Sighing, I nodded. "'Tis boneset. Aunt Martha says she's had great success in using it to bring down fever. When we get home, I mean to ask Mistress Blood about it too."

I spent the rest of the journey talking with Mother and Bethy. I also took uncommon interest in Concord as we passed through it, wondering why the men had been so set on going there. My curiosity was whetted even more when Father told Israel to stop the carriage at the Concord blacksmith's shop. After a brief conversation with the smithy, Father returned, saying only that Uncle William had asked him to convey a message to him. Though no further mention was made of the men on the road, the memory of them rode like two extra passengers in the carriage. Instinct told me they were why Father had stopped at the blacksmith's and that they were involved with General Gage. What I didn't know was what Father intended to do about them.

We arrived home about noon to find a warm fire burning in the kitchen and a meat pie baking on the hearth. As Mother was thanking Jane for having a meal ready for us, Father came in from the barn and asked Mother to join him in the study.

Bethy shot me a quick look, her face troubled as she came around the table and took hold of my hand. "What's wrong?" she asked in a hushed voice. "Why's he talking to Mother now instead of waiting until they go to bed tonight?"

I had a fair idea of what was being discussed, but I didn't want to worry Bethy. "Maybe something happened while we were away."

"Maybe," Bethy said, but her expression told me my explanation hadn't satisfied her.

Hoping to put her mind on more pleasant things, I said, "The cat looks plumper than she seemed last week. It looks as if she's going to have kittens."

Diverted, Bethy picked up the gray cat. It wasn't as simple to divert my thoughts. Seeing the men had upset Father more than he would admit. But whether they and his secret meeting with Gideon Whitlock were connected, I didn't know.

Bethy and I were setting the table when Mother returned to the kitchen. She paused in the doorway, her face grave and her eyes red from crying. "Your Father wishes to speak to you, Abigail."

My stomach tightened, and I almost dropped the fork I was placing next to Father's plate. Apprehension followed me as I crossed the kitchen to Mother. *What? I wanted to say. "Tell me what's wrong."*

Mother's dark eyes held mine as she reached and squeezed my hand. I hurried down the hallway to the study.

"Come," Father called in response to my knock.

He stood with his back to the fire, his head bent as if studying the silver buckles on his shoes. When he finally raised his head, I knew that what had passed between him and Mother had been difficult for him as well.

The barrier between us was suddenly of no significance. In three quick steps, I crossed to his side and laid my hand on his arm. "What is it? What's upset you and Mother?"

Father covered my hand with his. "I need your help, daughter. I wish with all my heart there were some other way to accomplish this, but since there isn't—" He paused to swallow. "What I ask will require great caution. It's also dangerous."

My mouth went dry, but I kept my eyes on his. "What is it?"

"I feel certain the men we saw were spying for General Gage."

"I wondered," I said.

"I know you did." Father paused as if uncertain how to go on. "I saw the men before they were aware of us. One was writing or drawing in a notebook, and the other was pointing out landmarks. As soon as they heard the carriage, the one quickly slipped the notebook into his pack, and they started walking along the road."

"What do you think he was writing?"

"I can't be certain, but . . ." He moved to the chair behind his desk and indicated that I take the other chair. "You had best make yourself comfortable, for there's much to tell you . . . much you must understand."

The last time I'd sat in this chair, I'd been nervous and contrite. Tonight, curiosity dominated my emotions. Was I about to learn why he and Mr. Whitlock had met? And what it was he wanted me to do?

Father leaned forward, his elbows on the desk. "All I tell you must be held in strictest confidence. Lives—perhaps the success of our stand against the King—will depend upon complete secrecy."

I nodded, my expression as grave as his.

"For weeks we've been stockpiling food, guns, and powder in preparation for a stand against General Gage. Much of it has been hidden in and around Concord."

I let out a slow breath. "Where the two men were going."

"Exactly." His mouth tightened. "Gage has his spies the same as we do, and I'm sure he's heard rumors about the supplies. The men were probably sent to map the terrain and find the best route for the redcoats to march to Concord. I think they were also sent to find exactly where the supplies in Concord are hidden."

I remembered how I'd looked at Concord with great interest as we'd crossed the north bridge on the edge of the village, but not once had I suspected that patriots had stockpiled supplies there.

"If you and your mother and sister hadn't been with me, Israel and I would have overpowered the men and taken them back to Lexington. Instead, I was obliged to wait until we got home to have Israel saddle Jumper and ride to tell your Uncle William and the Lexington committeemen what we saw."

The last of the uncertainty that had weighed on me since seeing Father in the study with Gideon Whitlock vanished. That he'd allowed someone other than himself to ride Jumper told me how concerned he was.

"Jon would have loved to be the one to warn them," I said softly.

Pain touched the corners of Father's mouth. "He would. And I would much rather have sent him than . . ." He stopped and studied his hands. "I know it will be difficult for you to believe, but Gideon Whitlock is not what he seems to be. He is no more a Tory than you or I . . . and he risks his life daily for the patriot cause."

I gaped at Father like a woman of limited brains. "But he—"

"I know," Father interrupted. "And I know you don't care for him. Even so, he's a man to be trusted. Not only does he have sources close to General

Gage, but he passes what he learns to the patriots. He also carries word from Sam Adams to us in the country."

My mouth tightened in chagrin. Hadn't a small part of me wondered if I'd misjudged Mr. Whitlock just as I'd done that day in the village? The arrogant man was a patriot, not a Tory. I remembered Father and him talking in the study. All made sense now. More than that, I felt great relief, one large enough to include Mr. Whitlock. Jarred by the thought, I turned my mind back to Father. "What is it you want me to do?"

"I want you to go to Boston and tell Gideon Whitlock about the men we saw today."

"But—"

"I would go myself, but it's not safe for me to be seen in Boston," Father hurried on before I could say more. "One of Gage's aides was given the names of those who attended the Cambridge Congress in February. Mr. Whitlock says my name is also on a list of men suspected of rebellion. Since I'm well-known in Boston, I fear that a meeting with Gideon might alert Gage's men to watch him too. Without his help, our cause would greatly suffer."

"Are you certain Mr. Whitlock can be trusted?"

"I am."

"Even after he quarreled with old Mr. Giles?"

"Such was done to make people think him a stalwart Tory."

I frowned, my feelings still in a quandary. "Where in Boston will I find him?"

"He keeps a room at The Rose and Crown. It's not far from the road entering Boston." His expression turned troubled. "I'd send Thomas or one of our committee men, but 'tis doubtful Gideon would recognize them. While you—" Father's face lost some of its grimness. "He'll not only recognize you but will seek you out."

I lifted my head to say I had no wish for Mr. Whitlock to seek me out. Then I realized that this had nothing to do with like or dislike and everything to do with helping the patriots. Excitement swirled through me. For weeks I'd longed to play an active role in the cause. "You mentioned danger."

Father nodded. "I didn't exaggerate when I said Boston was a hotbed of intrigue. I don't think you will be suspected of being anything other than a young woman who's come to Boston for whatever reason, but people may be watching Gideon. That's why you must pass the information to him in person instead of in a note." He paused to clear his throat. "Be discreet about letting Mr. Whitlock see you, then leave the rest to him. He's practiced in such things and will know what to do. You must be on your guard, however." His voice turned gruff, and he looked away. "Besides the chance that you might fall into one of Gage's agent's hands, there are men in Boston who prey on comely young women like yourself. 'Tis why Thomas and Jane will travel with you. I know Thomas will guard you with his life, just as I would."

I understood now why Mother had been crying and why Father's face had held concern. They had lost Jonathan less than year ago and two young daughters to a putrid throat. Now they were sending me into a situation that might prove dangerous.

I got to my feet and went to Father, who'd also risen. We stood without speaking, his eyes filled with emotion, mine brimming with tears. He gently pulled me to him, and I laid my head on his shoulder.

"I shall pray for you every hour you are gone," he whispered.

And I knew he would.

Chapter Six

WE LEFT EARLY THE NEXT morning, Thomas on his black gelding and Jane riding pillion behind me on Dolly, the gray mare. It would have been more comfortable if we'd ridden in the carriage or cart, but since the roads were still very muddy, Father and Thomas thought we would reach Boston sooner if we traveled on horseback.

Father had deemed it wise to tell Thomas as little as possible about my reason for going to Boston. He knew only that it had something to do with the men we'd seen on the road to Concord. As for Jane, she'd been told that Mother had been much taken with Aunt Martha's butter mold and that Father had sent me to Boston to buy one for her upcoming birthday.

The twenty-mile trip to Boston could be made in less than a day. We planned to stop to refresh ourselves and rest the horses in Lexington, where Thomas would make discreet inquiries about the men we'd seen. Hopefully after Israel's warning, the suspected spies had been apprehended before they could do any great harm.

From Lexington to Boston was the longest leg of the journey. For some years, the British had maintained a blockade on the narrow neck of land leading into Boston. A ferry also crossed several times a day between Boston's north end and the mainland at Charles Town. Since both the ferry and the gates at the blockade closed at sunset, we would need to reach our destination before then.

Jane was excited at the prospect of going to Boston. Her questions and chatter filled the time until we'd passed through Concord. Shortly after we'd crossed the bridge, we saw Israel riding toward us.

"How goes it?" his father asked.

Israel shook his head. "No luck, but the Lexington men are keeping watch." He gave me a polite nod and his sister a wide grin and continued on his way back to Mayfield. It took great control not to ask for more details.

The weather wasn't as warm as it had been the day before, and a steady breeze made me glad for the warmth of my woolen cape. In between listening to Jane's chatter and trying to avoid the largest mud holes, I looked for signs of coming spring. Even along the roadside, the drab brown grass showed definite signs of green.

Instead of stopping to see Aunt Martha, Thomas led the way to Monroe Tavern on the east side of Lexington. A red, two-storied structure, it was known for good food and hospitality.

We rode around to the back of the tavern, and after we'd dismounted and Thomas had seen to the horses, he led us inside, where we were served bowls of beef stew and thick slices of bread. In between bites, I furtively studied the faces of two men who ate at a small table. Although they wore the clothes of laborers, like the men yesterday, neither face was familiar.

The rest of the journey passed uneventfully. Each mile that brought us nearer to Boston increased my unease. In my mind, I rehearsed what I would say to Mr. Whitlock, but no matter how many times I rehearsed it, unease remained.

Instead of our entering Boston by way of the narrow neck and blockade, Father had deemed it best for us take the ferry between Charles Town and Boston's north end. Not only would it be shorter but also safer since no soldiers manned the ferry wharf.

The road between Cambridge and Charles Town wound in leisurely fashion past farms and orchards. A rock wall followed the road that wound around Breeds and Bunker hills and thence through Charles Town to the ferry wharf.

Jane gasped with delight when the inlet and bay came into view, with Boston peninsula sticking out into the blue water like a giant malformed thumb.

"Isn't it wonderful?" I asked.

Jane nodded and stared at the wide expanse of bay and ocean that stretched as far as the eye could see. Several large warships rode at anchor, their tall masts with slackened sails like a forest of bare trees.

While we waited for the ferry to return from Boston, I pointed at the outline of Noddle's Island. Not many minutes later, a flat-bottom scow with a small sail made its way into the inlet. Three farm women carrying market baskets were the first to leave the ferry. A carter and two men followed.

After we paid our sixpence for the crossing, we and the horses boarded the scow. With the briny wind blowing fresh on our faces, I pointed out Beacon Hill and the north end.

As soon as we docked, the bustle of the busy town surrounded us— the smell of brine and fish mingled with hammering from a shipyard and the strident voice of a woman selling hot pies. Remounting our horses, we rode to North Street and thence to Middle Street, winding our way among carts and barrows, burly stevedores and redcoat soldiers.

Jane's fingers tightened on my waist when she saw the soldiers, but when they passed without a glance, her hold slackened.

Since I was more familiar with Boston than Thomas, I led the way. Father had told me that The Rose and Crown was on Newberry Street, not far from The Black Swan, where we usually stayed.

Carts, wagons, and other riders joined us on Marlborough Street, then on to Newberry, where homes and buildings lined the street. Ahead was a two-storied building and a sign with a red rose and gold crown and the name The Rose and Crown painted on it. A Tory tavern if ever I saw one and a perfect cover for a man such as Gideon Whitlock.

I drew in an uneasy breath as I looked at the pink brick structure with white shutters. The purpose of my visit had never been far from my mind, but now the reality of what I faced made my stomach muscles tighten. What if Mr. Whitlock failed to recognize me or was away on patriot business?

The sound of Thomas's familiar voice stopped my runaway imagination. "We're here, Mistress Abigail," he said after he'd dismounted and come to help Jane and me down from the mare. The relief in his voice told me the last hours had been a strain on him too.

"It will take me awhile to care for the horses . . . what with havin' to scrape the mud from their hooves and get them fed and watered. As soon as I'm done, I'll bring your bag into the tavern." His gaze took in two men loitering near the stable. "'Twill be best if ye wait inside. They're sure to have a table for you."

I straightened my shoulders and beckoned Jane to follow me to the front entrance. As I opened the door, the sound of voices and laughter met us. A middle-aged man with a balding head stood behind a counter, dispensing mugs of beer and cider. As I returned his welcoming smile, a woman of similar age came to greet me, her brown hair tucked neatly into her cap and a clean apron covering her ample waist.

"I'm Goody Price," she said, dropping a curtsy. "I'll take you to the parlor, where there's tea or coffee to refresh yourselves."

Since I doubted I'd find Gideon Whitlock eating his supper in the parlor, I shook my head. "The main room, please." I glanced toward the wide, arched doorway leading to a large room where pipe smoke mingled with the sound of male voices.

Giving me a quick look, Goody Price called to a serving maid. "Meg, will you find a table for our guests?"

A comely young woman carrying a tray of empty mugs nodded and set it on the counter. "This way, mistress," she said, giving Jane and me a quick smile. Like Goodwife Price, she was neatly clad, her trim figure filling out her blue bodice and white fichu to advantage.

We hadn't taken many steps into the main room before a man hailed Meg. The smile she gave him was saucy, but she continued without pause toward an empty table. With senses heightened, I followed her, searching faces as I looked for Mr. Whitlock. Most of the customers were well-dressed gentlemen wearing wigs. Only a few were laborers.

Just before we reached the empty table, I encountered the startled gaze of Gideon Whitlock, his spoon poised between bowl and mouth, his green eyes staring.

Taking care not to slacken my pace, I met his gaze squarely so he knew I recognized him. It wasn't until I sat at the table that I realized how quickly my heart beat and that my throat felt like a piece of stale bread was lodged inside.

"May I bring you something to drink?" Meg asked.

"Coffee, please," I answered, though I would much rather have had tea. "And my maid will have the same."

Jane looked around, her eyes bright with interest as she took in the large room. Despite my show of nonchalance, I was aware that Mr. Whitlock covertly watched me, aware too that my blue cloak was badly wrinkled and that my bonnet—indeed, all of me—showed signs of the rigorous journey on horseback. My first instinct was to lift my chin to let Mr. Whitlock know I cared not a fig what he thought of my appearance. Then I remembered we worked for the same cause. Were we not allies, and didn't it behoove me to treat him with politeness?

The sad fact was that seeing Mr. Whitlock had put my mind in such a muddle I was uncertain what to think. Not liking the feeling, especially when it came at this critical time, I quickly took myself to task. Didn't I possess a quick mind and intellect, and hadn't Father sent me in his place because he trusted my ability to deliver his message? More than that, if I didn't play my part well, the arms and food hidden in Concord might fall into General Gage's hands.

Father's parting words seemed to ring in my ears. *"Leave matters to Mr. Whitlock. He's much practiced in such things. He'll know what to do."* Though it went against the grain, I settled myself to do just that. Mr. Whitlock had seen me. The next move was his.

Acting as if I frequently took refreshment in a tavern, I let my gaze casually travel around the bustling room. Most of the male occupants seemed bent on conversation while quaffing cider or partaking of large bowls of steaming chowder. We were seated but two tables away from Gideon and a well-dressed gentleman reading what looked to be a printed broadsheet.

I nodded my head ever so slightly when Gideon's eyes met mine with a questioning frown. Then I turned my attention to Jane.

"Mercy, 'tis even bigger than the tavern in Lexington," she said.

Before I could respond, Meg returned with our coffee. "Would you care to order your dinner now?" she asked.

I shook my head. "We're waiting for someone to join us."

Dropping another curtsy, Meg left, giving Gideon an inviting smile as she passed him.

Well, I thought.

I gave him a quick look, and to my irritation, I saw amusement in his eyes. How did he read my thoughts so well?

I longed to give him a quelling look, but before I could do it, Gideon rose, picked up his chair, and carried it to our table.

"What are you—" I began, only to be interrupted.

"I see that you and your maid are drinking coffee instead of tea. Has no one told you that doing so in a Tory tavern is frowned upon?"

I gave him a withering look. "Is this a new law passed by Parliament or an edict from the King?"

He laughed. "Neither. I only use it to bring color to a face. See . . . you're blushing, just as I'd hoped." He leaned close and covered my hand with his.

"Sir," I said, indignation taking precedent over reason.

He leaned close like a man wooing a woman and whispered in my ear, "Why are you here?"

"Fa . . . Father sent me." My heart pounded so hard it was difficult to think. "He sends a message."

Gideon's long fingers tightened on my hand. "And . . ." he prompted, his breath like a caress on my cheek.

I swallowed hard, and it was with effort that I brought my thoughts back to my purpose. "Yesterday we saw two men . . . probably General Gage's spies, making drawings of the countryside along the Lexington-Concord road."

"Ah . . ." A long moment passed, and I knew his mind was busy. His head moved closer to mine. "I want you to slap my face and walk out of the room. Leave the tavern as soon as you can."

I turned to look at him, thinking I hadn't heard correctly. Before I could blink, his lips closed over mine, my surprise such that I could neither think nor move.

When I came to myself, anger pushed me from my chair to slap him hard across the face. "Insolent cad! How dare you!" My indignation was genuine, as was the quelling look I gave him as I hurried from the room. Silence and a bewildered Jane followed me, the sound of the slap catching the attention of the patrons as surely as a musket crack.

"Is something amiss?" Goody Price asked as laughter followed us through the archway.

I wanted to turn and point an accusing finger at Gideon, but enough sense remained to tell me that such might unmask his cover.

"I find myself in need of a breath of fresh air," I said in a voice that shook despite my best efforts.

By now Jane had caught up with me, her pale eyes wide and an indignant look on her freckled face.

"Come," I said, taking her arm and hurrying her out the door. The less attention we brought to ourselves, the better it would be, though the slap was sure to provide conversation for the rest of the evening.

Jane's disjointed sentences matched our steps. "That terrible man! He— Are you a'right? 'Tis like Lucy Ames said. There's much sin in Boston."

Too distracted to answer, I quickened my pace. Since Gideon had told me to leave The Rose and Crown, I thought it wise to do so, though where we would go I didn't know.

"Where we goin'?" Jane asked. Like me, she was aware that the stable yard wasn't the best place for us to be.

"To find your father." Deeming it wise to call his name before we ventured any farther, I did so, conscious that the sun had set and that shadows had invaded the interior of the stable.

The sturdy outline of Mr. Boatrick emerging from the building was a welcome sight. He paused, clearly surprised. "Mistress Abigail."

"I think 'twould be best for us to find other lodgings," I interrupted before he could say more.

"But your father—"

"Things have changed," I said emphatically. "We must go elsewhere."

Conflicting emotions played across his broad face, and his lips moved as if to protest. Father had instructed him to lodge at The Rose and Crown, and now I was telling him to do otherwise. It was a minute before he spoke. "Where are we to go?"

"Our family lodges at The Black Swan. It should do."

He gave a reluctant nod. "It will take a bit to ready the horses."

As I watched Thomas reenter the stable, where lanterns had been lit to ward off the dusk, my mind replayed the scene with Gideon Whitlock. Only with strict control did I rein it back to think straight.

Slipping a hand into my pocket for the coins Father had given me to use in case of emergency, I extracted one and handed it to Jane.

"Go back to the tavern and give this to Goody Price. Tell her it's to pay for our coffee."

Jane made a tiny sound, and her gaze darted to the tavern as if she expected to see the horrid man who'd kissed me come out the door.

"'Twill be all right. Now go quickly."

"What if . . . ?"

I took her arm and walked with her to the nail-studded tavern door. "I'll wait here."

With an audible gulp, she opened the door and went inside. I waited uneasily, hoping not to draw attention to myself. A minute later, Jane rejoined me.

We moved away from the entrance as two men approached. Though they openly eyed us, they did no more than doff their hats and smile.

Only when they were safely inside did I turn to Jane. "Did you see the man who—"

"No. I walked straight in, like you said, and gave the coin to Goody Price." She opened her hand to show me the change she'd received.

I squeezed her work-roughened hand. "Thank you, Jane. You've been a great help."

Jane' grew teary-eyed. "You must tell Father what happened. That horrid man . . ." Her voice broke, and she shot a quick look back at the tavern.

"You mustn't tell anyone what happened," I insisted. "Not your father. Not anyone. Do you understand?"

Jane's thin lips trembled as she nodded.

"No one," I repeated, my mind veering away from what Father would think should he discover the means Gideon had used to receive the message. By now my anger had cooled enough for me to admire Mr. Whitlock's cleverness.

Seeing Jane's dejected expression, I went on in an optimistic voice. "It will turn out well," I assured her. "And here's your father with the horses. We'll be away from here in a trice."

I paid little heed to the ride to The Black Swan or to what I ate or to the details of the small room and bed I shared with Jane. But I remember the disjointed questions that jumped and flitted through my mind as I lay there. Not knowing on which path my thoughts would land, I firmly led them to one I thought safe.

I'd longed to be an active part of the patriot cause, and tonight I'd done just that, passing a piece of information that could keep patriot arms from falling into General Gage's hands. More than that, what I'd done could be done again. The thought pleased and calmed me enough that I thought is safe to think of Gideon Whitlock and the events at The Rose and Crown.

Now that anger and disdain no longer ruled my emotions, I recognized why Mr. Whitlock was a successful spy. Even so, I wished he'd chosen something less . . . less. Like waves of Boston's incoming tide, the fresh smell of his shaving soap and the whisper of his breath on my cheek washed over me. Then I thought of his kiss. Never in my life had I imagined a man's lips could feel so soft.

"Mercy," I whispered, glad Jane was fast asleep. Determined to put distance between me and the disturbing emotions, I set my mind on my purpose for coming to Boston. But somehow it got tangled around Gideon's warm lips and his kiss again. It was while I was thinking of them that I fell asleep.

Chapter Seven

THE SOUND OF VOICES DRIFTING up the stairway of The Black Swan wakened me the next morning. Lifting my head, I saw the sun well risen and Jane putting her nightgown into one of the saddlebags.

"Why didn't you wake me?" I asked.

"I tried, but you was so fagged from yesterday you didn't move."

"I'm sorry. Your father must be wondering where we are."

"Most likely." Jane's attention was on the sights outside the window. "I can't believe there's so many people and carriages and houses. It makes Mayfield look like nothin'."

"There are places bigger than Boston," I said while I donned my clothes. "London, of course, and maybe even Philadelphia."

Jane shook her head in amazement. Since I had no mirror, I had to depend on her to help me pin my hair in place and adjust my white cap.

"Come," I said. "I must see if I can find a pretty butter mold for Mother. If we hurry, there should be time for you to see the wharves on our way back to the ferry."

My spirits were high as we left The Black Swan. Hadn't I successfully delivered the message to Mr. Whitlock? Maybe even now it was being whispered into Sam Adams's ear. As for the kiss . . . Jerking my mind to other matters, I set out for Cornhill Street and the woodcarver's shop.

After I'd purchased a scalloped mold with flower petals carved into the bottom to decorate the butter, we made our way to King Street to see the marvel of Long Wharf that stretched half a mile into the bay. The naval blockade had left the wharf almost empty, though a few scows transporting goods from Boston out to the redcoats quartered on Castle Island were visible.

The tide was out, and the smell of fish and seaweed permeated the air as we made our way along Fish Street, where coils of rope and nets dried in the morning sun. A short time later, we were on the ferry to Charles Town.

Thomas took the lead from there, setting the horses to a brisk pace that said that while he'd enjoyed the bustling sights of Boston, he was eager to be back to a more familiar life where the air smelled of freshly plowed soil instead of fish.

Though I shared his feeling, part of me was loath to leave. In accompaniment to the steady rhythm of horses' hooves, I wondered if Gideon had successfully relayed my information to Sam Adams and if he were now safe. Thoughts of intrigue and how I could help traveled with me as the horses slogged along the muddy road back to Mayfield.

It was late afternoon when we reached home, where Father waited tall and solid with a smile on his face.

"I think 'twill be a very long time before I'll want to ride a horse again," I said when he helped me dismount.

He smiled and squeezed my arm. "Did all go well?" Tension left his face when he saw my pleased nod.

"And I found a lovely butter mold for Mother," I responded.

"Good girl."

Leaving Father talking to Thomas, Jane and I walked toward the house. "Was Boston what you expected it to be?" I asked.

"The shops and seeing so many people was like somethin' I dreamed, but I weren't so fond of all the noise. Just the same, I'm glad I got to go. I'll likely still be talkin' 'bout it when I'm an old granny."

"I'm glad you liked it . . . glad, too, that you were such a help to me." I gave her hand an affectionate squeeze. "Don't forget your promise. Not a word about what happened at The Rose and Crown."

She shot a glance back at Father and Thomas. "I won't."

Like Jane, I glanced back at the barn, where Father and Thomas still talked. Although I couldn't hear what they said, I was certain our having passed the night at The Black Swan instead of The Rose and Crown had been mentioned.

Mother's warm embrace and Bethy's excited questions greeted me as I entered the house.

"I prayed for your safety both morning and night," Mother said when there was finally a lull in Bethy's questions. "I can't tell you how worried I've been." She hugged me a second time, and grateful tears shone in her eyes when she pulled away.

"Did the redcoats carry guns?" Bethy asked. "Were they mean to you?"

"There were certainly a great many of them, and, yes, they carried guns and were unfriendly."

"Who was unfriendly?" Father asked as he came in the door and took off his coat.

"The redcoats," Bethy answered.

"Ah," he said. "Such is expected." He gave me a significant look. "Come with me to my study."

As soon as we reached it, Father closed the door and turned to me. "Now tell me how you gave the information to Mr. Whitlock. Were there problems? Thomas said you spent the night at The Black Swan instead of The Rose and Crown."

Though I was as impatient to tell Father about my success as he was to hear it, I had determined not to share that Gideon . . . Mr. Whitlock . . . had kissed me. It was my first kiss, and though I'd slapped him, it was nonetheless my first kiss. More than that, had the circumstances been different, I think I might have enjoyed it.

"I found Mr. Whitlock at the tavern, just as you said. He recognized me at once and was clever enough to provide opportunity for us to speak. I don't think anyone suspected what passed between us, but in case anyone did, I thought it prudent to seek lodging elsewhere."

"Good . . . good. When Thomas told me you'd lodged at The Black Swan, I began to worry." He nodded to himself. "I think 'twas wise of you to do so. Despite our worry for your safety, I never doubted your ability . . . or that of Mr. Whitlock . . . to carry this off." He nodded again. "By now, the information should be in patriot hands."

"Perhaps Mr. Whitlock passed it to Sam Adams himself." I hadn't realized until that moment how much pleasure I derived from speaking Gideon's . . . Mr. Whitlock's . . . name.

"I shouldn't be surprised. Mr. Whitlock has valuable contacts on both sides of the conflict."

"Have you heard from Uncle William? Have they caught the two men?"

Father shook his head. "As yet, there's been no sign of them. 'Tis feared they knew which home was Tory and were hidden until it was safe to leave."

"Then the maps they drew . . ."

"There's no way of knowing if 'twas a map he drew, though the fact that they disappeared as if they'd never ventured this way makes me think they were up to no good."

"Then all the more reason to be glad the patriots in Boston know they were here."

Father nodded and took my hand. "Thank you, Abby. 'Twas a brave thing you did . . . one that may well play an important part in the coming weeks." His hand tightened on mine. "Thank you."

★

My spirits remained high in the days following my return. Not only had my estranged relationship with Father been mended, but I had the satisfaction of knowing I'd succeeded in giving the message to Gideon Whitlock. Gone was my dissatisfaction with my life in Mayfield. In its place was a strong sense that if I exercised patience, other opportunities would come.

The message Mistress Blood had read in the tea leaves had something to do with it. But there was more—something I wasn't yet ready to explore or acknowledge.

A few days later, a letter arrived at the farm. Father had gone into the village to drill with the militia, so it was Mother who met the post rider. She stood for a long moment looking after him before she brought the letter into the house.

"What can this mean?" she asked, pointing to the address on the folded, wax-sealed paper.

I frowned and read the address aloud. "Master Silas Talbot, Stowell Farm, Mayfield, Massachusetts." I looked up as puzzled as she. "There's no one here by that name."

"I know." Mother looked uneasy. "Perhaps 'tis one of your father's friends in Boston or Cambridge playing a game of secrecy." The long look she gave me said she thought otherwise. "Put it on the desk in your Father's study. Most likely he'll know what to make of it."

As soon as Father returned, he went directly to his study, and we didn't see him until supper. Instead of mentioning the letter and the strange name on the outside, he spoke only of events in the village. Ignoring the expectant way I looked at him or that Bethy fidgeted more than usual, he spooned his soup into his mouth with maddening nonchalance. Only as he rose from the table did he ask Mother to come to his study. She delivered a similar summons for me an hour later.

I managed to hold my curiosity in check until I entered the study. "Who is it from? And why is it addressed to Silas Talbot?"

"The letter comes from William Brooks, a printer in Boston. I believe you know his bookshop. I placed an order with him in February for fifty broadsheets to tack on signposts and in taverns. He has written to tell me my order is ready."

"Are the broadsheets seditious?" Seeing him nod, I went on. "Was it not dangerous to order copies of such an inflammatory nature?"

"It was. That's why I gave my name as Silas Talbot. If Sam Adams and his cousin John can have letters published in the Boston Gazette under assumed names, why can't I?"

"But Silas Talbot?" I teased. "Why not something mysterious like Prinopolous?"

Father chuckled. "Such would attract even more attention." Looking down at the letter, he went on. "Mr. Brooks, in addition to saying my order for five copies of the Reverend Cooper's sermons are ready, goes on—"

"Reverend Cooper's sermons? I thought—"

"Reverend Cooper's sermons," he repeated, amusement twinkling in his eyes. "According to Mr. Brooks's letter, the good reverend's sermons are in high demand. 'Tis why it has taken him so long to complete my order."

I stared at him, not knowing whether to be amused or to look for deeper meaning.

"Mr. Brooks is a cautious man and refers to my order as sermons to protect himself." Tapping the letter with his finger, he said, "Since it's not safe for me to show my face in Boston, I'm left with no other recourse than to ask you to again go in my place."

"Which I'll gladly do," I said without hesitation. I didn't relish riding Dolly to Boston again, but the thought of outsmarting General Gage and his lobsterbacks strongly appealed to me.

★

Plans were quickly laid for another trip to Boston. Thomas and Jane would again accompany me, Thomas having been told about the broadsheets but Jane innocent of our true purpose. To my relief, instead of traveling on horseback, we would ride in the cart.

We left early the next morning, Thomas flicking Dolly's reins and Jane and I waving from the backseat of the cart. As before, we stopped at Monroe Tavern in Lexington and, from there, traveled without incident eastward to Boston. The day was overcast, but thankfully, the clouds weren't threatening. Even so, I was glad for my cape, for the wind was chill and belied the fact that we were almost into April.

Ever vigilant, Father had instructed Thomas to avoid the ferry where we might be recognized from before. Instead we took the longer way through Roxbury and thence down the narrow neck of Boston peninsula to the blockade.

The sun was lowering when we finally neared the guardhouse and saw the red-clad soldiers who manned the barricade. Though I tried for nonchalance, my heart jumped when a soldier stepped close to the cart and began to question Thomas. Jane reached for my hand, her fingers tight around mine.

I had a clear view of the young, freckle-faced soldier who wore his red uniform with pride, but it was his gun that held my attention. The long muzzle and metal trigger and firing pan were freshly polished, as if they were as prized as his uniform. I also knew that with one quick movement, the soldier could point his gun at Thomas should he not like or believe Thomas's answers.

There's nothing to fear. I only go to Boston to purchase copies of Reverend Cooper's sermons. Even so, I didn't breathe easily until the soldier gave permission for us to pass through the wide gate.

A second soldier standing at attention at the gate had been openly watching me. Fortunately, his eyes were admiring, not suspicious, and when his companion waved us on, he smiled. "Should ye be lookin' for a comfortable place to be stayin', The Black Swan is but a few streets from here."

I nodded and returned his smile, wondering what he would think if he knew I was on my way to Mr. Brooks's print shop to retrieve seditious broadsheets hidden among the pages of a sermon.

Leaving the blockade, we bumped along Orange Street to Newberry Street and The Black Swan, where we ate and spent the night.

My sleep was fitful as I worried about being discovered with the broadsheets and arrested.

After breakfast, we set out for Mr. Brooks's print shop and bookstore. Jane's excitement at seeing more of Boston swept us along, though we were obliged to take care not to step on horse droppings. Shops of milliners, coopers, and wigmakers were set close to the street, with upstairs living quarters for the owners and their families.

Thomas's eyes grew large when he saw a portly gentleman wearing a blue coat generously decorated with gold buttons and swirls of gold braid. His look of wonderment changed to anger when four redcoats with guns forced him into the street.

Father had warned us not to call attention to ourselves, and I shook my head in warning when an uncomplimentary epithet left Thomas's lips.

A short time later, we found the print shop. A bell tinkled, and a middle-aged man wearing spectacles looked up as we entered.

"May I be of service?" he asked.

My voice and manner were calmer than my fast-beating heart. "I'm on an errand for my father, Silas Talbot. He asked me to pick up some sermons he ordered last month."

The man rubbed ink-stained fingers on his canvas apron. "Silas Talbot, you say?" Muddy eyes the same shade of brown as his wig studied me intently.

"Yes."

"And you are his daughter?"

"I am." I wondered at his questions, wondered too why he studied Jane and Thomas as carefully as he studied me.

"And where, might I ask, does your father reside?"

Alarm and suspicion leapt at me. Was something wrong?

"Are you not William Brooks?" I asked.

The man pushed his spectacles more firmly onto the bridge of his nose. "I am."

"Since you sent my father a letter informing him that his order was ready, you should know where he lives."

"So I do." Some of the tension left him, and after giving me a quick nod, he turned to a drawer behind the counter.

Thomas moved to my side, a troubled expression on his face. "Mistress Abigail," he whispered, nodding in the direction of the back room. Following the direction of his nod, I saw a boy of perhaps thirteen listening intently from the half-opened door.

Realizing he'd been noticed, he stepped more fully into the shop. "I've finished setting the type," he told the proprietor.

Mr. Brooks laid a small bundle of papers on the counter. "Now set to work cleaning the type from yesterday." Returning his attention to me, he said, "I hope your father will enjoy Reverend Cooper's sermons. They are much in demand, and I'm hard pressed to print enough copies to meet the demands of his flock."

"Father said he is a popular preacher."

"Yes, indeed." Mr. Brooks went on smoothly. His finger lightly tapped the papers. When he'd gained my attention, he slipped his finger from the title page to the middle of the stack where one of Father's broadsheets lay.

Looking up from the broadsheet, I saw his silent plea for me to take care what I said. "Mother looks forward to reading them too." As I spoke, I heard a tiny sound from the back of the shop and saw the boy again listening at the partially opened door.

Mr. Brooks's attention was solely on wrapping the stack of papers with a piece of string. "That will be twenty shillings."

I reached into my pocket and took out Father's coins.

As I counted them, Thomas leaned close. "Hurry! The lad's run out of the shop. He's up to somethin'."

Mr. Brooks's head shot up. Breaking off the string, he thrust the package at me. "Go!" he said. "Quick, before he brings soldiers!"

Heart leaping, I hurried to the door.

Thomas yanked it opened and looked up and down the street. "Come," he said, motioning Jane and me through the door. As he closed it, the boy and two soldiers ran around the corner of the shop.

Chapter Eight

"'TIS THEM," THE BOY CRIED.

"Halt!" a soldier shouted.

My only thought was to flee or try to hide the papers. Before I could do either, the soldiers were upon us, one shoving Thomas hard against the wall of the print shop, the other pointing his gun at me.

Jane let out a piercing scream.

The redcoat struggling with Thomas planted his musket against Thomas's heaving chest. Anger and spots of color contorted his swarthy face. "One move and 'twill be your last," he warned.

The second soldier, whose eyes seemed pasted on me, didn't speak until Thomas had stilled. "Hand over the papers you're carryin'," he said in a clipped accent.

My heart beat so hard I found it difficult to breathe. *Think, Abigail. And remember to speak with care.* What came out surprised both me and the soldier. "Pray what is the meaning of this? Can a lady no longer leave her home without being accosted by soldiers?" My tone and manner were those of my Grandmother Reynolds, who could quell a man in midstride with no more than a look and a few well-chosen words.

The soldier, who looked no older than I, flushed. "The . . . the papers. Hand me them papers," he stammered.

"Since the papers are mine, not yours, I see no reason to comply. Not only did I pay for Reverend Cooper's sermons not five minutes past, but I had to wait for over a fortnight for Mr. Brooks to print them."

I paused to swallow, my legs and insides quivering so hard I feared the redcoat could see them. *Take care, Abigail.* Attempting to do so, I went on in a more conciliatory tone. "Perhaps you aren't aware that Reverend Cooper is famous for the excellent sermons he preaches. After I've finished reading them . . . and if you are of a religious nature, I shall let you borrow some." I lifted my head in the haughty manner Grandmother Reynolds sometimes used. "Borrow, sir," I said firmly, "not take them by force."

The soldier holding his gun against Thomas's chest made an impatient sound. "Just take the bloody papers, private."

Glancing past him, I saw two stevedores watching from the street. To my left, an older boy hurried toward us, followed by a burly man and then another. Hope surged through me. Sam Adams's Liberty Boys were gathering.

Something hard struck the older soldier's back. He turned, his eyes widening when he saw the gathering crowd. What had been but five was now a dozen. Two of them carried stout sticks, and another fingered a potato in his raised hand.

"Dirty lobsterbacks!" The man with the potato hurled it at the private, striking him hard on the shoulder. Its force drove the flush from his face and replaced it with fear.

"Steady," the older soldier said. He too heard the menacing sound of the crowd as it pressed closer.

"Go home, redcoat scum!"

"Stinkin' lobsterbacks!"

An amused voice cut through the epitaphs. "'Tis a right comely miss you have there, private. May I suggest that instead of using a musket to woo her, you try a wink and a smile? Such never fails to gain a lady's favor."

My gaze jerked to a man confidently threading his way to the front of the crowd. I didn't have to see his face to know who it was. The tone and cadence of Gideon Whitlock's voice, though heard but thrice, had embedded itself in my mind as surely as an arrow shot from a bow.

"Now, take note," Gideon went on, playing to the Liberty Boys as well as the soldiers. "See if I don't gain a smile from the lady with a soft word and a wink and smile." He moved between the two redcoats and made an exaggerated bow.

His wink, as he raised his head, was much like the one he'd given me at The Rose and Crown, but his smile appeared strained, as did his eyes, which pleaded for me to respond with a smile rather than anger.

I was so glad to see him I would have thrown myself into his arms had he asked me. Instead, I smiled sweetly and dropped a curtsey.

"See," Gideon said. "Now I will show you a better way to obtain the sermons you're so determined to have . . . though I have no notion why a few

sermons should be so important." He paused and smiled at me. "Nevertheless, I shall ask this charming lady with the sermons to accompany me to my
lodgings . . . her maid and manservant as well," he added when he heard the
snickers. "There I shall ply her with—" Gideon paused and whispered something into the older soldier's ear, then did the same with the younger. The
captain's mouth quivered with mirth, but a flush came to the private's face.

The Liberty Boys had stilled and pressed close, trying to see and hear
all what went on.

"We . . . we've been informed . . . that the lady carries seditious broadsheets," the private stammered.

"Surely not," Gideon retorted, the tone of his voice tightening. Without
saying more, he placed his hand on mine and loosened my vicelike grip
on the bundled papers. He let out an amused sound when he read the top
page. "If a sermon written by one Reverend Cooper of the Brattle Street
Church entitled 'The State of the Soul Laid Bare Before the Eyes of God' is
of a seditious nature, I fail to see it." Gideon's gaze held that of the younger
redcoat. "It appears that your information was wrong, private."

"But the boy said . . ."

Gideon thumbed through several sheets of sermons. "See for yourself. Your informant was mistaken." After giving the soldier a minute to
scan the top few pages, he went on, "Now if you will excuse me, I should
like to make myself better acquainted with this fair lady." He tucked my
hand protectively into the curve of his elbow.

Cheers and applause from the Liberty Boys followed his pronounce-
ment.

"Come," he said. "Your maid and servant also."

Jane, whose thin hands had gripped hard on my shoulders the minute
she'd spied the soldiers, loosened her hold when the sergeant reluctantly
lifted the gun's muzzle from her father's chest.

If challenging looks passed between Thomas and the redcoat, I didn't
see them, for I walked beside Gideon with my eyes straight ahead, each
step taking us away from danger.

In my state of mind, I paid little heed to the Liberty Boys's faces or
what was said as we walked between them to cross the street. But I did
take heed of Gideon's muscled arm and that my hand gripped it tightly.
I was also aware of his tailored brown coat and that my head came to but
an inch or two above his wide shoulders.

"Hurry," he said when we reached the other side of the street, "but
not so as to call attention to ourselves."

I nodded and quickened my pace, aware that Thomas and Jane did the same. "Thank you," I breathed, my voice and legs still trembling with fright. "How . . . how did you—?"

"I had business on Middle Street and heard you scream."

"'Twas Jane who screamed," I corrected.

Gideon glanced back at Jane and her father. "Keep close," he cautioned. "I think we'll be safe, but one can never breathe easy with so many lobster-backs roaming the streets."

As if his words conjured them up, two redcoats rounded the corner and walked toward us.

"I haven't had opportunity to ask how you are enjoying your stay in Boston," Gideon said in a polite voice.

I stared at him, wondering if he were jesting before I noted that his eyes were busy assessing the demeanor of the approaching soldiers.

"'Tis . . . much to my liking."

Though I told myself it was impossible for the soldiers to so soon know of the happenings at the print shop, my breathing quickened. My nerves weren't helped when I heard Jane whimper.

"Steady," Gideon said as if we were a regiment and he the captain. In a louder voice, he went on. "'Tis a pity you couldn't have been in town to attend the Governor's Ball on Saturday. 'Twas well attended. Even Major Layton and his wife were there."

Having no idea who Gideon was talking about, I forced animation into my voice and asked for more details. The redcoats were now so close I could see the seams of the shorter soldier's coat straining around his wide girth. They passed as if they didn't see us, forcing us into the middle of the street to give them room.

When Gideon deemed it safe, he bent his head and spoke. "Now tell me why you cling so tightly to the sermons and why the soldiers were so determined to take them."

"The Reverend Cooper's sermons hide broadsheets Father ordered from Mr. Brooks. His apprentice, who must be in the pay of the army, alerted the redcoats when we came to pick them up."

"I saw the rascal slip out the back door . . . but before we could leave, the soldiers came," Thomas put in.

Gideon looked back at him. "Have you checked to see if the lad follows us still?"

"I have, and he ain't. The redcoats are out of sight too."

"Well done . . . Thomas, is it? I should have known Nathan Stowell would send a capable man to protect his daughter."

"Thank you . . . though I don't understand why a Tory is helpin' us."

"Things are not always what they seem," Gideon replied.

Thomas's silence told me he was trying to puzzle this out. Finally, in a regretful voice, he said, "I fear I failed Mr. Stowell at protecting Mistress Abigail."

"Not entirely, but we must hurry to get the three of you safely out of Boston."

"If you'll tell me where you lodge, I'll fetch our horse and cart and meet you there."

"'Tis at The Rose and Crown."

Thomas made a sound of surprise.

"Travel at a normal pace so as not to call attention to yourself," Gideon admonished. "We'll meet you at the stable yard as soon as we can."

When Thomas left us, Gideon quickened his step. We hadn't gone far before he abruptly turned into an alley.

"'Tis a short cut . . . and you and your maid would do well to watch where you step."

Following his warning, as well as his lead, we hurried past clotheslines and necessaries and even a pigsty. Glancing ahead, I could see the rooftop of The Rose and Crown.

When we neared it, Gideon paused. "I apologize for taking you through the less seemly parts of Boston, but my lodgings back on the next alley."

I smiled. "You forget that Jane and I are country bred."

Gideon nodded and hurried us across a street and into an alley that smelled of garbage and the tavern's stable. A few chickens scratching for bugs at the back of The Rose and Crown were the only sign of activity. Yet after our fright at the print shop, I scanned the tavern with suspicious eyes.

"All is safe," Gideon reassured.

We halted behind a lilac bush, the half-opened leaf buds and thick branches offering cover. Though I'd followed Gideon without question thus far, I wondered what he planned next.

The tightness around his mouth told me he wasn't half pleased with the situation. "I don't think I need to tell you that 'twas very fortunate the Liberty Boys came to your aid. Their threatening presence did much to change the two soldiers' minds. Unfortunately, the guards at the blockade won't be so easily intimidated." His green eyes met and held mine. "I fear your only hope of getting them safely out of Boston is to hide the broadsheets on your person."

I nodded, knowing at once he was right, even as I looked around the alley for a place where I could accomplish this.

"You can use my room," he went on. He pointed to the back of the inn. "See the door under the far upstairs window?"

I nodded and studied the brick building.

Gideon retrieved a key from his coat pocket and handed it to me. "Inside that door is a stairway. My room is at the top of the stairs. Unlock the door and wait inside until I come."

"How can I know . . ."

"That you can trust me?" Gideon finished for me.

I blushed, not liking that he could read my mind so easily.

"You can't, which is the curse of what I do." His expression grew solemn, and his eyes bore steadily into mine. "One can only go by instinct. Mine tells me you will guard my secret well. 'Tis my hope that you will come to know you can trust me also."

All signs of the smug, confident man who'd kissed me a mere fortnight before and who only a few minutes ago had glibly spirited me away from the soldiers were gone. As our gazes held, something more binding than words passed between us to offer a hand of trust.

Gideon gave Jane a smile. "Hurry. We've no time to spare."

"What of you?" I asked.

"I shall enter The Rose and Crown by the front entrance and go directly to my room."

Jane and I hurried to the back door of the inn. Still holding tightly to the papers, I looked back and was reassured to see Gideon watching. Once inside, I stopped to get my bearings.

"There 'tis," Jane whispered, pointing to the stairway.

We climbed the narrow stairs to the landing where an empty corridor fronted by several rooms ran the length of the second floor. The key slipped easily into the end door, and the doorknob turned without sound. It seemed Gideon kept them both well oiled. Thinking to use similar caution, I relocked the door behind us.

In my relief to have reached comparative safety, I quickly noted the chairs, table, and desk with quill pen and inkstand, along with a partially opened door that revealed a bed and dresser in an adjoining room. Judging by the size of the rooms, Gideon didn't lack money. More importantly, his room had a sturdy door.

Jane let out a long sigh. "I ain't never been so scared nor so glad to see the man what rescued us from the redcoats. Just the same, I don't trust a man who kisses a lady without her say so . . . and if he tries it today, I'll scream louder than I did with the soldiers."

Setting the sermons on the table, I hid a smile. "Thank you. You've been very brave. Even so, I'm certain Mr."—I stopped, deeming it unwise for Jane to know Gideon's name—"the gentleman has things other than kissing on his mind today." I quickly took off my cape and draped it over the back of a chair. "We must hurry!"

"First you gotta tell me what we're doin' with broadsheets and why we gotta hide them." The tone of Jane's voice and the stubborn set of her pointed chin told me the time of secrecy had passed.

"Mr. Stowell ordered broadsheets that say things against the King. Mr. Brooks hid them among these sermons. If we're found with the broadsheets, we could be arrested."

Jane was silent for a long moment. Then she slowly straightened her shoulders and nodded. "Then we gotta hide 'em so no lobsterbacks can find 'em," she said determinedly.

Before I could say anything, a soft knock sounded on the door.

"'Tis Gideon," a voice whispered.

I unlocked it with shaky fingers. Gideon made straight for the papers on the table. Looking down at the top page of the sermons, he smiled. "I think 'twas the title of the sermon as much as the Liberty Boys that made the redcoats lose their zest to arrest you."

"Don't forget the part you played in it," I reminded him. With my former antagonism now past, I met his gaze squarely. "In our rush to get away, I fear I forgot to compliment and thank you for your quick thinking."

Instead of raised eyebrows or a sardonic smile, he returned my steady gaze. "You are more than welcome."

A tiny sound from Jane reminded us of her presence and sent us all to the table. It didn't take long to separate the broadsheets from the sermons, and as a precaution, Gideon looked through everything a second time.

"While I rekindle the fire and burn the sermons, you may use the adjoining room to hide the broadsheets on yourselves," Gideon said. "But hurry! Time grows short!"

Once in the other room with the door closed, I handed half the broadsheets to Jane. My fingers were clumsy as I folded a paper and rolled down my woolen stocking. Then, molding the broadsheet around my leg, I pulled the stocking up over it and did the same with the second stocking.

Mind and fingers racing, Jane and I conjured up other places to hide the broadsheets—rolling them to fit into pockets, folding them over the front and back of our petticoat waists. In not many minutes, all had been tucked into inconspicuous places between body and fabric, resulting in clothing that fit a trifle too tight. Darting a look at Jane, I saw at once that her brown skirt and bodice would need her cape to hide the bulkiness. Pray God the guards at the blockade wouldn't be so discerning.

Gideon was impatiently feeding the fire with the last of Reverend Cooper's sermons when we rejoined him. It was a moment before he spared a look at us.

"I think 'twill do, though . . ." His voice trailed away as he studied me more closely, shaking his head as he did. "Your fair hair and blue cape are certain to be remembered. You and your maid must exchange capes."

My mouth opened in protest. "I am a good half head taller than Jane!"

"You are also an unusually comely young lady . . . so comely the soldiers and Liberty Boys will talk for days about the young lady in a blue cape and wonder where she's gone."

I turned away, hoping he wouldn't notice my embarrassment. Retrieving my cape from the chair, I wrapped it around Jane's shoulders. She was so short it dragged on the floor. "Have you a pair of scissors?"

Gideon rummaged through his desk drawer for scissors. After kneeling to assess the amount of fabric I'd need to cut off, I spread my cape on the table and began to snip.

Though urgency shouted for me to hurry, I willed my hands to steadiness so my cuts were even. I tried not to think of the hours it had taken Goody Boatrick to weave the fine woolen fabric, or of the numerous nights Mother and I had sat up late to cut and sew it. But getting safely out of Boston with Father's papers was far more important than a ruined cape.

When I finished, I donned Jane's green cape. Though it came several inches above the hem of my green overskirt, I felt only gratitude for Gideon's caution and the fact that the blue hood of my cape would frame red hair, instead of blonde.

Gideon waited at the door. "Take the back stairs, use the alley, then turn to your right, where you'll see the front entrance to The Rose and Crown. I was on my way to meet a client when I heard Jane scream, so I must return on horseback and explain my lateness. If you see me at the stable, pretend you don't know me, and I'll do the same with you." His hand went to the doorknob.

"Thank you again," I whispered.

A smile lifted his lips, making the high planes of his face more prominent. "I would go to greater lengths than this to protect Nathan Stowell's daughter."

"My name is Abigail," I said, aware that we stood so close our shoulders almost touched.

"'Tis a name I'll not forget, for I've carried it in my mind since I first saw you some weeks ago."

His words and soft voice made me blush, and my heart acted just as strangely. "Thank you," was all I could think to say.

"You are entirely welcome." Turning the doorknob, he added, "Take care, and Godspeed, Mistress Abigail."

We found Thomas waiting with Dolly and the cart in the stable yard. His eyes widened when he saw Jane wearing my cape, but a finger to my lips silenced his questions.

"We must hurry," I said when he helped me into the cart. "And should you see the gentleman who helped us earlier, pretend not to know him."

He nodded as Jane scrabbled into the cart behind us. Thomas was climbing into the cart himself when Gideon came out the side door of The Rose and Crown. Acting as if he didn't see us, he hurried into the stable to saddle his horse.

No one spoke as Thomas called to the mare and the cart started toward the street. Keeping my gaze straight ahead, I sensed that Gideon watched us from the stable door.

Once we were on the street, Thomas set Dolly to a moderate pace. Though I knew his purpose, I wanted to scream at the slowness. I also knew he wouldn't take a relaxed breath until we were safely past the soldiers.

Then we were there. Keeping my eyes demurely downcast, I neither smiled nor did anything to attract notice. Had the redcoats been able to hear the rapid beat of my heart or listen closely, they might have heard the slight rustle of paper each time Jane and I breathed.

Luck and God were with us. After checking the canvas bag in the back of the cart and discovering it contained only two nightgowns, apples, and a wedge of bread and cheese, they waved us through without requiring Jane and me to get out of the cart.

Only then did my mind hearken back to Gideon. By now he should have met his client and explained his lateness with an excuse that didn't involve rescuing a young lady in a blue cape. Though he might downplay the part he'd played in our escape from the two redcoats, I would not soon forget the risk he'd taken.

Now that we were safely past the barricade, Thomas set Dolly to a brisk pace, and the cart bumped and jarred along the rutted road to Roxbury. The sooner we put distance between Boston and us, the better it would be. It wasn't until we had passed through Cambridge and were on the road to Menotomy that Jane and I felt comfortable enough to talk.

"I think your trip to Boston was not as you expected," I began in a low voice. Seeing her nod, I went on. "Am I also right to think that, like your father and brother, you are a loyal patriot?"

"Yes'm. I got no more use for the men in England who try to tell us what to do than Pa and Israel. Ben and Ma think the same."

I glanced at her as I held on to the side of the bumpy cart. "Then can I trust you not to say anything about what happened at the print shop?"

"Not even to Ma?"

"Not even to your mother or Israel . . . and especially not to Ben."

"Ben sometimes blabs," Jane agreed.

"If word got out that Mr. Stowell had ordered broadsheets that speak against the King and Parliament, he could be arrested for treason, just as we almost were."

"No . . ." Jane whispered.

"Yes," I replied.

Jane didn't say anything for a long moment. "What about the man what helped us get away from them awful lobsterbacks? Last time I saw him, I was so mad I wanted to slap him, but when he came today, I wanted to kiss him."

"He was a great help to us," I said. "But like Father, he needs to be protected." We ceased to talk, me thinking of Gideon, Jane with her eyes on the passing white daisies blooming among the thick grass on the road-side.

"I think he admires you," Jane finally said.

"Who?" I asked, though I knew full well whom she meant.

"The gentleman what helped us. Do you know his name?"

"I do, but 'tis best that you don't."

The mention of Gideon set me to worrying about him. Was he safe? What had happened? Tripping through my question was the memory of him saying he'd carried my name in his head since the day he'd met me. I smiled, thinking it wasn't just Gideon who remembered things. Didn't I remember things about him too?

We reached Lexington in time to sup and spend the night with Uncle William and Aunt Martha. My first act was to go with Jane to the necessary to remove the broadsheets and put them and the capes into the canvas bag with our nightgowns. It wouldn't do for ever-curious Aunt Martha to know what had happened in Boston.

Chapter Nine

EARLY THE NEXT MORNING, WE set out for home. When the cart rolled to a stop in front of the barn, both my family and the Boatricks came to greet us. One glance at Father's face told me of his concern, and a short time later, he invited me to his study.

"Thomas said there was trouble with soldiers when you picked up the broadsheets. What happened? Why were there soldiers?"

I quickly told him what had happened in the shop.

"Who would have thought?" Father asked when I'd finished. His expression turned apologetic. "Had I dreamed it would be that risky, I'd never have sent you."

"I wasn't overly worried until Thomas said the boy had left the print shop. But thanks to Mr. Whitlock's quick thinking, all turned out right."

"Mr. Whitlock?" Father's voice and brows lifted. "How did he come to be there?"

It took a while to explain. During the telling, Father sat behind the desk and I took my regular place opposite him. His eyes widened when I explained how Mr. Whitlock had bluffed his way past the crowd to reach the redcoats and had gambled us away right under their noses. I spoke of his cleverness and confidence and how he'd taken us to his rooms at the tavern.

Father scowled when he heard this.

"Mr. Whitlock was a gentleman in every way and most protective of Jane and me," I assured him.

"Well . . ." Father breathed. Conflicting emotions crossed his face— one of gratitude quickly followed by one that hinted of amusement. "'Tis what a father likes to hear, though I own you're quick to come to the man's defense."

"If it hadn't been for Mr. Whitlock's cleverness, your broadsheets would have been confiscated and we would have been arrested."

Father studied his hands for a long moment. When he spoke, his voice held anger. "To think that such a thing could happen in Boston in the brightness of day and with citizens looking on." He shook his head. "'Tis all the more reason for us to take up arms against such blatant tyranny."

Not wanting Father to become more upset, I hurried to tell him how Jane and I had hidden the broadsheets in our clothing and about the capes. "Mr. Whitlock burned Reverend Cooper's sermons, and when we stopped at Aunt Martha's, I put your broadsheets and our capes into the bag Thomas gave you."

Father's face was solemn when he arose and came around the desk. "The Good Lord most assuredly heard our prayers." He shook his head. "I shall eternally be grateful to Gideon Whitlock. I owe him a great debt of gratitude."

Before I could agree, Father put his arms around me and held me close. "Thank heaven you are safely home, Abigail. Thank heaven."

★

With the coming of April, the lilacs in the yard opened in clusters of lavender and white blooms. The heady aroma made the day seem like one made in heaven. Birds that had flown south for the winter were returning to blend the happy sound of their singing with that of bleating lambs.

Since my return from Boston, I felt as if I were awakening from the grayness of winter as well. I hummed to myself when I walked out to the pasture to watch the lambs gambol in spring-green grass, and I picked a lilac spray when I went to the well house to bring in water for Mother.

She looked up from the batter she was stirring. "Will you see if the chickens have laid more eggs? I used the last ones in this pudding. Your father will be unhappy if he doesn't have eggs in the morning for his breakfast."

Picking up the egg basket, I went out to the chicken pen. Still singing, I'd almost reached my destination before I heard someone call.

"Mistress Abigail."

I looked around and saw a tall man step from the shadows. The lowering sun was at his back, so I couldn't see his features clearly, but even if it had been midnight, I'd have recognized the voice. *Gideon!*

I hurried to him. "Gid . . . Mr. Whitlock."

"I wouldn't be offended if you called me Gideon. Indeed, I should like it, for 'tis what my friends call me." His voice was teasing, and I knew even before I reached him I'd see amusement dancing in his eyes.

Stepping close, Gideon looked as intently at me as I did at him. It was as if he had silent questions needing answers too. Awareness charged the air around us, and my gaze made a pleasurable journey over the high planes of his cheekbones, then down to his firm chin.

"You've come to talk to Father," I finally said.

He nodded, his gaze still intent. "I had to know you were safe."

Heat rose to my cheeks, and I tucked a stray lock of hair back under my cap.

His hand moved to stay me. The light touch of his fingers on mine sent pleasant shocks of warmth all the way down to my toes. "Don't," he said softly. "I like it that way." Clearing his throat, he dropped his hand. "Were there any problems at the blockade?"

"No, though I am ever so grateful for your help. Father is sure to thank you too. When I told him what happened, he said he would always be in your debt."

"I didn't do it just to please your father." Aware of my embarrassment, Gideon turned to study the orchard, then the barn and outbuildings. "Come," he said, taking my elbow and leading me into the trees, where we were less likely to be seen.

Like the lilacs, the orchard was in bloom, the pink and white blossoms covering the branches like froths of new-fallen snow.

"What of you?" I asked.

"All has been well, though I felt it prudent to stay close to The Rose and Crown for a few days. 'Tis fortunate most of my clients come to see me there."

"Clients?"

"I'm a lawyer."

I looked up at him in interest. "I wondered what you did when you weren't gathering information and spying."

His voice came light. "What makes you think I'm a spy?"

"I am not without brains, Mr. Whitlock."

"Courage either," he countered. He rubbed his cheek. "You also have a bit of a temper."

"'Tis true." I sighed. "I don't take kindly to being kissed in that manner, but I'm sorry if my slap hurt you."

"'Tis I who should apologize. 'Twas all I could think to do to cover our conversation and get you out of the tavern."

"When I left The Rose and Crown, my anger was genuine, but after I had time to think, I realized your ploy was really quite clever."

"Now you give me compliments?" He went on in a more serious tone. "Brave . . . with a bit of a temper. Clever as well. Your father told me how you and your brother were tutored together."

"Why were you and Father talking about me?"

"I wanted to know more about the young woman who'd called me an odious man and took me to task for quarreling with an old man."

"I don't like to see anyone bullied. Besides, I thought you were a Tory."

"For anyone to think otherwise could mean imprisonment . . . perhaps even the loss of my life."

I looked steadily into his eyes. "I promise that no one will learn it from me."

Silence stretched between us, and I hoped with all my heart that no one discovered the game Gideon played. Did he daily awaken to the knowledge that he might find himself imprisoned on Crown Island by the end of the day or that the breath he took in the morning might be snuffed out by nightfall?

I shivered and pulled my light cotton shawl more tightly around me.

Noticing my actions, Gideon fingered the shawl. "I'm sorry you had to cut off your cape. The blue color became you."

When I lifted my eyes and met his warm gaze, my insides quivered like leaves in a windstorm. Swallowing, I tried to think of something safe to say. "Jane is pleased to inherit it. After her mother hemmed it, the cape looked as if it were made for her, not me. Goody Boatrick is already weaving fabric for a new cape for me."

"There's no reason for you to worry," Gideon said as if he guessed the true reason why I shivered. "As long as I keep my wits about me, I shan't be found out."

"I hope not." I paused before going on. "When did you decide to spy and gather information from the redcoats?"

"While I was at college in Cambridge."

"My twin brother went there also."

"Your father told me about his death. I'm truly sorry."

"So am I." Unbidden tears clouded my vision.

Quickly clearing his throat, he went on, "While I was at Harvard, I frequently hired a horse and rode to Charles Town, where I caught the ferry to Boston. Hearing Sam Adams preach about gaining freedom from the heavy hand of England, I decided I wanted to be a part of the rebellion. The part I would play didn't come to me until after I graduated and was clerking for my lawyer uncle in Philadelphia. During the months I wrote briefs for him, I determined that when I opened my own practice, it would be in Boston, where I would pass myself off as a staunch Tory."

"An arrogant Tory," I corrected, my discomfort forgotten.

He chuckled and leaned against a tree. "'Tis my wish to play my part well."

"I think 'tis not entirely an act . . . that like me, you have a bit of pride."

"You admit to such, do you?"

"I do. And since you asked Father about me, he's certain to have told you as well. 'Tis a Stowell trait, and Father isn't shy about pointing out my faults."

"As any good parent should," Gideon remarked.

"Did your father do such to you?"

He looked down at the grass. My eyes followed, taking in his dun-colored breeches buckled at the knee, his long stockings, and scuffed boots. "My father died when I was too young to remember him, but thanks to a generous uncle, my mother and I were given a comfortable home and I a good education. Since my uncle has no sons of his own, he's also set me up at The Rose and Crown, where I've succeeded in building up a good clientele. Even so . . ." He looked up and met my eyes, the lowering sun outlining his wide shoulders and highlighting his brown hair touched with glints of copper. "Like your father, my uncle didn't mince words about my shortcomings. But he did allow me to go to Harvard instead of the college in Philadelphia, and he and my mother . . . who has since remarried . . . are reconciled to me practicing law in Boston instead of joining in partnership with him."

"You are from Philadelphia, then?"

"I am. And if you wish to know whether the male citizens there are as hot-headed as those in Boston, the answer is no. They claim to be of a more reasonable nature. My uncle is certainly so. He is also a dyed-in-the-wool Tory, and it's from listening many years to him that I learned to impersonate a Tory."

"Just the same, you must take care."

He pushed himself away from the tree trunk. "I intend to, Mistress Abigail, for I have every intention of seeing you again."

Color again rose in my cheeks. "I . . . I—"

He reached and plucked a spray of blossoms from the tree. Handing it to me, he said, "Now go and tell your father I am here."

I nodded. "I will also tell him to leave the door unlocked for you after dark."

His green eyes probed mine before I turned and walked away. I hadn't taken many steps before I heard him softly say, "Remember, you haven't seen the last of me, Mistress Abigail."

I gave him a teasing smile over my shoulder. "We shall see, Mr. Whitlock."

Basket still in hand, I left Gideon in the orchard. Twice I looked back, once near the barn and again at the chicken pen. The first time, he still stood under the apple tree, the top of his head half hidden by the blossoms, his hand lifted. By the second time, he had disappeared. I lifted my hand to shade my eyes against the lowering sun, but no matter how hard I looked, I couldn't see him. Like some figment of my imagination, he had vanished into the air.

My mind was so skittish with dancing, half-formed thoughts of Gideon, I paid little heed to the chickens as I gathered the eggs. When I entered the kitchen, I carried four eggs nestled in the basket and a spray of apple blossoms in my hand.

"I wondered what was taking you so long," Mother said, "but I see you've been out to the orchard."

I looked at the pink blossoms. If Mother hadn't been watching, I would have brought them to my lips and kissed them. "They're so lovely this time of year."

The spicy odor of bread pudding filled the kitchen and reminded me I was hungry. Gideon must be hungry too. If I were careful, perhaps I could take him something. That was, if I could find him. Something told me he wouldn't be an easy man to find if he didn't wish to be found.

A glance at Mother, who knew the contents of her pantry as well as she knew her book of common prayers, warned me that taking food to Gideon would be difficult. I wandered aimlessly around the kitchen, unable to keep my mind on any one thought for more than a few seconds.

"Whatever is wrong with you, Abby? I've never seen you so restless."

"I think I must have a touch of spring fever."

"We have no time for spring fever," Mother said in a brisk tone. "Can't you see the spit needs turning and the table isn't set?"

"Where are Jane and Bethy?"

"Jane wasn't feeling well and has gone home. As for Bethy . . ." Mother sighed. "She's as bad as you are today. The truth is I'm not sure where she is."

For the next few minutes, I busied myself turning the spit and setting the table. Gideon's name hovered at the edge of my mind like a bee darting from flower to flower in search of nectar. I tried to push it away, but in the end, I picked up the blossoms and slipped out of the kitchen. "I'm going to look for Bethy," I called.

Instead, I went up to our bedroom, where I poured water into a blue vial for the apple blossoms. After smelling and admiring them, I went outside to look for Bethy.

After I'd called to her twice, she poked her head out of the woodshed.

"Where have you been? Mother's looking for you."

"I'm looking for the cat. I think she's gone out to have her kittens."

"You can look for her tomorrow. It's almost time for supper."

Bethy sighed and followed me to the house. "I hope she has four."

"Why four?"

"I told Cousin Mary our cat was going to have more kittens than hers."

I smiled and wished my life were as simple as Bethy's. Yet if I were asked to trade it, my answer would be a resounding no, a response hopelessly tangled around Gideon's parting words.

After helping Mother finish supper, I went to look for Father.

"Abby," Father said when he saw me.

"Gideon Whitlock is here," I whispered.

Father looked around. "Where?"

"He was in the orchard, but he said he'd come to the house after dark."

Father nodded. "'Tis wise."

"I told him you'd leave the front door unlocked."

Father was unusually quiet throughout the meal, and I thought he must be wondering why Gideon had come. Only when Mother dished him a bowl of bread pudding did he smile and seem himself again.

"No one makes bread pudding as well as you, Goodwife," he said.

"There's no one I'd sooner make it for."

They exchanged a fond look, and his hand lingered on her shoulder when he rose from the table. "Instead of the sitting room, I'll be working late in my study."

Mother nodded and began to clear the table. With Bethy and me to help, it wasn't long until the kitchen was set to rights and we were sitting around the fire in the sitting room. I listened with only half a mind as Bethy and Mother talked. Soon I ceased to listen altogether, my mind and ears tuned for the sound of the front door quietly opening. No sound came, and when the clock struck eight, I began to worry that something had happened to keep Gideon away.

The stitches in my sewing were as erratic as my thoughts. Where was he? Had he been discovered? As if to answer my question, the sitting room door opened.

"Could you bring a tankard of cider to me, Abby?"

My heart skipped in happy anticipation as I left to fetch cider. Gideon was here! Although I'd listened, he'd slipped into the house so quietly I hadn't heard him.

Along with filling the tankard, I added bread with jam and dished up the last of the bread pudding Mother had saved for Father. Pleasing Gideon overrode the prospect of Father's displeasure in the morning.

I paused to pinch color into my cheeks and felt to see if any stray locks had escaped my cap. *"Don't,"* Gideon's voice seemed to say. *"I like it that way."*

Smiling at the memory, I hurried to the study and knocked on the door. Too impatient to wait for Father's bidding, I opened it and went in.

Gideon rose from his chair. Though his eyes showed pleasure, he gave no more than a polite nod. "Mistress Abigail," he said in a formal tone.

"Mr. Whitlock," I responded just as formally. I set the tray on the desk. "I thought Mr. Whitlock might like something to eat with his cider."

Father's look was unhappy when he saw the bread pudding. Hoping to divert him, I asked, "Did you wish to speak to me?"

He nodded. "Mr. Whitlock has devised a plan we thought would be wise for you to know about."

I had been waiting for an excuse to look at Gideon. Indeed, my senses had been aware of him the entire time I'd been talking to Father. Turning, I experienced the full force of his gaze. Something passed between us that made me swallow and Gideon to clear his throat.

"Something unusual is afoot with General Gage and the redcoats," he began. "His aides are strangely close-mouthed, and I can feel their heightened excitement. Instinct tells me something important is about to happen in your area. I came to warn your father and others before it's too late."

His news ate at my happiness. "What do you think it is?"

Father's expression was grave. "Mr. Whitlock thinks Gage's spies have learned about the arms and ammunition hidden in Concord. I'll ride there at first light to let them know."

"The men we saw on the road last month . . ." I said.

"Were spies who escaped us as well as Sam Adams."

"Whether a raid comes in two days or two weeks, it's sure to happen." Gideon paused before going on. "Since it isn't safe for your father to contact me in Boston, if a need arises and he needs to send a message—"

"Yes," I said, giving my answer before he could say more.

"'Twill be unwise to enter The Rose and Crown again . . . at least by the main door. But the back way can be used, though there's no guarantee I'll be in my room. I meet with clients in both the tavern's main room and my sitting room. You can also send a note. There are always boys roaming the streets, eager to earn a copper. Any of them can be trusted."

"You say this with confidence," I said.

Gideon gave a brief smile. "I do. Word has gotten out that I'll pay the boys another copper when the note is safely delivered into my hands." The tone of his voice changed, and he spoke as if making a solemn promise. "If you but tell me where to meet you, I will make every effort to be there."

His eyes held mine, their green depths deepening to seal the pact. Hoping Father hadn't noticed what had passed between us, I strove for normalcy. "Is there anything else I should know?"

"That the risk in Boston grows every day. If you come, you must act with caution. More important, remember things are not always as they seem."

"I will," I said.

"Good."

I looked at Father, who sat with his elbows on the desk. "Father?"

"I think all has been sufficiently covered."

"Then I shall rejoin Mother and Bethy." I moved to the door but stopped after opening it to look back at Gideon. "Please don't ignore our hospitality by neglecting to eat the food I brought for you, Mr. Whitlock."

"I shall eat every crumb." Turning his head slightly, he winked.

I could no more suppress my smile than I could stop breathing.

Gideon's next words stopped my smile, though, before it fully formed, his voice sounding so grave it gave me pause. "Should you be required to come to Boston, Mistress Abigail," he said, "you must use every care."

What remained of my smile trembled on my lips as I nodded and left the room. I leaned against the closed door, not knowing what to think or feel.

The sobering knowledge that General Gage was still determined to put down any show of rebellion coiled hotly in my middle. Father and dozens of others loyal to the cause could be arrested—carefully hoarded arms and ammunitions destroyed or hauled back to Boston—shots might even be fired. With all haste, the supplies stockpiled in Concord must be moved before the redcoats found them.

"Thank you, Gideon," I whispered.

When I returned to the sitting room, Bethy had gone up to bed. Instead of returning to my sewing, I told Mother I wished to retire as well. She nodded and gave me a long look. "First tell me what you and your father talked about."

Not wishing to reveal Gideon's presence, my answer was evasive. "The situation in Boston grows worse. Father might need me to take another message."

Mother's hand stilled on her sewing. "Is that safe?"

"Father will explain it to you," I said and kissed her good night.

Bethy was asleep when I undressed and said my prayers. Only when I'd snuggled into my pillow did I allow my thoughts to speed to Gideon. I remembered how he'd stayed my hand when I'd tucked back a stray lock of hair. And the apple blossoms. Tonight, their sweetness filled the room. Tomorrow they'd be there to savor, along with Gideon's parting words. The rich timbre of his voice seemed to echo from the orchard.

"Remember, you haven't seen the last of me, Mistress Abigail."

Chapter Ten

DESPITE THE SERIOUSNESS OF GIDEON'S news, my spirits were high as I helped Mother in the kitchen the next morning.

She looked up when she heard me humming. "'Tis good to hear someone singing."

"How could I not sing on such a lovely morning? The rest of the day looks to be fair too."

"I hope you're right, for your father rode to Concord at first light." Her expression was pensive, and the circles under her eyes told me she hadn't slept well.

I paused as I put on my apron. "Father told you what General Gage may be planning?"

"He did. He also told me how he came to learn of it." Her dark brows lifted in question. "Was the messenger present when you went to the study?"

"Yes."

Mother looked at me with furrowed brow. "I don't like it that a man I've never met slips into my home . . . partakes of my food, and who knows what else."

I was surprised by her sharpness. "I'm sorry I took the pudding without asking. The man had traveled far, and I thought he might be hungry as well as thirsty."

"Does this man have a name?"

"He does, though whether 'tis his true name, I don't know. I only know that to disclose it could endanger his life."

Mother turned contrite. "You needn't apologize for keeping your secret or taking the pudding. You are but being trustworthy and hospitable." She sighed and looked up from the griddlecakes she stirred. "I don't like change.

Lately, 'tis all I find. The threat of war . . . people taking sides and not speaking to each other . . . strangers stealing into my house at all hours of the night."

She paused and attempted a smile. "In time, I shall grow used to it, but there are moments when I wish we could go back ten years when things were more settled and when . . ." A look of sadness crossed her face, and I knew she thought of Jonathan.

"Ten years ago, you . . . we . . . didn't have Bethy."

She lifted her shoulders as if she were physically closing the door on her grief. "Yes," she agreed. "Sweet Bethy. What would we do without her?"

Though change didn't suit Mother, I welcomed it like the dawning of a new day. Not knowing what the next weeks or months would bring was exciting. I didn't delude myself into believing the future would be easy, but whether difficult or dangerous, I looked forward to playing an active role in whatever lay ahead.

★

Now that the weather was moderating, I began to spend more time outdoors. One particularly fine day, I saw Father pacing off the south field in preparation for spring plowing and planting. Seeing him, I hunted through the dead growth in the kitchen garden to see if any herbs or plants were beginning to sprout.

Even though I took pleasure in the warmer weather, thoughts of impending war were never far from my mind. The Mayfield militia now drilled three times weekly, and I came upon Israel teaching Ben how to clean and load the squirrel gun.

"'Tain't powerful enough to hurt anyone 'less you get up real close, but if me and Pa and Mr. Stowell march off to fight the redcoats, you'll be the man here." Israel paused and looked at his brother. "Besides defending Ma and Jane, you gotta take care of Goodwife Stowell and Abigail and Bethy. You hear me?"

The twelve-year-old boy nodded solemnly.

My heart constricted at Israel's words, and instead of joining them in the barn, I slipped quietly away so they wouldn't know I'd heard. "Not Ben," I whispered. "He's too young for killing."

The terrible picture weighed heavily on my mind, and the next day I found Father and told him what I'd overheard.

"You need to show me how to shoot Jonathan's musket."

Father's mouth opened, but before he could say anything, I hurried on. "Israel's squirrel gun can't be relied on. And with you and the Boatricks off fighting . . ." I straightened my shoulders. "I may not know how to shoot a gun, but I know enough about war to realize that when fighting starts, it may spread through the colonies . . . maybe even here."

Father looked away, his gaze moving over the barn and fields that made up our home. "I pray to God it will never come to that."

"So do I, but if it does—" I moved to face him. "If it does, I need to know how to defend Mother and Bethy."

"You are right," Father said after a long moment.

The following evening, Father retrieved Jon's musket from the rack above the fireplace. "Come," he said, leading me to the entryway. Handing the gun to me, he said, "First you must make yourself familiar with its weight and heft. Carry it around . . . lift it . . . aim it."

The gun's heavy weight surprised me, and I soon discovered that the long muzzle made it ungainly and difficult to balance and aim.

"It will come with practice," Father assured me.

I saw Mother and Bethy leave the sitting room to watch. Bethy's eyes were wide, but Mother's looked angry.

"This is not what I raised my daughter to do," she said in a voice that, despite its loudness, wasn't quite steady.

"'Tis not what I like either," Father replied. "But since all the men may be gone in a few days or weeks, I think it wise that one of you knows how to shoot a musket." That said, we returned to our lesson.

On the second evening, instead of sitting by the fire with my mending, I learned how to break down the musket and clean it. The next evening brought a lesson in loading and priming the gun. Since powder and lead balls were scarce, they were hoarded for actual fighting. Going through the motions without firing left me frustrated and feeling only partially prepared.

A week passed, and still there was no word of redcoats raiding Concord. I gave thanks every night, and each morning I listened for the pounding hoofbeats of a messenger coming to tell us of the raid.

It was George Hawks who brought the news that April morning, riding his lathered horse down the lane to our house. He called to Father, who was carrying a sack of seed out of the barn. "It's come, Nathan! War's begun!"

Dropping the sack, Father hurried to his friend. "Where?" he called. "Lexington!"

I set down the basket of eggs and hurried after Father, my blue skirt and petticoat tangling around my legs.

Mr. Hawks reined in his horse, the sound of the animal's labored breathing filling the morning air. "Redcoats left Boston last night, headed for Concord to destroy our arms." He panted. "They fired on the Lexington militia mustered on the commons . . . killed several and routed the rest."

Father's mouth tightened as he placed his hand on Mr. Hawks's booted leg. "What about Concord?"

Before Mr. Hawks could answer, the village church bells began to ring, their loud peal carrying the two miles to our farm.

"Reverend Whipple's sounded the alarm." Mr. Hawks looked down at Father. "As for Concord, I don't know. The rider only said the redcoats left Lexington and are marching toward Concord." There was a moment of tense silence. "Are we still to meet south of Millbrook fork in Ashley's pasture?"

Father nodded. "Pass along the word if you see any of the committeemen." His voice turned harsh. "We'll make them pay for what they did in Lexington . . . make them pay every step of the way back to Boston. The bells will bring men from all over the countryside to harass them so bad they'll wish they'd never left Boston. By nightfall, hundreds will have joined us."

Noticing me for the first time, Mr. Hawks gave me a quick nod. "I need to alert Josiah Ryder and those along Tipple Road in case they didn't hear the bell." Whirling his horse, Mr. Hawks lifted a hand and urged his horse back up our tree-lined lane.

Father started for the house. "Tell Ben to saddle Jumper and the other two horses," he called over his shoulder. "Then go help Jane fix food for us to take."

"Do Thomas and Israel know?"

Father pointed to the north field where both men were hurrying toward the barn. "They've heard the bells."

I left to find Ben, my basket of eggs forgotten. I spied him as I rounded the barn, coming at a hard run from the pasture.

"What's wrong?" Ben hollered. "Why're the bells ringin'?"

"Redcoats killed some Lexington militiamen this morning," I called. "Father wants you to saddle all the horses."

It took Ben a minute to reach me. "Redcoats!" he repeated, his voice cracking with excitement. He shook his head as he joined his steps with mine, looking like he didn't quite believe it had finally happened. His eager voice went on. "I'm gonna ask yer father to let me go with 'em. I've been practicing, and I'm right good at firin' the squirrel gun."

My stomach tightened at the thought of Ben tagging after the men— tightened even more as I pictured Father taking cover behind a tree or stone fence to fire at the well-trained redcoats. "You're to stay here," I replied. "'Tis the horses Father wants you to help with. Hurry and get them saddled."

I skirted the well house and made my way to the kitchen, where the smell of ham and breakfast still lingered. Jane came around the table as soon as I walked through the door. "What are we to do, Mistress Abigail?"

I knew by her worried expression that she'd not only heard the tolling bells, but Father's words as he'd hurried into the house as well.

"What did Mr. Stowell tell you to do?"

"He . . . he said to pack some bread and cheese . . . and a flask of water. Said to do the same for Pa and Israel."

"Then that's what you must do."

"Yes'm." She moved back to the table and began to slice off big slabs of bread. Though worry showed on her face, her strokes were quick and sure.

"It will be all right," I said in an effort to reassure her. "Mr. Stowell and your pa and Israel know how to take care of themselves."

She nodded, her ruffled cap slightly askew. "Yes'm," she repeated, and I sensed that like me, she hoped my words proved true.

I lit a candle and ran down the steep steps to the cellar, where rounds of yellow cheeses sat next to crocks of butter on a shelf above casks of cornmeal and salted fish. In my haste, I almost dropped the cheese as I grabbed three apples. They were starting to shrivel, but I hoped the men would still enjoy them.

Urgency drove me back up the stairs where Bethy waited. As soon as I set down the food and the candle, she wrapped her arms tight around me and buried her face in the waist of my apron.

"I'm scared, Abby," she whispered. "What if the redcoats shoot Father like they did those men in Lexington?"

I pulled her close and ruffled her dark curls. "They won't, Bethy."

"How can you be sure?"

"Remember that Father fought in the French and Indian War. He knows how to fight and take care of himself."

Bethy pulled away and looked up at me, her large eyes dark with worry. "Are you sure, Abby . . . sure nothing bad will happen to him?"

I returned her steady gaze. "As sure as anyone can be without actually knowing."

"Like faith?" she asked.

"Like faith."

She nodded and seemed to take comfort in my words. They comforted me as well. Perhaps if I said them often enough, I'd come to believe them.

I had just finished slicing cheese when my parents came into the kitchen. Though the spring day was warm, Father wore a coat over his vest and carried his long rifle with a powder horn and lead balls secured by a strap over his shoulder.

For a moment, no one spoke. In the silence, I noted that Mother's dark eyes were unusually bright. Seeing them and her unsteady mouth almost undid me. Then Mother and Father both began talking at once, Mother asking if the bread and cheese were ready and Father reminding Jane to fill a flask with water.

My fingers were clumsy as I folded the cheese and bread in a cloth and put the bundle and the apples into Father's knapsack. All too soon, the five of us were walking out to the barn, where Ben and his father and Israel stood by the horses.

Goody Boatrick was there too, her plump arms folded tightly at the waist of her bibbed apron, her white-capped head shaking vigorously as she spoke firmly to Ben. "No," she said. "Your pa already said ye was to stay home with me'n Janie."

"But, Ma . . ."

Father's voice brought Ben's tongue to a halt. "Your place is here to look after the women. They'll need someone to chop wood and see to the milking, and I expect all the rocks the plow turned up in the cornfield to be piled next to the fence."

Ben knew better than to say anything besides, "Yes, sir," to my father. Even so, it was obvious how badly he wished to go with the men.

Father cleared his throat and looked at Bethy and me—she standing as tall as she could and trying to be brave, me with a hand on her shoulder and my head held high. We were all that remained of the Stowell children.

Bethy ran to Father and circled his waist with her arms. Father bent his head and spoke in a low, comforting voice, and I saw Bethy nod her head. After Father had untangled her arms from his waist, she went to Mother.

I approached Father, and though I didn't hug him, I badly wanted to. Instead, I met his eyes and set my trembling lips in a firm line. The dreaded war had finally begun, and if nothing else, I would show him a brave face.

"Keep safe, Father."

"You know I shall, just as I know you and your mother will look after things while I'm away."

I nodded and continued to hold his gaze.

"Then I can leave with my mind at ease."

Head high, I remained where I was as he made his farewell to Mother. With so many watchful eyes, there was no outward display of affection, but I knew they had not been so restrained in Father's study.

Then the three men mounted their horses and rode up the lane, our calls of Godspeed following them.

Disappointed at being left behind, Ben looked ready to burst into tears, and Jane was openly crying. Only Goody Boatrick stood solemnly with Mother and Bethy and me.

Her face was anxious as she turned to Mother. "I can't believe 'tis begun. Even with all the talk and drillin', I kept hopin' 'twould never happen. Didn't you, Mistress Stowell?

"I did. Hoped and prayed." Mother lifted her narrow shoulders like she was inwardly telling herself she must be strong. "Pray God they'll all come home safe."

Goody Boatrick sighed and set out for the laundry house while Jane dejectedly followed us back to the house.

As soon as we entered the kitchen, I turned to Mother. "When do you think they'll be back?" It was a question in all of our minds. Jane waited at the door to hear her answer.

Mother took a deep breath. "I do not know. I truly do not know."

"A day? A week?"

"I don't know," she repeated. Moving from the fireplace, she placed her hands on my shoulders. "If the militia means only to harass the soldiers back to Boston, they may be back by the morrow. Thursday at the latest. But if"—she stopped, and her fingers tightened—"if the redcoats engage the militia in battle—" She paused again, and her gaze shifted to Bethy, then to Jane. "We must each be brave and pray," Mother said. "Now . . . at meals . . . at bedtime. Each time you think of your fathers, you must be brave and pray." Mother reached out a hand to Bethy and nodded to Jane to join us in prayer.

"But 'tisn't meal or bedtime," Bethy stated.

"God has invited us to call out to Him in times of trouble," Mother answered. "This is a time of trouble."

Though she smiled at Bethy, I knew that behind the smile was the urge to cry. I saw tears shimmer in her eyes as the four of us joined hands and knelt on the wooden floor of the kitchen, heard them quiver through her voice as she, instead of Father, led us in prayer.

★

Although we attempted to return to our chores, no one was successful. Mother twice left off making a chicken pie, once while cutting up the chicken and again when she crimped the edges of the crust. Her pie crusts were always flaky and tender, but I feared the one today would be lacking in both. As for Jane, she flitted from room to room as if she weren't certain what to do next, and Bethy followed me so closely I seemed always to trip over her.

Never one to wait patiently, I'd resolved what I would do while watching the men ride away. Instead of enduring the endless waiting to learn what our militiamen and the redcoats were doing, I intended to ride after them and watch from the height of Hardy Hill.

The year before, when Jonathan had been so sick and I'd made my frantic ride to fetch Prudence Blood, I'd flung myself without thought onto Jumper's back, riding bareback with my dress bunched up as I'd clung to the horse's mane. Not so today. Today I would don breeches to better stay on the horse.

It was close to noon before I could elude Bethy and carry out my plan. Hurrying up to Jonathan's darkened room, I opened one of the shutters and went straight to the drawer that held the clothes I needed: the pair of breeches and shirt Jonathan had left behind when he'd gone to Harvard College in Cambridge three years before. Once I was dressed, I pulled on his old, scuffed boots and snatched his wide-brimmed hat from the peg. Not wanting to be seen, I used the front door to leave the house and slipped out to the barn.

The inside was dim and cool, and though I'd vowed not to ride a horse for a good long while, Dolly was my quickest means of seeing what was happening along the Concord-Lexington road. Taking Ben to open gates would also be helpful. Besides, he was as eager as I to see the soldiers.

He was carrying a large rock from the cornfield to the stonewall separating the pasture from the meadow, his scrawny frame struggling with each step. Instead of calling to him, I set out across the pasture, finding unexpected pleasure in not being encumbered by my long skirt and petticoat, especially when I climbed the wall.

Ben didn't see me until I was almost there. Lifting his hand to shade his eyes, he stared for a long moment, his stance wary.

Waving, I called in a soft voice. "'Tis I . . . Mistress Abigail!"

Ben continued to stare as if he doubted his eyes. To reassure him, I removed Jon's hat so he could see my blonde hair.

Reassured, he scrambled over the wall. "For a minute, I thought 'twas Master Jon. Why are you wearin' his clothes?"

"I mean to ride to see what's happening between the militia and redcoats. Would you like to come?"

"Would I!" Ben's freckled face split into a grin. "Better'n most anything, though my ma'll likely give me a lickin' when she finds out." He paused and shook his head. "Ma won't like it above half, and I doubt yours will either."

"We'll ride cross county so no one will see us."

Seeing me in Jon's clothes seemed to have unsettled him so much that he followed me to the barn without saying another word. Leading Dolly to the mounting block, I was soon astride her. Ben furtively led Dolly out of the barn and through the gate. After closing it, he climbed atop the gate and scrambled on behind me.

The songs of robins in newly leafed trees reassured me that all of Massachusetts hadn't suddenly gone mad, and the cows and sheep grazed as placidly as they'd done the day before, which added to the reassurance. Over the past months, tension and rumors had increased—some true, others exaggerations or lies. Pealing church bells had twice sent militia and committee men streaming into Charles Town and Cambridge. The sight of so many had been enough to quell General Gage's enthusiasm for sending redcoats out of Boston to search for hidden stores of gunpowder and ammunition in Salem and Mystic. Until now.

As Ben opened and closed gates, his excitement was such that he couldn't stop talking. "When do ya think we'll catch up with them? Do ya think there'll be actual fightin', or is it but another scare?"

"I don't know, Ben. I truly don't know."

Today, shots had actually been exchanged between colonists and soldiers. I knew without doubt Uncle William and Cousin Enoch had been among those gathered on Lexington common. Pray to God they hadn't been wounded or killed.

We were nearing Hardy Hill when we heard the sudden crack of musket fire and saw distant puffs of smoke.

"Fightin'!" Ben said, the excitement in his voice joined by a quiver of fear.

My heart slammed hard against my chest as I urged the mare toward Hardy Hill, where I hoped to catch sight of Concord village and the road leading back to Lexington. What was happening? Was it redcoat or patriot guns we'd heard?

Someone was already on the hill when we reached the top. At first I thought 'twas a boy left behind like Ben, but then I realized the petite form on the horse was Prudence Blood.

When I halted the mare, Mistress Blood spoke, her voice raspy as if from lack of use. "Mistress Abigail." Clearing her throat, she pointed to the valley below us, the greening pastures and meadows, stone fences and trees. "War and fighting," she went on, "same as I dreamed two nights past. Many will be wounded or die before this day is done."

I stared in amazement at the rows of tightly formed redcoats marching in retreat along the Concord-Lexington road. Seen from the hill, they looked like the red toy soldiers Jonathan had once played with. Unlike toys, though, these soldiers had fired on the Lexington militia, killing and wounding.

A stone wall bordered the length of the snaking road. Crouched behind it, I saw dozens of militia and committeemen, the glint of their muskets clearly visible from the hilltop—simple farmers and storekeepers and black-smiths setting themselves against better-armed and -trained soldiers. As if by some unheard command, the patriots fired quick shots at the advancing soldiers, then ran, still crouching, and took cover behind the wall farther along the way.

Ben and I dismounted and hurried to peer between trees at the fighting. I pressed a hand to my suddenly dry mouth as several redcoats crumpled and fell and others broke ranks and fired at our men. Smoke from the conflict obscured my view, but the cacophony of rapid shots continued, interspersed with screams of pain.

I momentarily closed my eyes to shut out the horror. "Dear Lord," I prayed. "Please don't let it be Father." A ragged sound from Ben made me amend my words. "Please keep all our men safe."

Hearing me, Mistress Blood turned, her small black eyes filled with compassion. "Your father and the Boatricks will come to no harm this day, nor will any of the Mayfield men and boys. But the soldiers—"

Her voice broke, and for a moment, there was only the sound of gunfire and the distant pealing of bells to the south and east of the battle. "I have dreams from time to time but never one as vivid as this last one." She swung her arm in a wide arc. "Men are gathering from everywhere—Lincoln, Bedford, Watertown—and they'll hound and shoot at those poor soldiers every step of the way back to Boston."

"You sound like a blasted Tory," Ben said.

"I'm naught but Prudence Blood, and I care naught for politics. I feel sorrow for all who die or who need my help . . . yea, even those ye call lobster-backs."

Giving me a nod, she set her horse down the hill toward the fighting. Unlike Ben and me, who'd come empty-handed to watch, Mistress Blood had come prepared to help. I noted the bag tied to the back of her saddle and heard the clink of water and tincture bottles. I suddenly felt childish and selfish. In my rush to find out what was happening, I'd failed to give any thought to how I could be of help in our first fight for freedom from England.

Chapter Eleven

As WE RETURNED TO THE farm, my thoughts were on the scene of horror we'd witnessed from atop the hill. Despite Prudence Blood's assurance that none of our men would be killed or wounded, the words of my silent prayer ran in endless circles through my mind. *Please, God, keep them safe.*

When Ben opened the gate to the cow pasture and climbed back onto the horse behind me, I caught a glimpse of movement at the side of the barn.

"I see 'em. They're comin'," Jane shouted.

I had hoped no one would notice we were missing, but I should have known better. Mother and Bethy hurried around the side of the barn, and Goody Boatrick came at a half run from the orchard.

"Where have you been?" Mother demanded after we'd crossed the pasture.

"We've been worried sick," Goody Boatrick added.

Ben slid off Dolly's broad back. "We went to watch the fightin'." His chest expanded, and I think in his eyes, he'd grown several inches.

"Fighting?" Mother asked.

"I told you I heard guns," Jane said.

Like Ben, I slid off the mare. "The redcoats are retreating from Concord and have opened fire on our men who wait behind trees and fences. Our men are firing back. We watched them from Hardy Hill."

A tiny moan escaped from Goody Boatrick. "Dear heaven," she whispered.

"Your Father?" Mother asked. "Did you see him?"

"My Thomas and Israel?" Goody Boatrick echoed.

"As near as we could tell, they are safe," I said.

"Prudence Blood said not one of the Mayfield men would be hurt or killed," Ben put in.

"Mistress Blood to you, young man," his mother corrected, though it was obvious from her expression that Ben's words had lifted her spirits.

"Mistress Blood was there too?" Mother asked.

I nodded and began to explain, with Ben interrupting and giving his opinion every time I paused for breath.

To satisfy Goody Boatrick, we were obliged to go over the details of what we'd seen more than once. It wasn't so much that she was particularly dense as it was that she needed reassurance that her husband and son were safe.

I noticed then that Mother was frowning. "What are you doing in your brother's clothes?" she demanded. "And why did you leave without telling me where you were going?"

"Because I knew you'd forbid it."

"As I would. You have no business riding off . . . or taking Ben with you. His mother has been beside herself."

To prove her right, Goody Boatrick gave her son a hard swat across his behind.

I returned Mother's frown with a steady gaze. "I'm sorry for the worry and that Ben got a whipping . . . but I'm not sorry we went. If we hadn't, we wouldn't know what was happening or that, so far, Father and Thomas and Israel are all right. Most likely we'd have had to wait for days . . . worrying, not knowing . . . thinking the worst. Now we not only know, but we have Mistress Blood's assurance that the Mayfield men will be safe."

Silence settled over the pasture. Goody Boatrick pulled Ben close. "I was right worried," she said softly. "But now I know what you done . . . and why ye done it, I'm right glad you went." Her voice turned stern again. "Such don't mean you can run off whenever ye please, so ye'd best be watchin' what ye do."

Jane's voice broke past her mother's. "Can Mistress Blood be trusted . . . what she said about none from Mayfield being hurt?"

"I think she can," I replied, glad to have words other than those of justification leave my mouth. "The old woman has a way of knowing things before they happen. She told us she had a dream two nights ago. There was shooting and fighting, but when she saw the Mayfield men, none had been killed or hurt."

In the silence that followed, I became aware of the sun beating down on the shoulders of Jon's jacket and that the heavy woolen fabric that had been welcomed earlier was now too warm for comfort. I glanced up at the clear, blue sky of the perfect April day. It seemed unfitting that fighting and killing had commenced on such a beautiful spring day.

After the final questions had been asked and answered, Goody Boatrick and Jane returned to the laundry house and Mother, Bethy, and I went back to the kitchen. Ben stayed behind to see that Dolly was properly taken care of.

"Please change out of your brother's clothes," Mother said after she'd closed the back door. Pain showed in her eyes, and I realized how it must hurt her to see me, instead of Jonathan, wearing them.

Had all gone as planned, Mother would never have seen me in my brother's clothes. Even so, I wasted no time in doing her bidding. When I went to close the shutter, I pressed a finger against the glass pane to feel the radiating warmth of the sun. It was the warmest day we'd had in more than six months. With the thought came the realization that it had now been a year since Jonathan's death, twelve long months of pain and sorrow.

"I miss you, brother. How you would have enjoyed riding off to battle with Father." I blinked back tears as a new thought slipped into my mind. Perhaps Jon's spirit had been there today, riding with me on the gray mare, an essence of him lingering in the fabric and seams and stitches of the clothes I'd been wearing.

Mother was busy at the hearth when I returned to the kitchen. Using tongs, she lifted coals onto the lid of a cast-iron pot sitting on a bed of coals. Only when she finished did she turn to me, her voice still holding remnants of anger. There was a plea for conciliation too. "After all these years of living with you, I still don't fully understand you, Abby. Why you're so impetuous and quick to speak your mind. Why you—"

"If I didn't speak and act so, none of us would know what our men are doing and that the redcoats are in retreat. Nor would Father have his broadsheets . . . and the message he sent to Boston wouldn't have been delivered." I paused, knowing that in my reply, I'd shown the very qualities she didn't understand.

Mother slowly rose to her feet, her face looking as if she wanted to cry.

I regretted speaking so frankly and feared I was about to receive another scolding.

"I'm sorry, Abby," Mother said instead. Tears brightened her eyes as she crossed the space between us and pulled me into her arms. "I feared you'd run off to fight and . . . and that I'd lose you as I had your brother."

"No, Mother . . . I went only to watch."

Taking a deep breath, she went on. "Though I criticize, I also have great admiration for you, Abigail. You're brave . . . just like your father and Jonathan . . . and 'tis a great comfort to me to have you with me when there's just the three of us." She pulled me close in another embrace.

Father and the Boatricks didn't return the next day, nor did they return on Thursday. Thursday night when Mother led us in prayer, her voice was strained with worry. After fastening the bolts on the outside doors, her steps, like mine and Bethy's, were slow on the stairs. Over the following days, our ears were turned for the sound of hoofbeats and a rider bringing news. Had a battle taken place when the redcoats had reached Boston? What was happening?

Besides worrying about Father, thoughts of Gideon were never far from my mind. How had the events at Concord-Lexington affected him? Was he safe? While I helped Mother, I sent a prayer heavenward that he sat in his room and not in some dank prison cell. Surely after the redcoat retreat, General Gage's officers had more to occupy their minds than a Tory gentleman at The Rose and Crown.

Impatient for news, I decided to visit Prudence Blood to see if she had returned. After telling Mother where I was going, I asked Ben to ready Dolly and the cart. A few minutes later, I was on my way. Many of the farms lay idle, their men harassing the redcoats back to Boston. Only the Tory men remained.

My heart lifted when I saw the old woman working in her garden. She looked up when I stopped at her sagging gate and was on her way to open it before I could get down from the cart.

"I've been expecting you," she said by way of greeting.

"How did you know I'd come?"

"'Twas a feeling I had."

"Have you news of the Mayfield men? Did you see them when you went to help? Were they all right?"

"They were . . . at least when I left them two days past." Her eyes looked beyond me as if she saw something other than Dolly and the cart.

"'Twas a terrible day of bloodshed and killing," she went on in a voice hollow with sorrow. "Those poor soldiers. So many killed . . . picked off like birds sitting on a fence." She shivered as if she were there again, caught in the slaughter and the noise of guns. "Those poor soldiers," she repeated, "harassed all the way to Boston, their ranks getting smaller while the number of those who fired at them grew with every mile."

"You seem to have more concern for the redcoats than you do for our men."

Mistress Blood's dark eyes fastened on mine. "They were men who needed my help. 'Twas what I did that entire day . . . offering sips of water, staunching blood, trying to ease the pain. It mattered naught to me whether they wore coats of red or homespun brown. They were God's creatures needing my help."

Taken aback by her fervor, I said not a word, though several skittered around in my head—words like the rightness of the patriot cause and the need for us to govern ourselves. But when I set my words next to hers, I found them lacking. Instead, I asked, "Weren't you afraid you might be shot?"

The little woman shook her head. "I was too busy to give any thought to that." She paused and went on in a subdued voice. "I followed them all the way to Cambridge, staying a safe distance from the fighting and trying to help any who fell. Men from both sides helped too . . . carrying a friend or dropping behind to assist as best they could."

"And Father?" I prompted.

"I saw him in the distance a time or two. When the redcoats finally reached Boston, those that had fired at them camped on the hills around . . . hundreds . . . thousands . . . so many I couldn't find the Mayfield men. I continued to nurse and help those I could and slept on the ground by their fires."

My admiration for Mistress Blood increased—risking her life to help others instead of holding back and thinking of her own safety.

She paused, and a look of wonder crossed her wrinkled face. "There were so many campfires it looked like heaven had lowered itself to spread her stars across the hills . . . hundreds of stars lighting the hills and the night. Tired as I was, I couldn't help but stare. "'Twas a sight that told those in Boston as surely as if the men on the hills had shouted it. They had come, and they meant to stay."

I pictured the lights outlining Boston and the sweep of the bay— Bunker, Breed, and Charles Town hills covered with innumerable fires and men and guns. It would be a sight those both within and outside of Boston would long remember.

The sound of Mistress Blood's voice brought me back to myself. She had turned to stare across the meadow to the east. "This fighting is but the beginning," she said as if she could see all the way to Boston.

I wished she could and that I could know of Gideon's safety too.

"'Twill go on for years . . . so long men will weary of fighting."

"Will we win and be free from King George's rule?"

Mistress Blood suddenly looked weary, the deep seams of her numerous wrinkles proclaiming every one of her seventy-odd years. "The dream didn't tell me." As she spoke, her narrow shoulders lifted. "Though my dream was grim, it also spoke of hope. 'Tis what I cling to . . . what you must do too, Mistress Abigail."

The dread around my middle lessened at the mention of hope. At least for now, Father and the Mayfield men were safe. As for Gideon . . . Like Prudence Blood, I stared long and hard toward the east, wishing I could see and know. How had the return of the defeated redcoats affected him? Was he safe, or had their return only made his life more perilous?

Chapter Twelve

Not wanting Mother to worry, I didn't tell her that fighting would soon begin in earnest or that it might last for years. Instead, my first words were, "Father and the Mayfield men are unhurt."

"Thank God," she whispered. "I have tried to hold tight to faith and not worry, but . . ."

Seeing her face crumple, I moved to the chair where she sorted peas for planting and laid a hand on her shoulder. "I have prayed too. Not only are Father and the militiamen unhurt, but they were joined by thousands of other committee and militiamen who followed the redcoats back to Boston. Mistress Blood said they are now camped on the Charles Town heights. The redcoat losses were far greater than ours. If our men number in the thousands and hold the heights, General Gage's army won't be able to leave Boston without a big battle."

Jane came in through the kitchen door in time to hear this last. "Ma and me been prayin' these last two days. Ben too. If anything happened to Pa or Israel, I don't know what we'd do."

"We must all continue to pray," Mother admonished.

I nodded and refused to let my mind dwell on the long years of fighting Mistress Blood had seen in her dream. Instead I would take each day as it came and look for joy in every corner and crevice of it. I also would let Mother and others cling to the hope that the conflict would be over in a month or two.

★

Four days later, Father rode Jumper down the lane. Ben saw them first, and his shout of "Mr. Stowell!" sent everyone hurrying to meet him. From the welcome Father received, one would have thought he'd been gone a year rather than a week. Laughter and happy tears were shed as we gathered around him after he'd dismounted.

Goody Boatrick's voice came loud. "Where's my Thomas and Israel? Has harm come to them?"

"They are fine and send their good wishes," Father told her. "In fact, all the Mayfield men do well."

"Thank the good Lord," Mother said.

"Amen," Goody Boatrick agreed, her red hands clasped tightly below her ample bosom and a smile stretching her face.

"What of the redcoats?" I asked. "Mistress Blood said many were killed and that you harassed them all the way back to Boston."

"We did . . . much to their surprise and dismay." His satisfied smile was outlined by a week-old growth of beard. "I think General Gage has learned a powerful lesson and has spent the past days licking his wounds and trying to decide what to do." His smile grew larger. "I'm certain neither Gage nor his soldiers had any idea so many would oppose them. Even I was surprised. Our men control the heights above the peninsula, and there's nowhere for Gage and his soldiers to go except the sea . . . unless, of course, he wants a battle."

Ben's eyes brightened. "There'll be more fightin', then?"

"I'm certain there will be." Father clapped Ben on the shoulder. "After you take care of Jumper, I'll tell you more. Give him an extra measure of oats too. As for me, I want a meal cooked by skilled hands rather than scorched over a campfire."

We turned to the house, Father with his arms around Mother and me while Bethy ran ahead to open the door. Goody Boatrick and Jane followed, as eager for news as we.

Father hung up his hat and removed his jacket while Mother heated a pan of leftover soup and Jane sliced bread. While the soup warmed, I fried bacon and two fresh-laid eggs.

"What about Uncle William and Cousin Enoch?" I asked. "Are they safe?"

"Thankfully, they're fine. Some of their friends weren't as fortunate."

Bethy's voice mingled with the sizzling bacon. "Did you shoot any red-coats?"

"Why do you ask?" Father responded.

"Because you were mad at them for shooting those men in Lexington."

Father sat and reached for her hand. "Come here, Bethy," he said. "I did shoot some redcoats, but I don't say it with pride. God has commanded us not to kill. But there are times . . ." He paused, and stillness settled over the kitchen. "There are times when it seems the only thing left to do. They came in search of arms and meant to make us defenseless." Both his voice and expression were regretful. "Now is one of those times. Do you understand?"

"I . . . I think I do."

Father looked at me. "And you, Abigail?"

"You know I do." My voice was strong and carried conviction. "We've tried words and diplomacy too long. Now it's time for something stronger."

Father nodded and turned his gaze on Mother. Before he could say anything, she spoke. "I understand, though I wish freedom didn't have to be won by killing and bloodshed." Leaving the wooden spoon in the soup pot, she went to him. "I doubt you realize how much you've been missed. We've worried and prayed much for your safety. All of us will sleep better now that you're home."

Father put his hand on hers. "A feather mattress will be welcome after sleeping on the ground. Being home with those I love . . ." His gaze included Goody Boatrick and Jane. "I can only stay a day or two . . . just long enough to try and catch things up on the farm. Then it's back to the heights above Boston to prepare for a battle against the redcoats."

Goody Boatrick made a tiny sound. "What about Thomas?"

"Next week Thomas will come home to work the farm, and Israel will come the next week. Although we want General Gage and his soldiers to feel our presence, we know we must grow crops to feed our families and the army."

Awe pricked the hairs along my arms. "Army. At last we have an army."

"We do, though I doubt General Gage would call it such. Few are trained in fighting, and as yet, there is no order or discipline. Hopefully, this will change when congress in Philadelphia appoints a general."

An army! A general! Part of me rejoiced at the words and that so many men had risen to support the cause. But would they be enough against General Gage's better-trained and well-armed soldiers?

I lifted the bacon and eggs onto a plate and carried it to the table, where Goody Boatrick had spread a cloth and laid utensils and a tankard of cider. Pausing only for grace, Father set to the meal with great appetite while the rest of us gathered around him, anxious to hear what else he had to say.

Ben had slipped into the kitchen in time to hear Father's last remarks. "We'll show them lobsterbacks!" Ben said. "They'll be high tailin' it back to England afore ya can say Jack Nipper."

"I fear 'twill not be that easy," Father said. "We have little powder and balls while they are well equipped. They also have cannons that can take out several men with one shot."

I knew Father regretted his words as soon as he heard Goody Boatrick's gasp. We were a roomful of women and children, not men sitting around a campfire readying to fight.

"I'm confident we'll do well," he added hastily. "More men are gathering daily . . . some walking, others riding. I was talking with a man who'd ridden all the way from Pennsylvania. He said he'd been toting a gun since he was eight and claimed he could drop a squirrel out of a tree from three hundred paces."

"No matter how many men join you, Nathan, they'll be shooting at armed soldiers, not squirrels," Mother said. "Those soldiers also will have cannons."

Stillness settled over the kitchen, leaving only the soft hiss of the fire to fill the silence. Father nodded, then dropped his gaze to stare at the toes of his boots while I studied the tablecloth as if the gravy stains that no amount of scrubbing could remove were the most interesting thing I had ever seen.

Father stayed with us two days, the bulk of his time taken up with working the farm. Mother and I prepared and gathered supplies and food for him to take back. It wasn't until Father was about to leave that I had a chance to speak with him alone.

"What of Mr. Whitlock?" I asked, trying to keep my voice nonchalant. "Has he been able to get information out to you?"

Father shook his head. "General Gage has reinforced the blockade at the neck and posted sentries along the docks and shoreline to ensure that no ferries or boats cross between the mainland and Boston." He paused and sighed. "Even if Mr. Whitlock managed to slip past the sentries, finding me in the confusion on the heights would be difficult."

Over the next fortnight, Thomas, then Israel returned to help on the farm for a day or two. It was a busy time for all, with Goody Boatrick and Jane helping Ben with the heavier outside work and Mother, Bethy, and I caring for the house.

Each time the men returned, they brought news. "We're close enough we can see the lobsterbacks fortifying Prospect Hill," Thomas said. "They're preparing for a fight the same as we are. When it'll come . . ." He shrugged.

Goody Boatrick pressed her fingers to her mouth and held hard to her husband's arm as we gathered around him.

"When?" The word seemed to hang in the April sunshine, distracting my mind from my chores. Next week? In a month?

It was from Israel we learned that General Gage had relaxed the blockade so Tories in the countryside could flee into Boston.

"What about the patriots in Boston?" I asked, my mind hearkening like an arrow to Gideon.

"General Gage is lettin' 'em leave so's to make room for the Tories."

I thought about this for the rest of the day. If people were both leaving and going into Boston, then perhaps Gideon had been able to send information about the general's plans. Maybe he'd even left Boston.

Not being able to see and hear more, my frustration mounted. I was miles away and had to rely on others to pass along bits and pieces that might well be no more than rumors.

★

Hoping Father would have something more definite to tell us, I anxiously awaited his next visit. A week passed, then ten days. The worry lines in Mother's face deepened, and tension, rather than easy conversation, filled the house. Was an attack imminent? Had Father taken ill? What kept him?

Two days later, I looked up from hanging out the wash and saw Father riding down the lane. I dropped a damp petticoat back into the basket and ran to greet him.

"Father! 'Tis Father!" I cried.

Though I was the first to reach him, the others weren't far behind. I welcomed the solid comfort of his arms around me and minded neither the rasp of his beard or the odor of dirt and sweat and smoke that clung to his shirt. He was safely home. As before, Goody Boatrick and Jane followed us into the kitchen to hear the latest news.

Ben ran into the kitchen just as Father dipped water from a bucket by the door. "Has there been fightin'?" Ben panted.

"Not yet." Father drank thirstily from the dipper. "We can see them drilling . . . and they're building fortifications on three of Boston's hills. No one knows why Gage waits so long to attack."

"Why don't we attack them . . . send 'em back to England, where they belong?"

"They have cannons," Father reminded Ben. "We may outnumber them, but to attack, we'd have to cross the lowlands and board boats. We'd be exposed to their gunfire like sitting ducks, and most of our force would be wiped out before we could reach Boston."

I tried not to think of the bloodshed and falling men . . . some of them those I loved and knew. My mood was somber for the rest of the day.

That evening when we gathered in the sitting room, I questioned Father more closely. "Israel said patriots who wish to leave Boston may now do so. Is this true?"

"'Tis true. Those who wish to go elsewhere are leaving daily. When I visited George Smyth in Cambridge, he said he'd spoken to a family who'd just left."

"What of the Linds?" Mother asked. "You said Caroline was so frail she spent most of her time in bed."

Father's face turned grave. "'Tis not only true but also likely that the rigors of leaving could endanger her life." He shook his head. "I can't see Joseph doing such. Nor can I see him leaving all that he's spent his life accumulating." He reached for his pipe. "The family George spoke to said Caroline's personal maid has left Boston too."

"Poor Caroline, and their Henry is still in England," Mother said.

Father nodded. "I feel great sympathy for her and their son, but with Joseph . . ." He paused and frowned. "Despite our long friendship, I've long seen that he puts greater store in a fine home and prosperous business than is perhaps wise. This year has also shown me that our cause is not as dear to him as it is to me."

Mother's face showed disappointment. "I've always thought highly of Mr. Lind."

"I know you have. Though I'll always count Joseph as a friend, I believe he will be more comfortable living among Tories than those opposed to the King."

He tamped tobacco into his pipe and lit it with a candle. For a second, I pretended Lexington had never happened, that the four of us sat in companionable silence broken only by the peaceful sound of crickets outside the open window.

Father's grave voice broke into my daydream. "Although General Gage now allows patriots to leave Boston, they must surrender all weapons. And once they leave, they cannot return."

"Not even if they forgot something?" Bethy asked.

"Not even then. George Smyth said some patriot men are sending their wives and children to live with relatives outside Boston while they remain behind to guard their property."

Bethy had ceased to knit. "Why must they guard it?"

"Soldiers and others sometimes steal. Tories coming from the country also need a vacant house to live in."

Instead of listening, my mind slipped to thoughts that had niggled at me since I'd learned General Gage was allowing people to leave and enter Boston. Why couldn't one of those entering be me? Until Father had mentioned that the Linds wouldn't be leaving, I'd thought the idea impossible. But now . . .

I carried the idea to bed and mulled it over long after Bethy had fallen asleep. If war came, I knew I wouldn't be content to wait at home for occasional visits and news of the fighting. Instead, I wanted to be where I could see for myself what was happening—in Boston where I could gather information about General Gage and his army and relay it to the patriots.

And then there was Gideon. I was drawn to him in ways I didn't entirely understand. I'd never wished for a man to touch or kiss me before, but I did so now. If I remained in Mayfield, I'd never see him again. The thought brought a stab of panic. If the love and marriage Mistress Blood saw in the tea leaves was to happen, I must see that it did. It would be much easier if I had Father's aid and approval, but with or without it, I would go to Boston. On the morrow, I intended to talk to him.

Chapter Thirteen

"CAN I SPEAK WITH YOU in the study?" I asked Father after supper. "Just for a few minutes," I added when he hesitated, though I knew full well it could take longer. Unless, of course, he stopped me in midsentence and refused to listen further.

After motioning me to a chair, he went around his desk and sat. "What concerns you so much that you feel you must speak to me in private?" Though his smile was tolerant, he studied me as if he sensed my nervousness.

I was aware of my nervousness as well, feeling it in the fast pulse of my heart and the urge to moisten my lips. Even so, my voice was steady and filled with determination when I spoke. "I have made up my mind to go to Boston. I wish to ride with you when you return."

Father's mouth opened in astonishment. "What . . . ?"

"I wish to go with you when you return to the army."

"Have you lost your senses? I've never heard such outrage!"

I ignored his outburst. "How can you think being a part of the cause is outrageous? I can be of help, just like you and the Mayfield men . . . but I can't do it stuck away in the country. I need to be in Boston where I can learn what General Gage plans to do."

"And where you will daily be in danger from roving redcoats and those looking for spies," Father added. His face had colored, and the tone of his voice was one I didn't often hear. "I'll not have you risk your life! My answer is no."

I stood and leaned across his desk. "Please listen to me, Father. I have thought long on this, and I'm certain I can gain information that will help our army . . . learn what General Gage is doing too. I can draw maps of their fortifications and count the soldiers who man them."

"And how, pray tell, do you intend to accomplish all of this?"

"I hope to stay with the Linds." Before he could protest again, I quickly went on. "Since Aunt Caroline's personal maid has left, I can take care of her. What better way to learn what's being planned than to live among those with Tory leanings?"

"'Tis not as simple as you think, Abigail. Do you imagine Gage and his staff tell their plans to any and all Tories?"

"Of course not, but doesn't Mr. Whitlock pass himself off as a Tory and isn't that how he gleans his information?"

"Mr. Whitlock has lived in Boston these last two years . . . time enough to have made acquaintances in high places. More than that, he's a man."

"And many men act as if women are invisible and have no opinion." I smiled across the desk at him. "You might be surprised what I've learned from you and your friends while stitching in the corner while you talked and smoked your pipes."

My smile seemed to soften him, for when he spoke, he sounded more himself. "I was not unaware that you were listening. What better way for a young woman to learn of the world and politics than by listening to her elders converse?"

"You are not like most men, Father, something I constantly give thanks for. But would I not be doing the same in Mr. Lind's parlor . . . quietly stitching and listening and learning?"

"Since his wife is an invalid, 'tis doubtful Joseph does much, if any, entertaining. When I last conversed with him, it wasn't at his home but over a tankard of ale at The Black Swan."

His words gave me pause, as I was certain he'd intended, but I wasn't my father's daughter for nothing. Readjusting my tactics, I responded, "Even if the Linds seldom entertain, the fact that I reside there should work to my advantage and open other doors."

Determination crept back into Father's voice. "No matter where you stay, it will be too dangerous."

"How will it be too dangerous? Won't you and the Mayfield men face danger when you next encounter the redcoats?"

"We will be armed . . . while you—" He shook his head in frustration. "Boston is a town under siege, with soldiers roaming everywhere."

"I know how to be careful. Besides, I'm a woman. Who will suspect a woman . . . a mere maid running errands? If I can learn anything that will give our army an advantage . . . perhaps where and when they plan to attack—" I paused, then hurried on. "Has Mr. Whitlock smuggled out any word of their plans?"

Father shook his head. "I have received nothing. William Heath, General Artemas Ward's aide, hasn't heard from him either. 'Twas Mr. Heath who introduced me to Gideon."

I struggled against rising unease, and my voice wasn't quite steady when I spoke. "Do you think something has happened to him?"

"'Tis hard to say. I only know there's no word from or of him." Father's voice held regret. "We hear conflicting stories and know not what is true or what is rumor. I'm concerned something unfortunate has happened . . . that he's been arrested and is in prison or, heaven forbid, he's been hanged as a traitor." Father broke off and shook his head. "Can't you see why it's not safe for you in Boston?"

His words filled me with dread, but before they could take root and weaken me to tears, I plunged ahead. "Perhaps nothing has happened to Mr. Whitlock," I countered. "Perhaps 'tis only that circumstances are such it would be unwise for him to send word. If such is the case, I could help him. The two of us can work together."

Father stared at me, but I thought I read speculation in his eyes.

"When last we spoke, Mr. Whitlock mentioned he practices law at The Rose and Crown. I can pass myself off as a new client seeking his services."

"Abigail . . . Abigail." Father looked at me as if he didn't know what else to say.

I leaned forward, our faces but inches apart. "I know I can do it. I've never had such a strong conviction that going to Boston is what I'm meant to do. Whether 'tis God's will, I cannot say, but please don't shut the door until you've taken time to give it serious consideration. Please, Father."

He straightened and pursed his lips, his blue eyes looking at the wall behind me. Silence dominated the study. "I am thinking about it, Abigail," he finally said. "Now go. I'm sure your mother and Bethy are waiting for you in the sitting room."

My mind was too agitated to sleep well that night. Although Father had agreed to think about my plan, I knew much of the credit for him doing so lay in the fact that I would be staying with the Linds—Caroline, whom

I called aunt, and her husband, Joseph. Then my mind slipped back to worry about Gideon. Was Father right? Had he been arrested? "Surely not," I whispered into the darkness. Father had to be wrong.

I went downstairs the next morning not knowing what Father's decision would be. At breakfast, he talked only of farm matters, and he largely ignored me for the rest of the day. When, after eating our noontime meal, he bid Mother go with him to the study, I didn't know whether to take heart or prepare for disappointment.

It wasn't until night that he called me to come to his study. He'd no more than closed the door than he spoke, both of us still standing, me poised for argument and he looking stern.

"Your mother and I talked late into the night and again this afternoon," he began. "She has no liking for your scheme either." So it was to be disappointment. Before I could speak or prepare for argument, he went on. "However, I've been thinking over what you said about the Tories not suspecting a woman. There is merit in this, one we also talked about at length."

My heart lifted from where it had fallen, but I waited, warning myself not to get my hopes up.

"If you could, indeed, make a map of Boston's fortifications or study the movement and placement of the soldiers and discover some indication of what Gage intends to do . . ." He paused, his expression serious. "Such information would be invaluable to General Ward and our army. Though we outnumber Gage's soldiers and hold the heights, our lack of powder and ammunition gives the advantage to them." He paused and pointed to the chair. "Sit. Sit. There is much for us to discuss, and we'd best be comfortable."

My heart quickened as I sat and Father moved behind his desk, his final words echoing in my mind. *Much to be discussed.*

"You are strangely quiet," he said. "Have you nothing to say?"

It was on the tip of my tongue to say, *You have told me to think before I speak,* but I cast it aside as being too impertinent. "I'm waiting for what you say next."

Amusement touched his face. "Why . . . that if you could succeed in your plan, it would help our cause immensely."

I stared in surprise. "Then . . . you'll let me go with you?"

"Only if you promise to use great caution and think carefully before you say or do anything. There is much confusion there with patriots pouring out and Tories pouring in. Even so, there will be those who watch and look for anyone who seems the least suspicious."

Relief and excitement flooded through me. "I promise to be very careful."

"'Tis our prayer also. It isn't lack of intelligence that concerns your mother and me, Abigail, but your impulsiveness and penchant to rush into things. Did you not put on Jonathan's breeches and ride after us on the day of Lexington?"

"Yes . . . but only to watch from Hardy Hill. Didn't that exhibit caution?"

"It did. It would have been better, however, if you'd stayed home."

"We wouldn't have known what happened, that the redcoats were in retreat."

Father nodded, but his voice remained firm. "Your mother is afraid you'll follow me if we don't allow you to go, while I . . ." Father's voice trailed away. "Though I have great concern for your safely in Boston, I also see the merits of your plans. Not only will you be under the protection of Joseph Lind, a man of great consequence in the town, but you are also a woman. I doubt the redcoats will be unduly suspicious of a mere woman." He paused, and his eyes looked deeply into mine. "'Tis a terrible risk you'll be taking, daughter, but I've long known you don't lack for courage."

I wanted to fly around the desk and hug him, but I knew he would take it as but another example of my impulsiveness. "Thank you, Father. I know I can help."

"I think perhaps you can."

He couldn't help but see my pleasure. Perhaps that was why he projected such a solemn mood—to keep my emotions tamped down so I didn't forget the seriousness of my undertaking.

"There are still many details to be worked out. Your mother is writing a letter to Mistress Lind tonight, and I shall add one to Joseph." There was a slight pause. "I'm not a man who looks constantly for the hand of Providence in his life, but I own such seems to be the case now. Mistress Lind's fondness for you has been evident on each occasion our family has been together. And now—"

"Mother is writing to offer my services to Mistress Lind," I finished for him, a smile stretching my face.

Father nodded. "You will carry our letters with you when you arrive at their home. Give them to Mr. Lind."

"Father!" I said, scarce believing what I heard.

"Do not let your enthusiasm carry you away, Abigail. Most invalids are less than amiable and are often demanding. More than that, you must keep caution at the forefront of your mind. There are things I must tell you about Joseph before you arrive at his door."

The seriousness of his tone cut at my enthusiasm once more and held me tight to my chair.

"I have recently learned that some three years ago, after Joseph met with Governor Hastings, he was given an advantageous contract on Long Wharf for unloading goods from English ships. As his friendship with the Governor thickened, more favors came his way. Later, after the King appointed General Gage the new governor of Massachusetts, George Smyth says Joseph started receiving favors from him." Father's voice hardened. "Bribes, more like, though what he gives in return, George cannot say with any certainty, but . . ."

Though I didn't gape, I was nonetheless astonished by Father's revelation. Sadness washed over me as well. Although I'd never thought as highly of Joseph as I did Aunt Caroline, I had thought him as committed to the patriot cause as Father and George Smyth. "Do you think he spied for Governor Hastings and now does the same for General Gage?"

"That, neither Mr. Smyth nor I know, but 'tis a strong possibility . . . one you must constantly keep in mind while you live under his roof."

Neither of us spoke for a minute—me looking at the shelves of Father's leather-bound books, he looking down at his hands on the desk.

"As I said last night, I have sensed for some time that Joseph has changed, but I wasn't aware of just how much until I spoke with George Smyth when I attended the congress in Cambridge in February. 'Twas well he alerted me, and I took care to guard what I said when I later visited with Joseph in Boston."

"I don't like to think such a thing, but did Mr. Lind pass bits and pieces of your conversations with him to both governors?"

Father raised his head. "There's a strong possibility that he has. In February, Gideon Whitlock saw my name on a list of men General Gage and his staff is watching. I thought 'twas only because I attended the congress, but it could well be because of things Joseph told General Gage about me."

Anger surged through me. "How could he? He's been your friend for years!"

"And for years Joseph has been focused on building one of the most successful shipping and trading companies in Boston," Father countered.

"Ambition can sometimes blur the line between right and wrong—between friendship and betrayal." He shook his head sadly. "What Joseph has chosen to do saddens me, but I can see how this knowledge can be used to your advantage. Your eyes will be opened to what he might be doing, but 'tis doubtful he'll suspect your coming to care for his wife is founded on anything other than friendship."

Before Father could say more, Mother tapped on the study door. Her mouth trembled when she saw me, but after we'd embraced, she made a valiant effort not to cry. The three of us talked and planned and shed some tears until the brace of candles on Father's desk had burned down several inches.

Father agreed to delay his departure another day so I would have time to ready myself for what lay ahead. "You will need your wits about you when you go to the Linds. 'Tis best that you take time to think carefully about the ruse you will play. Consider carefully what to pack as well. If you forget something, it will be nigh impossible for you to get it later."

I nodded. What I'd told Father about my reasons for going to Boston was true. But there was another reason that burned like a flame inside my heart. Gideon Whitlock!

★

The next morning, Mother and I began an inventory of my wardrobe. Skirts and bodices were laid out on the bed, stockings and handkerchiefs taken from drawers. Finally, Mother reached for my pink silk bodice and overskirt.

"Although you'll spend most of your time caring for Mistress Lind, you'll be in polite society at times and will need something nicer to wear." It had been fashioned two years before by my Aunt Rachel's seamstress in New York. Both bodice and skirt were silk and trimmed with expensive ribbon and wide lace. Though I'd told my aunt I wouldn't feel comfortable wearing such a beautiful creation in Mayfield, she'd insisted.

"I've a notion you'll not spend many years in Mayfield," she'd said. "Mark my words, Abby, you'll find bigger fish to catch than some village farmer."

I ran my fingers along one of the long silk sleeves. I hoped 'twould be me, not shimmering silk, that would gain Gideon's admiration. *Gideon. Pray God, he was safe.*

In not many minutes, I'd finished packing.

As I closed the lid, Mother spoke. "I promised myself I'd be brave. But not to be able to hear from you . . . to know how you are—" She put a hand to her mouth. "Take care, Abby. Please . . . take care."

"I will," I promised in a voice as unsteady as hers. "I'll be careful for you and Father." Looking past Mother, I reached for Bethy, her dark eyes bright with tears. "For all of you."

For the first time, I wondered what I was doing leaving everyone I loved. Goody Boatrick, who over the years had scolded and laughed with me and taught me how to weave—loyal Jane, whom I cherished like another sister. Then thoughts of Gideon and the good I hoped to accomplish pushed past my tears and strengthened my resolve. *'Tis the right thing to do,* my heart told me. Holding the thought close, my arms tightened around Mother and Bethy, and I smiled through my tears.

As the family gathered around the table for our noonday meal, the mood was somber, and the few words that passed for conversation centered mostly on my upcoming departure.

"Have you remembered to pack your sewing box?" Mother asked.

"I have . . . the new petticoat I was hemming as well." I spooned a small serving of Dutch cheese into my bowl. "There's something else I need to do though."

Father looked up. "What's that?"

"I want to take some of Mistress Blood's herbs and tinctures to help Aunt Caroline."

As Father took a bite of bread, the look he gave me was skeptical.

"The lady slipper and valerian root tea she gave me to cure my headache worked far better than our chamomile tea," I hurried on. "Maybe she'll recommend something for Aunt Caroline. I'll need to write down her directions and some of her recipes too."

Mother nodded. "I put great store in Mistress Blood's physics and remedies."

As if remembering the great care the little woman had taken to nurse him through the typhus, Father's expression cleared. "'Tis true."

A short time later, with my writing box in hand, I called to Ben to ready the cart.

He came at a run and seemed his usual self until he eased Dolly between the tongues of the cart. "Is it true you're goin' off to Boston?"

"It is."

"Why you doin' that for?"

"A sick friend needs someone to take care of her."

He looked up from Dolly. "Such don't sound like you one bit . . . goin' off to take care of a woman who could just as well get someone in Boston to care for her." A frown settled on his face. "If you was goin' off to fight or do somethin' exciting, it'd be just like you. But to take care of some old lady—"

I laughed and rumpled his red hair. "She's not an old lady."

Ben acted as if he hadn't heard me, the freckles on his face standing out like tiny brown currants when he scowled. "'Tisn't right," he muttered, bending to adjust the harness. He continued to mutter in a low voice. Even so, I managed to make out "old grouch" and something that sounded like, "not like her a'tall."

He was more himself when he helped me into the cart and handed Dolly's reins to me. "You make sure you take good care of yourself," he said like I was leaving for Boston that very minute.

"I will, Ben."

"Promise?"

"Promise."

I clicked to Dolly, and the cart slowly rolled up the lane. When we turned onto the road and I looked back, Ben still stood by the barn, looking after me.

As I flicked the reins and set Dolly to a brisk pace, I became aware of gathering clouds. With luck, I could be back home before rain began.

Not many minutes later, I brought the gray mare and cart to a halt at the sagging gate. Though I didn't see any sign of the old woman or her cats, I got out of the cart with my writing box. Had she gone to help someone in the village?

Calling her name, I opened the gate, noting the vigorous growth of her plants as I followed the mossy stone path around the side of the cottage. I hadn't gone many steps before the two cats ran to meet me. Ebony purred and circled my skirt while Griselda gazed inquiringly at me.

"Where's your mistress?" I asked.

As if she understood, Griselda trotted back the way she'd come and scratched at the herb room door.

The old woman gave me a welcoming smile as she opened the door. "So, 'tis you," she said. "My hearing's not what it used to be. I wasn't sure if 'twas someone calling or but the wrens chattering in the tree."

"'Twas me," I said, aware of the puzzled look she gave my writing box as she invited me inside. The sharp, musky odor of herbs and roots met me as I entered.

"What brings you today?" she asked. "You haven't the look of a headache."

"I came seeking your advice and to buy some herbs. Perhaps even some tinctures."

Her brows lifted, and without saying anything, she led me into the keeping room, where the sharp tang of something simmering in a pot made my nose wrinkle.

"'Tis a mixture of aniseed and fennel I'm fixing for Goody Brown's new babe," she said when she saw my reaction. "He's poorly since I birthed him. A few drops of this in a sugar teat will calm and help him take his mother's milk better."

After stirring the concoction, she motioned me to a chair and fixed me with an inquiring gaze. "Now," she said, in a tone inviting me to explain myself.

"I go to Boston tomorrow to take care of a sick friend. I've packed snakeroot and blue iris. What else can you recommend for me to take?"

"What ails your friend?"

"I know only that she's now an invalid and seldom leaves her bed." Watching Mistress Blood's impassive face, I added. "I want very much to help her. Can you recommend any helpful herbs?"

The old woman's gaze shifted to the pot simmering over the fire. After a long moment, she said. "To heal the hurt or sick cannot be done by everyone. Mixing and brewing herbs and physicking those who are ill is an art . . . a special gift. I, my mother too, believe 'tis bestowed on some by our Maker. The gift should not be taken lightly." She paused and fixed me with her deep-set eyes. "When I birthed you, I sensed you had the gift . . . saw it later when you were a girl and came to see my garden." She nodded to emphasize her words. "It takes years to learn all there is to know about plants and healing. You are but beginning. Still . . ." She led me to the herb room. "Since you leave tomorrow, I'll tell you a few things that if used with care can help your friend."

She moved behind her worktable, talking softly to herself as she searched the bags on the wall. One by one, she set several of them on the table.

While she checked the bags, I sat at the worktable with my writing box. Dipping the quill into the ink bottle, I wrote while Mistress Blood told me the herbs' names, uses, and directions for preparation. While talking, she ground roots with a pestle or measured and poured leaves and bark onto pieces of paper, folded them into packets and sealed them with wax from the candle burning on the table.

The scratch of my pen blended with the raspy cadence of the old woman's voice. The flickering glow of the candle at my elbow fell across each page as it filled with the curving swirl of ink. Two pages, then three were soon covered with strange-sounding words and recipes that sometimes gave me pause but slipped from Prudence's tongue like the names of old, dear friends—*For nervous complaints, take wild cherry bark and the green of elder. Boil and add saltpeter the size of a walnut. Then add blue flag root steeped in one half pint gin and oil of checkerberry.*

I was scarcely aware of Ebony's purr as he curled at my feet or of the rising whisper of wind scurrying around the cottage. Only when the distant rumble of thunder penetrated the little room did Prudence Blood cease her instructions.

"Rain is coming. You must hurry." Taking the candle, she sealed the last of the packets, her movements surprisingly quick for a woman her age.

While I packed the recipes and writing supplies into the box, she took a canvas bag from a peg and put the packets inside.

"I'll leave your bag with Mother when I go," I said, taking out money to pay her.

Mistress Blood shook her head. "I do not take money from a friend."

"But . . ." I began, knowing her income was meager.

She shook her head again. "Keep it . . . the bag too." She ran her fingers over the worn material. "'Tis my hope that it will whisper some of my secrets to you as you brew the herbs for your friend."

I thanked her. "I'll treasure it and think of you each time I use it." Tears threatened like the rain as I moved toward the door. Gusts of wind whipped my skirt as I opened it, and the clouds I'd seen earlier had closed in to fill the afternoon sky with gloom.

Mistress Blood followed me outside, the gusting wind emphasizing the thinness of her small frame.

"Thank you," I repeated.

She nodded, and though she'd told me I must hurry, the gaze she turned on me was deep and searching. "Although you go to help a friend, you also go to meet your destiny, Mistress Abigail."

I looked at her in puzzlement.

Her thin fingers closed around my wrist, their touch gentle and surprisingly warm. "Did not the tea leaves say you would find love?"

"Yes."

A fond smile lifted the corners of her narrow lips. "Go to him. He is waiting."

Chapter Fourteen

EARLY THE NEXT MORNING, MOTHER and Bethy and the Boatricks gathered at the barn for good-byes. My throat ached from the need to cry as I hugged Goody Boatrick and Jane. Ben shied away when I tried to hug him, but Bethy openly cried. My eyes were moist, and my lips trembled when I said good-bye to Mother. Father was strangely silent as he lifted me onto Dolly and tied the trunk onto the saddle behind me. Only then did he turn and pull Mother and Bethy close.

Sadness engulfed me as Father mounted Jumper and the two horses started up the lane. I turned for a last look—the house rising tall in the morning sky, Mother and Bethy clustered by the barn with the Boatricks.

Seeing me turn and wave, Ben scrambled up on the fence and, waving both arms, shouted, "Hurry back, Mistress Abigail! Hurry home, and Godspeed!"

"I will, Ben." Just saying the words lifted my spirits.

Once we reached the main road, Father set the horses to a brisk pace. I made attempts at conversation, but Father's lack of response and the set of his mouth told me he wasn't in the mood to talk.

Though part of me ached from leaving, I also eagerly looked ahead to Boston and finding Gideon. Perhaps by next week, I would have seen him, maybe even begun to learn more about General Gage's plans. I knew such wouldn't be easy, but I had great hopes of success.

Adjusting myself to Dolly's rhythm, I looked out on meadows sprinkled with wildflowers and rolling hills dotted with sheep. Songs of peewees and warblers filled the spring air, and I broke into song myself, ignoring Dolly's twitching ears when I did.

Instead of stopping at Aunt Martha's or Monroe Tavern in Lexington, we pressed on, munching on the roast chicken and bread Mother had wrapped in cloth. It wasn't until we'd left Menotomy that Father fell back to ride abreast.

"Rather than have you arrive at the Linds so late in the day, I think 'twould be best for you to spend the night in Cambridge with George Smyth and his wife."

"And you?"

"I shall rejoin the Mayfield men camped on Lechmere Point."

"Can I not—"

"You may not." Father's voice cut me short. "Thousands of unknown men cover the hillsides. I don't wish my daughter around them."

I stared at him in surprise. These men were patriots, not redcoats . . . men born and reared on New England soil, the same as I.

"Don't misunderstand me, Abigail. I'm most encouraged at our troops' fervor for freeing us from the oppressive grip of the King and Parliament, but men being men . . . especially when they're away from home . . ." He let out a frustrated breath. "Reverend Whipple and I have so far succeeded in keeping order among the Mayfield men, but others—" He shook his head. "There's too much rum, gin sling, and grog available and far too little discipline. Congress is choosing a general for our army. Hopefully he'll bring order, but until he arrives, we must make do as best we can."

His words painted a different picture of the army than I'd carried in my head. Before I could ponder his words further, I caught my first glimpse of the ranks camped on the hills and ridges to the northeast. In my wildest imagining, I'd not properly pictured the sight of the teeming crowd covering the grassy hills. 'Twas like a hodge-podge of tiny creatures clothed in shades of brown, blue, black, and gray. Their so-called uniforms had no more rhyme or reason than their disorganized placement on the hills.

"So many," I breathed.

"Aye," Father agreed. "And more arrive daily from other colonies . . . some as far away as Virginia."

When we reached the outskirt of Cambridge, two drunken men staggered out of a tavern, men who no more looked like soldiers than I did. Their breeches were of brown homespun, their once-white shirts grimy, the fastening on their vests undone. Small wonder Father was concerned. Pity the poor man appointed as general who must face the task of building an army out of such men.

As we neared the Smyth's home, Father spoke again. "Instead of me, Thomas will take you to Boston tomorrow."

I looked at him in surprise.

"If there are spies in Boston, there are bound to be men posing as patriots among our troops. 'Tis best if it isn't known that you are my daughter."

I nodded reluctantly. Though I knew I'd be perfectly safe with Thomas, I'd hoped to have Father's company as long as possible. Instead, we rode along the tree-lined streets of Cambridge without speaking and arrived at the home of Father's friend sooner than I wanted. After Father lifted me and my trunk down from Dolly's back, he placed his hands on my shoulders and looked deeply into my eyes. "We will say our good-byes here, daughter." Before I could think, he pulled me close, his voice but a whisper in my ear. "I love you, Abigail. May God and all His angels watch over you."

My eyes welled up with tears, for I hadn't heard him express his love for me since I was a small child. "I love you too, Father."

★

I spent a restful night at the Smyth's and, after breakfasting with the family, was ready to leave with Thomas early the next morning. Though I greeted him with a smile, he didn't return it. The fact that he didn't and that his mouth was set in a firm line told me he wasn't half pleased at what I was doing.

After I thanked my host and hostess and Thomas lifted me and my trunk onto Dolly's back, we rode away from the Smyth's stable. We were not the only ones traveling through Cambridge that morning. Instead of a sleepy town whose main activity centered on the red-brick buildings of Harvard college, it had changed to one that bustled with carts and people. Some were Tories or patriots either leaving or going to Boston, others farmers and tradesmen bringing supplies to the army.

After we crossed the bridge over the Charles River, I reined in Dolly for a last look at the army, for army it was, despite the lack of order or uniformity in clothing. The open view from the rise near the bridge allowed me a closer view than the one I'd had yesterday. Smoke from hundreds of campfires still hugged the ridges, while makeshift tents, shelters, and fortifications marred the symmetry of the grassy hills.

As had been the case in Cambridge, there were others on the road leading to Roxbury besides Thomas and me. Coming from the direction of the neck, a boy of about twelve drove a cart piled high with furniture and household goods. His mother, sitting on the seat beside him, held a baby while an older girl and her sister walked beside the cart.

A man traveling behind us called to the boy. "You're like rats leaving a sinking ship, but methinks this ship won't be sinkin' and you'll be wishin' ye'd stayed in Boston a'fore long."

I looked back intending to give the man a quelling look and remembered just in time that I must act the part of one sympathetic to the King rather than a rebel.

The middle-aged man who'd spoken rode in front of his family's carriage, which was followed by a wagon heavily loaded with baggage and furniture. It had joined us near the outskirts of Roxbury and bore out Father's words that Tories were seeking safety in Boston even as those like the family with the cart were leaving.

Thomas's face remained grim, and he made no attempt to talk as we traveled along the rutted road. It wasn't until we started down the neck that he broke his silence. "I gotta leave you afore we get to the blockade. If I ride with you all the way, the lobsterbacks guardin' the blockade won't let me leave without a lot of questions."

"I understand," I said. Instead of feeling uneasy at the prospect of having only myself to rely on, I felt a surge of excitement. There was so much I wanted to see and do and limitless ways for me to prove I was capable of helping the patriots.

"I don't agree with what yer doin'," he said. "Just the same, I'll be prayin' for you."

"Thank you, Thomas. I'll be praying for you and Israel and Father . . . those I left at home too." I gave him a smile. "I'll be fine."

The look he gave me was dubious, his unshaven face shadowed by his sweat-stained hat, his large, sun-browned hands loosely holding the reins. I'd known him all my life, and though he was our hired man, my affection for him was like that for a favorite uncle.

As the blockade loomed close, Thomas eased his horse to the side of the road. "'Twill be best if I leave you now," he said as the Tory family passed us, the man on horseback nodding, his wife and children staring from the carriage. "Stay close to them," he added.

"I will." I met his eyes full on so he could tell Father I looked and acted myself when he left me. Setting Dolly to follow after the family, I looked back in time to hear Thomas call after me.

"Godspeed, Mistress."

I lifted my hand in reply. "Godspeed, Thomas."

Then I turned my face toward the excitement of Boston and the man Mistress Blood said awaited me there.

Chapter Fifteen

BOSTON, MASSACHUSETTS
May–June 1775

THE BREEZE BLOWING OFF BOSTON Bay lifted the brim of my straw hat and sent the pink ribbons under my chin fluttering as I approached the blockade that May morning. Since the tide was out, mudflats instead of seawater bordered the narrow neck, and the pungent odor of mud and sodden reeds saturated the air. I took a deep breath, knowing that in time, the smell would become as familiar to me as the grassy aroma of the pastures and fields at Stowell farm.

Tension warred with excitement when I saw four armed redcoats manning the blockade, the glint of the sun on their muskets visible from Dolly's back. When we'd passed here in March, only two soldiers had been present.

"All will go well," I told myself. "They will think me but a Tory seeking safety from the patriot army camped across the bay." *Rebels. If you mean to carry off your masquerade as a loyal Tory, you must remember to think and speak of them as rebels, not patriots.*

"Next!" A loud voice called.

Realizing the Tory family had been waved on, I urged my mare forward.

The gaze of the young soldier who motioned to me was admiring, his manners pleasant. His sturdy build set off the white knee britches and wide lapels of his red coat to advantage. Had circumstances been different, I might have smiled, but caution bade me do nothing that would call attention to me. Still, I answered his questions in pleasant tones while his companion lifted the lid of my trunk. Thankfully, he gave it no more than a cursory inspection. As I'd hoped, he thought me but another Tory lass seeking refuge in Boston.

I continued to follow the carriage and wagon up Orange and Newbury streets, but when I saw the gray roof of The Rose and Crown looming through the trees, I pulled Dolly to a halt. It seemed like months rather than mere weeks since I'd entered the tavern's door.

I stared long at the upstairs window where Gideon Whitlock lodged. Was he downstairs eating a late breakfast, or was he meeting with a client? I willed myself to optimism, reasoning that just because no one had heard anything from him, such didn't mean he wasn't alive. As I urged the mare toward the home of Joseph and Caroline Lind, I purposely pictured Gideon in his comfortable room instead of in a cold cell on Crown Island.

The mare and I threaded our way past carts and carriages until I reached the Lind home. The white, two-storied structure with a cupola topping the gabled roof was awash with light from the morning sun. Spring-blooming shrubs edged the wide front steps, the lavender blooms seeming to call a welcome. I fervently hoped Joseph Lind would do the same.

Instead of dismounting at the front steps, I guided Dolly to the alley behind the Lind's stable and carriage house. The wrought-iron gate opening off the alley stood open, and a Negro boy of about ten was sweeping the cobbled area by the stable.

Seeing me, the boy dropped his broom and hurried into the stable. A moment later, a tall, broad-shouldered black man emerged.

"May I be helpin' you, mistress?" Though his voice was deep and warm, his dark eyes registered surprise at seeing me and the mare.

I was surprised as well. Although I knew several Boston families kept Negro servants, I'd never seen one at the Lind's home. Apparently the man and boy were recent acquisitions.

"I have come to visit Mr. Lind and his wife."

"Yes'm." And in a quieter voice to the boy, "Go fetch Mr. Gridley." After I handed him Dolly's reins, he led her to the mounting block.

Recognition crossed Mr. Gridley's face when he saw me. "Mistress Stowell, is it?"

"It is. I've come to visit the Linds," I explained again. "I'd be obliged if you'll see to my mare and have someone carry my trunk to the front door."

"Of course, though perhaps you aren't aware that Mistress Lind isn't well and doesn't receive visitors."

"I do know. 'Tis why I've come."

He gave me an uncertain look, but in the end, he said no more.

Not wanting to put myself at a disadvantage by entering through the back door like a servant, I thanked Mr. Gridley and walked toward the house, aware as I followed the oyster-shell path around to the front door that the black man had lifted my trunk onto his shoulders and was just a few steps behind me.

Looking back, I said, "Mr. Gridley failed to tell me your name."

"Jake. 'Tis Jake, Missy."

"Thank you for carrying my trunk, Jake."

His surprised nod told me he wasn't accustomed to being thanked for his services.

My steps slowed as we approached the front door. What if Joseph Lind's welcome was no warmer than Mr. Gridley's? Or that he'd already hired someone to care for Aunt Caroline? Taking a deep breath for courage, I lifted the brass knocker and let it fall heavily against the oversized door. After a minute, a maid opened it—one who bore a familiar face and, despite showing surprise, also smiled a welcome.

"Mistress Stowell. Won't you come in?" Alice pulled the door wide so Jake could set my trunk on the floor. When he retreated back down the front steps, her gaze followed him as if she expected to see my parents.

"I've come alone," I said. "We were told that Mistress Lind is unwell and that her personal maid has left and . . ."

"Not only did she leave but the housekeeper too. We're all at sixes and sevens. Mr. Lind is in the library talkin' to a woman he hopes to hire as housekeeper. 'Tis why I'm answering the door, and Mina, 'stead of cookin' and runnin' the kitchen, is lookin' after Mistress Lind." Running out of breath, Alice was forced to stop.

My heart lifted at her words. "Then 'tis fortunate I came to help."

Alice's eyes widened. "You came to help?"

I nodded just as a door off the high-ceilinged entryway opened and a woman of perhaps forty years came out.

"I will send a note to let you know what I decide," I heard Mr. Lind say.

"You won't be sorry if you hire me," the woman said. Her pale eyes narrowed when she saw me. *Competition*, they seemed to say, and her nod was less than friendly as Alice ushered her out the door.

"I'll tell Mr. Lind you're here," Alice said. Her voice, which had sounded harried, had taken on a note of optimism.

As soon as she left, I removed my hat and ran quick fingers over my hair. As I did, my eyes were drawn to the carved railing of the staircase and the woven burgundy carpet covering the polished wooden floor. They and the large gold-framed mirror on the wall were evidence that no expense had been spared on the home or its furnishings.

I recalled Father making a similar observation when we'd visited the Linds two years before. Then, we'd been close friends. Now, Father suspected Joseph of working hand in glove with General Gage and other prominent Tories, and I'd come to live with him to play a cat-and-mouse game of my own.

"Abigail!"

My heart jumped as I saw Mr. Lind come out of the library. Though not overly tall, he was still a fine-looking man. His tailored blue vest, white shirt, stockings, and dark knee breeches showed off a fit frame for a man his age. He extended a hand, and the smile on his broad, strong-boned face was one of warmth and welcome.

I dropped a curtsey. "I hope I haven't arrived at an inconvenient time."

"No, indeed. 'Tis just the opposite." Looking pleased, he motioned me toward the library. "Come along. We can talk in here."

When he'd closed the door, he turned, his gaze as it traveled over me admiring. "Lovely, just as I predicted." His smile widened. "But I believe I told you this when you were here . . . was it two years ago?" His expression sobered. "'Twas a great blow when we heard of Jonathan's death. We were . . . are so sorry. So very sorry."

Tears came to my eyes.

When Mr. Lind saw them, he cleared his throat. "He was such a bright and capable young man. Like your father, I had great hopes for Jon."

When I made no reply, he cleared his throat again and invited me to be seated.

Since I was fond of books, I'd often explored the tall shelves in the Lind library. Mr. Lind's fondness for books was shown by the number that sat on his large desk.

After he'd taken the chair behind it, he said, "Though I'm happy to see you, I must own I'm surprised that you're in Boston in such troubled times."

His words sent caution knifing through my middle. Momentarily lulled by his warmth, I'd forgotten the true purpose for my coming. "Perhaps the letters my parents wrote can explain why I've come better than I can."

Willing my hands to steadiness, I took the letters from my reticule and handed them to him.

Joseph Lind studied me briefly before he turned his attention to the letters. Since I'd already read them, I was well acquainted with their contents.

Against my better judgment . . . In view of our long friendship . . . Abigail has long held Caroline in high esteem . . . Wishes to care for her during her time of need.

I watched him closely to gauge his reaction while scraps of prayers from my heart fluttered upward. Father had often commented on Mr. Lind's astute talent for business. Such was evidenced when, except for the movement of his gray eyes as they followed the trail of words across the paper, not a muscle moved in the rest of his face.

"Hmm . . ." he said when he'd finished. Though his tone gave away nothing, his eyes were warm. "You should know that your affection for my wife is reciprocated."

I gave a small smile. "Thank you."

"However . . ."

His words hung on the air and made my hands resting quietly in my lap with my reticule suddenly grow damp.

"You have never been shy about expressing your opinions." The corners of his mouth lifted, but his gaze remained steady. "I should like to hear from you why you come to Boston at this unsettled time."

My heart skipped a beat as I recognized that my success at aiding the army might well hinge on the outcome of my next words. Taking a deep breath, I chose them with care. "A family leaving Boston spent the night with Mr. George Smyth in Cambridge. Father was there, and when he learned Aunt Caroline was still unwell and that her personal maid had left . . . he felt great concern . . . one Mother and I felt, as well, when he conveyed the news to us."

I smiled at him as if we were talking of nothing more important than which book I should read. "I have great affection for your wife. She has unfailingly shown me the greatest kindness and has several times gone out of her way to ensure that my time in Boston was enjoyable. When I heard she'd been left"—I put a slight tremble into my voice—"with no one to look after her, I wanted to come and care for her myself . . . that is, if you'll let me."

Mr. Lind's gray eyes hadn't left me the entire time I'd spoken. He continued to hold my gaze, his broad face framed by a brown wig, his manicured hands absently playing with a paperweight. "And your father allowed you to come?"

"Not without much talk and argument. Fortunately, Father's long friendship with you, along with Mother's great affection for Aunt Caroline, weighted the scales in my favor. Nevertheless, gaining his permission didn't come easily."

His lips twitched as if he enjoyed hearing that Nathan Stowell had been outmaneuvered by his daughter. Not wanting to be lulled the second time, I reminded myself that he was still a man to be reckoned with.

A long moment passed before he spoke. "Over the years, I've become familiar with your father's opinions . . . especially those on colonial rights. I'm not as well versed on yours, Abigail. Do you sympathize with the farmers and blacksmiths who chased the King's soldiers back to Boston and now hold us under siege? And am I correct in assuming your father was among those who did the chasing and that he's now camped with the patriots across the bay?"

I nodded. "He is there, along with many from Mayfield. I would be lying if I said I didn't pray for their safety and hope they can keep the redcoats from invading our peaceful farms. But as for this present stalemate . . ." I leaned forward and held his gaze. "I shudder to think of outright war . . . of hundreds, perhaps thousands, of men on both sides bleeding out their lives . . . their final moments a torture." I closed my eyes, and the shiver that ran down my spine was not feigned. "I wish for peace, not war, and I wish to repay your wife's kindness by caring for her in her time of need. 'Tis what I think our Lord would want me to do as well. That's why I have come."

Mr. Lind's eyes shifted to the clock on the mantelpiece, its tick the only sound to fill the room and count the minutes. Father had warned me his friend might meet my offer with suspicion and that he would be a hard man to deceive. Had my carefully chosen words convinced him? Had I succeeded?

"Hmmm," Mr. Lind breathed after a long moment. "I'm not by nature a praying man, but I've prayed this past week to find someone suited to care for my wife. I believe my prayers have been answered by your arrival, Abigail." Clearing his throat, he got to his feet. "You have arrived at a household functioning like a mill wheel out of kilter. Not only has Mistress Kent, my wife's personal maid these six years, left us, but so has Mistress Holbrook, the housekeeper. To say I was taken aback by their leaving would be an understatement." He shook his head like he still couldn't believe it. "Mina . . . our cook, has been sitting with Caroline. She is kind, but she is better suited to cooking and looking after the kitchen. While you—" He paused, and though his expression remained sober, his eyes were warm. "There is much I'll need to explain about her illness and the medicine and your duties, but they can wait until you've had time to settle in and see Caroline for yourself." Coming around the desk, he added, "Thank you for coming, Abigail. I know my wife will be as happy as I am that you are here."

Chapter Sixteen

INSTEAD OF TAKING ME TO see Aunt Caroline, Alice helped me carry my trunk up the elegant staircase to the second floor. "Take care," she cautioned. "If we scratch somethin', no tellin' what'll happen to us . . . leastwise to me."

We paused to catch our breath on the landing.

"Mr. Lind said you're to stay in this guest room and that after you've had a chance to freshen yourself, I'm to take you to see Mistress Lind . . . that is, if she's not sleepin'. 'Tis what she mostly does."

Besides a bed with a blue coverlet and hangings, the guest room held a small desk, a stand with a patterned bowl and ewer, and a tall wardrobe. I'd hoped for a view of the ocean, but the two windows looked out over the homes and streets of Boston.

Hoping to catch a glimpse of The Rose and Crown, I leaned closer to the window only to discover that my view of the south end of Boston was obscured by the tall façade of the governor's mansion. Tomorrow I must try to slip away and familiarize myself with the changes in Boston since the siege. Perhaps, like the day when a crowd had gathered outside Brooks Prints Shop, I'd be fortunate enough to see Gideon.

I'd just finished unpacking when Alice came to tell me Aunt Caroline was awake and wished to see me. Following her along the upstairs corridor, I wondered how much change the illness had caused in her.

Part of me recoiled from the stale air and smell of sickness that permeated Aunt Caroline's darkened room. Since heavy drapes covered the windows, I was able to see little until I'd stepped into the room.

"Abigail." Aunt Caroline's frail voice came from the shadows of the bed. "Joseph and Alice . . . told me you had come."

"I have," I said, walking across the room to take her hand. It was frail, like her voice, and cold, and I instinctively covered it with my other hand to warm it. "If it pleases you, I would like to stay and take care of you."

Aunt Caroline's hand tightened on mine. "I should like that . . . though Mina has been good . . . to help me."

Only then did I notice a tall Negro woman standing in the shadows on the other side of the room. Rather than speaking, she nodded.

"Please pull the drapes so I can see Abigail better," Aunt Caroline said.

Wordlessly, the black woman pulled the folds of burgundy fabric away from one of the windows. The light pouring through the panes revealed a gaunt woman propped among the pillows. It took great effort to hide my dismay. Instead of the vibrant, handsome aunt of two years before, I found one with pasty, sunken cheeks, her blue eyes dull instead of brimming with life.

Aunt Caroline spoke before I could think of what to say. "You're so lovely . . ."

"Thank you," I said in a voice still unsteady from shock.

A shimmer of tears brightened her dull eyes. "I . . . I know I'm . . . much changed."

I patted her frail hand. "I've come to help you get better."

"Better," she repeated in a listless voice lacking hope. Her eyes slowly closed, and it was a moment before she spoke. "Nothing helps."

"There's sure to be something. Though I'm country bred, we have remedies too."

Aunt Caroline's eyes gave another weak smile. "'You were always one . . . to try new things."

I laughed in an effort to lift the despair that filled her voice and the room. "You are right. I mean to make you well again."

"If . . . only." She fell quiet so long I thought she'd fallen asleep. "I wish to . . . rest now," she finally said, her voice so soft I had to lean close to hear it. "Thank you . . . for coming." She withdrew her hand—warm now instead of cold—and her head turned tiredly into the pillow.

Mina picked up the lunch tray, one that looked untouched. "I be takin' this back to the kitchen."

"Please . . . close the drapery," Aunt Caroline whispered.

When Mina moved to the window, I noticed that her ebony face was slightly scarred by smallpox and that she wore a bright-blue-and-yellow turban around her head.

Mina followed me from the room. After closing the door, she spoke in a low, melodic voice. "More'n anything, the missus need to know she ain't a gonna die. I try to tell her, but she don't believe me." Her dark eyes held my blue ones. "I'm thinkin' that if you was to tell her sich, she'd believe it comin' from a white woman."

"I'll do that," I said.

As I watched Mina start down the narrow back stairs to the kitchen, I thought of the despair and sadness I'd sensed in the bedroom—it penetrated the walls and fabric of the sickroom and clung like a heavy gray fog around Aunt Caroline.

"I will do that," I repeated in a determined voice. "Along with Prudence Blood's teas and tinctures, I'll give Aunt Caroline hope."

Later that day, Alice tapped on the door to tell me Mr. Lind wished to see me in his library. I descended the stairs with a mind full of questions about Aunt Caroline's health. What disease had left her so thin and frail, and what could I do to help her?

Although Joseph greeted me with a smile, his somber mood was apparent. "Thank you for coming." He motioned to the chair I'd sat in earlier. "Please be seated, for there's much I need to explain about my wife's condition." Instead of taking the chair behind his desk, he remained standing, his back to the window, his head slightly bowed as if inspecting the expensive silver buckles on his polished black shoes.

"I purposely waited until after you'd seen Mistress Lind before I spoke to you about her illness," he continued. "That she is greatly altered from what she was but six months ago is a daily tragedy for her and me . . . for all of us."

"I scarcely recognized her," I said, blinking back sudden tears. "What disease has ravished her so?"

"It's not so much a disease as a condition . . . one that isn't contagious . . . so you can rest easy. 'Tis called female hysterics. Dr. Barnes, a highly respected physician and surgeon brought from London by General Gage, made the diagnosis."

"Female hysterics?" I echoed, having never heard of such a thing.

"Dr. Barnes says it isn't uncommon among genteel females in London. He's treated a case or two here in Boston as well. It shows itself in various forms—headaches and vague aches and pains, difficulty in sleeping, crying, and instability." He paused and expelled a long sigh. "In Caroline's case, she began to talk nonsense, accusing me . . . others too . . . of doing things that aren't true."

His shoulders drooped, and he turned to stare out the window. Sadness gathered around my heart as I watched him standing so still. Lost in thought, neither of us spoke.

Mr. Lind finally broke the silence, his voice low as if he struggled to find the words. "When I tried to tell Caroline I would never do the things she accused me of, she became hysterical . . . crying, screaming . . . so angry she threw her hairbrush at me."

He turned away from the window and fingered a place on his forehead. "Despite Caroline's hysteria, her aim with the brush was true. The bruise it left required a tale that was less than truthful."

The vivid word picture sat at sharp contrast to the delightful woman I'd known in the past. It was with difficulty that I spoke. "I can hardly believe such—"

"Nor can I. It was as if a wild person had invaded the body of one I loved . . . some terrible demon. I sent Jake for Dr. Barnes, yet even the doctor had difficulty subduing her. Caroline fought like a woman possessed . . . kicking and screaming. In the end, the butler and I were required to hold her down while the doctor forced a dose of laudanum down her throat."

A sick feeling pulsed through my stomach. "How awful," I whispered, my clasped fingers tense, my voice unsteady.

"Yes," he agreed. He sat down and studied me. "I've shocked you, which wasn't my intent . . . though I thought it needful for you to know what to expect. I don't want you to be taken by surprise should your aunt act or speak strangely."

I nodded, though I wished with all my heart that I hadn't been subjected to the scenes he'd described—talking irrationally, screaming, and throwing things. "Now she's weak and listless," I finally said.

He nodded and ran his hand along his jaw. "It was a painful choice Dr. Barnes gave me—a wife who raves and talks nonsense or one placid and prone to sleep."

While I sat numbly in my chair, doubts niggled at my brain. Some of what Joseph Lind was telling me didn't seem quite right. "Is there no place in between?"

"Dr. Barnes says no." His mouth firmed resolutely. "And thus you find us, Abigail—our lives much changed and Caroline dependent on others instead of presiding over her home as she once did. As I said this morning . . . your coming was a Godsend."

"What would you have me do for her?"

He sighed again. Did he realize how often one slipped past his lips? "Your first charge is to see that she is kept clean and is well cared for."

"She is so thin."

"Laudanum is the culprit. It takes away her interest in food. Other things too."

"Then why not curtail its use?"

"Because . . ." Mr. Lind's voice turned irritable. Taking a deep breath, he spoke more softly. "Because she becomes agitated and quarrelsome and says things that aren't true."

"What things?" I asked, disliking his vagueness.

He blinked and seemed not to know what to say. "Why . . . things so preposterous, they don't bear repeating." Though he smiled, it was evident he didn't like my question. "Either Caroline remains thin and without energy, or she is impossible to manage."

"I see," I responded, though in truth, I didn't. Sensing that he wouldn't brook any further discussion on the subject, I said nothing. Wasn't he a successful businessman accustomed to others following his decisions without question? Just the same, I questioned them.

Seeming pleased at my silence, Mr. Lind went on. "As to your other duties, each morning you must check on my wife. If she's still sleeping, you may breakfast in the kitchen and take a tray of food up to her when you're finished. Dr. Barnes left instruction that she be given her first dose of medicine with her breakfast."

He rose and retrieved a brown bottle and a small wine glass from a bookshelf. "I asked Alice to bring the glass and medicine to me so you can see how to measure the dosage." Picking up the glass, he ran a fingernail around the middle of it. "The medicine is strong so you must take care not to fill it more than half full." He paused to see that I watched him closely. "Give one dose to her at breakfast, another in midafternoon, and the last one at night before you settle her for bed. To keep her docile and manageable, it's important that it's given to her on a regular schedule."

Docile. Manageable. The words pulsed with anger through my mind. Was Aunt Caroline no more than an animal to be kept docile and manageable? Had it not been that I needed to remain with the Linds, I would have protested. It took great effort to make my face expressionless and keep my thoughts to myself.

"Dr. Barnes keeps a standing order for the laudanum at the apothecary on Cornhill Street. You'll be obliged to procure a new bottle when the medicine runs low." He picked up the wine glass and laudanum bottle and handed them to me. When he saw me hesitate, he chuckled. "It isn't poison, Abigail, though Dr. Barnes tells me an overdose can be fatal. Laudanum is also very bitter tasting. To make it more palatable, the apothecary mixes the opiate with wine and cinnamon and saffron."

I reluctantly took the items. "I feel so very sorry for her."

"As do I. As do I." Stepping away from the desk, he added, "Other than myself and those who care for her, Dr. Barnes has deemed it wise that Caroline have no other visitors. Though the doctor comes weekly to examine and bleed her, I fear there has been little improvement these past four months."

I wanted to say I meant to change it, but prudence bade me do no more than nod.

Mr. Lind moved to open the door. "When my wife is sleeping, you are free to use your time as you see fit. I believe Mistress Kent spent considerable time gossiping with the servants in the kitchen, but I can't see you finding much pleasure in that." Pointing to the crowded bookshelves, he smiled. "Most of my books are of a scholarly nature, so I doubt you'll find them to your liking. But those on the lower shelves are yours to read and enjoy." He paused and gave me a patronizing smile. "Knowing your love of books, I suspect you'll make use of my offer."

"I shall," I said, though the words came without pleasure. Had he so quickly forgotten that I'd been tutored with Jonathan as he'd prepared to go to Harvard? More than that, Father had always given me free access to all of his books.

My mood was pensive as I carried the glass and bottle upstairs. How I wished I could ask Ben to ready the cart so I could consult with Mistress Blood. On my last visit to the wise little woman, I'd written down the names and dosages of herbs and roots to help relieve headaches and dropsy and ailments of the stomach, but not once had she mentioned such a thing as female hysterics.

"Female hysterics." Just running the name over my tongue and letting it out in a whisper set my nerves jangling. Doubt raised its head again. Despite Joseph Lind's numerous sighs, his words and manner had struck me as rehearsed . . . his concern for his wife not entirely genuine. More than that, if what Father suspected was true, he was much practiced at pretending to be other than what he was.

As I paused outside Aunt Caroline's bedroom door, my resolve to help the woman who'd been so kind to me deepened.

Chapter Seventeen

OVER THE NEXT FEW DAYS, I spent many hours with Aunt Caroline, encouraging her to eat and reading to her from one of Mr. Lind's books. Through it all, my true purpose for coming to Boston was never far from my mind. Each morning while she napped, I slipped away to explore Boston.

The town was a warren of alleys that bisected the streets at irregular intervals, some mere paths to drive cows to graze on the common, others wide enough to accommodate carts and wagons. All had one thing in common: with so many soldiers and unemployed dockworkers present, they were not safe for an unescorted female.

I took note of the alleys, and each night I sat at my desk with quill and ink and paper and carefully added street names and lines to the map I drew. Whether 'twas for my own benefit or to help the army, I didn't yet know, but I felt strongly that an accurate map of streets and fortifications would prove to be important.

It was not difficult to invent a reason to leave the house each day. Although Mina went to market each morning, other items were needed—medicines, tobacco, or a copy of the *Boston Gazette* for Mr. Lind. These and other errands I took as my own. With my white cap, apron, and basket, it was easy to blend in with the goodwives and maids.

Unlike in March, a somber mood hung over the besieged town. Faces wore uneasy expressions, and I saw many of the citizens cast worried glances across the narrow bay to the mainland. Did they wonder if the rebels on the hills were about to attack? Or was their focus on General Gage and the puzzle of why he still waited? The answer to this plagued me as well. If only I could discover his plans.

On my daily sojourns through the streets, soldiers were everywhere, some drilling, others digging fortifications on the common or patrolling the town in pairs. One morning, I saw redcoats stop a boy running down the street. After questioning him as to his hurry, they ordered him to remove his cap and to empty his pockets. When they found a scrap of paper under the lining of his cap, they marched him off to the guardhouse.

"Good," a woman said. "'Tis good to see our soldiers on the alert for spies. In times like this, 'tis hard to know who's for the King and who's for the rebels."

As I moved away, the image of the young boy being marched off to the guardhouse wouldn't leave me. Hadn't Gideon told me to use such a boy to carry a message to him if I came again to Boston?

I glanced often at the faces of those on the streets that first week, but of the man I sought, I saw nothing. Finally, I determined to visit The Rose and Crown under the guise of seeking legal advice from a lawyer by the name of Gideon Whitlock.

I knew I risked being recognized as the young lady who'd been kissed and had promptly slapped Gideon, but the need to find him pushed caution aside.

After I'd made certain Aunt Caroline was sleeping soundly, I put on my straw hat, adjusted the brim to lie low over my forehead, and tied the ribbon so the bow covered part of my chin. Hoping the change would prevent recognition, I set out for the tavern.

A strong breeze blowing off the bay buffeted my skirt and lifted the brim of my hat so I was obliged to hold on to it. When I neared the tavern, my steps slowed. Would I have to wait while Gideon finished with another client? What if he was off on an errand?

Since it was midmorning, I heard only a few voices when I opened the door. All was as I remembered it—the main room to my left, the ladies' parlor on the right, and the proprietor presiding behind the bar.

He greeted me with a nod as he polished a tankard. "How may I help you?"

"I'm in need of legal counsel. A friend directed me to a lawyer who lives here . . . Mr. Gideon Whitlock."

"Lived," the proprietor said. "Mr. Whitlock is no longer with us."

Numbness closed around my throat. Had my nightmare of Gideon being hanged or shot been carried out? "Is . . . is he dead?" I managed to get out.

The balding man chuckled. "He's alive . . . leastwise he was when I last saw him. 'Tis just that he don't live at The Rose and Crown no more."

Relief washed over me. "Can you tell me where I might find him?"

"At a house on Summer Street. Number 28, I think it is . . . though I know for a fact his room there don't compare to the one he had here." Shaking his head, he went on, his vexation at losing his lodger evident. "'Twas that army officer he spent so much time with who got him to leave. He even helped him pack his belongings and papers."

Though I longed to know more, I thought it unwise to query any further. "He's at number 28 Summer Street?"

"That's the address he told me to give to clients seeking his services. Since General Gage's officers and a good many of his soldiers now lodge free in private homes, I expect the officer resides there as well." Holding the tankard up to the light, he went on, "Mr. Whitlock is a fine lawyer. All speak highly of him."

Seeing the proprietor's wife approaching, I hastily murmured my thanks and left.

My mind was in a jumble as I reached the street. From my forays into town, I knew the location of Summer Street. What I didn't know was whether it would be wise to go there. What if Gideon hadn't left The Rose and Crown willingly and he was being held prisoner? Or maybe the home was a trap to learn who helped Gideon gather and smuggle out information. Such would certainly explain why no one had heard from him. In the end, I decided I would only walk past it. Surely no harm could come from that.

The address of the white clapboard home was clearly marked in black letters above the door. I walked at a leisurely pace, trying not to show undue interest in the dwelling while wondering if one of the front windows was Gideon's. I cast a furtive glance at the house. Nothing. No one.

Disappointment dogged me as I returned to the Linds' home. That night, after much thought, I penned a short message to Gideon. *Apple blossoms are not forgotten. Do you recall the promise you made? M. A.* Would Gideon remember the apple blossoms he'd given me? And would he know the initials *M. A.* stood for Mistress Abigail? So many question, yet as each one arose, I failed to find an answer.

★

The next morning, it was difficult to exhibit my usual patience with Aunt Caroline as I attempted to cajole her into eating a piece of toast topped with marmalade. Instead, my mind was on the tightly folded missive in my pocket, and my nerves clamored to be off to find a boy to take the note to Gideon.

As if she sensed my thoughts were elsewhere, Aunt Caroline became agitated and not only refused to eat any toast but had difficulty falling asleep too. Ordinarily, I would have welcomed it, for I was concerned by the numerous hours this radically changed woman slept. But not today.

It was after ten o'clock before I could leave the house. More than that, I had to walk to Marlborough Street before I could find a boy to carry my note.

"I can do it . . . though fast as folks is movin' in and out, 'tis hard to say who's livin' where anymore," the grimy faced boy responded.

"'Tis for Gideon Whitlock, the lawyer. At Number 28 Summer Street."

"I know of him."

Pleased, I handed him the folded note and a coin. "There'll be another coin from Mr. Whitlock when he receives it."

"Where can I find you if Mr. Whitlock sends an answer?"

"There," I said, pointing across the street to a tinsmith shop. "I'll be there until the clock strikes eleven."

As soon as the boy left, I crossed the street to the tinsmith shop, pausing to look at a display of tin cups in the front window before going inside. What exactly I looked at I cannot say, for my mind was on the boy instead of the items in the shop. Was he to Summer Street yet? What if Gideon didn't send a reply? The expectancy that had carried me through the morning suddenly fell flat, the interior of the shop seemed stuffy, and the shopkeeper's hovering presence was annoying. Excusing myself, I exited the shop.

After walking but a few steps, I saw the boy ambling along a side street connecting with Marlborough. As soon as he saw me, his steps quickened.

"Is there a message?" I asked before he reached me.

The boy shook his head and darted a quick look over his shoulder. "Never saw Mr. Whitlock . . . but a soldier said he'd give it to him." Without breaking pace, he passed me. "Two soldiers been following me since I left Summer Street," he whispered.

My heart gave a frightened leap when a quick look revealed two red-clad soldiers coming at a quick pace along the connecting street. Their steps were determined, and I had no doubt they had come to find me. Without thought, I hurried off in the opposite direction. My mouth went dry, and my steps were quick and hard like my heartbeat. I scarcely noted the shops as

I passed them. Instinct bade me lift my skirt and flee while caution warned that to do so would shout my involvement with Gideon to the soldiers.

Not knowing whether they followed the boy or me, I kept my focus ahead and my pace like a maid but hurrying home from an errand. In my haste, I almost missed an alley bisecting the street. I quickly turned into it, hesitating only long enough to look over my shoulder. Not only were the soldiers following, but they were also gaining!

"Halt!" one of them shouted.

Ignoring the command, I quickened my steps.

Hurry! Hurry! The unspoken words cried through my fear-clogged mind. Lifting my skirt, I broke into a run—past a chicken coop and clothes pegged to dry on a rope. Spying a gate, I sped through it and along a tall boxwood hedge that stretched across the back of the yard.

Not seeing the soldiers, I left the cover of the hedge and ran across the yard and hid behind a bush. The rapid thud of my heart mingled with my harsh breathing as I waited. Was I safe?

After waiting and watching, I left my hiding place and hurried to the front yard. A quick look at the street showed only a carriage and a mother walking with a child.

Fearing the soldiers would cut through a yard from the alley too, I hurried on, zigzagging down streets and across alleys until I became so lost and confused I had no notion of where I was. But at least I had evaded the soldiers. When I stopped to get my bearings, I spied the great wharf stretching into the Atlantic and knew I was only a few streets from home.

Exhaustion and disappointment dogged my steps as I returned. Was I never to find Gideon? Even as the question formed, I realized the mistake I'd made by giving in to fear and fleeing. I'd not only raised the soldiers' suspicions but had also endangered Gideon.

"Foolish girl!" The accusing words came in a harsh whisper. The house on Summer Street had been a trap, and I was extremely fortunate to have escaped. My lack of experience had shown. In the future, I must be more careful and think before I acted.

By the time I reached the Linds', I'd determined to stay close for the next few days. Although the soldiers had seen me only from the back, they might remember the lavender color of my skirts. For safety's sake, I decided that in the future I must wear them only at home.

Jake looked up from mending a harness when I crossed the stable yard. "Mornin', mistress," he said with a nod and smile.

"Good morning, Jake."

He went on in a low voice. "Alice been lookin' for ya."

I nodded and whispered my thanks as I hurried past him. I was almost to the house when I saw Alice.

"I been lookin' all over for you," she exclaimed in relief. "Mistress Lind was asking for you. Thanks to Mina, she's finally sleeping again."

"Thank you. I would have been back sooner, but . . ." Seeking to divert her attention from my absence, I said, "You'll not believe what I saw."

"What?" Alice's eyes brightened with curiosity.

I launched into a description of the boy who'd been stopped by soldiers and taken to the guardhouse a few days before.

"The poor lad," Alice said, then added, "though I expect they were only doing their duty. 'Tis perilous times we live in, Mistress Abigail, and I daily thank my Maker the rebels ain't at our very door."

"Times are certainly unsettled," I agreed. Looking past Alice, I went on. "I need to talk to Mina. Is she upstairs or in the kitchen?"

"In the kitchen."

Nodding, I opened the kitchen door, where a massive brick fireplace took up one wall, with two ovens flanking each side and numerous nooks for warming dishes until serving time. Mina stirred a pot over the fire, and Hettie, the kitchen maid, was chopping an onion.

"Something smells good," I said as Hettie scooped the chopped onion into a bowl and dumped it into the pot.

Mina nodded. "Chicken soup's what you'll be havin'."

"It would be good for others in the house as well."

Mina gave me a quick look, then glanced at Hettie. "I need you to go out to the coop and find six eggs for the puddin' I'm startin'," she said to the maid.

"Six?"

Mina nodded. "And don't come back till you find 'em."

Mina waited to speak until after the maid had gone. "You meanin' the missus?" she asked. Seeing me nod, she went on. "The doctor don't like her havin' more'n tea and toast. He say she too sickly to have anything more."

"She'll never improve on a diet of tea and toast," I countered. "My mother gave us strengthening broths and custards when we ailed."

Mina nodded. "Twice I slipped such up to her, but . . ." She paused and shook her head. "Gettin' the missus to eat ain't easy."

"I know." I studied Mina, her turbaned head outlined by the fire, her brown eyes holding steadily to mine. "I want to make her stronger and persuade her she isn't going to die . . . but I'll need your help. Going against Mr. Lind will be a big risk . . . especially for you." I paused and took a deep breath. "I don't know your situation . . . whether you and Jake are slaves or hired servants, but . . ."

"We free, Missy." Pride punctuated her words. "We free."

"It's still a risk. Before we go further, you must talk with your husband."

"I done talk with Jake when Mistress Kent left and I took her place lookin' after the missus. He know what I did 'bout her food."

"You're a brave woman."

"I only doin' what the good Lord want me to do." She continued to hold my gaze. "I knew that first day you was the woman I'd been prayin' to come here."

"I want to help her get well again."

She nodded and turned back to the pot of chicken.

"Noontime should be best to begin this," I said after a minute. "Mr. Lind is gone by then, and he doesn't come home until evening. If I were to start taking my meals with the mistress instead of in the kitchen . . ."

Mina flashed me a quick smile. "I kin send up a tray with the usual tea and toast along with two spoons and a bowl of broth or custard for the two of you."

"How clever."

"We best be hopin' no one else be clever too," Mina reminded.

I immediately sobered. "What about the maids? Can they be trusted?"

Mina frowned. "Hettie don't think about much 'sides doin' what she told to do, but Alice—" Her frown deepened. "Alice, I ain't so sure 'bout."

"Me either. We're going to need to pray and keep our wits about us."

"Amen," Mina said. "Amen to that."

Chapter Eighteen

AFTER BEING OUTSIDE IN THE fresh air and sunshine, the stuffiness of Aunt Caroline's bedroom was more noticeable than ever. Since she was sleeping, I pulled back the drapery and opened the window a few inches. A slight breeze carried not only fresh air but also the cheerful song of birds into the room. "There," I whispered in satisfaction.

As I stood at the window, my frightening encounter with the redcoats jumped back into my mind. With it came the knowledge that Gideon's freedom had been curtailed. After today, I saw why it was so difficult for him to smuggle out information. But thank heaven he was alive.

Glancing at the bed, I realized that part of the reason for Aunt Caroline's restlessness while I was gone might be the result of me lessening her dose of laudanum. Though I'd only reduced it by the slimmest amount, her sleep wasn't as deep or her actions as placid as they'd been three days ago.

I moved restlessly myself. I'd thought my purpose in coming to Boston was finding Gideon and helping the patriots. But in just a week, my path had diverged into two—Gideon and the patriots on one side, helping Aunt Caroline recover on the other.

Hearing a small sound from the bed, I saw that she'd wakened. Her gaze moved to the open window. "Light and air," she said in a low voice.

"It's such a lovely day; I wanted you to enjoy it too."

"Yes." She lifted a hand to shade her eyes from the brightness.

"Would you like me to close the drapery a little?"

She shook her head and smiled as if she took as much pleasure in fresh air and birdsongs as I.

Sitting down on the chair next to her bed, I took her other hand. As usual, it was cold. I gently rubbed and chaffed it.

"Thank you," she said. "You're so kind."

Before I could respond, a soft knock sounded on the door.

"Yes," I called.

"'Tis Alice with the lunch tray." As she set it down, her eyes widened at the sight of the open window. For a moment, she looked ready to speak. In the end, she only curtsied and left.

"Mmm," I said, inhaling the appetizing aroma of the soup. "It smells like Mina's fixed some of her delicious chicken soup. She and I want to make you well again." When I unfolded the napkin, I found a second spoon.

Aunt Caroline gave a wan smile. "You're so kind," she repeated, but instead of having to be coaxed, she opened her mouth and took a sip of the broth. After the second sip, a knock came again. Before I could respond, a gentleman I'd never seen before entered the room.

Tall, thin, and impeccably dressed in black and white, I felt his dark gaze sweep across my person, then jump to the window. "Who has opened the window?" he demanded.

My hand jerked at the loudness of his voice, and only Providence kept me from spilling the soup. Before I could speak, the man, whom I presumed to be Dr. Barnes, strode across the room, shut the window, and loosed the drapery to shut out the light.

As he strode to the bed, Aunt Caroline spoke. "Dr. Barnes, this is . . . my good friend Abigail . . . who's come to care for me."

Acting as if he hadn't heard her, the doctor set his bag on the bed, took a Sulphur match from his pocket, and lit the twin candles on the table. As they flared to life, he gave me but a cursory nod and fixed his attention on his patient. "I see that you haven't eaten your tea and toast yet."

Aunt Caroline's gaze flicked from me to the doctor. "I was about to."

"Make certain you do."

She nodded and quietly allowed him to lift each eyelid and peer into her eyes.

I wanted to ask why he did so, but his haughty manner discouraged questions.

He wasn't averse to asking them himself, however. "Has Mistress Lind exhibited any sign of agitation since you've come?"

Thinking of her actions today, I was aware that both the doctor and his patient watched me—his gaze stern and demanding, hers soft and pleading. Not liking to see her acting like a fearful child, I answered with only the slightest hesitation. "She's been nothing but amiable."

"Good."

Aunt Caroline's expression immediately relaxed.

"How often do you give Mistress Lind her medicine?"

"Three times . . . just as her husband instructed."

"Should she ever become agitated, you can increase the dosage to four times."

Wondering what he would say if he knew I'd decreased rather than increased the laudanum, I picked up the tray with the half-eaten bowl of soup and set it on the floor. When I straightened, Dr. Barnes had unbuckled his satchel and taken out a small bowl and a leather case.

Since Prudence Blood had always attended our family, my curiosity was pricked as I watched Dr. Barnes extract a knife from the leather case. Sliding up the white sleeve of Aunt Caroline's nightgown, he slipped the bowl under her elbow.

She lay with eyes closed, seeming to have moved to another place as he took a strip of cloth from the satchel and tied it tightly around her upper arm. After kneading the inside of her elbow, he pierced the skin with the point of his knife.

I sucked in my breath as tiny drops of blood trickled from the wound into the bowl. "Why are you . . ." I began.

"I tolerate no distraction in my sickroom," the doctor snapped. Like his voice, his brown eyes snapped as he gave me a censuring glance. "If the sight of blood upsets you, leave. I have no time or patience for squeamish young women."

"I'm not upset but curious as to why you're making Mistress Lind bleed."

Dr. Barnes kneaded a few more drops of blood from the pale arm. Only when he seemed satisfied did he speak. "Unhealthy humors live in the blood of the sick. For the patient to heal, the humors must be extracted."

His dark eyes bore into mine. "Unhealthy humors are also present in outside air. This is why I have ordered the windows to be kept closed and the hangings drawn." The nostrils of his thin nose flared with distaste. "No poisonous air is allowed in this room."

Though I nodded, I remembered Prudence Blood's claim that fresh air and sunshine were healing gifts from our Maker—recalled how, while dispensing teas and tinctures, she told those who were recuperating to spend time each day sitting in the sunshine.

As I followed Dr. Barnes's instructions to rinse the blood from his bleeding bowl, I recalled how hard we'd worked to stop the bleeding when Jon had cut a deep gash in his leg while chopping wood. Instead of helping, the weekly bleeding of Aunt Caroline could only be making her weaker. It took great control not to say such when I handed the bowl back to the doctor.

By the time I returned from emptying the basin of bloody water down the necessary, the candles were snuffed, the doctor gone, and the room again in darkness. Disregarding Dr. Barnes's instructions, I went to the window and opened it an inch.

Though I wasn't yet confident enough of my place in the Linds' home, I promised myself that when the time came, I'd not only open the window wider but help Aunt Caroline sit in a chair so she could see the beauty that awaited her outside.

★

Leaning on the side of caution, I stayed home for the next three days, my mind focused on helping Aunt Caroline rather than finding Gideon. The more I thought about the doctor's nonchalant bloodletting from a woman already pale and listless, the more it upset me. As for his talk of harmful humors, I preferred to think as Prudence Blood did: that patients were better cured by strengthening foods and the warmth of healing sun.

I had taken a strong dislike to Dr. Barnes. Not only did I think him arrogant, but I disliked his narrow features and fastidious dress too. The silver buckles on his shoes were bigger than Mr. Lind's, his white powdered wig more elaborate than what was commonly seen in Boston. If the man thought his demeaning words and curt manners would cow me, he was sadly mistaken. Even so, I knew I must use care.

Now, instead of taking my meals in the kitchen with the servants, I fixed a tray for me and Aunt Caroline with an extra fork or spoon hidden under the napkin and her toast and cup of tea set beside my more substantial fare. To Alice's query about the change, I said I hoped Mistress Lind would eat better when someone ate with her.

My explanation proved true. Not only did she eat without complaint, but her appetite seemed improved as well.

"How often does Dr. Barnes come to see you?" I asked the next morning.

Aunt Caroline frowned as she chewed a bite of toast. "I'm not certain. The days . . ." She frowned and sighed. "One day seems to slide . . . into another."

"Don't you remember?"

She stared past me for a minute. "At first . . . I think he came every day. Now . . ." She shrugged. "Perhaps once a week."

"Does he always bleed you?"

"Always," she whispered. "I can't bear to watch . . . so I close my eyes."

"I'd close my eyes too."

She smiled as if my words pleased her.

"When my brother cut his leg, Father said if we didn't stop the bleeding, Jon would die. And yet the doctor . . ." My voice broke in frustration. "Why does he bleed you if he's trying to make you well? Isn't there some way you can make him stop?"

Aunt Caroline gave a harsh laugh. "I tried . . . fought. He didn't care." Tears slipped from her closed eyes. "Then I was tired . . . and didn't care anymore."

I leaned close to her, my voice fierce. "I'm not too tired to care!"

Her eyes flew open, and she gave a sad little smile. "You were always so bold."

"And so were you!" I took hold of her hand. "I have a plan . . . one I think will succeed if we are careful. My plan will make you care again."

"If only I could," she whispered.

"You can."

A flicker of hope brightened her eyes. Seeing it, I tightened my hold on her hand. "We can."

Hers lips began to quiver, and tears trickled down her cheeks.

Seeing her distress, I went to the armoire and found a handkerchief. After she wiped her cheeks and blew her nose, she apologized. "My nose and eyes keep running."

I'd noticed the running nose when I'd arrived with the breakfast tray and hoped she wasn't coming down with a summer cold. Watching her, I saw her fuss with the sleeve of her nightgown.

Thinking that our talk had upset her and that it was time for her medicine, I went to the shelf and took down the laudanum bottle and glass.

Aunt Caroline stopped fussing when she saw the bottle. "Surely you know . . . what that medicine is," she said.

"I do."

"And you . . . still give it to me?"

"I don't know what else to do. Until Mr. Lind told me this was laudanum, I'd only heard of it once before. Prudence Blood told me that at first laudanum brought pleasure, but in a short time, it became a curse . . . the devil's curse, she called it."

"'Tis a curse . . . but I can't do without."

"Perhaps in time you can." Seeing her skepticism, I went on. "As a mother, didn't you gradually wean your babies to a cup?"

She gave me a puzzled nod. "What has that . . . to do with this?"

I held up the wine glass. "See these leaves etched around the middle?" At her nod, I went on. "When your husband gave me the laudanum and glass, he told me to fill it up to the top of the leaves. But in the ten days since, I've decreased it a little each day."

"Oh, Abigail," she said on a trembling breath.

"See this petal here," I said, pointing to a leaf in the middle of the etching. "This is where I filled it today."

She wiped her nose. "I've felt different . . . but I didn't want the doctor to know."

"Nor did I. If this is to succeed, we must see that he and your husband don't suspect."

"Especially . . . Joseph," she whispered. "He . . . he—" Tears filled her eyes, and she began to shake. "Please . . . the laudanum."

Uncorking the bottle, I carefully poured the amber liquid up to the petal. "There."

Craving showed in her eyes as she eagerly reached for the glass with unsteady hands.

Fearing the contents would spill, I guided it to her lips. She drank it in three quick swallows. Then licking her lips, she closed her eyes and gave a contented sigh.

I looked with pity at her gaunt cheeks and pale skin, the slight tremors that shook her body. Had the laudanum ravished her so, or were the frequent bleedings partly to blame?

As if sensing my gaze, she opened her eyes. "Thank . . . you for caring."

Setting down the glass, I again took her hand. "I'll always care about you, but you must realize that what we attempt involves great risk for us both. I don't know what might happen in the days ahead. You're already more alert than you were. Restless too. What if by decreasing the laudanum, you suffer worse things? What if I do wrong?"

The confidence that had set me on this path had faltered. Who was I to think I could cure something I knew nothing about? Or to match wits against Joseph Lind and Dr. Barnes? *Think before you act or speak,* Father's voice seemed to say. But I had thought and had lost numerous hours of sleep as I wondered and worried. *Please, God, make it right.*

Seeming to sense my turmoil again, Aunt Caroline spoke with slurred words. "You didn't . . . do wrong . . . but came like. . . the angel I prayed for."

I blinked back tears. "Thank you."

Her fingers returned my clasp, and with a sigh, she settled into the nest of pillows.

Still holding her hand, I sat with her for some time, felt her fingers gradually relax, watched as little by little the agitation subsided and calm settled over her features.

"Sleep well," I whispered, praying that in a fortnight her sleep would come naturally instead of from the clutches of laudanum.

Chapter Nineteen

AGITATION AND RESTLESSNESS CONTINUED TO plague Aunt Caroline over the next three days. Her nose continued to run, and she complained of itching as well. Not knowing whether 'twas a summer cold or being weaned from the laudanum, I concentrated on keeping her comfortable.

On Saturday, as I was reading to Aunt Caroline, her husband came to see her. The light and shadows of the candles flickering over her fine-boned features made him smile.

"Candlelight always becomes you, Caroline."

She gave a tight smile and closed her eyes, her fingers clenched as she strove to keep the fidgeting under control. His daily visits were a test for us both. On my first day, I noticed his coming didn't please her. Though she didn't speak of it, she must recall him holding her down and dosing her with laudanum. He, on the other hand, ignored the strained atmosphere his visits brought.

Though I couldn't bar his entry, I'd taken pains lately to keep his visits short. "I fear now isn't the best time for your visit. She has slept most of the day and isn't at all responsive to conversation."

"Small matter, for 'tis you I came to see." Still standing by the door, he went on. "Tomorrow is the Sabbath, and I thought to invite you to attend meeting with me and my mother and sister. There's ample room in the carriage."

Surprised by his invitation, I smiled my pleasure. I'd missed attending church, and the outing would provide opportunity to look for Gideon. "I would like that very much . . . though I'll have to ask Mina to sit with Mistress Lind."

The following morning, I dressed with care in my green dress. I also took pains with my hair, twisting it into a coil at the back of my head and leaving a few wavy tendrils to curl around my face. When I was finished, the guest room mirror reflected a face that didn't displease me.

As I adjusted a lock of hair, I seemed to hear Reverend Whipple's voice. *Pride, Abigail. Remember pride paves the way to hell.* I pushed the annoying thought aside and descended the stairs, filled with excitement and hope.

It was but a short drive to the home of Mr. Lind's mother and sister. His sister—one Elizabeth Corbin—looked to be at least ten years his junior. She was finely turned out in a stylish polonaise of bottle-green silk, and her looks were not unattractive. His mother, who looked to be in her late sixties, wore a bodice and overskirt of a subdued shade of blue.

After introductions had been made, Mr. Lind explained that his sister's husband was in England on business for the King. His pleasure in letting me know she'd married well was obvious. It also reminded me to watch my words and actions.

Despite this, the friendliness of the two women put me at ease. Although my attire wasn't as stylish or expensive as theirs, neither made me feel as if I were a country cousin.

When we reached the Anglican Church, Jake's son, Ezra, let down the steps of the carriage. The church was larger than the one I attended in Mayfield, and those I followed into it were more finely attired. But my mind was more taken with the hope of seeing Gideon than on anything else.

I scanned the pews as I followed Mr. Lind and his mother up the aisle to their pew near the front of the church and looked again before I sat next to his sister. Although several red-clad soldiers were there, I didn't see Gideon sitting with them.

Disappointed, I had difficulty keeping my mind on the sermon, and only strict control kept me from turning to look for Gideon. Had he arrived late? Why, oh, why wasn't the Lind pew at the back of the church so I could more easily see who was present?

I arose as soon as the service ended, but as I turned to look, a gentleman with his wife and two grown children crowded close to walk with us from the church. The height of the two men and the press of people blocked my view. More than that, the son openly watched everything I did.

When we'd passed through the vestibule and out into the spring sunshine, Elizabeth Corbin introduced me to Mr. Nichols and his wife and son and daughter, Edward and Emma.

"My pleasure, Mistress Stowell," Edward said as I rose from my curtsey.

Thinking to make the best of the situation, I smiled up at him, noting his good looks and dark hair and a good-humored smile that put me at ease. His sister, Emma, was an attractive young woman of an age similar to my own.

"Since Mistress Stowell will be staying with my brother and his wife for an indefinite time, I hope you can become friends," Elizabeth went on.

I was thankful for her tact in not mentioning that I was taking care of her invalid sister-in-law, grateful also that none knew the true reason for my being to Boston.

I responded to Edward and Emma's friendly overtures, but I did so with only half a mind, my gaze more often on the people exiting the church than on them. Then, just as I was about to give up hope, I saw Gideon. My heart leapt hard against my ribs as he and an officer stepped out of the vestibule. I drew in a quick breath, and happiness swirled around me at the unmistakable evidence that he was alive!

My entire attention was centered on Gideon, though some part of my brain registered the fact that he was taller than the officer. The officer's red-and-white uniform, with buckle and braid, might have caught the eye of most, but 'twas Gideon dressed in a blue coat and tan breeches that held my notice.

At first he didn't see me, his attention taken by a gentleman and two ladies who warmly greeted him and the officer. Only as they excused themselves did his gaze happen upon me. Shock and disbelief momentarily crossed his rugged features. Then, with only the slightest hesitation, he walked toward me, his face devoid of expression, though twice he gave his head a tiny shake. Was it one of surprise or meant as a warning?

Knowing it wouldn't be wise for others to know that Gideon and I were acquainted, I quickly turned my attention back to Edward and Emma. What was it Edward had just asked? Did I enjoy playing games? "I do," I replied, hoping I didn't sound as distracted as I felt.

Edward's face lightened. "Good, for Emma and I are planning a small dinner and social with games. We'd like very much if you would attend."

Since my attention was divided between Edward and Gideon, who'd paused to speak to Joseph Lind and Mr. Nichols, my answer took a second to form. "I . . . I should very much like to come, though since I'm staying with the Linds, I shall have to wait upon Mr. Lind's permission."

"I understand," Edward responded, though his pleased expression said he expected an affirmative answer.

Using this as an excuse to look at Joseph standing next to his mother, I saw Gideon nod at something Mr. Lind said, his manner relaxed as if my being there was scarcely noted. Then he turned to greet Mr. Lind's mother and sister.

Elizabeth Corbin's face lit with pleasure. "How nice to see you." Turning to me, she touched my arm with her fan. "This is Mr. Gideon Whitlock, my dear."

My mouth wanted to break into a wide smile, but I held it tightly in check and allowed the corners to do no more than lift slightly.

I felt the full force of Gideon's green eyes as he bowed. Though his expression held only politeness, his eyes were full of questions.

"May I present Mistress Abigail Stowell, who is newly come to town and is staying with my brother and his wife," she went on.

"My pleasure, Mistress Stowell." The hard edges around his mouth said otherwise, and I sensed that learning where I stayed had stunned him. Despite this, his voice held a touch of warmth as he went on. "One so lovely is bound to add luster to Boston society, is that not so, Edward?"

Edward readily agreed, though he didn't seem pleased that Gideon had complimented me before he'd thought to do so.

Before I had time to respond, Elizabeth introduced me to the officer. "Colonel Paxman, may I present Mistress Stowell."

As I smiled and curtsied, I felt certain he was the officer who'd "persuaded" Gideon to leave The Rose and Crown. I also suspected he'd set soldiers to monitor all who contacted Gideon at the home on Summer Street. Proud in bearing, with a lean but not unhandsome face framed by a curled white wig, Colonel Paxman nodded as I rose from my curtsey. As his appraising gray eyes made a quick assessment of me, I was struck with the knowledge that not much escaped his probing gaze. Did they sense that I was other than what I pretended to be? My white gloves hid the fact that the palms of my hands were suddenly clammy, and only I knew how my heart quickened with unease.

"Mr. Whitlock is a lawyer, and the colonel serves as one of General Gage's aides," Elizabeth Corbin said. "We're honored to count them both as friends."

"I hope that in time I shall become your friend as well," I responded.

Gideon nodded, but the colonel, whose gray eyes reminded me of a fish recently taken from a stream of cold water, showed little sign of friendliness.

We began to move toward the waiting carriages. In the polite jostle for position, Gideon gained my side long enough to speak low in my ear. "What are you doing in Boston?"

"Looking for you," I whispered from behind my fan.

Gideon's lips tightened, and he managed to whisper before Edward gained a place on my other side. "Take care, Abigail." Then he moved to join the colonel.

Edward scowled at Gideon's broad back. "You should know that Mr. Whitlock has a reputation for flirting."

"Does he?" I asked in mock concern. Touching his shoulder with my fan, I teased, "What of you, Mr. Nichols? Should I be warned of you as well?"

Edward laughed, and color rose in his cheeks. "I am but a gentleman bent on ingratiating himself with a pretty young lady."

"Then I shall take your warning with a grain of salt."

When we reached our carriage, Gideon and the colonel doffed their hats and moved in another direction. I schooled myself not to look after them. Instead, I listened to Edward ask Mr. Lind if I might accept an invitation to their social.

Mr. Lind looked pleased that I had so quickly been invited into Boston society and readily gave his consent.

"We will send an invitation around to you with the details," Emma said.

Not many minutes later, we took our leave.

On our way home, Mr. Lind assured me that the Lind carriage would be at my disposal for the Nichols's social.

"Thank you," I said, though it went against the grain to accept favors from a man for whom I felt increasing dislike. I hadn't failed to notice the number of people who'd stopped to ask about Aunt Caroline's health. Rather than being saddened by her condition, he seemed to take pleasure in the attention it afforded him.

"There will be other opportunities for you to go into society while you're in Boston. I heard but yesterday that General Gage is planning to hold a ball."

I raised my brows. "A ball when the rebels are camped just across the bay?"

"I have it on good authority that he hopes to raise spirits and take people's minds away from the fear of attack." He gave a little smile. "I have long noted that General Gage always has good reasons for what he does."

"But why does he wait so long to attack?" his sister asked. "Surely our soldiers are better trained and armed than the rabble on the hills?"

"'Tis for General Gage to decide, not those who know nothing of the true nature of the situation." A dismissive expression slipped over his features, one that made the rest of us reluctant to speak as he settled back into the cushions of the carriage.

In the silence, my mind flew to Gideon. He was alive! More than that, I'd spoken to him, albeit only a few words. But at least he knew where I was staying. As for Edward's assertion that Gideon was a flirt, hadn't I known that the first morning I'd seen him? In the days ahead, I would pin my hopes on future meetings—the Nichols's social, even the governor's ball. Perhaps Gideon would even try to contact me.

When I returned home and reached Aunt Caroline's bedroom, Mina's face wore concern.

"How is she?"

Mina put a finger to her lips and tiptoed to meet me. "Ain't never seen her so restless," she whispered. "She sleepin' now, but it took her a long time gettin' there."

Watching Aunt Caroline twitch even as she slept sent pangs of guilt tripping through me.

"Things don't seem quite right," Mina went on.

Before I could decide whether to take Mina more fully into my confidence, Alice knocked on the door. "Mr. Lind said he wants to eat at once," she said.

"So soon?" Mina questioned.

Alice nodded. "A soldier left a message for him while he was at meeting."

"I best hurry and slice the cold chicken." Mina sighed. As she left, she gave me a quizzical glance.

Seeing it, I realized again what a dangerous path I'd taken. What if, like Mina, Mr. Lind came to suspect what I was doing? As for Dr. Barnes . . .

Over the next hours, concern for Aunt Caroline kept me so occupied that I had no time to worry about Joseph Lind or the doctor. Nor was there room for thoughts of Gideon and the Nichols's social. Not only was her sleep restless, but she shivered too, and beads of perspiration formed on her forehead and upper lip.

I dampened a cloth and gently sponged her face. Though she flinched, she didn't waken until Alice arrived with the lunch tray. Not wanting the maid to see her mistress's condition, I took the tray before she could approach the bed.

Carrying the tray to the table, I noted that despite the perspiration on her face, Aunt Caroline shivered as if she suffered a chill. "How are you feeling?"

"Not good," she whispered. "My head aches. I feel like . . . I have the ague."

My concern for her mounted. First a runny nose and tearing eyes—now aches and chills and fever. Had she, indeed, contracted ague? Her twitching and restlessness had also increased. I again dampened the cloth and wiped her face, noticing as I did that her skin, rather than hot, was clammy.

"Thank you," she whispered. Scratching her arm, she added, "I feel so strange."

"I think 'tis ague. After you've eaten, I'll fix you a cup of boneset tea. Mistress Blood says 'tis very helpful in curing ague."

Aunt Caroline's only action was to shiver and pull the covers more firmly about her.

Yesterday, I'd attributed her restlessness to the reduction of the medicine, but now, to have her beset with ague—what if the sickness weakened her frail body and sapped her resolve to be quit of the laudanum?

I took the bowl of broth from the tray and sat next to the bed. "Some of this broth should help you."

Aunt Caroline closed her eyes and turned away.

"Don't you want to become stronger?"

She acted as if she hadn't heard me.

I continued to coax her, and finally she opened her mouth.

I smiled my encouragement each time she took a swallow. To take her mind away from her discomfort, I told her about meeting the Nichols family and of their upcoming social. Her only response was to shudder and wave the spoon away. "No . . . more."

I set down the bowl. "Rest while I fix some boneset tea."

Another bout of shaking overtook her. "Hurry . . ."

I quickly retrieved the packet of boneset from my trunk and carried it and the recipe down to the kitchen. Silence pervaded the lower level. Even the kitchen was deserted, the fire banked and everything scrubbed and put to rights. The servants, including Mina, had been given a half day off for the Sabbath.

In not many minutes, I had rebuilt the fire and measured water and boneset into a pot to warm and steep over the flame. While I waited, I opened the kitchen door to breathe in the fresh air. My gaze followed the neat rows of vegetables edged by sage and thyme and rosemary that made up Mina's kitchen garden. Then it moved to take in the rest of the backyard with the whitewashed necessary and small shed for gardening tools tucked into the back corner. What had earlier been a sunny day had given way to an overcast afternoon, the faint sunlight turning the bright-colored brick of the circular well house to a subdued shade of red. Voices came from the stable yard—Jake's deep and teasing and Mina's laughing with a retort, followed by Ezra's delighted giggle.

A wave of homesickness washed over me, making me long for Stowell farm and the people I loved. How I missed them and Father. Were he and the Mayfield men waiting and wondering when the redcoats would attack?

Waiting. Everyone seemed to be waiting—those on the mainland—the people in Boston—perhaps even General Gage himself. Wasn't I waiting as well? Waiting for Aunt Caroline to heal and waiting to talk to Gideon Whitlock.

Chapter Twenty

DESPITE TWO DOSES OF BONESET tea, Aunt Caroline continued with chills and complained of aches and pains. When she finally slipped into fitful sleep, I went to the window and pulled back the drapes. Night was fast coming on, sucking the color from the trees and flowers to paint the world with a pallet of black and gray. How I wished Mistress Blood were here to tell me what else to do.

Worried, I started to pace the floor. Should I make up more boneset tea or reread Mistress Blood's directions to see if another herb might be more helpful? Before I could do either, a soft knock sounded on the door. Not wanting to disturb Aunt Caroline, I slipped quickly to open the door.

"A gentleman waitin' out back to speak to you," Mina said as I opened it.

I raised my brows.

Mina leaned close. "Mr. Whitlock," she whispered.

My heart gave a happy leap. Though I'd hoped Gideon would try to contact me, I hadn't expected it to be so soon. "Where?"

"By the tool shed."

I glanced back at Aunt Caroline.

"I'll stay with the missus while yer gone. Best hurry before Mr. Lind and the servants come home."

I moved past Mina and took the steep back stairs down to the kitchen, where embers still glowed from the fire I'd made for the boneset tea. Leaving the kitchen, I skirted the well house and Mina's kitchen garden, then made my way across the grass toward the tool shed. Seeing no sign of Gideon, I softly called his name.

The slight movement by the lilac hedge signaled his presence. When I reached it, strong fingers pull me into a gap between the hedge and shed.

Before I could speak or move closer, he set his hands on my shoulders, their weight like a stone bulwark between us.

"What in heaven's name are you doing in Boston?" he hissed. "Don't you know how dangerous it is for you?" His fingers tightened on my shoulders as if he wished to shake me. "I've done nothing but worry about you since I saw you at meeting."

"There's no need . . ." I began.

"No need," he echoed in a harsh whisper. "How can I not worry when you're staying with Joseph Lind? Other than General Gage or Colonel Paxman, you couldn't have chosen a more dangerous man."

"He and Father have been friends for years," I defended.

"He's not your father's friend anymore. Don't you know he gave your father's name to General Gage as a suspected traitor?"

"Yes."

"And yet you still came to live with him?" Exasperation filled the space between us.

"When you didn't come or send word after Lexington, I . . . everyone . . . was worried that you'd been found out . . . perhaps imprisoned."

"As you can see, I'm fine. What I don't see is why your father, knowing what he does, let you come."

"The patriot leaders are desperate to know General Gage's plans. When we learned that Mr. Lind's wife needed someone to care for her, it seemed the perfect plan." In the tiny bower of spent lilac blooms, I told Gideon about Aunt Caroline being dosed with laudanum and the note I'd sent to him after I'd learned he'd left The Rose and Crown.

Silence followed my words.

"I never received your message," he said.

I hurried on to tell him about the soldiers and how I'd managed to evade them.

"Thank God," Gideon whispered. Shaking his head, he asked. "What did you say in the note?"

"Only something about apple blossoms . . . nothing that would make sense to anyone but you. And I signed it M.A. for Mistress Abigail instead of my real initials."

"Good girl."

"I was afraid the house on Summer Street was a trap or that you were being held prisoner there," I added.

Gideon let out a long sigh. "Not a prisoner yet . . . nor do I plan to be, though sometimes 'tis hard to tell whether it's Colonel Paxman who watches me or me who watches him in the double life I lead on Summer Street."

I eased away from a branch poking my side. "Double life?"

"It was from Colonel Paxman that I learned Joseph Lind had given your father's name to General Gage. Later, he let slip that soldiers were being sent into the country to search for arms." Gideon paused and shook his head again. "I would give anything if you hadn't been introduced to Colonel Paxman this morning."

"Why?"

"Not only is the colonel one of General Gage's favorite aides, but he has a mind like a steel trap that absorbs all and forgets nothing. We hadn't taken more than a dozen steps away from the church before he mentioned that your last name and that of Nathan Stowell were one and the same."

Unease pricked my mind as I recalled the colonel's cold assessment of me. Did he suspect my true purpose in being in Boston?

As if reading my thoughts, Gideon bent his head close to mine, and when he spoke, there was tenderness in his whisper. "I want you home in Mayfield, Abby, not caught in a game of pretense in Boston, where one false step could mean your life."

I tilted my chin. "I'm not afraid." Though in truth I was, now that I knew about Colonel Paxman. "Who's going to suspect the woman who cares for Joseph Lind's invalid wife, especially since I've been coming to visit them since I was a girl? I even called them uncle and aunt. I don't think Mr. Lind suspects why I'm here. Since I see and talk to him every day, I hope to learn something of use. I know that a soldier came with a message for him while we were at church and that he left a short time later and hasn't returned."

Gideon nodded. "Jake told me."

"How do you know Jake and Mina?"

"I did some—" Gideon stiffened at the sound of hoofbeats entering the stable yard. "Go, Abby, and whatever you do, be careful!"

Putting aside caution, I reached up and touched his cheek, something I'd wanted to do the moment he'd touched me. I heard his quick intake of breath before he covered my hand with his. The small space in the hedge was suddenly charged with emotion. If he thought me bold, I did not care. Then I turned and hurried across the yard to the kitchen, fumbling at the latch in my haste to get inside before Mr. Lind saw me.

The embers from the fire lit my way across the kitchen, but I stumbled twice while climbing the dark back stairs. The light from Mina's candle was a beacon of welcoming light when I reached the corridor.

Mina gave me a questioning look from the chair next to the bed. "You all right?"

I nodded. "Mr. Lind just rode into the stable yard."

"Whatever was in that note done keep him away longer than usual."

I wondered at this as I looked down at Aunt Caroline and saw the nervous twitch of her fingers. "How has she been?"

Before Mina could answer, a loud curse and bellow for the butler punctuated the night air. "Been drinkin' again," Mina muttered. Touching the flame from her candle to the wick on the one on the table, she quickly moved to the door. "I best be gone. No one be safe from his tongue when he be like this."

I sat and focused on the poor woman lying in bed shivering with chills one moment, moaning in pain the next. I tried to soothe her, taking her hands in mine, then gently massaging her arms, both of us aware of stumbling steps and curses as Briggs helped Mr. Lind up to bed.

Only after Aunt Caroline and her husband had quieted did I let my mind turn to Gideon. Though I thanked God again that he was alive and well, I was disappointed that restraint and warning had dominated our meeting. Had my feelings for him caused me to misinterpret his words that day in the orchard? Though I'd known for some years that men both young and old found me a pleasure to look at, was Gideon not among them? The thought cast me into gloom, and it wasn't until later that I realized we'd been interrupted before a time or place for another meeting could be made.

I spent a restless night trying to sleep on the padded settle in Aunt Caroline's room. The next morning as I was sponging her forehead, Alice came with the breakfast tray.

Aunt Caroline refused it all. "My stomach . . ." she began. A sick expression crossed her face. "Quick . . . the night jar!"

I scrambled for the porcelain pot under her bed and had no sooner retrieved it than she spewed out the contents of her stomach. The next few minutes were not pleasant for either of us, but when at last the poor woman's stomach had settled and I'd sponged and cleaned her again, I put the lid back onto the night jar and carried it downstairs and out to the necessary. Where was Mina? Maybe she'd know what to do.

As if she'd heard my inward cry, she came around the corner of the house. "Mornin', Missy."

"Mina." I hurried to her. "The mistress is sick. Ague, I think . . . and she's vomiting." Swallowing my pride, I rushed on. "I'm not sure what to do. Please, can you come and tell me what you think is wrong?"

"I kin." She set down a large market basket and followed me into the house and up to the invalid's bedroom.

The smell of the sickroom was even worse than usual. Ignoring Dr. Barnes' instruction, I went to the window and lifted the sash. After taking a deep breath of fresh air, I joined Mina by the bed. The sight of the once beautiful and vivacious woman lying like a wraith on the rumpled pillow tore at my heart.

"Poor thing," Mina mouthed as she felt Mistress Lind's forehead and cheeks. "Clammy, just like I suspected." As if she were Dr. Barnes, she gently lifted the sick woman's eyelid. "Yes," she said, nodding as if to confirm her suspicion.

Grateful that Aunt Caroline still slept, I leaned closer and whispered. "Is it serious?"

"No . . . though she gonna be right miserable for the next day or two."

"What does she have?"

"Ain't got nothin'." Seeing my puzzled expression, she smiled. "You been weaning her off the laudanum, ain't you, Missy?"

My heart started. "How . . . how did you know?"

"'Cause I seen a woman bein' weaned off it before . . . heard 'bout it from others too. In Virginie, where I come from, tain't uncommon for rich ladies to get in the habit of dosin' themselves with laudanum. My master's ol' mama took to usin' it. She got real bad . . . sleepin' all the time like the missus here. When the master's sister came to visit and seen how bad her mama be, she threw all the laudanum down the privy." Mina's full lips tightened. "It was a bad week for the poor ol' lady . . . for me too 'cause they set me to watch and nurse her. But after the vomiting and loose bowels passed, she got on much better."

"Loose bowels?" I repeated stupidly.

Mina met my gaze and nodded.

Torn between relief and embarrassment, I hurried to explain. "I expected her to be restless and sleep less, but when she started with chills and sweating . . ." I touched the black woman's arm. "Thank you, Mina."

"You welcome . . . though I ain't done nothin' but tell you what be botherin' the missus." She gave me a sympathetic smile. "She ain't done with it yet, so you best be prepared. It be a good idea to have an extra night jar and plenty of water and clean rags."

"Alice and Hettie are sure to notice," I pointed out.

"Leave them to me. All I gotta say is she got the summer complaint."

"I wish the doctor could be as easily fooled."

"He be a problem, all right." Mina gently lifted one of the sick woman's eyelids. "See," she breathed.

I was surprised to see that the size of her pupil was now normal.

I remembered Dr. Barnes lifting Aunt Caroline's eyelids on his last visit. What day had he come? How soon before he came again? "We must pray the doctor doesn't come this week." Caught in momentary panic, I failed to see my aunt's eyes open.

"Yes . . . he mustn't know," she said.

"Did you hear what Mina said?" I asked.

Nodding, her gaze shifted to Mina. "Throw the laudanum . . . down the necessary." The words came weakly through dry, cracked lips.

"It'll be hard for you," Mina warned.

"Throw it!" she rasped.

★

The remainder of the day passed much as Mina had predicted. Thankfully, Dr. Barnes didn't come, although toward evening, Mr. Lind tapped on the door.

My stomach tightened as I hurried to intercept him before he could enter the room. "Your wife has a touch of summer complaint, so perhaps it would be better if you didn't visit her today," I said in a rush.

My words and the unpleasant odor of the room caused him to quickly step back. "Yes," he said, reaching for his handkerchief and dabbing at his nose. "It's early in the season for the sickness, but she's not the first case this week. Dr. Barnes sent word that several soldiers wounded at Lexington have come down with it too. He's so busy caring for them on Castle Island, he won't be able to visit Caroline this week."

Relief stilled my tongue for a minute. "With Mina to help, I'm certain we'll be able to give your wife the care she needs."

"To be sure," he agreed, dabbing at his nose. "Hopefully the illness will be of short duration so you can attend the Nichols's social."

"Yes." I dropped him a curtsy as he left. After I closed the door, I leaned against it and gave a sigh of relief. "Did you hear what he said?"

Aunt Caroline nodded and managed a weak smile.

"Hopefully the soldiers on Castle Island will continue to require the doctor's attention for a good long while."

Caroline's "amen" was no more than a whisper, and despite the closeness of the warm room, she began to shiver. Although Mina had assured me her withdrawal would be miserable, not fatal, her weakness with vomiting and loose bowels gave me concern.

I spent the next two nights sleeping on the uncomfortable settle, rising often to care for her. Weak and miserable as she was, I noted that Aunt Caroline was more alert and bore her suffering without complaint.

Even so, as I looked at her, I smiled. "You're coming back. Though you're still uncomfortable, the Caroline Lind I knew is coming back."

★

By Friday, the worst had passed. Though the rigors of the withdrawal had taken a toll on Aunt Caroline, her eyes were alert and her mind lucid. She also spoke at greater length than she'd done ten days ago.

After breakfast, she took my hand. "Thank you. Without your help . . ." Her gaze flicked to the shelf where the laudanum bottle had been, and her dry lips quivered. "You were an answer to prayers . . . muddled though they were . . . but prayers just the same. I . . . I was a prisoner . . . my bedroom a cell. The laudanum robbed me of my will." Her grip on my hand tightened. "How can I ever repay you?"

"Seeing you alert and more yourself is all the payment I want." I leaned down and kissed her brow that felt like that of a healthy woman. "One day soon you'll be strong enough to sit in a chair."

"Yes." Her pale cheeks flushed with a bit of color. "There's much I'd like to do, but—" The animation left her face. "We must take care . . . Abby."

"I know. Your husband told me a tale about you being afflicted with female hysterics. Unfortunately for him, I didn't believe it."

"Thank God you didn't." She looked past me for a moment. "There's much to tell, but . . ." She put a hand to her head as if to clear it. "Beware of Joseph. He's a powerful man . . . and not what he seems."

Though the words were softly delivered, they struck me with great force. Hadn't Father said the same? And he hadn't known about the laudanum or that, in a sense, Caroline was being held prisoner in her own home. Why?

What had occurred between husband and wife to cause Joseph to do such a cruel thing?

Seeming to read my mind, she closed her eyes and sighed. "Later . . . Abby . . . later."

Later, I straightened and aired her room and took the evidence of her stomach upset downstairs for Hettie to empty and clean. After lunch, Mina helped me move Aunt Caroline into a chair so we could wash her and replace her soiled nightgown and bed linens.

Often as we worked, Aunt Caroline's gaze would fasten on the shelf where the laudanum had been. I read the craving in her eyes and knew that although the chills and stomach upset had passed, the need was still alive. Anger at Mr. Lind and the doctor swept through me. Had they any idea what they'd done to her? Did they even care? Would that they, along with the laudanum, had been thrown down the hole in the necessary.

Mina's eyes met mine over the pile of soiled bed linen in her arms, and she nodded. Not saying anything, I followed her out into the corridor.

"Someday he gonna have to pay for what he done to her," she said.

"Yes." Looking to make sure no one was near, I asked a question that had been on my mind all week. "How long have you known Mr. Whitlock?"

Mina gave me a quick look. "We met him right after we come to Boston . . . goin' on two years now. There was some trouble 'bout our freedom papers and folks told us to go see Mr. Whitlock . . . he take care of you good." A smile touched her full lips. "He done that a 'right, but when we went to pay, he wouldn't take no money. Said keepin' folks free was all the payment he want."

She paused, and her face broke into a big grin. "Since then, we see him from time to time . . . him helpin' us, we helpin' him . . . 'specially since we come to work here."

I met her dark eyes, which looked as pleased with the friendship as her grin.

"Yer Mr. Whitlock be a right fine man . . . a good friend too, though I 'spect you'd like him to be more than a friend?" Her smile widened when she saw my surprise. "He feel the same way 'bout you, Missy."

Heat that had nothing to do with the weather rose to my cheeks. "You're right about him being a good man . . . right about the other too," I admitted.

Mina laughed and winked.

After she left and Aunt Caroline napped, my mind turned to my other purpose for coming to Boston. Caught up in worry about Aunt Caroline's health, I'd had little time to think of the patriot cause.

Just then, Joseph knocked and opened the door before I could answer. "How is my wife?" he asked, his handkerchief at the ready.

I strove to make my voice pleasant. "She's weak but improving." Realizing the windows were still opened, I added, "I've been airing and freshening the room."

As Joseph stepped inside, Aunt Caroline gave a soft moan. Glancing at the bed, he said, "I've been much concerned for her."

Liar, I wanted to say. Instead, I nodded and looked at her. Eyes closed and lying as if she were sleeping deeply, she showed no response to him.

He turned to me. "I fear that caring for my wife has proven to be a heavy burden on you these last days, my dear. Let me get Mina or Alice to sit with her so you can rest."

"Thank you, but now that she's doing better, I'll be able to rest and do just fine."

"If you're sure. I don't want anything to take the bloom from your lovely cheeks."

I gave him a startled look.

"Yes," he said smoothly. "I couldn't help but notice how taken Edward Nichols was with you on Sunday . . . Mr. Whitlock and Colonel Paxman too, or I miss my guess."

"Except for Edward, I think you are mistaken."

"Perhaps." The look he gave me held a touch of smugness. Whatever did he mean?

Changing the subject, he went on. "How fortunate that Caroline has improved. I've already made arrangements for Mina to sit with her while you attend the Nichols's social tomorrow evening." He nodded as if her improvement had been his doing, a pleased expression on his face as he walked to the door. Everything about him bespoke a man of assurance and wealth. Power too, as Father and Aunt Caroline had said. It was something I would be wise to remember.

As soon as the door closed, I returned to my chair. My aunt lay so still I wondered if she'd slept through her husband's visit. Looking more closely, I saw the corners of her mouth quiver as she strove to hide a smile. Then her eyes flew open.

"Did I not play my part well?" she asked, her eyes filling with laughter.

"You did, indeed. Even I was taken in."

"I've practiced all afternoon. Joseph . . . everyone . . . must believe . . . I spend my days sleeping." She sighed, and petulance crept into her voice. "I don't like how Joseph . . . spoke to you. He's clever and—"

"I know." But despite my confident nod, a shiver of unease slid down my back.

Chapter Twenty-One

WELL BEFORE SEVEN O'CLOCK on Saturday evening, Mina came to sit with Aunt Caroline. Though the ravages of the withdrawal from laudanum had taken a toll on her fragile health, she roused enough to ask if I knew who else would be at the dinner party.

"Edward and Emma Nichols and their parents, of course. Emma hinted that a few young officers had been invited too."

She smiled. "Then it should be . . . enjoyable for you."

My steps were light as I left her to go to my room to dress. After a tiring week of nursing Aunt Caroline, I looked forward to the social. Not only was it my first venture into Boston society, but I hoped it would also be an opportunity to learn something of value for the patriot army. Weren't young officers to be there? Maybe Gideon as well.

When Alice had learned about the dinner party, she'd offered to help me dress. "I sometimes helped Mistress Lind before she took sick," she'd told me.

I was grateful for her nimble fingers as she arranged my hair and fussed with the rose-colored robe until it draped gracefully over the lighter pink underskirt of my gown. Not satisfied, she tightened my embroidered stomacher to better show off the slimness of my waist.

Stepping to the mirror, I smiled at the results of my hair drawn into a high pompadour with ringlets framing my face. All in all, I was pleased with the outcome.

After thanking Alice, I made my way down the wide front stairs and out to the waiting carriage. A short time later, Jake stopped the carriage in front of a white, two-storied home with windows alight with candles.

Emma was waiting for me and took me into a lovely drawing room papered in deep blue and adorned with windows richly draped in floral silk. Though it wasn't as grand as the Linds' drawing room, the numerous unfamiliar faces made me glad for Emma's small gloved hand on my elbow. She introduced me first to Arabelle Cole, a friend since childhood with fine gray eyes and unremarkable looks. As I dropped a curtsy and murmured my pleasure, I was aware of three red-clad officers conversing with two young ladies. But of Gideon, I saw nothing.

Before Emma could introduce me further, Edward was at my side, his smile and words welcoming. After complimenting me profusely, he introduced me to two gentlemen friends. Though they were pleasant, my main interest was in the officers, and I was grateful when Edward finally took me across the room to make their acquaintance.

Captain Russell bowed low, his manner stiff, and Captain Burns's lean face looked as if it hadn't had much practice at smiling. Captain Tercel was the most amiable of the three, and his sandy brows lifted in appreciation as he took my hand. Even so, there was aloofness in their manner, as if they felt themselves above the company of mere colonials.

Despite my smile, I felt their rebuff. More than that, anger shouted that they were the enemy. Had Captain Burns led soldiers to Lexington? Perhaps Captain Tercel's teasing eyes had squinted down his musket as he'd fired at Father. It took great effort to remember that my purpose was to attract and charm, not to challenge with anger and a cold shoulder. With this thought firmly in mind, I set out to do just that.

Unfortunately, before I could say more than a dozen words, a servant announced that dinner was served. Edward put a possessive hand on my elbow and whispered, "I hope you don't mind that I've set myself to partner you for dinner."

"How could I mind when I've looked forward to getting to know you better?"

My words pleased him, as I'd intended, and a minute later, Edward and I followed his parents into a room dominated by a long, covered table set with snowy napkins and crystal goblets. Along with Edward's parents, twelve young people sat down to dinner.

We had no sooner reached our places than Mr. Nichols rapped with his spoon on a goblet. "As you know, our dear friend Arabelle Cole is leaving us to live with her widowed aunt in Salem."

Mistress Cole's cheeks flushed as gazes turned to her.

He lifted his wine glass. "A toast of farewell to Mistress Cole. Godspeed, my dear. Know that our best wishes go with you."

"Godspeed!" a chorus of voices echoed as we raised our glasses.

After we resumed our chairs, the servants brought in steaming bowls of chowder and flaky rolls with butter and a variety of preserves. The meal passed pleasantly, for Edward had a ready sense of humor and was bent on holding my attention. Charming as he was, I would much rather have been partnered by one of the officers.

I wasn't displeased when the meal ended and we returned to the drawing room, where tables had been set up for games. Before we could find a table, Edward's mother approached, Captain Burns but a step behind.

"I apologize for interrupting your time with Mistress Stowell," she said to Edward, "but others are eager to enjoy her company . . . Captain Burns among them."

Hearing his name, Captain Burns bowed stiffly and asked if he might have the pleasure of partnering me at a game of cribbage.

I readily accepted his invitation, smiling up at his lean face as he led me to join Arabelle Cole and Captain Tercel at the cribbage table. Counting my good luck, I sat at the table and gave the captain another smile.

"Having lived all my life away from Boston, I've never had opportunity to meet an officer before." My gaze traveled over him in an admiring manner. "I must say I find it to my liking."

For a second, Captain Burns looked as if he'd lost his power of speech, his cheeks flushing and his Adam's apple working in his thin neck. "Why . . . why thank you."

"You are most welcome," I replied. "Welcome, too, for asking me to join you for a game of cribbage. Did you know 'tis one of my favorite games?"

"Mine too," he said, his tone conveying the hope that our mutual liking for cribbage would make our time together even more agreeable.

As the pegs were laid out, Captain Tercel and Mistress Cole joined our conversation, and I continued to exert my wiles on Captain Burns, flashing him a smile when our glances met and giving him my undivided attention each time he spoke. Though part of me cried shame for doing such to a man who must seldom bask in the glow of female admiration, the rest claimed fair in a time of spying and war.

"Have you been long in Boston?" I asked after the game had commenced.

"Nigh onto a year now, and no hope to leave until this blasted rebellion is put down. No offence to you," he hastily stammered. "Even in England, I never saw a face more lovely, but—" His Adam's apple moved erratically.

I scarcely believed what I was doing when I fluttered my eyes at him. "Yes . . . ?" I prompted when he seemed to lose his train of thought.

"'Tis your climate that makes me want to leave. I nearly froze last winter, and now this heat—" He ran a stubby finger around his collar as if he'd like to rip it off.

I nodded sympathetically as I took my turn in the game.

This was all the encouragement the captain needed. "If it weren't for dinner invitations like tonight, we'd be eating no better than the men in the ranks," he confided.

I leaned toward him and murmured my dismay.

"It isn't just the soldiers who lack," he went on. "Our horses don't have hay. If things don't change soon, they'll be nothing but skin and bones."

"How awful!"

"Isn't there grass for them to eat on the common?" Mistress Cole asked.

Captain Tercel shook his head. "'Tis fiercely guarded by town folk for their cows, and for once, General Gage agrees with them."

"They say there's plenty of hay on Noddle's Island and hogs for the taking on Hog Island," Captain Burns said importantly. "There's talk of raiding both islands . . . perhaps as soon as a week, but—" Something— most likely Captain Tercel's foot kicking him under the table—stopped Captain Burns's tongue.

My mind whirled with what he'd said, remembering the green of Noddle's Island sitting not far from the ferry crossing between Boston and Charles Town and Hog Island to the east—both with ready food for redcoats and horses and none but a few farmers to hold off a raid.

Captain Tercel hastily turned to Mistress Cole. "Though I'm sorry to see you leave Boston, I'm pleased that I was here tonight to wish you Godspeed."

Quick to recover from his blunder, Captain Burns seconded the sentiment.

Flushing at their attention, Mistress Cole murmured a soft, "Thank you."

"When do you leave for Salem?" I asked.

"Hopefully on Tuesday, though as yet, I haven't obtained a pass for the blockade."

"A pass?"

Captain Tercel nodded. "Since you're recently arrived, you probably aren't aware that a pass to leave Boston is required at the blockade. Otherwise we have no way to stop rebel sympathizers from smuggling aid to the rabble across the bay. Every care must be taken, and sometimes the passes are slow to be approved."

"I didn't know."

"I thought not." Haughtiness edged his words as he opened his snuff box and put a pinch of it to his nose.

Remembering the part I played, I smiled and gave him a look I would have despised in another woman. Trying not to think what Reverend Whipple would say if he saw me openly flirting with two redcoat officers, I lowered my lashes.

This act sent Captain Burns to recapture my attention, and the rivalry between the two men to gain a smile from me added an undercurrent of excitement as we played cards.

In Mayfield, I seldom lost at cribbage, but I lost that night. My mind was so full of charming the two captains while trying to suppress my excitement about Noddle's and Hog Islands that it had little room for anything else. The army needed to know that a raid was forthcoming. But how could I get a message to them?

★

The answer came to me as I was taking my leave of Edward and Emma. As Edward was expressing the hope of seeing me at church on the morrow, I caught a glimpse of Arabelle Cole standing by the front door. Hadn't she said she was leaving Boston on Tuesday? Excusing myself, I went to intercept her.

"Will you be passing through Cambridge on your way to Salem?" I asked after I'd wished her a pleasant journey.

The flame from a candle cast light and shadow across her plain features as she nodded.

"Would it be possible for you to carry a letter to my mother? She was worried about me coming to Boston, and I want to let her know of my safe arrival."

"Does your mother live in Cambridge?" Arabelle asked.

"On a farm to the west, but friends in Cambridge will see that she receives it."

My stomach tightened as I waited for her to answer. "I'll be happy to, but you must make certain to have it to me before Tuesday."

"I will," I promised. After asking for her directions, which I quickly committed to memory, I nodded and took my leave.

During the carriage ride home, I mentally composed the letter I intended to write to Mother and the note I would add in invisible ink for Father and the army. Hopefully by Wednesday, Mr. Smyth and Father would be alerted to the redcoats' plan to raid Noddle's and Hog Islands.

★

As soon as I reached my room and donned my nightgown, I sat at the writing desk to compose a careful letter to my mother, one so normal and commonplace that it wouldn't arouse suspicion. I also left enough space between the lines to pen a second letter to Father in the invisible ink he'd told me to use should the need arise.

I arrived safely in Boston and was warmly greeted by Mr. Lind, who was most grateful for my visit. Aunt Caroline's poor health saddens me, but I feel my presence here helps and cheers her. Boston is much changed from when we visited it last—the mood is more somber, and soldiers are every-where. But I am well received and treated kindly.

A young lady traveling to Salem has graciously agreed to leave my letter with the Smyths as she passes through Cambridge. My prayer is that all of you are kept safe and well by a loving God. May that same God continue to watch over me.

Your loving daughter,

Abigail I

I added a capital I after my name so Father would know there was another letter written with invisible ink. As I did, the memory of Father telling me about invisible or sympathetic ink filled my mind. "Lemon juice is best, but apple or other juice . . . even the juice of an onion will work. If worse comes to worst, you can even use your own spittle."

I wrinkled my nose at the memory, glad that both apple juice and cider was in plentiful supply in the Lind household. Either should provide the results I needed, but the actual writing would have to wait until I could obtain one or the other.

★

I awoke the next morning, eager to find the juice with which to write the message to Father. Unfortunately, Aunt Caroline's mind was of a different bent when I entered her room.

"You've come," she said as soon as I entered the room. The eagerness in her voice surprised me, as did the sight of her propped up on pillows instead of lying abed. Before I could respond, she went on. "The party. Did you . . . enjoy it?"

"It was wonderful, and I enjoyed myself very much."

"Good." Other questions followed as I helped with her morning oblations.

I answered as best I could, though I sensed her interest wasn't entirely engaged. Like me, something else crowded her mind. Moments later, someone knocked on the door. After Aunt Caroline slid down from the pillows, I called, "Come in."

Alice curtseyed after opening the door. "Here's porridge and toast for you and tea and toast for Mistress Lind when she wakes," she said on noting Caroline's closed eyes. When I rose to take the tray, she eagerly asked, "How was the party?"

"Very nice, thanks to you and your clever fingers. I received compliments on my hair and gown."

Alice's face flushed. "'Twas naught . . . though I do take pleasure in doing such."

Though I was eager to ask her to bring me a glass of apple juice, I was also familiar with her penchant to linger and gossip. Siding with caution, I nodded to her in dismissal.

Aunt Caroline's hand wasn't quite steady as she took a bite of porridge, but she showed improvement over the day before. She'd just taken a second bite when another knock sounded on the door. Our eyes met, and I took the spoon from her hand and laid it on the tray.

Unlike Alice, Joseph opened the door and came inside without my bidding. "Breakfasting, I see," he said in a cheerful voice.

His wife turned her sleepy gaze on him but didn't speak.

"How are you feeling?"

"Not well," she answered in a weak voice.

"But well enough for Abigail to attend church with me and Mother and Elizabeth."

Aunt Caroline shook her head. "No."

"Mina can stay with you as she did last night. We'll only be gone two hours."

She continued to shake her head, her fingers plucking nervously at the sheet. "No."

Disappointment washed over me, for I'd hoped to see Gideon again. I was about to add my voice to that of Mr. Lind when I caught the pleading look in her eyes.

"As ill as she's been, perhaps it would be best if I didn't leave her again." Swallowing my disappointment, I added, "I do thank you for thinking to ask me, however."

Mr. Lind's lips tightened, but when he spoke, his voice was resigned. "Very well, but I shall expect you to attend with me next week."

"Yes," I said, even as I wondered what the week would bring.

Aunt Caroline sighed with relief when her husband quit the room. When she started to speak, I put a finger to my lips and went to the door to listen for his retreating footsteps.

"I'm sorry to . . . keep you from meeting," she said when I returned to my chair. "I feel stronger. There's much . . . to tell you."

"I have many questions," I said, "but first you must finish your breakfast."

In but a few minutes, the dishes were empty, and I'd returned the tray to the kitchen. As I climbed the stairs, I also carried a glass of apple juice. Nerves made me want to glance over my shoulder to see if anyone watched me. Though I chided myself for my foolishness, I felt uncommon relief when I finally gained my room and closed the door. Everything cried at me to hurry and write the letter, but I'd promised Aunt Caroline I'd be gone but a minute.

I'd scarcely taken the chair by her bed before she took a deep breath and leaned toward me. "Don't trust Joseph. He's evil and . . . has . . . caused a man's death."

I stared at her in disbelief. "He killed someone?"

"Not with his own hands . . . but he's responsible."

I shook my head in bewilderment. Watching her trembling lips, I realized what effort it had taken to say the damning words.

"You've heard of . . . Dr. Williams's hanging?"

I nodded. Everyone in the colonies knew about the terrible incident. Charged with treason for stealing vital information from one of General Gage's aides, he'd been hanged in Boston Common but a half year before. Only the overwhelming presence of armed troops had prevented rioting throughout Boston, and resentment over the incident had done much to rally the patriots against those same troops in the encounter at Lexington and Concord.

"Did Mr. Lind report Dr. Williams to General Gage?" I asked.

She nodded. "I don't know the details . . . but, yes."

"How did you find out?" Realization suddenly struck me. "That's why he drugged you, isn't it? To keep you from telling what you know."

"Yes." Anger stiffened the word.

"How did you find out?" I repeated.

"I . . . I overheard him talking . . . in the library. I thought to leave, but . . ." She paused to gather strength. "I heard a woman's angry voice . . ." Tears filled her eyes. "'Twas Dr. Williams's widow . . . accusing Joseph of double-crossing her husband."

I stared, scarce knowing what to say.

"Yes," she said when she saw my horror. "The men had purchased a shipment of smuggled ammunition . . . Dr. Williams to help the Sons of Liberty but Joseph to—" She paused and shook her head. "Joseph wanted to sell them to General Gage at a large profit. 'Twas then they quarreled and"—her voice sank to a whisper—"and Joseph planted the false evidence . . . and Dr. Williams was hanged."

I pictured Aunt Caroline with her ear pressed against the door as she listened in disbelief to the distraught widow.

"She demanded to know where he'd hidden the arms," my aunt finally went on. "Joseph laughed and said there were no arms . . . but 'twas a lie Dr. Williams told to hide his gambling debts."

"What did she say to that?" I asked.

"The widow started to cry . . . and Joseph can't abide tears. In the end, he gave her money . . . to go to relatives in Pennsylvania."

Neither of us spoke for a minute—she to rest and me to wonder at the unsettling story I'd heard. Not only had Joseph Lind betrayed Father but Dr. Williams as well.

My aunt's voice was low when she said, "I hid so the widow wouldn't see me when she left, but—" She paused to clear her throat. "When I opened the library door . . . Joseph was returning a hollowed-out book to the shelf. He was so startled to see me that he dropped it and—" Her gaze shifted away as if to better picture what had happened. "Coins and papers spilled everywhere. I dropped to my knees and picked up . . . a paper that looked like a lease . . . but Joseph—" She shivered, and her words came fast. "He pounced on me and grabbed at the paper . . . shoving and hurting while I screamed that I knew what he'd done."

"When he realized what I'd said . . . he grew very still . . . and his face turned cold and hateful. Before I could think . . . he struck me hard on the face . . . then again . . . while I screamed for help."

The horror of what she'd told me filled the bedroom, and Aunt Caroline began to shiver as if with the ague. I reached for her hand, but she moved it away as if the touch came from her husband, not me.

"While I cried and screamed, Joseph yelled for Briggs: 'She's snapped . . . gone mad and insane! Help me get her up to her bedroom!'"

Aunt Caroline shuddered as she repeated his shout. Overcome from reliving the terrifying experience, she closed her eyes and turned her face into the pillow.

Anger and shock rendered me speechless while I absorbed the wrenching scene. "Perhaps you should rest," I finally said in a voice as unsteady as hers.

"No . . . no." Opening her eyes, she stared past me at the wall, her dark plait falling across her shoulder while I listened with tightly clasped hands.

Her voice was faltering but grew in strength with each word, as if some unseen presence helped her tell of that awful day. "I fought and called for help as Briggs and Joseph forced me upstairs. Mistress Kent rushed out with a poker, but Joseph told her the same story he'd told Briggs. Everyone believed him."

"Not I," I declared.

But Aunt Caroline was so caught up in those terrible moments that she ignored me, her words painting vivid mental pictures of her fighting and clawing as Briggs captured her hands in his larger ones, her words so intense that I could feel her shuddering panic as Mistress Kent sat on her legs so Joseph and Briggs could tie her to the bed and gag her.

"You know the rest," Aunt Caroline concluded in a weak, trembling voice.

"Dr. Barnes was sent for . . . told I was raving . . . out of my mind." Her voice choked with tears. "Then I was dosed with . . . laudanum and fell asleep."

I took her hand between mine. "I'm so sorry. So very sorry."

"So am I," she whispered. "Sorry that I married . . . such an evil man." She paused for a moment. "Dr. Williams birthed both of our children . . . saw them through measles and whooping cough. He even pulled Joseph . . . through a painful case of quinsy." Her voice stilled again. "I know 'tis a sin to hate . . . but that's what I feel. Hatred and disgust."

I wished Reverend Whipple were here to say some comforting words about how prayer and time are great healers. Instead, I could only continue to hold her hand.

She closed her eyes and lay so still I thought she'd fallen asleep. "Joseph can't be trusted," she rasped. "His passion for wealth . . . has robbed him of honor. If he would move the smuggled goods to a new hiding place . . . and do what he did to Dr. Williams . . . and to me . . . who knows who he might betray . . . or harm next?"

"We must be very careful." I didn't have the heart to say that her husband had also betrayed Father. "You need to rest. And we must pray for guidance to outwit this vile man."

Chapter Twenty-Two

WHILE AUNT CAROLINE SLEPT, I paced the bedroom floor. Each time I thought of what Joseph Lind had done, anger made me want to rush to the church where the hypocrite sat with his mother and sister and scream to the congregation what he'd done.

"*Easy, Abigail,*" Father's voice seemed to say. "*Easy, daughter.*"

Little by little, my pacing slowed. Small wonder Father and Aunt Caroline had warned me about him. The detestable man thought only of himself, success, and money. Anyone who stood in his way or posed a threat was rendered harmless or was disposed of.

You as well, Abigail, a warning voice whispered.

The thought made my insides tighten and brought my feet to a halt. Unable to think clearly, my gaze wandered around the room until it rested on the shelf where the laudanum bottle and wine glass had stood. Fear sliced through my stupor when I realized my mistake in not having Mina return them to the shelf after they'd been emptied. If Mr. Lind noticed they were gone, it wouldn't take many minutes for him to realize what I'd done.

My first impulse was to rush to the apothecary shop and buy another bottle. Then I remembered it was the Sabbath and the shop was closed.

Willing myself not to panic, I went to the window and pulled aside the drapes, my mind twisting and turning as it sought a way to keep Mr. Lind from visiting his wife until after I'd obtained another bottle of laudanum. In my quandary, I saw a bright spot of color by the back gate that materialized into Mina carrying the egg basket. I hurried downstairs to intercept her before she came inside.

She looked up in surprise from admiring the red-sprigged blooms on the valerian. "Thought you was off to church this mornin'."

"Mistress Lind needed me."

"She all right?"

"Just worn out from doing a lot of talking."

Mina gave me a quick look, the bright red and pink colors on her turban rivaling those of the valerian. "Imagine she got lots she wanna talk about."

"She does." I moved closer, pretending to admire the flowers. "After what she told me, I . . . Mr. Lind . . . He's . . ." The words wouldn't come out properly.

Mina's eyes filled with understanding. "I know, Missy. Knowed it for a long time."

"To make matters worse, I just realized the big mistake I made by not returning the laudanum bottle to the shelf. If Mr. Lind notices it's gone, who knows what he'll do."

Mina sucked in her cheeks. "Won't be good for neither of us."

"First thing in the morning, I'll go to the apothecary shop."

"And I kin get another wine glass."

"I can't thank you enough for what you've done already."

She nodded, and the understanding in her eyes warmed me as surely as if she'd given my hand a reassuring pat. "You need to stop worryin' so, Missy. Things is sure to work out . . . 'specially since Jake and me always say extra prayers on the Sabbath." She nodded and smiled. "Just like Paul was struck blind by the angel, we'll pray that Mr. Lind won't be able to see what's missing from the shelf."

★

The unsettling events of the morning had pushed all thought of Noddle's and Hog islands out of my mind. Only when I'd checked on Aunt Caroline and found her still asleep did I go to my room to complete the letter. I took an extra quill out of my writing box and sharpened it. After dipping it into the apple juice I began to write. The carefully rehearsed words came easily.

Lacking hay for their horses and enough food for themselves, a party of redcoats plan to raid Noddle's and Hog islands. I have talked to our mutual friend who is well but closely watched by General Gage's aide.

Although my quill moved quickly between the black lines I'd written before, no visible trail of words followed its progress. Invisible, just as Father had said, and it would stay thus until a flat iron was taken from the hearth and run across the surface of the paper to bring color and form to the words I'd written.

Waiting for the apple-ink to dry, the full impact of what I'd just done struck deep. Along with the heady excitement of being an actual spy came the knowledge that my life was forever changed. Caution must guard all of my thoughts and actions. Starting today, I must take even greater care.

I smiled in satisfaction as I looked down at my handiwork. To all eyes but Father's, it was no more than an innocent letter from his daughter. There. It was done, or nearly so. All that was needed on my part was to seal it with wax from my bedtime candle and deliver it safely into the hands of Mistress Arabelle Cole.

Just before lunchtime, someone knocked on the door. Aunt Caroline broke off talking and slipped under the covers just seconds before Mr. Lind opened the door.

"How is she?" And before I could reply, "I hope she hasn't overtaxed you."

"She and I are both doing well, but as you can see, she's sleeping."

He moved closer to the bed and looked at his wife longer than was his habit. I held my breath, fearing he might notice her better color and fuller cheeks. In an effort to deflect his attention from her and the empty shelf, I moved to the end of the bed, taking heart when his attention turned to me.

"Rather than my wife, it's you I wish to speak to. I've come to invite you to join me for luncheon."

I stared in surprise while trying to dampen my alarm. Now that I knew what he'd done, I didn't like even being in the same room with him. How could I eat an entire meal with him without divulging my true feelings?

"Aunt Caroline hasn't eaten lunch yet," I said in a voice not entirely steady.

"I have already spoken to Mina. She will see that my wife is fed and cared for."

Trying to gather my scrambled thoughts, I gave him what I hoped was a convincing smile. "Then of course I'll join you."

Mr. Lind nodded in satisfaction as he stretched out his arm to invite me to precede him from the room. As I did, I saw Mina waiting in the corridor with Aunt Caroline's lunch tray. Worry clouded her dark eyes when our glances met, and I wondered if mine showed similar concern.

Willing myself not to give way to nerves, I used the time it took to descend the wide front stairs to bolster my confidence. Since Mr. Lind didn't know his wife was strong enough to tell me of his treachery, I must act as I had when I'd first arrived—open and eager to help. Not for a second could I let my true feelings show.

Filled with resolve, I paused with one hand on the railing and smiled back at the man I detested and feared. "Thank you for inviting me to eat with you. Though I have great affection for my aunt, her health is such that few words pass between us."

"Since eating alone leaves me in similar circumstances, my intent is that we enjoy our time together." Nodding, he took my elbow and escorted me down the final steps and into the dining room.

It was as I remembered it, with a long table dominating a room wall-papered with burgundy flowers entwined with green leaves. Burgundy drapes outlined two windows, and crystals from the chandelier reflected onto the polished wood of the table. One end had been covered with linen and set with two places.

Joseph helped me into my chair, then took one across from me. We looked an unlikely pair—me in plain cotton and he still wearing his curled white Sunday wig, white knee beeches, and black coat and vest with silver buttons.

Mr. Lind seemed not to notice but spoke instead of the fine sermon the reverend had given. "Several people asked about you after meeting," he went on. "Edward Nichols in particular and two of General Gage's officers. Their comments lead me to believe you made several conquests at the dinner party last night."

Disappointed that Gideon hadn't asked about me, I modestly looked down at the blue-flowered pattern on my plate. "I think 'tis only that I'm newly arrived in Boston."

"'Tis more than that, my dear," Joseph countered. "Though I've known you since you were a child, I can't fail to notice the lovely young woman you've become."

It took great control to keep my head and eyes lowered. How I wanted to fly at the man and tell him what I thought. Thankfully, Alice and Hettie entered the room with the luncheon, their presence taking the place of conversation as the cold Sabbath meat was served.

My mind was so busy selecting, then rejecting something to say that I scarcely remembered what was on my plate. It could have been wet newsprint for all the notice I took. *Remember the smuggled ammunition Aunt Caroline told you about. Use your head and turn the conversation to your advantage.*

Mr. Lind's voice broke past my thoughts. "Before Caroline took ill, it wasn't unusual for us to have frequent dinner guests. Now—" He indicated the length of the empty table. "This is the result of having an invalid wife. Friends ask me to dine from time to time, but when I eat at home, it's lonely." He paused to pour himself a glass of wine and did the same for me. After taking several swallows, he went on. "Now you must tell me what you think of Boston. I'll wager you find it much changed from when you last came to visit."

I nodded, wanting to say that the biggest change was in his home— Aunt Caroline drugged and betrayed, he a traitor to his wife and friends. Instead, I answered in a careful voice. "The mood is more somber, and food is not as plentiful. One can scarcely walk the street without seeing soldiers. All in all, 'tis not the bustling town it once was."

Joseph's mouth tightened. "'Tis the da . . . the blasted blockade of the harbor that's done it . . . that and the nest of rebels camped across the bay. Why Gates doesn't —" He broke off and drained his glass. Licking his lips, he said, "You mustn't get me wrong. General Gage is my friend, but the harbor blockade has seriously hurt my business. Nothing can come into Boston . . . nothing can go out, except for military frigates and ships, of course."

Thinking this an opportune time to lead the conversation to the hidden ammunition, I asked, "Doesn't smuggling go on any more?"

Preoccupied with refilling his wine glass, he set down the decanter with such force that some of the wine splashed onto the table linen. "None!" he said emphatically. "Small military vessels ply the coast line looking for just such activity. King George is determined to end the rebellion. Someone needs to tell him that the blockade is hurting loyal Tories like me far more that it's hurting the rebels."

Taking a large swallow of wine, he went on, his cheeks flushed with emotion. "It's the rabble across the bay that I should be cursing. Yes, rabble," he said when I lifted my head. "I have nothing but enmity for your father and the ilk he's sided with. Uncouth trash, most of them, and why General Gage doesn't blow them to bits with his guns and cannons, I know not."

Unable to stop myself, I put down my napkin and rose to my feet. "I won't listen to such talk. 'Tis Father, a worthy man and worthy friend, whose death you crave."

Mr. Lind's steely gray eyes met mine. "So . . . a rebel, are you?"

Praying God would forgive my lie, I shook my head. "Didn't I say I try to keep an open mind? Regardless of Father's politics, he's still my father, and I love him deeply."

Mr. Lind's gray eyes narrowed in a manner that made my mouth go dry, changing the amiable façade of family friend to that of a cold and shrewd businessman. "I wonder," he said softly.

The Stowell backbone kept my eyes steady on him, the taut seconds stretching until I feared they'd break. Finally, I detected a slight softening of his mouth, and his eyes lost some of their iciness.

"Though a man may blunder," he said in that same soft voice, "he never loses hope that his child will love him no matter what he does. Nathan Stowell has received great honor this day." Pausing to take another sip of wine, he nodded. "Please . . . let's finish our luncheon."

After taking a deep breath, I returned his nod. My nerves and muscles were so taut that I sat down without grace. Neither of us spoke, me striving to still my trembling hand when I took a quick sip of wine, Mr. Lind resuming his role of amiable friend.

Smiling at my reaction to the strong-tasting wine, he spoke in a hearty voice. "Now, tell me about the Nichols's dinner party. Did you enjoy it?"

Loathing threatened to pull my mouth into a sneer while anger at his callous wish for Father's death tightened the cords in my throat. I had to clear my throat before I could speak. "It was . . ." I cleared my throat a second time. "It was very pleasant. Edward and Emma and their friends were much to my liking." Using details of the evening to cover my true feelings about the man who sat across from me, I went into a lengthy description.

Mr. Lind listened attentively, nodding from time to time and smiling when I recounted an amusing story Edward had told. Through it all, I was aware that he didn't touch his food but that his wine glass was refilled frequently. Even so, I knew he was aware of my effort to cover my anger. Men like him were not easily deceived.

Remembering what Mina had said about Mr. Lind's temper when he drank, I searched for an excuse to return to Aunt Caroline's room. As if conjured up by my thoughts, Mina's tall figure appeared in the doorway.

"Excuse me, Mista Lind, but ya wife be upset and carryin' on again. She say she want Missy Abigail this very minute . . . won't listen to nothin' I say. Just cry for Missy Abigail." I saw Mina's gaze travel to the near-empty decanter, and I knew she heard Joseph's none-too-quiet curse.

For a minute, I feared he'd explode in rage. Instead, he clenched his jaw and shook his head in disgust. "Has she been given her drops?"

Seeing me nod another lie, he fell silent. "I'll have to send Briggs for Dr. Barnes and have him increase the amount of her laudanum."

A small sound escaped Mina's lips. To cover it, I rose from my chair. "Before you send for the doctor, let me see if I can calm her." Not giving Mr. Lind a chance to argue, I hurried from the room and up the stairs, my breath coming fast from fear and exertion. As I neared the top of the stairs, I heard Aunt Caroline call my name. Quickening my steps, I reached her room and opened the door to see her calmly sitting up in bed.

"Aunt Caroline?"

Instead of answering, she put a finger to her lips and motioned for me to close the door. Before I could, Mina appeared, her breathing hard and drops of sweat beading on her face.

"There," she said, closing the door and leaning against it.

Realizing Aunt Caroline's hysterics had been a ploy to get me away from Mr. Lind, I walked to the bed and took her hand. "Thank you, though things really weren't that dire."

"Joseph's very clever at concealing his motives. When Mina said she heard raised voices . . . my only thought was to get you away from him."

Mina's brightly turbaned head nodded. "Me and the Missus don't trust him. He might be plannin' all sorts of things."

Knowing I had two staunch friends, though one be an invalid and the other but a servant, brought a swell of warmth to my heart. "Thank you."

Mina's head nodded again. "Now what we gonna do?"

"If Mr. Lind sends for the doctor, he'll discover you're not taking the laudanum . . ." I let my words hang in the air.

Aunt Caroline drew a quick breath. "I didn't think of that." Her gaze flew to the empty shelf.

"He'll only have to look at the size of your pupils to know you're not taking the drops."

A troubled silence settled over the room.

After a long moment, Mina spoke. "I got a confession to make. When you done tol' me to throw that awful stuff down the necessary . . . I didn't do it. Beggin' your pardon for disobeyin', but I thought we might need it sometime." Her dark eyes turned to me. "I think that time be now. As soon as it's safe, I'll put the laudanum back on the shelf."

Before anyone could say more, I heard Mr. Lind loudly call for more port. I'd witnessed his liking for it. Maybe his weakness could be used to our advantage. After today, we needed to look for and use every possible advantage.

Chapter Twenty-Three

By late afternoon, the laudanum bottle and wine glass had been returned to the shelf. Even so, my mind was too busy to sleep well that night. Like water in a brook skipping over rough stones, my mind bounced from place to place—Noddle's and Hog islands and the letter written with invisible ink, the terrible things Aunt Caroline had told me about her husband, and my uncomfortable luncheon with that very man. How I detested him and his hold over Aunt Caroline. His hold over me if I weren't careful. Yet satisfaction was there too. In my first attempt at spying, I hadn't done too badly.

As I breakfasted with Aunt Caroline the next morning, she confessed that, like me, she hadn't slept well.

"So much can go wrong. If Joseph suspects about the laudanum . . . or Dr. Barnes comes—"

"That's why it's important for you to perfect your game of possum while I keep watch for the doctor." As I started for the door with the empty breakfast tray, I added, "I must go to the apothecary to get a new bottle of laudanum. While I'm gone, you must rest."

Except for Hettie washing up, the kitchen was empty. After I set down the tray, I picked up an empty basket. "Tell Mina that Mistress Lind is sleeping and that I've gone to the apothecary shop." Then with the comforting feel of the letter in my pocket, I set out for Arabelle Cole's home.

Although it had been a fortnight since I'd been chased by the soldiers, I'd taken the precaution of wearing a hat rather than my white cap, and I'd put on my green dress instead of the lavender one I'd worn that day.

The sky was overcast, but I was in too fine a mood to pay it any mind. Being able to act instead of only thinking about it added a lilt to the wordless tune I hummed as I crossed the stable yard. Pausing at the large gate into the alley, I waved to Ezra.

It was only a few streets to the Cole residence, the clapboard home shaded by a tree whose leaves fluttered in the breeze. A maid answered the door and led me into the front parlor after I asked for Arabella. Not many minutes later, she joined me.

"Mistress Stowell," she said in greeting. "I hoped you'd come today, for our servant returned with the blockade pass but an hour past, and I'm to leave first thing in the morning."

"Then 'tis well I came today." I extracted the sealed letter from my pocket. "I've addressed it to my parents, along with the name of Mr. Smyth. He's well-known in Cambridge, and you have only to ask and someone will direct you to his home."

That Arabella only glanced at the letter when I gave it to her added to my ease.

"I'll put it in my reticule so I don't forget it," she said.

I left her home, and the press of horses and wagons and people increased as I neared the apothecary shop. When I entered it and stated my purpose, the proprietor nodded. "You're late," the round little man said. "I've had a bottle of laudanum waiting for you this past week."

I silently scolded myself for another oversight. "My mistress has suffered from summer complaint, and her stomach wouldn't always tolerate the medicine," I said.

He gave me a quick look over the top of his spectacles as he wrapped the bottle in paper. "I hope she's feeling better." At my nod, he added, "In the future, you must take care not to alter her dosage."

Assuring him I'd take more heed, I took the package and set out for home, grateful the shopkeeper hadn't alerted Mr. Lind of his concern.

I'd scarcely left the shop when a male voice called to me. Startled, I looked up and saw Gideon Whitlock, accompanied by a soldier, cross the street to intercept me.

"Mistress Stowell," he said, removing his hat and bowing.

"Mr. Whitlock." I made no attempt to hide my surprise, but of my gladness to see him, I tried to be more circumspect.

"I was disappointed when I failed to see you at meeting yesterday," he said. I suspected his words were as much for the soldier as for me.

The soldier's suspicious brown eyes studied me as if he were committing my description to memory. He was young and probably not above the rank of a corporal, which gave me hope that he wasn't as dangerous as

Colonel Paxman. Recalling the effect of my smile and the slow flutter of my lashes at the dinner party, I favored the young soldier with the same. Though his back remained stiffly erect, quick color mottled his cheeks.

"Mistress Lind was unwell and required my attention," I told Gideon. "Otherwise I would have been at church."

A wagon filled with casks that smelled of pickled herring passed us, the driver giving a nervous look over his shoulder at four soldiers on the corner.

Moving us more firmly onto the path, Gideon handed a packet to the soldier. "In view of the skirmish this morning, I think it wise for me to escort Mistress Stowell to her home."

The soldier opened his mouth in protest. "Colonel Paxman will . . ."

"I'll explain to the colonel," Gideon said smoothly. "Your responsibility is to see that these papers are in my client's hands by ten o'clock."

The corporal shot me a sharp glance before he nodded and walked away. As soon as he did, Gideon tucked my hand in the curve of his elbow and set our course toward the Linds'.

"Was that wise?" I asked in a low voice.

"Probably not, but it was all I could think to do to get you alone so we can talk." He gave me a sideways glance. "You didn't need to smile and look at that poor man like that."

"Like what?" I asked innocently, enjoying myself more than was perhaps wise. Trying not to smile, I looked up at Gideon in exactly the same way.

"Like that," he said emphatically, though he smiled. We walked a short way in silence before he spoke again. "When Colonel Paxman can't be with me, he sets one of his lackeys in his place. The skirmish earlier between soldiers and idle dock workers makes a convenient excuse . . . that and my desire to be in the company of a very fetching young lady."

"'Tis my hope that instead of giving Colonel Paxman a detailed description of me, his lackey will keep it to himself. I am, after all, but a maid running errands."

He glanced at my basket.

"'Tis medicine for Mistress Lind. I also entrusted a letter for my parents to Arabelle Cole, who leaves Boston in the morning with the charge to give it to Mr. Smyth in Cambridge."

Gideon's thick brows rose. "What did you say in the letter?"

"That I arrived safely in Boston and that Mr. Lind and his wife are pleased to have me stay with them."

"That's all?"

"Not quite." Only the need to act as if Gideon and I were but casual acquaintances kept me from turning to him in excitement. "I added in invisible ink that a raid on Noddle and Hog islands is imminent."

Gideon's even gait faltered. "How . . . how did you come by this information?"

"A captain remarked about it at the Nichols's dinner party on Saturday." Pride led me to take inordinate pleasure in telling Gideon of my successful evening. As I concluded, an expression of chagrin mingled with admiration showed in his slow-breaking smile.

"Well," he said. His smile widened into a grin, and his green eyes filled with warmth. Thankfully we were away from the center of town, and no other people were in sight as our steps slowed. Perhaps my hope that day in the orchard hadn't been misplaced after all.

"Dear . . ." His jaw clamped down to cut off the rest of his words. Instead, he covered my fingers resting on his elbow with his other hand and squeezed, then covered them gently with his palm again. We took a few slow steps before he spoke again, all softness having left his voice. "Today is but more proof that we need a safe way to communicate. If I had but known in time about Arabelle Cole . . ."

"Perhaps it isn't too late for you to send a letter as well."

He shook his head. "Unfortunately, I have little to report. Colonel Paxman . . ." He shook his head in frustration. "But such doesn't mean I won't learn something soon."

I caught sight of the Lind chimneys rising through the trees when we turned the corner.

"Can you meet me in the Lind stable after dark tonight?" he asked quickly.

I nodded, trying not to think of what might happen if Mr. Lind saw me.

Gideon steered me into the alley behind the stable yard where our steps slowed and he turned me to face him in the shelter of a tree. "It seems we're destined to shortcuts through alleys. Do you remember our flight to The Rose and Crown?"

"I do. I didn't mind then, nor do I mind today."

"Nor do I." His eyes, like his voice, were solemn. After a moment, he lifted his head to scan the trees and alley. "We must take care, Abby . . . and yet we need to meet." Seeing me nod, he went on. "There's a niche in the back of the gatepost into the Lind stable yard we can use to exchange messages." He stopped me when I turned my head to look. "Look at me, not the gate. Someone may be watching." Then, with his green eyes holding mine, he said, "The gatepost is almost covered by a vine so it's hard to see the niche unless you know it's there."

"I'll find it. I already feel less alone now that I have a way to get in touch with you." Seeing him frown, I hurried on. "Not that you need to worry. But I have so much to tell you. Important things."

"Tonight," he said. "Unless something unexpected happens, I'll be in the stable as soon as it's dark." His hand lifted as if to stroke my cheek. Before it reached me, he let it fall to his side. "Tonight," he said in a whisper. Then he turned and walked away.

I found the hiding place, just as Gideon had described, the splintered crevice on the post inconspicuous and mostly covered by a vine. I pretended to drop my basket so I could study the crevice more closely. It would do very nicely.

I was crossing the stable yard when I saw Ezra motion to me.

"Mama say she need to talk to you and for you to wait by the lilacs while I run tell her you back," he said in a low voice.

He hurried across the backyard to the kitchen while I followed at a more leisurely pace, pausing to smell a snowball bloom before I reached the hedge. It was several minutes before Mina joined me in the cover of the lilacs.

"Did you get the laudanum?" she whispered.

I lifted the wrapped bottle from the basket.

"Good," she breathed, "'cause Mista Lind done go to the missus bedroom while you was gone. Don't know what he done, but he was there longer than to see she was sleepin'."

I tensed and wondered if Aunt Caroline had truly been asleep or only pretending. Just as quickly, I remembered the bottle and wine glass, grateful they'd been replaced on the shelf yesterday evening. "I wonder what he wanted. Did he say anything to you afterward?"

Mina shook her head. "Didn't say nothin' to no one . . . just walk out the front door, where Jake be waitin' with the carriage to take him to the wharf."

"Or maybe to take a message to Dr. Barnes on Castle Island."

Mina's dark eyes met mine. "What we gonna do if that doctor come?"

I'd wrestled with that problem during the night. "The only thing I can think to do is to give Mistress Lind a dose of laudanum."

Mina's frown told me she didn't like the idea any better than I did.

"If I don't and Mr. Lind finds out, no telling what he'll do to me . . . or her."

The morning air suddenly seemed uncomfortably warm. Mina swatted a fly, and I tried to ignore the unpleasant odor of the necessary.

In the sultry silence, an idea came to me. "Do you think Jake could find out if and when Dr. Barnes is coming? If I knew, I could give Mistress Lind the laudanum in time for it to change the size of her pupils before he saw her."

A hint of a smile crossed Mina's face. "Now that be a idea . . . one what just might work." She nodded, her expression taking on hope. "Mista Lind always be tellin' Jake his plans . . . get de horse saddled . . . be out front with the carriage. When Jake get back, he might know if the mista sent for the doctor."

"What would I do without you?" I said, wanting to hug her.

She gave a low chuckle. "Most likely go hungry. That what be happenin' if I don't get back to the kitchen. But I thought you should know 'bout the mista goin' in her bedroom."

"Yes, thank you."

A few minutes after Mina returned to the kitchen, I also made my way into the house and upstairs to Aunt Caroline's bedroom. At first she appeared to be asleep, but as I neared the bed, she opened her eyes.

"You're back."

"I am." Instead of sitting, I went to the wardrobe and put the wrapped bottle on the top shelf. "Were you able to sleep?"

"A little." Her voice sounded distracted. "Joseph came into my room after you left. When I recognized his step, I pretended to be asleep."

"What did he do?"

"I could feel him watching me, and it made it hard to lie still. Then—" She paused and licked her lips. "When I heard him move, I peeked and saw him hold up the laudanum bottle to see how much was left."

The muscles in my throat tightened. If he started monitoring the amount of laudanum used each day, the danger of being found out would be even greater.

The strain Aunt Caroline felt showed on her face, and I purposely made my voice light when I replied. "Then 'tis good I bought a new bottle this morning."

I quickly exchanged the two bottles. "Since your husband has thought to monitor your medicine, I'll need to pour a little from the new bottle into the old one each day. Hopefully he'll think the decreased amount is proof that you're being properly dosed."

Relief lifted the corners of Aunt Caroline's mouth. "'Tisn't just Jonathan who was clever. Your father has reason to be proud of his daughter as well."

"I hope so," I said, sitting to take her hand. "But the important thing is to stay one step ahead of the man responsible for our worry."

Aunt Caroline's words about her husband monitoring the laudanum were with me as I stealthily made my way down the back stairs to the kitchen that night. The sun had long been down, and I'd heard the servants climb the back stairs to their third-floor rooms some time ago. It was Joseph I worried most about. Was he still in the library, or had he retired to his bedroom?

With slippers in hand, I tiptoed across the kitchen to the back door. Except for the rhythmic tick of the clock, the house was wrapped in silence and darkness. I felt along the door until I found the bolt and carefully eased it back. The resulting click sounded loud to my ears. Had someone heard it?

I waited, scarcely daring to breathe. On hearing nothing, I put on my slippers and hurried across the backyard to the gate.

"This way, Missy," Mina whispered.

Realizing that Gideon had sent her to wait for me, I veered toward her voice, grateful for the direction it gave me in the dark, overcast night.

"Here," she said.

I saw a slight movement, and a moment later, I felt the touch of a hand on my arm. "There," she whispered. "Jake waitin' under the tree. He'll show you the rest of the way."

I wondered at their caution as I walked toward Jake. Didn't they think I could find my way in the dark?

Jake's dark figure emerged from the shadows of the oak. He nodded and motioned me to follow him past the carriage house, where Mr. Gridley lived upstairs.

I followed Jake's light-colored shirt into the even darker stable, where the smell of hay and horses and the occasional sound of shifting hooves greeted us as we walked down the aisle between the stalls.

When we reached the back of the stable, Jake paused. "Mr. Gridley be a light sleeper so we can't use no lantern," he said in a voice so soft I had trouble hearing it. "The gentleman's waitin' up the ladder there."

It took me a moment to make out the ladder's outline. Nodding my thanks, I lifted my skirts and began to climb the wooden rungs.

I was almost to the top when a voice whispered, "Take my hand."

I reached up and felt the grip of strong fingers that drew me up into the loft. I was deeply aware of Gideon's touch, though I had scarce gained his side when he moved away.

"Come," he whispered, leading me farther into the hayloft. "Here's a stool you can sit on. We have much to say and little time to say it."

Once I was seated, Gideon dragged a sack of oats next to the stool and sat down. "'Twas fine work you did in finding out about the upcoming raid on Hog and Noddle's islands and sending word to your father. Still—" He paused and leaned toward me. "I don't think you fully understand Joseph Lind's treachery."

"I know that in addition to betraying Father, he planted false evidence in Dr. Williams's physic office that led to his trial and hanging."

Startled silence followed my words. "How did you— Who told you?" he stammered.

"Mistress Lind. That's why I said I needed to talk to you."

"But she—" He paused as if to gather his thoughts. "'Tis common knowledge she's so ill she's rarely conscious."

"'Tis a lie her husband gave out."

Gideon shook his head in disbelief. "Why would he lie and say such about her?"

"It wasn't always a lie." With Gideon leaning close in the darkness, I told him what Aunt Caroline had discovered about her husband and the terrible things he'd done to her. "Mistress Lind's so-called illness was the result of being given heavy doses of laudanum," I concluded.

Gideon cut off a muffled oath. "What of her now?"

"Over the past fortnight, I've managed to wean her off the laudanum."

A small sound bespoke his amazement. "'Tis clever and brave." His words lifted my heart, though what came after showed more concern than amazement. "You take a terrible risk in being found out."

"I know. As soon as Aunt Caroline is stronger, I must find a way to get her away."

"Get both of you away," Gideon corrected. "I won't rest until I see you safely in Mayfield. I've already talked to Jake about using the Lind carriage. And tomorrow I'll see about getting passes for the two of you to go through the blockade. It may take a few days, but I know someone who can help." We sat for a moment without speaking, our knees almost touching, the smell of oats and hay mingling with the soft sound of our breathing.

"There's more you need to know," I said in a low voice. "Some time ago, Mr. Lind and Dr. Williams invested in a shipload of smuggled balls and powder. Aunt Caroline doesn't know the details, but she heard Dr. Williams's wife accuse Joseph of moving the ammunition so the doctor couldn't find it . . . perhaps to another warehouse. Think what it would mean to our army if we could find where it's hidden." Although softly spoken, my words sounded loud in the stillness.

Gideon didn't say anything for a long moment, but his excitement pulsed through the space between us like charged air before a summer thunderstorm. Powder! Ammunition! A chance for victory! "It would mean much if we could find it," he said.

"I think I can. That same night, Aunt Caroline thought she saw a lease spill onto the floor of the library. Perhaps it's the lease to the hiding place."

"What if it isn't?"

"Then I'll search until I find it."

"No." Gideon's voice was firm. "You mustn't put yourself in any more danger."

"It won't be any more dangerous than what I'm already doing. Mr. Lind is gone for several hours each day and . . ." The shuffle of hooves in a stall drifted up to the hayloft.

"Jake and Mina are keeping watch," he assured me. "Just the same, we must leave. Sometimes Colonel Paxman doesn't stay long with his lady friend." He got to his feet and helped me to mine, the two of us standing just inches apart. My pulse quickened as I looked up at the shadowy outline of his face and saw the glint of his eyes in the darkness. With the night shrouding us like a fragile mist, his hands reached to cradle my face, his touch sure and gentle, his fingers spanning it as if to measure the bones and planes and flesh so as not to forget it . . . or me.

"I was afraid you would forget me," he whispered after a moment.

"How could I?"

Rather than answer, he took me into his arms, his mouth claiming mine, the hard, rapid beat of his heart calling to mine to match its rhythm. My arms stole around his neck, the breadth of his shoulders and the soft queue of his hair but more to be savored as his lips made a soft trail across my cheek and closed eyes. "Does this make up for the shabby kiss I gave you in The Rose and Crown?" he asked against my ear.

"I certainly don't want to slap you."

He laughed and pulled me closer. "I'm so glad I found you. But I hesitate—" His tone turned hesitant, like his words. "My life is very uncertain right now and . . ."

"Shhh," I whispered, placing a finger to his lips. I didn't want to hear about danger, only that his feelings matched mine. "For now, this is enough."

His answer was to continue to hold me close and to gently stroke my face. With a tiny sigh, he again spoke. "We must leave. If Colonel Paxman returns to Summer Street before I do, it will arouse his suspicions even more."

A moment later, we were down the ladder and standing at the stable door, where he placed his hands on my shoulders and turned me to face him. "I wish with all my heart for time to know you better, Mistress Abigail Stowell . . . your thoughts and feelings about things both trivial and deep. But—" His fingers tightened on my shoulders. "If you need me, leave a note," he whispered.

"I will."

The gray-black sky devoid of stars silhouetted his head. Turning me away from him, his hands dropped from my shoulders. "Go," he whispered. "I'll follow you to the gate to make sure you get safely into the house."

I quietly slipped from the stable, aware that Jake and Mina kept watch too. At the gate, I paused and looked back for Gideon. A movement by the oak told me he wasn't far behind. My attention returned to the black façade of the three-storied house. All was in darkness, and I saw no evidence that anyone watched. Lifting my skirt, I hurried toward it.

When I reached the paving stones outside the door, I stopped to remove my shoes, letting out a breath of relief when the door opened easily to my touch. As I turned and waved, an answering movement by the back gate told me Gideon watched, just as he'd promised.

Senses alert for sound or someone's presence, I tiptoed through the kitchen, up the back stairs, and on to my bedroom. Once I was inside and the door closed behind me, I leaned against it and smiled. Gideon cared, and although my life was still fraught with danger, being in his arms had driven away much of my fear.

Chapter Twenty-Four

I OPENED MY EYES TO the sight of golden sunrays on my bedroom wall. Stretching, my mind turned at once to Gideon. The memory of his lips on mine was as fresh as if it had happened but minutes before, and it caused me to smile and hum while I dressed and prepared for the day.

Aunt Caroline was sitting up in her nest of pillows when I entered her room. "You look to be in better spirits than you were when you left me last night," she observed.

"A bright sunny day always lifts my spirits."

"Is it sunny?"

"Let me pull back the drapery so you can see for yourself."

I took perverse pleasure in disobeying Dr. Barnes's charge to keep the bedroom in near darkness. Though I might fear his next visit, the sight of blue sky and sunlight swallowed the dread. "When you're stronger, you'll be able to sit in the sun." I gave her a questioning look. "Are you ready to try walking?"

She sat up taller. "Before you came, I dangled my legs over the side of the bed." Pushing back the covers, she proudly showed me what she'd done.

I held out both hands to her. "Can you stand?"

On her first attempt, she sat back before she gained her feet, but on her second try, though her legs trembled, she stood for some time, her hold on my hands steadying her, the smile on her thin face triumphant.

"Wonderful!" I said.

Though she beamed, I could tell she was glad to sit on the bed again and rest.

"We can't go on many more days without someone discovering you're not taking the laudanum," I said. "The maids or your husband could come in before you can pretend you're asleep or . . ."

A rap on the door sent a jolt of fear through the room. In a trice, Aunt Caroline lay down, and I tucked the covers around her.

"Missy," Mina called.

Relief spilled through me as I hastily pulled the drapes across the window and went to the door. When I opened it, I was aware of Mina's worry.

"Jake just sent word by Ezra that Mista Lind told him to wait at the wharf for the boat that be bringin' Dr. Barnes from Castle Island," she whispered. "He be bringin' the doctor to see the missus."

Neither of us spoke, Mina's eyes full of questions while my mind scrambled to find the answers.

"Thank you, Mina," I said in my normal voice. Stepping closer, I whispered, "I'll have to give her laudanum."

"Yes'm," Mina said, though her nod was reluctant and her face still showed worry as I closed the door.

"What is it?" Aunt Caroline asked.

"Dr. Barnes is on his way to see you."

"Dear heaven," she gasped. In the next breath, she added, "He's sure to find out I'm not taking laudanum."

"I'm going to give you a small dose before he arrives."

She lifted her lips in protest. "But . . ."

"Remember how the doctor checked your eyes when he came? One look at the pupils and he'll know you're not taking it."

She shook her head as if to argue, but her next words surprised me. "If he can tell so easily, Joseph might notice too."

"Not if you have your eyes closed and are playing possum."

Though she nodded, her expression remained troubled. "'Tis a dangerous game we play, Abby. So much can go wrong."

"I know . . . just as I know you must leave Boston as soon as possible."

Her eyes widened. "How?"

"I have a friend who said he'd help."

"A friend?"

"We'll talk of it later. Now we must get you ready for the doctor."

I went to the shelf and picked up the wine glass. How large of a dose was I to give her? Up to the circle of leaves as I'd done when I'd first arrived or less?

In the end, I settled on half a dose, hoping it would be enough to fool the doctor without causing problems for Aunt Caroline afterward. I felt her eyes on me as I poured the laudanum into the glass, saw them fix on the glass as I carried it to her.

She took the glass without speaking and drank it down in two quick swallows. Then with a sigh, she settled into the pillows and closed her eyes.

As I looked down at her still figure—her dark lashes a graceful arc against her pale skin, the plait of her black hair lying against the whiteness of her nightgown—I wondered if I'd done wrong.

As if she sensed my concern, Aunt Caroline spoke. "Don't worry, Abby. I'm only practicing playing possum."

Even so, a prayer formed in my mind that Dr. Barnes wouldn't notice that her skin wasn't as sallow or that her cheeks had more flesh.

I prayed the same words when Dr. Barnes entered the bedroom less than a half hour later, his tall frame but a silhouette in the room's dimness, his movements quick and impatient, just as I remembered.

"Mr. Lind sent a note saying his wife is given to hysterics again. Instead of increasing the dosage of her medicine as I suggested, he sent a second note insisting that I examine her myself." He set his bag on the bed and bent to look at Aunt Caroline. He studied her for a long moment before he lifted the lid of one eye, then the other.

Both my breathing and heartbeat quickened. Although Aunt Caroline had genuinely fallen asleep within minutes of taking the laudanum, I didn't know if the dose had been enough to change the size of her pupils.

"Light a candle," he ordered.

My hand was unsteady as I lifted the flint to do his bidding. Were her pupils too large? Too small?

As Dr. Barnes took the lighted candle, the flame cast flickering shadows onto his thin face, his nose seeming to grow longer, his chin more pointed. Then my attention was on his fingers as they lifted Aunt Caroline's eyelids and peered long at her pupils.

Stifling a shudder, I put my hands behind my back so he couldn't see how tightly I clutched them. What did he see? Did he know?

Aunt Caroline roused, and her eyes fluttered opened. "What is it?" she asked, her voice slightly slurred.

"Dr. Barnes has come to see you," I said.

Her head moved on the pillows. "Don't bleed me," she pleaded.

"'Tis for your own good," he said dispassionately. As he spoke, he handed me the candle and lifted Aunt Caroline's wrist to check her pulse. "Too fast," he muttered.

"She is fearful of the bloodletting."

The doctor lifted his head, his hard gaze locking on mine. "Did I ask for your uneducated opinion? One more word and you shall leave the room."

"No . . ." Aunt Caroline pleaded.

"Then be quiet, both of you."

Biting my lip, I took Aunt Caroline's hand while she grimaced and closed her eyes.

My mind was full of worried questions as Dr. Barnes removed the bleeding cup, tourniquet, and scalpels from his satchel. Had bringing the candle close to Aunt Caroline's eyes been a good or bad omen? And what did her quick pulse mean?

'Twas hard to say if the doctor's foul mood, the stuffy room, or heavenly intervention made the bleeding little more than a quick formality, for as I rinsed the cup, the blood it held was much less than before. After the utensils were dried, I handed them to the doctor.

"'Tis just as I suspected. Mistress Lind's only trouble is that she needs a larger dose of laudanum. How much are you giving her now?"

I quickly retrieved the wine glass and ran my fingernail through the etched vine.

His narrow brow furrowed. "Increase it to here," he instructed, pointing to a tiny flower above the vine. "That should keep her docile enough."

And no more trouble than a rag doll, I wanted to say. Fearing the doctor would see my anger, I returned the glass to the shelf while he placed his instruments back into the bag.

"I'll be giving the same instructions to Mr. Lind when I stop by his place of business to collect my fee. I trust that you can be depended upon to do as both he and I say."

Only then did I turn to face him, taking great care to keep my expression and voice impassive. "I have always been known to be trustworthy," I replied.

"Then see that you continue to do so." He picked up his black bag and strode to the door without giving so much as a second glance to his patient.

Aunt Caroline's eyes flew open as soon as the door closed. "Do you think . . . ?"

Fearing that Dr. Barnes suspected and listened, I put a warning finger to my lips and quietly went to the door. Hearing nothing, I carefully eased it opened and let out pent-up breath when no one was there. Closing it, I said, "He's gone. I don't think he suspects."

"Thank God." Aunt Caroline sighed. "When he took so long looking at my eyes, I feared we'd been found out."

"For now, I think we're safe . . . but there's still your husband to worry about."

"If only Joseph weren't so clever." She sighed. "Every day is a risk, and the sooner I leave Boston, the better it will be." Though her speech was slightly slurred, her voice held determination. "I'd like to go to my daughter in Philadelphia, but that's the first place Joseph will look."

"Stowell farm would welcome you."

"Even when your father and Joseph no longer agree on politics?"

"To Father, friendship is more important than politics."

"Is your father at Stowell farm?"

I shook my head. "He's camped with the Mayfield militia not far from Cambridge . . . Reverend Whipple too."

She studied me for a long moment. "What truly brought you to Boston, Abigail?"

Much as I wanted to tell her, caution stayed my tongue. "Are we not more like mother and daughter than friends?" I asked. "What other reason than wishing to care for you would bring me here?"

"The wish to help your father and the rebel army."

I stared at her, not knowing what to say. Though her eyes were half closed, her thinking was clearer than I'd thought. "I think we should wait and talk when you're more yourself."

Aunt Caroline gave me a sleepy smile. "But we will talk, Abby. We must talk."

Her eyes closed, and in less than a minute, her heavy breathing told me she'd fallen back into the laudanum-induced sleep. I, on the other hand, was tense with worry, aware that by one small misstep on my part, Joseph Lind would realize what I'd done and that I, along with his wife, knew he'd caused the death of Dr. Williams.

Trying to calm myself, I went to the window and parted the drapes. I needed to know that despite the dangerous path I trod, the sun still shone, flowers bloomed, and birds still lifted their heads to the sky and sang.

★

It was late afternoon when Joseph knocked briefly and opened the bedroom door. Nodding to me as he approached the bed, he said, "Dr. Barnes told me he's increased the dosage of Caroline's medicine."

I became uneasy when he studied her. Thankfully, either Aunt Caroline was truly asleep or she had perfected her game.

"It pains me to see her agitated and giving way to hysterics," he went on. "The doctor says the new dosage should keep her calmer." His gaze lifted to me. "Have you given her the larger amount?"

I nodded and crossed my fingers behind my back. "At lunchtime."

"The new dosage will require you to visit the apothecary more often."

"I don't mind." It took effort to keep anger out of my voice and expression. *It pains me to see her so agitated.* A feeling of loathing gathered inside me.

I fervently prayed none showed while he lingered to express his gratitude for all I did for his wife. I played my part, smiling and nodding whenever I thought it needful, though his words made me want to shudder. Even so, I was obliged to look after him with a smile fastened on my face until he left.

"Thank heaven he's gone," Aunt Caroline whispered when the door closed.

"And for now, he doesn't seem to suspect." When she stretched and yawned, I asked, "How are you feeling?"

"Well enough, though I don't like feeling like my brain is clogged with porridge." Sitting up, she said, "Now, more than ever . . . we must be on our guard. His seeming gratitude is but a hoax."

"Father said he was a clever man."

"Unscrupulous as well," she countered. She paused before going on. "We must decide what to do next. You said you had a friend who could help me leave Boston?"

I nodded, wondering how much to tell her.

"Is he also a friend of your father's?"

"He can be trusted," I said evasively.

Aunt Caroline smiled. "For now, I'll let that suffice, though you should know that when I wasn't sleeping, I had time to think and put things together . . . little things that told me Abigail Stowell is very much her father's daughter."

"Thank you." Eager to change the subject, I said, "The main thing is for you to be able to walk so you can leave."

Her mouth tightened in chagrin. "If only I weren't so weak."

"You must practice walking every day . . . eat more too. I don't entirely trust Alice, so either Mina or I will bring your tray."

"Alice is curious and likes to gossip," she said.

"We need to talk about the safest and best time to leave Boston too. Sunday afternoon when everyone has their half day off seems a good time."

"What about Joseph?"

"I've noticed that he usually naps or visits friends on Sabbath afternoons." As I spoke, a thought came to me. "Maybe my friend can arrange for a fake message to take Mr. Lind away."

Her eyes lit with amusement. "Mine isn't the only mind that's been busy."

"I'm determined to get you safely away from your husband."

"And what of you, Abby? You can't stay in Boston if I go."

"I'll have to leave too," I conceded. "But my hope is that I won't leave empty-handed."

My aunt straightened and took my hand. "What can I do to help?" When she saw me hesitate, she added, "Rest assured, Abby, Joseph's politics aren't mine. Your father was well aware of this."

"I don't want to put you in any more danger."

She gave a short laugh. "Nothing you could ask me to do could be more dangerous than what I already face from Joseph."

I leaned close to her. "Are you sure?"

Her steady gaze held. "Yes . . . very sure."

My fingers tightened on hers. "On the night you learned what your husband had done to Dr. Williams, you said a box spilled onto the floor and you saw a paper that looked like a lease."

"I did." The bright look on her face told me she'd guessed my purpose. "And if the lease is to the place where the powder and ammunition are stored, the address would be a great prize for your father and the rebel army."

"Yes." I waited, not knowing if, as Father often said, I should have guarded my tongue. Yet every instinct told me I'd done right.

"It would be unsafe for you to go to the library tonight," she said after a moment. "But tomorrow, after Joseph leaves, I'll tell you where to look."

"Tomorrow," I said. And with a squeeze of our hands, we sealed our bargain.

Chapter Twenty-Five

I RETIRED THAT NIGHT WITH a mind filled with all that needed to be done before we could leave Boston. Although I knew Gideon was trying to obtain passes for the blockade and that he'd talked to Jake about using the Lind carriage, there was still the challenge of getting Aunt Caroline down the stairs and out to the stable yard. Threaded through my thoughts was the anticipation of finding the lease and perhaps the location of the powder and ammunition.

Strangely enough, I slept well. Aunt Caroline seemed to have done the same, for she expressed her intent to practice walking as soon as I entered her room with the breakfast tray.

Her effort to stand was more successful than the day before, and after she'd done so twice, she took two steps, leaning on my arm as she reached the chair on trembling legs.

"Wonderful," I encouraged.

Though her breathing was hard, she managed a smile. When she'd rested, we repeated the process back to the bed, where she lay down.

"You did better than I expected."

She gave me a tired smile. "Our time is short. I'm determined to be ready." She closed her eyes. "Now would be a good time for you to go to the library and look for the hollowed-out book."

"What does it look like?"

"Dark in color, I think, but whether 'twas black or brown . . ." She shook her head. "I was in such a state that night, I really don't remember. But I do know that Joseph was returning it to the top shelf behind his desk and that the book was over large."

Armed with this information, I picked up a book as if to return it to the library and went downstairs.

I heard voices in the kitchen, and a quick look across the foyer showed Alice counting out the tableware on the dining room table. I slipped quietly into the library and softly closed the door.

As I did, the pleasant room changed to the place where Aunt Caroline had struggled and fought with her husband. Despite the warmth of the June morning, a shiver ran down my back, and for a moment, it was as if the evil of that night still clung in cloying folds to the walls and ceiling.

I straightened my shoulders and looked up at the top shelf behind the desk. Several oversized books were bracketed between heavy bookends. All were dark in color with titles embossed in gold lettering along the spines.

I pushed the chair over to the shelves and climbed onto it to reach the books. I started with the widest volume, but a peek inside it and three others revealed nothing unusual. When I picked up the fourth book, I heard a clink, and the heft was different.

Climbing down and setting it on the desk, I opened the cover and found not the lease but dozens of gold and silver coins. Taking a minute to run my fingers through them, I resolutely climbed back onto the chair and renewed my search. Unless Mr. Lind had moved the lease, there had to be a second false book.

After I looked through two more volumes, I impatiently picked up the third. Still standing on the chair, I opened it and saw two folded pieces of paper and more coins.

"Yes," I whispered. I lifted the top paper and saw a list of men's names with my father's among them. Sickness caught in my throat at the unmistakable proof of Joseph Lind's treachery. As I reached for the second piece of paper, the book slipped from my hands, the thud as it hit the floor like a drum and the clatter of coins like the clanging of church bells. I immediately thought of Alice and Hettie and scrambled to pick them up, my fingers clumsy with fear, my thoughts tumbling. Hurry! Hurry!

As soon as the coins and papers were retrieved, I picked up the two fake books and started for the door. As my fingers closed around the knob, caution stopped me and sent me back onto the chair to arrange the remaining volumes between the bookends. Only when the room was as I'd found it did I open the door. Seeing no one, I quietly slipped out of the library and up to Aunt Caroline's room.

Her eyes were closed when I opened the door, but they opened as soon as I called her name.

"I found them. There were two false books, not one."

"Two?" she echoed as I laid them on her lap.

She let out a gasp when she opened the first. "How could so much money be in the library? It can't have come from Joseph's business. He keeps it in a secret place at his warehouse."

She stared at the wall for a long moment. Then, with a shake of her head, she said, "I feel certain he didn't come by it honestly. Didn't he cheat poor Dr. Williams?" She shook her head a second time. "I'm sure 'tis all ill-gotten gain."

After a moment, she set it aside and opened the second book. "The lease," she said, reaching for a torn, wrinkled paper.

It was all I could do not to snatch it from her. I wanted to see the address! The time it took her to unfold and read it seemed like an eternity. Finally, she handed it to me.

"I think we've found what you're looking for."

My eyes hurried past the date and other details, not stopping until it reached the address—Number 26 Grind Street.

"Where's Grind Street?" I asked, not bothering to read further.

Aunt Caroline shook her head. "I don't know, but such doesn't mean it doesn't exist. Jake will know."

I wanted to rush out to the stable to ask him, but my aunt put a restraining hand on my arm. "Don't go. It might arouse Mr. Gridley's suspicion. Let Mina ask him."

I knew she was right, but the urge to act persisted. I wanted to know at once if the building at 26 Grind Street held the cache of ammunition or something entirely different.

With effort, I quelled my impatience and watched Aunt Caroline take out the second paper. Her expression changed as she read it. "Nathan Stowell," she whispered. Holding the paper out to me, she asked, "What's this?"

"I believe it's a copy of a list your husband sold to General Gage's aide in exchange for favors from him as governor. At least that's what Father was told."

A sick expression crossed her face. "Surely Joseph wouldn't do such to your father?"

Not answering, I asked, "Is George Smyth's name on the list?"

She looked at the paper. "Yes." She shook her head in disbelief. "Joseph and Nathan have been friends for years . . . Mr. Smyth too. I . . . I can't believe he'd do this." Tears trembled through her words. After she'd regained control, her attention returned to the box. "Gold guineas," she said, sifting them through her fingers.

"A great many," I agreed as her gaze traveled to the wardrobe.

A frown slowly crossed her face. "Would you bring me the red box on the wardrobe shelf?"

I did her biding without asking why.

"My father gave me one hundred gold guineas as part of my dowry," she explained when I put the red box on the bed. "Joseph used part of them when he began his business, but being proud, he insisted that I keep the rest for our old age." She ran her fingers over the red lacquered pattern on the lid. "I keep them in here. You'll find the key inside the sachet bag with my nightgowns."

I found the key and handed it to her. With unsteady fingers, she unlocked and lifted the lid. Inside was a velvet drawstring purse. Without speaking, she unfastened it and poured the contents into the box.

She made a tiny sound when she saw them. "Just as I suspected! He's taken more guineas."

Though they covered the bottom of the box, I doubted there were more than twenty. "How many should be there?"

"Sixty. I remember counting them last Christmas. We were making ready to go to Philadelphia to visit Eleanor and her husband. She'd been feeling poorly since the loss of her baby, and I hoped a guinea might cheer her."

"Do you think your maid . . . Mistress Kent . . . might have taken them while you were gone?"

"She went with us." She shook her head. "No, 'twas Joseph. I know without a doubt 'twas Joseph." Her voice was emphatic. "He's the only one who knows where I keep the key. Remember, until January, we shared this bedroom."

"But why when he's so wealthy?"

"I . . . I don't know." She fell silent, and when she finally spoke, her voice held rancor. "Joseph ignored me when I asked him not to borrow money to build our new home . . . said he'd have it paid back in a trice. But after the tea party, when the King ordered the harbor blockade—" She shook her head. "Since there are no new goods coming from England and he's unable to ship anything out, his business must be in greater peril than he's let on."

"That would explain why he did what he did to Dr. Williams."

Aunt Caroline shut her eyes as if to blot out the terrible memory.

"With matters so desperate, he may try to take the rest of the guineas," I ventured.

"Then we must hide them." She began to put them back in the purse.

"Wait," I said before she picked up more. "Mother once told me of a woman who, for safe keeping, sewed her dowry money into the hem of her petticoat as she traveled to meet her husband-to-be. If we did the same, perhaps it will keep them safe from Mr. Lind, as well as the guards at the blockade."

Aunt Caroline smiled. "What a wonderful idea! It will also give me the means to care for myself after I leave Boston."

"What about the coins in the other book?"

"Sort out enough guineas to replace the ones Joseph stole from me, but the rest . . ." She paused and thought for a moment. "We must divide what is left between the two books. Hopefully, Joseph won't be suspicious should he chance to open them."

Although her plan held flaws, I could only pray that such an occasion wouldn't occur.

Ten minutes later, the money had been divided between the two books, and the red lacquer box was returned to the wardrobe. By then, it was lunchtime, and Aunt Caroline looked badly in need of a nap.

When I went to the kitchen for the lunch tray, only Mina was there. While she ladled soup into a bowl, I asked if she knew the location of Grind Street.

"I heard of it a time or two, but I don't know exactly where it be. Most likely Jake'll know. Ezra too since he runs errands."

"When you find out, will you let me know?"

"I will, Missy." Though her look was speculative, she didn't question me further.

As soon as I returned with the lunch tray, Aunt Caroline asked me to return the fake books to the library. "I won't rest easy until they're back where they belong."

Although it wasn't time for Mr. Lind to return, I was as anxious as she to have them safely back in their places.

I quickly returned the fake books to the top shelf and was just getting down from the chair when I heard the front door open and Mr. Lind's voice.

"Ask Alice to bring a glass of cool water from the well into the library," he told Briggs. "The heat today has brought me home early and made me thirsty."

My heart thudded so hard it knocked all thought from my mind. Panic pushed my hands to set the chair in its place, snatch up a book, and hastily sit down in the window seat.

"Oh!" I exclaimed when Mr. Lind entered the room. The hammer of my heart made my voice unsteady. "I . . . I didn't realize it was so late." Closing the book, I stood.

Rather than seeming startled, Mr. Lind looked pleased. "What a pleasant surprise." He held out his hand to stop me when I moved toward the door. "Stay . . . stay. I was planning to go upstairs to see how Caroline was doing. You being here will save me the trip."

My desire to escape was so strong it was all I could do not to rush past him. Thankfully, sense returned and reminded me to smile. "She's much calmer," I said. "That's why I was able to come here to read. It's much cooler in the window seat."

"Then you must stay and enjoy a cool glass of water with me as well."

Not daring to be rude, I waited while he pulled a chair away from the wall for me to sit on. Before I could sit, Alice arrived with his glass of water.

"Serve Mistress Abigail, then bring another glass for me," he instructed.

"Yes, sir." She looked over her shoulder at me with an expression that made me uncomfortable.

Unaware of my discomfort and desire to leave, Joseph took the chair I'd but minutes before put back, a genial smile stretching his face. "Now, tell me about your day. I hope it was pleasant."

"It was." I took a nervous sip of water. Something about his smile made me want to jump to my feet and run.

"It pleases me that you feel at ease enough in my home to come here to relax. Seeing such a charming face in my library makes my home-coming much more enjoyable."

Ignoring his pretty speech, I asked the first thing that came to my mind. "Your return this afternoon was earlier than usual, wasn't it?"

He made a grimace. "This—this blockade," he said, "leaves me with little business to transact. I . . . along with many, am anxious for Gage to attack the rabble on the mainland and show them they've bitten off more than they can chew. When they've left with their tails between their legs, life can get back to normal."

The week before, I would have challenged him for speaking so disparagingly about Father. Today, because I feared his growing suspicion, I took another sip of water and nodded. "It must be difficult for you."

Before he could reply, Alice came with another glass of water. A bit of a breeze blew through the open window, but neither it nor the water cooled my nerves. My unease increased when he asked Alice to close the door after she left.

As I watched her leave, my eyes caught the glint of a gold coin on the rug next to the bookcase. Trying to hide my panic, I made a try at more conversation. "Do you think the war can end so quickly?"

"I have no doubt of it. Most of the rebels will soon tire of playing soldier and go home where they belong. Food is running short . . . even our soldiers aren't fed very well."

My mind was so occupied with the coin, I scarcely heard what he'd said. How much longer until Mr. Lind saw it? What would I do? How could I escape?

My mind darted in a dozen directions as I tried to think of what to say. "Mina told me she set Ezra to guard our chickens," I blurted.

Joseph gave me a quick look. Thankfully, it was me, not the coin he saw. "Good. I shall be upset if I have to miss my morning eggs."

Looking for an excuse to leave, I opened my mouth to say that I really must return to his wife, but before I could speak, the loud rap of the knocker sounded on the front door.

Mr. Lind, who'd settled back into his chair, looked irritated. "Who can that be?"

I heard the murmur of voices and, a moment later, a knock on the library door.

"Yes?" Joseph said.

Briggs opened the door. "A note for you, sir." He walked to the desk and handed him a folded piece of paper. As he waited to see if there would be an answer, he gave me a sideways glance. I didn't doubt there would soon be talk among the servants.

Anger boiled inside me as I watched Mr. Lind read the note.

"Will there be a reply?" Briggs asked.

"No." Mr. Lind got to his feet and slipped the note inside his waistcoat. "I do need to leave, however." He gave me a quick nod as he moved to the door. "I look forward to conversing with you again, Mistress Abigail."

Once he'd left, I quickly snatched up the coin. Only when it was safely in my pocket did I breathe more easily. Thank heaven Mr. Lind had seen neither the coin nor me returning the fake books. Even so, I would have given much to read the note he'd tucked into his waistcoat.

Chapter Twenty-Six

I WAITED TO COLLECT MYSELF before opening the door to Aunt Caroline's bedroom. Though I was grateful for my escape and for Mr. Lind's apparent lack of suspicion about his wife, the way he'd looked at me had set my nerves jangling. Country lass I might be, but even country lasses recognize the ulterior intent of certain looks from a man. Dear heaven! He was old enough to be my father!

In the end, I didn't say anything to Aunt Caroline. To her question about returning the fake books, I told her they were back in their places. "Mr. Lind returned early, but a note came for him, and he's left again."

"Good," she said. "Every hour counts, and I'm anxious to begin sewing the coins into one of my petticoats."

With ears alert for approaching footsteps, we began to unpick the petticoat's hem. When we'd finished, she counted out thirty gold coins and bade me take the other half and sew them into the hem of my petticoat. "In case something unexpected happens."

After I returned with my extra petticoat and sewing case, I found Aunt Caroline staring blankly at the wall.

"You're not to worry," I said.

"I'm thinking, not worrying."

She looked down at the gold guineas pooled in her lap. "Our risk is steadily growing, Abby. Dr. Barnes's visit. Joseph coming home early." She shook her head. "We must leave this Sunday. I don't dare wait longer."

"Nor do I," I said, thinking of the look in Joseph's eyes.

We spoke of other things as we sewed guineas into the hems, taking stitches between to prevent them from sliding. Though I kept my ears tuned to the sound of footsteps and a sharp eye on the clock, my nerves wouldn't let me rest. "Your husband could return any minute."

At her nod, I bundled the remaining coins and my sewing case into my petticoat and put them and Aunt Caroline's petticoat into the wardrobe. "We can finish in the morning."

It was well we took the precaution, for Aunt Caroline had scarcely slipped back between the sheets before, following a quick rap, Mr. Lind entered the room.

My heart jumped, but Aunt Caroline lay with closed eyes as if she slept.

"I wanted to see for myself how much the larger dose has calmed her," Joseph said by way of greeting.

I strove to match my aunt's apparent calmness. "She sleeps more often," I said as he approached the bed.

After looking down at her, he shook her shoulder and spoke brusquely. "Caroline."

Knowing that the size of her pupils might give her away, Aunt Caroline's eyes only fluttered.

He spoke her name again.

"What . . . do . . ." she said in a slurred voice.

"I want to talk to you."

"I . . ." The word drifted away in a sigh, and her head sank deeper into the pillow.

Her husband nodded in satisfaction. "The larger dosage seems to be working well."

"It does."

"That being the case, will you dine with me on Friday evening?"

Aunt Caroline's mouth jerked slightly, but since her husband's attention was focused on me, he didn't notice.

"Friday?" I echoed, hoping my sudden panic didn't show.

"I'll ask Mina to fix a special meal," he went on in a smooth voice. "And wear the pink gown you wore to the Nichols's dinner party."

I stared at him, not knowing what to say.

"Young Nichols mentioned how lovely you looked. Since I was deprived of the pleasure, I wish to claim the honor on Friday."

"But . . ."

"No false modesty, my dear." With a smile like the one he'd given me earlier, he started for the door. When he reached it, he turned and added, "By the by, I noticed that the laudanum bottle is running low. Make certain you don't let it run out."

"I plan to go to the apothecary in the morning," I said, my voice not entirely steady. Thank heaven I'd continued to empty the bottle.

"Good." With another unsavory smile, he quit the room.

Aunt Caroline and I stared at each other after he left, her eyes filled with worry, mine likely mirroring her dismay.

"He's despicable!" she finally hissed. "His friend's daughter!"

"And he's still monitoring the laudanum," I added, though my mind, likely like hers, still heard his caressing tone as he'd said, "My dear."

"We must think of an excuse . . . though we can't use my illness or hysterics again."

Before we could say more than a word or two, another rap came.

"Missy," Mina called.

My heart resumed its regular tempo as I called, "Come in."

The sight of Mina's dark, placid face eased some of my tension.

"I brung you some dinner," she announced. As she set the tray on the table, she gave me a measured look. "What's wrong, Missy?"

"Mr. Lind asked me to dine with him on Friday evening."

Mina's large brown eyes widened. "Laws! Why he want to do such a no 'count thing?"

"Because he's a no 'count man," my aunt stated.

Mina's shoulders lifted in a big sigh. "He that all right, but I never thought he'd do it in his own house . . ." Her voice broke off. "We cain't let it happen." But as her gaze met mine, I think she realized that too many excuses had already been made and that we might do more harm than good if we tried to prevent it.

When Mina made to leave, she jerked her head at me in an invitation to follow her. Neither of us spoke until we were in the corridor.

"Jake and Ezra know where Grind Street be," she said in a low voice. "Jake cain't get away to take us, but Ezra can."

"Us?" I asked.

"Jake said it not the best part of town for a lady to be goin'. Said it best if Ezra and I go with you."

"Where is it?"

"In the west end, not far from the mill pond."

"I need to buy more laudanum in the morning. Can you and Ezra take me to Grind Street after that?"

"We kin."

She left with a troubled face, and neither my aunt nor I had any appetite for our dinner.

★

The next morning, after Aunt Caroline and I had eaten and the breakfast tray was returned to the kitchen, she again attempted walking. This time I moved the chair a step farther away from the bed, and she had strength enough to reach it without mishap. After she'd repeated the process, I left her to rest.

A few minutes later, basket in hand, I was on my way to the apothecary shop.

When I failed to see any sign of Jake or Mr. Gridley in the stable yard, I paused at the gate into the alley and slipped a folded paper with the address of the lease into the hiding place with the hope that Gideon would check the gatepost before the day was over.

Then I set my steps to a brisk pace and soon reached the cobbled street fronting the apothecary shop. The owner greeted me cheerfully, and but a few minutes later, I was back on the street with a paper-wrapped bottle of laudanum in my basket. I spied Mina across the way, her height and brightly colored turban setting her apart from others on the street.

"Where's Ezra?" I asked when I reached her.

"Had to run an errand on King Street. Said he'd meet us there."

Goodwives and maids made their way along the street with us, their intent likely the fish market near the wharf rather than King Street. Red-coated soldiers were in abundance, usually in groups of two or three, the heavy sound of their boots and the sight of their guns making me all the more eager to find the ammunition.

Mina's expression was worried, and she said little as we walked.

"Is something wrong?" I finally asked.

"Just havin' a bad day."

Before I could ask more, Ezra jumped down from a wooden crate to join us. His brown eyes were bright with anticipation, and the gleam of his white teeth was wide against the black of his skin. That he was pleased at the importance of being our guide was evident, and his gait as he led the way was a wee bit cocky.

The day was overcast, and a bank of lingering fog obscured Castle Island. Even so, the heat was building.

As we made our way west from King Street, homes replaced businesses in a mixture of clapboard houses and the taller brick homes of the rich.

Missing Mina's cheerful conversation, I said, "I hope you're not worrying about the dinner with Mr. Lind on Friday."

She shook her head. "Just havin' a bad day," she repeated.

"A bad day in the kitchen?"

Sensing that my questions wouldn't end, she finally said, "I don't want to worry you none, but Jake don't like us goin' to Grind Street. He said it no place for his wife or a lady . . . Ezra neither."

"Surely it can't be that bad."

Her steps slowed. "You ever hear of Mount Whoredom?"

I shook my head, but since I read my Bible, I had a fair idea of what she meant.

"The street you're lookin' for is close to that hill, and the kind of women it was named after live in houses next to Grind Street."

Understanding came, not only of Mina's meaning but also of why Mr. Lind had leased a building in such a disreputable area. No wonder Dr. Williams couldn't find the hiding place. I gave Mina a level glance. "I still want to see it."

Her full lips tightened. "Figured you would."

"You don't have to come with me if . . ."

"You think I let you go there alone? Ain't you or Ezra goin' to such a place lessen I go with you." Straightening her shoulders, she called to Ezra who was a ways ahead. "You stay close. You hear?"

Ezra gave a reluctant nod and waited.

Crossing a street, he led us into a cobbled courtyard where a large wash pot sat on a fire and a woman pumped water into a bucket while a small child clung to her drab-colored skirt. Clothes flapped in the breeze from a rope strung between a pole and a house, and a thin dog growled and barked at our approach.

The woman quickly quieted the dog and returned my nod, and I felt her curious gaze follow us as Ezra led the way across the courtyard and into yet another street.

Suddenly we were in an area of taverns, foul-smelling garbage, and ramshackle buildings gray with grime and age. Mina took hold of my arm and hissed for Ezra to stay close. We hadn't gone many steps before we saw an ill-dressed man collapsed in a drunken heap near a tavern door. Mina's hand slipped under the towel covering her basket, and I saw her clutch the hilt of a long-blade kitchen knife.

I was greatly relieved when we left the street of rundown taverns and houses and spied the dilapidated sign of Grind Street.

"Jake said walk fast and don't stand 'round lookin' at nothin'," Mina cautioned as we started down the short street fronted by four or five buildings.

Looking down the seemingly deserted street, I wondered why Jake had given such cautious words. When a burly man stepped out of the second building, I knew why.

"What's yer business here?" he demanded.

Mina's answer came quick. "We're lookin' for Green Lane. Is it here 'bout?"

The man gave a derisive laugh that revealed several missing teeth. "Lost, are ya? Keep goin', and ye'll find it."

Mina thanked him, and Ezra gave him a strained grin.

My eyes scanned the next ramshackle structure with broken windows and a sagging door. Then I saw it, the 26 almost indiscernible on the front of the end building. Instead of broken glass, the windows and door were boarded up, the color of the newer boards a contrast to the grimy gray wood of the rest of the building.

Before I could study it more, a man pushing a wheelbarrow covered with a tarp rounded the corner. He gave us a suspicious look as he passed, and I thought that a white lady accompanied by a black woman and boy would not be forgotten.

"Don't look good," Mina breathed when we'd quit the street.

I nodded, keeping the image of the boarded-up building in my mind.

Our return home was uneventful, with Ezra leading us on a more roundabout route through a better part of Boston. Mina kept up a steady stream of talk, the main point being that she hoped seeing Grind Street would be the end to my foolishness.

"It's not foolishness. It's important. If those men hadn't been there, I'd have tried to peek through the boards to see what was inside."

"Jake said not to—" Her voice broke off. "Important to who, Missy?"

I didn't answer, the two of us standing in front of a tailor shop while a wagon rolled past and Ezra looked back in impatience.

"Important to who?" Mina repeated.

"To Mr. Whitlock."

Mina blinked, her expression immediately changing. "You sure 'bout this?"

I met her uncertain gaze. "I am."

The black woman let out a long breath. "Then I guess I gotta help you." Shaking her head, she muttered, "May the Good Lord help us."

I made no answer, already determined not to put Mina or Ezra at any more risk. Instead, I set my mind to making plans. Mina wouldn't approve, and I knew Gideon, in his concern and need to protect me, would be furious. Nonetheless it was something that needed to be done. By the time I reached home, I knew I would return to 26 Grind Street that night to see if that building actually housed ammunition.

Chapter Twenty-Seven

AUNT CAROLINE AND I SPENT the rest of the morning and early afternoon sewing the remaining guineas and some of her jewelry into the hems of our petticoats. As I stitched, I planned my excursion to Grind Street. Since I was more familiar with the more roundabout route we'd taken on our return, I decided that it would be the safer and wiser course. I also decided to disguise myself as a man.

When we'd sewn the last of the guineas into the petticoats, Aunt Caroline was more than ready to nap. As soon as she'd fallen asleep, I went to her son's bedroom. Unlike his father, Henry's build was short and slender. Although he'd been in England for two years, I hoped he'd left some of his clothes behind.

Hot stagnant air engulfed me as I quietly closed his door and made my way through the dim, shuttered room to the wardrobe, where I found a dark-colored jacket whose sleeves were only a little long. My luck continued with the discovery of a pair of knee-length breeches that fit me better than I'd hoped. A short time later, I quietly left the room with not only a jacket and breeches but a white shirt, neck cloth, and an old hat. The shoes and stockings would have to be my own.

After hiding the clothes under my bed, I found the map I'd drawn when I'd first reached Boston. From it, I devised a route from King Street to Green Lane that looked easy enough. From there, it would be only a short way to Grind Street. Pleased with my plan, I returned to Aunt Caroline.

She stirred as soon as I opened the door. "I'm glad 'tis you, not Joseph," she said with a yawn.

"He'll likely be here soon," I reminded her.

She frowned. "I do wish it was next week and we were safely away from here."

I nodded, although the thought of leaving Gideon distressed me, especially when I knew how closely Colonel Paxman watched him.

Not wanting to think about it, I said, "I'm pleased at how quickly your strength is returning."

She smiled, as I'd hoped she would. "Each day I feel better . . . just as each day I perfect my game of possum."

It was well she had, for but five minutes later, Joseph knocked on the door and entered the room. This time he made no pretense of concern for his wife but spoke directly to me.

"I came to fetch you to join me in the library, where it's cooler. Alice is bringing cool glasses of water for us to enjoy there."

Taken by surprise, it took me a moment to reply. "What of Aunt Caroline? I've been trying to cool her, but she frets with the heat."

She stirred and made a tiny sound when I dipped a cloth into the basin and gently sponged her face and neck. "Since she's trapped upstairs, I don't feel right leaving her for the cooler library."

"It will only be for a short while."

"My guilt would make it seem an eternity." I gave him a pleading look. "Please, don't ask it of me."

Clearly taken aback, Mr. Lind looked torn between ordering me to do his bidding and trying to ingratiate himself. Luckily the latter won. "It would pain me to know I'd caused you guilt, my dear. Perhaps I can still show my concern for you by having Alice bring a glass of cool water up to you."

I gave him a smile that was almost genuine. "That would be wonderful . . . and one for Aunt Caroline, of course."

"Of course," he agreed, but his words sounded insincere.

A short time later, Alice came with a tray holding two glasses of cool water. Though Aunt Caroline and I took pleasure in my small victory, we were wise enough to know that such a farce couldn't last.

"He will soon demand payment," she cautioned. "It has always been Joseph's way."

I shuddered when I thought of dining with him on Friday.

The hours until I could don Henry's clothes seemed endless. Though he had often fretted to me about his lack of stature, tonight I was grateful. Using a ribbon as a belt for my overlarge beeches and with my hair pulled back in a queue under the hat, I felt that if I kept to the shadows, I might well pass for a young man.

Needing something to pry the boards away from the warehouse window, I'd gone earlier to the garden shed and found a metal bar, one small enough to fit into the pocket of Henry's breeches. Now, well after ten o'clock and with the house wrapped in silence, I cautiously left my room, holding my breath as I crept past Mr. Lind's bedroom, then went down the stairs, through the kitchen, and out the door.

I waited and listened, senses alert. The morning fog had crept back in fingers of mist that half obscured the moon and stars, and the peak of the stable roof was no more than a vague outline. Moving toward it, I wished more than ever that I had a lantern. Jake or Ezra would know where one was, but I didn't want them to know my intentions.

I was grateful the Linds didn't keep a dog as I moved stealthily through the stable yard and past the carriage house. The gate to the alley had been locked for the night, but thanks to the breeches I wore, I climbed over it without trouble or noise. When I found the crevice in the gatepost empty, my heart lifted. Gideon had been there.

I hurried down the dark alley and onto the street without incident, the sound of my slippers on the cobbles muted by the fog. At this late hour, few people were abroad, but I still feared patrolling soldiers.

I'd just entered the next street when the sound of approaching hooves made me flatten myself against the wall of a shop and wait while a carriage rolled past. When it was gone, I ran to the other side of the street and turned the corner, moving west toward my destination.

I hadn't gone far before a glimpse of white alerted me to an approaching soldier. I pulled the jacket lapels across my white shirt and darted behind a bush, heart pounding wildly as I crouched, knees drawn up, arms wrapped tightly around them. Listening to the boots' cadence, I realized there was more than one soldier. I could see them now, the outline of muskets and hats barely discernable in the swirling fog.

As they scanned the yards and silent houses, I shrank even smaller, scarcely daring to breathe as the sound of their approach grew ever nearer. Then they were past, the faint smell of rum and a clearing of a throat melding with the rhythmic cadence of their retreating feet.

I didn't move until they turned the corner. Rising on cramped legs, I resumed my journey, my progress more cautious as I quickly moved from shadow to shadow. I had to hide once more when a man rode by on a horse.

On I went, not stopping to get my bearings until the muffled sound of laughter and revelry penetrated the thickening fog. Grind Street should be close, but in the mist and darkness, it was hard to tell. Moving but a few steps at a time, I stopped to listen again for laughter. What a cruel joke it would be if I became lost and couldn't find either Grind Street or my way back home.

Engulfed by thickening fog, I shivered and remembered being lost and cold and afraid as a child. Then, Father had found me, but tonight I was alone.

Taking a deep, steadying breath, I peered ahead and found that the fog, like a fickle mare, had suddenly parted. Instead of impenetrable grayness, I saw the outline of ramshackle buildings and knew I'd arrived.

Because I was coming from the opposite direction, number 26 was now the first building on Grind Street. The stillness made an eerie contrast to the noise and laughter coming from the taverns and houses behind it. I prayed the burly man who'd confronted us earlier wasn't still there.

The fog closed in again, forcing me to find my way to the back of the warehouse more by touch than sight. Finally, a raised board told me I'd found the back boarded-up window.

Taking the rod out of my pocket, I cautiously pried away the bottom board. Each sound came loud to my ears, and a nail's protesting squeal set my heart clamoring. Had someone heard? Hearing and seeing no one, I started on the second board, scraping a knuckle in my haste and feeling frustrated at my slow progress.

Panic shot through me when a muscled arm caught me around the neck and a hand grabbed my wrist and forced me to drop the rod. I thrashed frantically, trying to break the suffocating hold, but the arm tightened until I couldn't breathe. My ears rang, and in a frantic effort, I braced my feet against the wall and pushed.

As we fell, the hold on my neck slackened enough for a strangled breath, but as we hit the ground, my attacker was atop me, his weight pinning me so I couldn't move. Still struggling, I saw his hand pulled back in a fist and the glimpse of a shadowed face.

"Gideon!" I croaked.

His arm fell back, and for a moment, there was only the sound of harsh breathing. "Abby?"

I nodded, my heart pounding hard against my ribs while my lungs gasped for air.

Before I could say anything, he rolled off and pulled me so that we both sat. "What are you doing here? I could have killed you!"

"The ammunition," I managed to get out. "I had to know . . ." Instead of finishing, I burrowed my head into his shoulder, needing to feel his closeness. "You frightened me," I finally whispered.

"And you scared me." His arms tightened around me. "I'm sorry. Are you all right?"

I nodded, savoring the feel of his fingers in my loosened queue, the steady rhythm of his heart. After a moment, I raised my head. "What if there's only furniture or bolts of fabric inside? I had to know."

"So did I." He jerked his head at the sudden sound of revelry. "We must hurry and get the rest of the boards off."

We worked together, Gideon's strong hands making short work of the remaining boards while I kept watch. When there was enough room to climb through the opening, he stopped and put his head inside.

"Can you see anything?"

"No, but I brought a lantern."

Not far from where our hats had fallen, he retrieved a lantern and lit the candle inside with the flint he took from his pocket. The flickering flame glowed weakly in the thick fog, and it grew even dimmer when Gideon lowered the shutters and handed the lantern to me.

"I can't risk taking it with me if there's gunpowder." Giving my hand a reassuring squeeze, he climbed inside.

For a minute, he neither moved nor spoke, the shuttered lantern of little help as he tried to get his bearings in the black interior.

"Lift one of the shutters," he whispered.

Worried that someone might see the flame, my fingers were clumsy on the metal. Then the splash of light picked out stacks of wooden kegs, and I could think only of our find.

"Powder!" Gideon whispered. "Lots of it!"

His elation matched mine as I moved the lantern to see what else was in the warehouse. The dim light only penetrated a short distance, but it was enough to see several wooden crates.

"Keep watch while I check them."

I shivered as I looked behind me, the oppressive gray fog seeming to take on life, becoming a cloak worn by something inhuman and too horrible to have a name. A burst of laughter from the next street made me jump and almost drop the lantern. It also brought back my good sense.

"It's safe," I whispered, but it was all I could do not to add, "Please, hurry."

"Good."

The deep resonance of Gideon's voice braced my sagging courage as I watched him pry open a crate. Even so, the sound of protesting wood made me draw in a quick breath and again look over my shoulder.

Then he was back, his low voice filled with excitement as he climbed through the window. "Lead balls . . . just what the army needs."

The next minutes passed quickly as Gideon refastened the boards across the window and I retrieved our hats and blew out the candle.

We wasted no time in leaving Grind Street. Gideon, like me, seeming to feel an urge to be away. We moved stealthily from shadow to shadow until we reached the better part of town. Even then we kept watch for patrolling soldiers. I led the way, and Gideon followed, his presence like a solid, comforting shield at my back. It was well past midnight, the streets deserted except for the town crier calling the hour.

When I reached the alley behind the stable yard, Gideon quickened his pace to join me, his arm circling my waist to draw me under a tree.

"Well done, Abby, though I don't like that you took such risk."

"I was afraid you couldn't get away from Colonel Paxman . . . and besides—"

"You were curious," he finished for me.

"You're coming to know me well," I said. With his lips but inches from mine and his breath warm on my cheek, I had thoughts other than conversation.

Gideon seemed to be of a different mind. "You're at great risk living in the same house as Joseph Lind," he reminded me.

I thought it best not to tell him of the unwanted advances. Instead, I said, "His wife is anxious to get away. When can we leave?"

"My friend expects to have the passes by Saturday."

"Sunday, then?" I asked.

He nodded and looked beyond me into the swirling fog.

"How will you get the powder and balls across the bay without being discovered?"

"It won't be easy. . . and it will take time. But my friends and I have done difficult things before."

"Even with Colonel Paxman watching?"

In the uncertain darkness, I thought he smiled. "I was able to divert Colonel Paxman's attention from me tonight. I can do it again."

Before I could ask more, he pulled me close, his chin resting on my forehead, a hand cupping my chin.

"I don't want you to leave Boston, but the risk . . ." He shook his head. "'Tis too dangerous for you to stay."

I nodded, feeling the prick of tears as I reached up and touched the shadowy outline of his cheek.

Then his lips were on mine, bringing warmth with their touch, joy with their closeness, and my fears vanished like fog giving way to the morning sun.

Chapter Twenty-Eight

THE LINGERING EXCITEMENT OF THE night opened my eyes shortly after dawn the next morning. My mind immediately leapt to what the powder and balls would mean to Father and the army—greater fire power and confidence and hope as they challenged the better-equipped redcoats.

Not wanting to worry Aunt Caroline, I hadn't told her about my trip to Grind Street, but my excitement when I went to her room was such that she immediately asked its cause.

"My friend went to the warehouse on Grind Street," I whispered. "It's filled with ammunition!"

Her face broke into a smile. "How exciting, and what a boon for your father and the army."

"Getting it to them will be a challenge, but my friend seems confident it can be done."

Her smile widened. "Your friend seems a most enterprising young man. When do I get to meet him?" The knowing look she gave me made me blush.

"Perhaps on Sunday."

"Then I must practice walking."

She set to the task with determination, and that afternoon, she walked all the way to the window. She dropped with a sigh onto the chair and smiled when I pulled back the drapes and opened the window.

"Wonderful!" Though her voice was breathless, her smile stretched wide. "Do look at the sky . . . the fog is gone and hardly a cloud in sight. And look . . . my roses are starting to bloom."

As enjoyable as it was for her, Aunt Caroline soon asked to return to bed. But as she closed her eyes in exhaustion, I knew it wouldn't be long until her husband noticed her returning health.

Thankfully, when Mr. Lind came a short time later, his attention centered on me, not his wife.

"I hope you're looking forward to our dinner tonight as much as I am," he said in greeting. "You're much too young and pretty to be closed away in a stuffy bedroom with a sickly woman. Tonight I'm taking you away."

"We'll only be downstairs," I reminded him. "And I truly don't mind taking care of Aunt Caroline. It gives me time to read, and in my free time, I'm able to enjoy Boston."

"Still, I mean to make it a pleasant respite for you. I have asked Mina to prepare her best meal."

"Then I shall look forward to it."

He smiled, his eyes moving over me in a manner I didn't like. "We will be dining at eight," he said in parting. "And remember to wear the pink gown young Nichols said so became you."

My reply was a weak smile, and I spent the hours until it was time to dress for dinner alternating between fits of anger and dread. For both Aunt Caroline and me, Sunday couldn't come soon enough.

Since Alice was needed to help Mina with dinner, I had no one to help me dress or arrange my hair. Having no desire to impress Mr. Lind, I didn't greatly mind. Even so, there was pleasure in again donning such a beautiful creation and feeling the silky fabric against my skin. Finally, I was done, the last of the silk strings tied, the final hairpin fastened into my curls. Taking a long, steadying breath, I left my room and slowly made my way down the curved flight of stairs where Mr. Lind waited at the dining room door.

He was dressed as if he were going to a ball, in white knee-breeches, a dark-blue coat with frills of lace at his neck and cuffs, and a white curled wig covering his shaved head. He bowed deeply in return to my curtsy, his eyes alight with pleasure as he met my gaze.

My lips moved in a stiff smile as he gallantly offered his arm and escorted me into the dining room. When he looked down at me and patted my hand, I felt a growing revulsion and dread. How was I going to get through the long evening?

Only when we reached the table did I realize just how long and uncomfortable it was going to be. Instead of our places being set across the table from each other, they were set side by side.

"I have put great thought into our time together," Joseph murmured as he pulled out my chair.

Not knowing what to say, I nodded, inwardly cringing when his hand brushed my shoulder, then traveled down to my waist, where it lingered as he helped me be seated.

As I watched him take his chair, anger warred with the knowledge of my precarious position, and something in between came out. "I wish Father could be with us tonight as he was when our family last dined with you and Aunt Caroline," I said with forced brightness. I pulled away from him as I went on. "I remember how lovely Aunt Caroline looked in a red silk gown, and you were smiling down at her as if she were all you could wish for in a wife."

Joseph picked up his napkin and snapped it in annoyance before placing it on his lap. "I fear I don't remember," he said stiffly.

"'Twas a lovely evening. Henry hadn't yet left for England, and everyone was laughing and talking . . . you and Father, especially."

Seeing Alice come to the door, Joseph nodded at her to begin serving the meal. "Can we not talk of something other than your father?" he said in a voice that was more command than question.

"Of course."

Falling silent, I took what pleasure I could find in how the patterned china and goblets and polished silver shone in the reflection from the glow of the chandelier. Through it all, I was aware of the hard lines of disapproval on Alice's face as she stood by my chair with a serving platter. It didn't take much effort to know what they thought or of the gossip that would follow. How I hated it and the way Joseph leaned close each time he spoke to me, his manner that of a man who was courting.

"I planned the entire evening for your enjoyment," he said in a silken voice. "I even asked Mina to prepare her famous chicken."

"I hope you thought to have some sent up to Aunt Caroline so she will know you were thinking of her too," I said sweetly.

Joseph's mouth tightened. "You know Dr. Barnes has ordered that she have only tea and toast."

"Even so, she needs to know you are thinking of her."

I knew my words rankled him, but 'twas better than having him lean close with his head but an inch from mine, the strong smell of port overpowering. It was also a reminder that he drank more often from his goblet than he ate from his plate.

Once, I saw Mina standing by the doorway, her steady look willing me to courage and her nod applauding my adeptness at avoiding his advances.

'Twas well Joseph didn't see the look she directed at him, else he would have sprung to his feet to defend himself.

Still, he persisted, his words those of a man sure of his charm. The more he sipped his port, the more bold he became in his advances.

"Sir," I said loudly when his leg brushed against mine.

Thankfully Alice was refilling the wine decanter and gave him a withering glance. Still, it didn't keep him from ofttimes placing his hand on my arm as if to make a point when he spoke.

My nerves were so on edge I could scarcely eat. Indeed, Mina's special chicken could as well have been porridge cooked without salt for all the pleasure it gave me. How long could I keep up my pretence without anger or disgust breaking through?

Finally, the last of the dishes were served. While Alice was still in the room, I made my play for escape. "Though dinner has been lovely, I fear I've developed a terrible headache . . . one so fierce I must ask to be excused," I said as I moved to push back my chair.

Joseph scrambled to his feet to help me. By now, he'd imbibed so freely of the port that his stance wasn't quite steady, nor was he at his best. Even so, he managed to place his hand on my waist and look down at me with a caress in his voice. "You're so lovely," he whispered.

It was all I could do not to push him away, but like an actress playing a part, I gave a little laugh. "I fear your liking for port has colored your discernment. If you aren't careful, you shall suffer the headache as I do," I teased.

Though he bowed and smiled at my teasing tone, when I glanced back as I climbed the stairs, the look in his gray eyes increased my unease.

"Thank you. Thank you," I whispered to my room when I reached it and closed the door. But disquiet stayed with me, eating at my relief when I recalled the look in his eyes. They'd told me more powerfully than words that he was not a man to be crossed or underestimated, even when he'd partaken too liberally of wine.

After I changed into my nightgown, I went to the window and leaned out the sash to search for a cooling breeze. Dusk had fallen, and the sleepy night song of a robin mingled with the clatter of pans and the faint murmur of voices from the kitchen.

Nerves sent me away from the window to pace the room. As I did, I recalled that the brass key to the bedroom door was in the bottom drawer of the wardrobe. "Get it! Use it!" a warning voice seemed to say.

Only after I'd inserted the key and locked the bedroom door did my unease dissipate enough for me to go to bed. I'd expected the evening's events to hold sleep at bay, but as subtly as the sun's lazy course across the sky, I rode the hypnotic crest of slumber until I was jerked from its edge by a noise at the door. The furtive turn of the doorknob stilled my breathing and set my heart beating an erratic dance. The knob turned again, this time more loudly, as if Joseph—I knew 'twas he—couldn't believe it was locked.

I sat up, my ears tuned, hoping he would leave. The knob turned again.

"Open the door, my sweet," a raspy voice entreated.

Anger pushed past fear and sent me to the door. "Go away!" I hissed. Gaining courage from the solid oak door, I repeated my words. "Go away!"

"I only want to talk to you . . . to thank you . . ." His whisper, though slightly slurred, was pleasant.

"You can talk to me in the morning."

He cursed. "Open this door at once!" To give emphasis to his words, he threw his shoulder against it.

Joseph was a strong man, and no one slept on the second floor except him, Aunt Caroline, and me. No one would hear. No one!

"If you don't go away, I'll scream!" I breathed.

The force of his shoulder hitting the door was his answer.

Panic sent me to the opened window. My scream echoed loudly through the quiet of the night. "Help! Jake! Someone! Help!"

Startled silence followed by the sound of hastily retreating footsteps came in response to my screams. A long moment later, I heard Jake call from the stable yard, "Comin'" and Briggs calling from the third floor.

"What's wrong? What happened??" Briggs called, his voice closer.

Reassured by their nearness, I unlocked the door with shaky fingers and opened it enough to see Mr. Lind clad in a purple robe and holding a candle coming down the corridor. Preceding him was Briggs, his bare legs showing below his nightshirt.

"Someone tried to break into my room," I said.

Even Briggs momentarily lost his unruffled demeanor.

"I'm sure Mi . . . Mistress Abigail has only experienced an upsetting nightmare," Mr. Lind said. His tone, though slurred, didn't invite argument and was one I felt certain he'd used the night Aunt Caroline had discovered him returning the false book to the shelf in the library.

Determined not to let him win again, I stepped more fully into the corridor and said in a voice that closely rivaled that of my Grandmother

Reynolds. "It was not a nightmare. Someone tried to open my door . . . not once but several times."

Mr. Lind glared at me, the message in his narrowed eyes unmistakable. *Don't try to cross me!* On seeing Alice and Hettie in the corridor, he motioned them back. "'Twas only a nightmare," he called.

Through it all, Briggs continued to look from me to Mr. Lind, a slight frown furrowing his narrow brow, one that didn't ease until someone pounded on the kitchen door.

"It's Jake. Let me in!"

A flick of unease crossed Mr. Lind's face, but his voice was firm when he spoke to Briggs. "Go down and tell Jake it was all a mistake . . . just a silly dream."

Briggs gave me a quick look before he hurried away. He hadn't gone many steps when Aunt Caroline called in a quavering voice.

"Abigail! Abigail!"

Inwardly praying she wouldn't open her door, I hurried to her room. If Joseph saw her—if anyone saw her out of bed—our masquerade would be over!

"Hush," I said, quickly entering her room and closing the door. Relief poured through me when I saw her dark outline sitting on the bed.

"Is Caroline all right?" Mr. Lind asked.

"Yes . . . though she's very upset. I think 'twill be best if I give her another dose of medicine and spend the night with her."

"An excellent idea," he replied. "Who would think something as silly as a nightmare could disturb the whole house?"

His condescending tone raised my hackles, and I had to bite my tongue to keep from calling out the truth. I took a deep breath, knowing that if I meant to leave Boston on Sunday with Aunt Caroline and the information about the ammunition, I must think and act with great care. Even so, after he left, I found pleasure in inserting the key into the lock and listening to its hard, metallic click as I turned it. Then I crossed the room to Aunt Caroline.

"What happened?" she whispered.

She gasped when I told her. "The beast," she hissed. "I was afraid this might happen."

"It won't happen again," I assured her. "I'm certain Briggs suspects what really happened."

"Joseph will continue to say it was a nightmare . . . just like he did when he claimed I was mad and hysterical."

"What happened then isn't going to happen again," I said. "I mean to tell Mina. More than that, we'll be gone on Sunday."

"Yes." Her hand took mine as if making a pact, and when she spoke, her voice held determination. "We will outwit that evil, arrogant man, but until we leave, the two of us must stay together."

Nodding, she lay back on the pillows, but it was a long time before her even breathing told me she slept.

Still too agitated to lie on the padded settle, I went to the open window hoping the fresh air might cool and calm me. Finally, I lay down, but fear and uncertainty wouldn't let me sleep. When the sky finally began to lighten, my thoughts turned to the morrow. How could I avoid Mr. Lind until we left, especially when I'd promised to attend church with him on Sunday?

I was awakened the next morning by the sound of Aunt Caroline's feet slowly padding to the window.

"Aunt Caroline," I said in surprise.

Her face lit with a satisfied smile. "I'm more determined than ever to be ready to leave tomorrow. When I heard you scream last night, I tried to go to help." A look of chagrin crossed her face. "After only a few steps, I realized I didn't have the strength to reach the door."

"I'm glad you didn't. If your husband had seen you . . ." I paused and shook my head. "The consequences would have been terrible . . . probably fatal . . . for us both."

"I realized that as soon as I got back to the bed." Her voice firmed with determination. "Our only way to thwart Joseph is to leave. And leave we will tomorrow."

Her words set the tone for the day. After eating a hearty breakfast, which I retrieved without incident, despite Alice's numerous questions, Aunt Caroline walked three times to the window, sitting well back from it so no one could see her as she rested.

As soon as she lay down to rest, I returned to my room to retrieve my trunk from under the bed and began to pack my things. Each item folded and placed inside added to my conviction that Aunt Caroline and I would safely be gone before Joseph Lind learned of our plans. Even so, thoughts of him lurked like threatening shadows at the back of my mind. What would he do? Avoid me or brazen it out like nothing had happened when he came to visit his wife?

When Prudence Blood's herbs and tinctures had been safely put back into the trunk, I fastened the straps and slid it under the bed. There. It was done.

Chapter Twenty-Nine

AFTER LUNCH, I WENT TO the kitchen to speak to Mina. The smell of freshly shucked oysters hung in the air, and Mina's voice greeted me from the back of the kitchen.

"There you be," she said. Before saying more, she went to the dining room to make certain no one was there. After she quietly closed the door, she gave me a worried look. "You all right, Missy?"

"Thanks to Jake and Briggs, I am."

"Jake and me know it wasn't no nightmare you had . . . lessen you call Mr. Lind a nightmare."

"He's a nightmare and worse." My bravado suddenly left me. "I worry about tonight though."

Mina placed a big hand on my shoulder. "Jake think Mr. Lind too smart to try such again . . . least not for a night or two." She gave me a reassuring smile. "Just to make sure, I'm plannin' to stay with you and the missus tonight."

"Then we leave tomorrow afternoon."

Mina nodded, and her fingers tightened on my shoulders. "We gotta be awful careful. You. Us'n. Mistress Lind. If one little thing was to go wrong . . ." Her voice trailed away. "I swear Mr. Lind be workin' with the devil. We gotta pray harder than we ever pray before, Missy. Pray Mr. Lind don't find out what we gonna do."

★

After our midday meal, Aunt Caroline tried walking again. Though she only went as far as the chair at the window, her steps were surer than they'd been before.

"Good," I said when she'd covered the distance twice. Despite my effort to encourage her, I felt far from good myself. Mina's words were clamped like a vise around my mind. *We gotta pray hard Mr. Lind don't find out what we gonna do.*

I glanced at the bedroom door. All would be lost if he opened the door without knocking and saw Aunt Caroline sitting at the window. I reached into my pocket for the key, and I didn't relax until I felt the lock click firmly into the hasp.

Aunt Caroline nodded when she saw what I'd done. "We'll both feel better now."

And we did. Each step she took added to her confidence and mine.

"I plan on walking to the carriage by myself," she said.

"If you can't, Jake and my friend will help you."

Her eyes widened. "Jake?"

"He'll be driving the carriage."

"Our carriage or a hired one?"

"Yours."

Amusement sprang to her eyes. "How Joseph would hate it if he knew his own carriage and trusted stableman were being used to help me escape."

Delighted at the thought, her steps quickened, and it wasn't until she'd made another trip to the chair and back that she sat on the bed to rest.

As she did, a soft knock sounded on the door. Without saying a word, I returned the chair to its place, and Aunt Caroline lay down and pulled the sheet up to her shoulders.

"Who is it?" I called.

"Mina."

Relief spilled through me when I unlocked the door and urged her inside. "We were afraid you were Mr. Lind."

Mina grimaced. "I don't want to be mistaken for that man." Stepping to the bed, she addressed Aunt Caroline. "I know it ain't my place to tell you what to do, but it seem like if Missy and I was to spend the night with you . . . the three of us together might discourage Mr. Lind from tryin' anything again."

A slow smile spread across Aunt Caroline's face. "I'm sure Abby and I will sleep better with you here, though where you'll sleep—" Her voice turned apologetic.

Mina chuckled. "Don't worry none 'bout me, Missus. I done spent more years sleepin' on the floor than any place else. I'll do just fine."

Aunt Caroline pushed herself up onto the pillows. "Has Abby told you I'm able to walk now?"

"She did, and—"

A knock on the door stilled Mina's voice. Without hesitation, she helped Aunt Caroline slide under the sheet before she sat on the chair.

"Who's there?" I called, hoping my voice sounded natural.

"Mr. Lind." He tried the knob. "Why's the door locked?"

A quick look showed Aunt Caroline feigning sleep and Mina trying to arrange her face in a calm expression. "Just a minute," I called. At Mina's nod, I went to the door and unlocked it.

Mr. Lind's face wore an angry scowl. "I don't take kindly to having to ask permission to enter my wife's room."

I made a point of meeting his gaze and slipped the key into my pocket. "Mistress Lind is so upset she asked me to keep the door locked."

He opened his mouth to speak, but when he saw Mina sitting on the chair next to his wife, it snapped shut.

"Afternoon, Mr. Lind," Mina greeted in a low, drawling voice.

Ignoring Mina, he walked to the bed. "What's wrong with my wife?"

"The noise last night has left her much agitated," I repeated.

He shot me an annoyed look. "I should think so. I've never heard such screaming and carrying on . . . all because of your silly nightmare."

"You know it wasn't a nightmare."

The tone of my voice and my steady gaze brought a flush to his face. "I—"

Aunt Caroline's whimper and restless movement interrupted him.

I leaned across the bed and touched her cheek. "It's all right," I soothed. Giving Mr. Lind a quick glance, I added, "She's been like this since last night."

"That's why Missy asked me to come have a look at her," Mina added, her large black hand holding Aunt Caroline's thin white one. "I be stayin' the night so two of us kin look after the missus real good."

Mr. Lind turned his frowning gaze on me. "I thought you said you'd increased her laudanum."

"I have . . . but with the heat—" I went to the basin and dipped a cloth into the tepid water. Turning, I saw his eyes narrow in concentration as he looked at his wife. I wanted to thrust the damp cloth over her face, but I could only dab at her brow and cheeks and fervently pray he hadn't noticed her healthier appearance.

Aunt Caroline gave a little sigh.

"Me and Missy's gonna take good care of you," Mina said.

"Make sure you do. I have far too much on my mind to be distracted by a—" After shooting me an angry look, he turned on his heels and went to the door. Opening it, he looked back at Mina. "I'll be dining with friends this evening."

Mina's turbaned head nodded.

Her silence seemed to anger him more. "You do remember that you were hired to be my cook, not my wife's nursemaid, don't you?"

She nodded again. "I know my duties, Mr. Lind."

"Then see that you don't neglect them."

"Yes, sir."

Then his gaze locked on mine, the icy glint in his narrow gray eyes making me draw in a quick breath. For a second, I couldn't look away, held like a fear-frozen rabbit pinned by the gaze of a crouching wolf. Reaching deep inside for strength, I lifted my chin and ended the terrible moment.

No one moved or spoke until Mr. Lind closed the door behind him. That same strength sent me across the room on unsteady legs. I leaned my head against the door and listened until I finally heard the faint whisper of retreating footsteps.

"Mercy," Mina breathed after I relocked the door. Beads of sweat glistened on her dark skin, and her face lost its calm expression.

"Are you all right?" Aunt Caroline asked.

"Yes." I looked long at them from across the room. "He's onto our masquerade."

Aunt Caroline nodded. "It was only a matter of time." She paused and shook her head. "We've been so careful. How did he guess?"

"He looked at you . . . really looked at you. Instead of gauntness, he saw color and fullness." I let out a frustrated sigh. "Why couldn't he have waited one more day?"

Mina shivered. "His cold eyes like to froze me to the chair." She shivered again. "What he goin' to do next, you think?"

Aunt Caroline's head stirred on the pillows. "Before he makes a decision, he'll think on it. That's his way." Pushing herself to a sitting position, she went on. "Then he'll kill me."

Mina gasped, and I hugged myself against an icy shudder.

"Why he didn't kill me as soon as Dr. Barnes agreed to give me laudanum, I don't know. Every day I've lived since then, I've been a threat to him. He can't help but wonder when my garbled talk might make someone suspect. With me dead . . . the threat is gone."

"Perhaps Dr. Barnes coming to bleed you so often was a blessing in disguise," I ventured. "Maybe he feared the doctor might suspect."

"Perhaps . . . though it galls me to give credit to that detestable man. But now—" The look she gave me was steady. "It won't be long before he realizes I've told you everything."

Turning to Mina, who sat with her large hands tightly clasped in the lap of her apron, she went on. "He'll likely think I've told you too." Something like satisfaction crossed her face. "Having to explain the deaths of three people will be much harder than one."

"It won't be easy," Mina agreed in a surprisingly calm tone.

Even so, hearing Aunt Caroline speak of our deaths sent a chill down my back. "We must pray to be gone before he tries."

"Does your friend know we must leave tomorrow afternoon?" Aunt Caroline asked.

"He does."

"What would I do without such loyal friends?"

"We want you away from that no-good husband of yours the same as you do," Mina said.

Though I knew Mr. Lind was clever and far more practiced in scheming than we were, I also realized that the three of us were not without talents too. Wasn't Aunt Caroline freed from laudanum's debilitating grasp and growing strong again? Hadn't I thwarted Joseph's unwanted advances and discovered the location of the ammunition? Mina wasn't without strength and ability either. As the three of us held hands, the warmth of our sisterhood dispelled the cold threat that had entered the room with Mr. Lind.

Dusk was coming on, and for the first time in days, a cooling breeze stirred the air. Eager to take advantage of it, I joined Aunt Caroline at the window. Leaning on the sill, I looked out at the fading light that tinged the sky with soft orange and peach and pink. The scent of early roses hung on the air, and the soft colors pooling in the western sky soothed my frayed nerves.

I closed my eyes and lifted my face to the breeze, letting it and the beauty wash over me.

"How lovely," Aunt Caroline murmured. "And a needful reminder that beauty and goodness still reign in the world."

"Yes." Before I could say more, a knock came on the door. My heart leaped, and my voice was unsteady when I responded. "Who is it?"

"It's Mina."

I was aware that her knock had sent Aunt Caroline hurrying back to bed. When I unlocked the door, Mina held a brown leather trunk.

"Thought while the servants be eatin' in the kitchen, I'd fetch your trunk from the attic," Mina explained.

"Thank you, Mina. I was wondering how to get it without arousing anyone's suspicions," Aunt Caroline said.

Mina carried the trunk to the wardrobe. "Thought we best get yer clothes packed tonight while Mr. Lind be gone." After setting the trunk on the floor, she turned to me. "Ezra say someone want to talk to you, Missy." Her gaze held mine, and she gave a smiling nod.

My heart lifted as it always did when I anticipated seeing Gideon.

"Missy." Mina's voice held warning as I started for the door. "Everyone still in the kitchen. Best if you use the side door."

"Thank you." I handed her the key. Mr. Lind wasn't the only who shouldn't see the leather trunk.

My feet fairly flew down the stairs while I straightened my cap and brushed at my apron. I stopped at the back gate to catch my breath and peer through the shadowy twilight. Seeing a familiar figure move from the oak tree, I hurried through the gate.

When strong arms pulled me close and eager lips met mine, thoughts of Joseph Lind receded until there was only Gideon and me.

"That was a very nice greeting," he whispered.

I burrowed my head more firmly into the warmth and strength of his shoulder, letting my happiness at being with him wash away the knots and sharp edges of fear.

"Come," he whispered.

I admired his rugged profile and thick hair pulled back in a queue as we walked to the stable. No wig for Gideon Whitlock, not for Sabbath meeting nor for an assignation in a stable with the woman he loved. He was who he was, genuine and without pretense, except when he engaged in spying. Having him at my side lifted a heavy burden from my shoulders.

As soon as we were inside the stable, he turned me to face him and took both of my hands in his. "Jake said there was trouble with Joseph Lind . . . that he knows what you've done."

I nodded. "I've known all along that one day he'd notice the improvement in Aunt Caroline's health. Though he didn't let on that he actually knew, the terrible way he looked at me—" Despite my resolve to be brave, shivers ran across my shoulders. "There was menace there . . . his eyes threatening and cold. All of us felt it. There's no doubt he knows. Thank God we're leaving tomorrow."

Gideon's hands tightened on mine. "Everything is arranged," he assured me. "Mina will dose Mr. Gridley's cider with laudanum when she takes his noon meal to him. . . enough so he'll sleep long and hard while Jake gets the horses and carriage ready." His voice, like his touch, conveyed confidence and assurance. "Then we only have to wait for the servants to leave and for Mr. Lind to take his usual Sabbath afternoon nap . . . one made deeper by the laudanum Mina will put in his wine."

"Were you able to get the pass for the blockade?"

He nodded. "It's one of my reasons for coming." I heard the rustle of paper as he reached into his vest. "This should get you and Mistress Lind safely through the blockade . . . Jake, Mina, and Ezra too. Since I'm closely watched, it will be best if the pass is with you."

I took the pass and slipped it into my pocket. "What about getting the ammunition out of Boston?"

"There are rebel sympathizers still in town. If need be, we can smuggle it out shot by shot, powder sack by powder sack, just as a cannon was taken apart and smuggled out piece by piece last week."

I looked up at him in amazement. Besides being a lawyer involved in spying, it seemed that dismantling a cannon and obtaining counterfeit passes were also part of his occupation.

"Why your puzzled expression?"

"I've realized again that you're a man of many talents and that there is still much I don't know about you."

Gideon chuckled and pulled me close. "My hope is that after you come to know me better, you won't decide I'm no more interesting than a post."

"Never that." I laughed.

His expression sobered. "Tomorrow, as soon as you're clear of Boston, make straight for the patriot army headquarters. Tell them about the powder and balls and that we'll smuggle them out as soon as we can."

"I thought to tell Father's friend George Smyth in Cambridge. He's in constant touch with the army and should be reliable."

Before Gideon could respond, an owl hooted in the trees, closely followed by a dog bark. Gideon's head lifted, and he stiffened. "I must go."

"So soon?" I was sorry as soon as the words left my mouth. Gideon needed someone who was strong and capable, not a clingy woman who wept at the mention of good-bye. Straightening my shoulders, I smiled up at him. "Keep safe."

"You too. I won't rest easy until you're safely away from Boston."

He kissed me then, long and hungry as if he couldn't get enough of me. After a moment, he pulled away. "I plan to post a letter tonight to Colonel Paxman saying Joseph Lind is selling ammunition to the rebels. Trying to prove it isn't true should thwart Mr. Lind even more."

"What a clever idea."

"My aim is to cause as much grief for him as I can."

We moved from the stable saturated with the smell and soft sounds of horses and stepped out where the night sky seemed spread with a quilt embroidered with dozens of early stars. Gideon walked with me to the back gate.

"Wait," Gideon whispered when I opened it.

I turned to look at his tall frame silhouetted against the starlit sky.

"Whatever you do tomorrow, don't let Mr. Lind separate you from his wife. No matter what happens, stay together."

I nodded and went through the gate. "Good night, and God bless, sweet Abby," he whispered after me.

Aunt Caroline's trunk was packed and standing on end behind the closed door of her wardrobe when I returned. Tired as Mina and Aunt Caroline were, their pleasure at what they'd accomplished mingled with the heat. With Gideon's reassuring words still echoing in my mind and the pass inside my pocket, I felt a renewed confidence too.

"Look," I said, retrieving it from my pocket. "'Tis our pass to get through the blockade and out of Boston."

Together we scanned the words and the official-looking stamp and seal, our spirits rising as we did. On that note, we prepared for sleep. I agreed with Aunt Caroline when she suggested that I share her bed so Mina could sleep on the settle. Uncomfortable from the heat, I chose to sleep on top of the bed clothes, but Aunt Caroline was so thin, she still required a sheet. As for Mina, after wishing us good night, she simply removed her colorful turban and dress and shoes and curled her long frame onto the padded settle.

The minutes slowly slipped by, none of us sleeping, no one talking. In the darkness, some of the bravado that had carried me through the past hour was replaced by uncertainty and questions. Wasn't Joseph Lind a powerful citizen of Boston? Who knew what he might do when he returned home tonight? Or tomorrow? The locked bedroom door was only a door, after all, a door that could be broken down if he put his mind and shoulder to it.

He won't, I assured myself. *Not after last night. Besides, he knows Mina and Aunt Caroline are here.*

Not liking the path my thought had taken, I turned my mind to the small successes that had come: Mina staying with us, our trunks packed and waiting, the pass in my pocket. And, of course, Jake and Gideon.

Slowly, I began to relax, the chirp of crickets and the distant croak of frogs carrying to me on a rising breeze. Hopefully it would blow the oppressing heat inland as it brought in cooler air from the ocean.

The sudden sound of footsteps jerked my mind away from the weather. All of my senses gathered in my ears as I listened to the creak of the stairs, then footsteps moving along the corridor. Though I felt confident Mr. Lind wouldn't try the door, the passing seconds stretched as if pulled by the hands of the ticking clock. After a pause, his steps moved on.

I felt a slight movement as Aunt Caroline reached across the bed and took my hand. "He's playing a game of nerves," she whispered, "but we won't join him."

We lay in a companionable silence, and then slowly and surprisingly, I fell asleep.

Chapter Thirty

I AWOKE THE NEXT MORNING with nerves coiled and ready for action. Deep inside, something warned that although today was the day I was leaving, many things could still go wrong. Unable to lie still, I eased myself to the edge of the bed.

"Good, you're awake," Aunt Caroline said.

Seeing her watchful eyes and slight frown, I asked, "Are you all right?"

"Yes, though I haven't been able to sleep since sunup. I wish we could be gone this very minute, yet part of me—" She paused and sighed. "Boston has been my home for more than forty years."

"Maybe someday you can come back."

"Yes, though if Joseph is still here . . ." She shook her head.

"Things will work out," I said.

"It's the Lord's day," Mina said from across the room. "Things allus go good on the Lord's day." Unlike Aunt Caroline and me, she was already putting on her shoes and reaching to rewind her multicolored turban around her kinky black hair.

Watching her, Aunt Caroline spoke. "Before you go down to the kitchen, would you offer a word of prayer for us, Mina? I have a strong feeling we'll need the Lord's help today."

Mina didn't seem surprised by the request. "I'd be right glad to, Missus." She lifted her hands toward the ceiling and, in a hushed, mellow voice, began to pray.

I'd never heard such a prayer before or one given with so much trust and feeling. It sounded as if God were Mina's best friend and that she talked to Him several times a day. I knew I wouldn't remember all she said, but the feelings that washed over me would stay for as long as I lived. It felt like God was standing with us, His love and warmth encircling the room, its rays telling us He was there to help.

After finishing our cold Sabbath breakfast, an uneasy, edgy feeling came over me. Putting a finger to my lips and taking the spoon from Aunt Caroline's fingers, I waited with quickened pulse, listening for I knew not what. The act was no sooner done than a knock sounded, and Joseph Lind walked into the room. His eyes raked the walls as if to assure himself there were only two of us—me sitting on the chair holding the bowl and Aunt Caroline propped on the pillows as if waiting for another bite.

"Breakfasting, I see," he said in a genial voice. The expression on his face matched his voice, a smile stretching its contours but stopping before it reached his eyes. Not waiting for an answer, he went on. "How are you feeling, Caroline?"

That he addressed his wife instead of me told me again that he was much more practiced at playing games than we were.

"I . . . I'm not sure," she said in a faltering voice. She reached for my free hand, her grip like a frightened child's. "I'm afraid . . . so very afraid," she went on, her voice turning high and thin like it might become hysterical at any moment.

Mr. Lind gave me an amused glance as if we were playing a game with a petulant child. His voice when he spoke, however, was soothing. "There, there, my dear. There's no reason for you to be afraid. I'm only going to take Abigail to Sabbath meeting."

I lifted my head and glared at him. "After Friday night, I'm not going anywhere with you."

Surprise momentarily flashed across his face. Then his gray eyes narrowed and turned cold. Acting as if I hadn't spoken, he said, "We won't be gone long, only . . ."

The rest of what he said was drowned out by Aunt Caroline's high-pitched voice. "Don't take her! You can't take her!" She thrashed around on the bed, holding up her hands as if to fend off blows, her words soaring to high-piercing screams.

Joseph cursed. "Get the laudanum!" he ordered. "Give her another dose of medicine!"

"But, sir . . ." My thoughts whirled so fast it was difficult for me to catch them. Had the tension of the last few days caused Aunt Caroline to snap, or was she playacting?

"Get the laudanum!" he repeated. Fear edged his voice, and I realized he was afraid of what his wife might say next—about Dr. Williams—about the deed and money.

I rushed to the shelf and grabbed the laudanum bottle and wine glass, my hands unsteady and my mind racing with half-formed thoughts. Shielding the wine glass with my body so he couldn't see, I poured a drop or two of the laudanum syrup into the glass.

Her incoherent words and sobs and occasional shrieks continued, and I was aware on some level that Mina had rushed into the room.

Help me, I prayed as I walked to the bed where Aunt Caroline thrashed about. Should I drop the glass or spill it and blame the mishap on her?

Before I could do either, Aunt Caroline dashed the fragile container from my hand, the sound of breaking glass joined by her violent, "No!"

My gaze flew to the shards of glass scattered on the floor, then to Aunt Caroline's contorted face.

"Get out!" she screamed. Her gaze fastened on Joseph, then flitted to those by the door. "All of you . . . get out!"

I think it was only then that Joseph realized Mina and the maids had rushed into the room. After throwing his wife a hateful look, he turned his rage on me. "Get her under control! I don't care how you do it. Just get her under control!" He moved away from the bed. "I'm going to send Briggs for Dr. Barnes." He hurled this last over his shoulder as he stalked to the door. Aunt Caroline shrieked when she heard the doctor's name.

Mina recovered more quickly than I. She stood solidly at the door while the housekeeper and maids scattered. "There's no need to send for no doctor, Mr. Lind. Me and Missy can get her to settle down. Just give us a few minutes."

"Then do it!" Joseph spat. "I don't want to hear another scream or word out of her."

He was scarcely out of the room before Mina closed the door and locked it. Even so, Aunt Caroline continued to moan and cry and move restlessly about on the bed. Was she truly hysterical?

Then her eyes met mine, clear and lucid and filled with satisfaction. "I'm all right," she whispered before giving another softer but incoherent cry.

"There, there," Mina said in a voice loud enough for Mr. Lind to hear if he listened at the door. "Don't stop all at once," she whispered.

Aunt Caroline nodded and resumed her performance, her cries slowly becoming less frequent and terrified. After a few minutes, they stopped altogether. Perspiration shone on her forehead, and she looked exhausted when she finally relaxed onto the pillows with a sigh.

"Mercy," Mina said, laughter brimming through her voice. "I can't remember when I heard such carryin' on."

"Nor I," I agreed. An impulse to giggle washed over me, but I pushed it away, fearing if the giggles started, they would turn to hysterics that would put Aunt Caroline's performance to shame. My nerves were stretched so tight I wondered that they didn't break, and from the looks of Mina and Aunt Caroline, they suffered in a similar fashion.

Mina looked at the broken glass. "Better get this cleaned up."

"I'm sorry for the extra work," Aunt Caroline said. "It was the only thing I could think to do."

"Don't you go bein' sorry. After what you did, I think Mr. Lind won't be so sure you're better."

"That's what I hoped . . . that and to get Joseph to stop badgering Abigail about going with him to meeting."

I gave an involuntary shudder. "I doubt his plan was to take me to meeting. Did you see his rage when I refused to go with him?"

After warning me to take care not to step on the broken glass, Mina went to get rags and a broom to clean the floor. When it and the bed had been put back to rights, Aunt Caroline walked across the room to the settle. Her steps weren't as sure and quick as they'd been earlier, and I knew the pretended hysteria had sapped much of her strength.

I looked out on the stable yard and was rewarded a short time later by the sight of Jake driving the carriage around to the front of the house.

The two hours while Mr. Lind was away seemed to drag on endlessly. While Aunt Caroline napped, I occupied myself as best I could. What I did, I can't remember, only that all of me clamored to be gone. My heightened senses jumped and stuttered each time I heard an unexpected sound, and I couldn't sit still for more than two seconds.

Finally, I heard the carriage enter the stable yard and Jake call for Ezra to help him remove the harness. At the same time, I heard Joseph's steps on the stairs. He was back!

Sitting tensely on the chair, I heard his approaching footsteps. My heart jerked when they stopped at the locked door. After a pause, he moved on. Aunt Caroline's eyes flew open. Though she'd been napping, some part of her had been listening too.

Later, when Mina came with our lunch tray, her face wore a pleased expression. "The Lord surely be watching over us. After meeting, Mr. Lind told Jake he want the carriage brought 'round at one o'clock."

I stared at her in disbelief. "But how. . . ?"

Mina held up her hand. "Wait till you hear what Jake done." Her face broke into a grin. "There's times my Jake be right clever. Instead of doin' what Mr. Lind said, he sent me to tell him that when he unhitched the horses, he found a crack in the front wheel. Said it's not safe to drive but that he kin have his horse ready and waitin' instead."

"What did Joseph say?" Aunt Caroline asked.

"He scowled at me like I was the one what broke the wheel. Then he say 'All right' and for Jake not to be late bringin' the horse 'round."

Unease flicked through Aunt Caroline's eyes, but her words were firm when she spoke. "God is still with us. He will not fail us." Looking at Mina, she asked, "Did you put laudanum in Joseph's port?"

"Soon as I heard he was leavin', I thought it wouldn't be wise."

"Good." Seeming to relax, she added. "Thank Jake for his cleverness. Now, if Joseph will leave when he said he would and the servants leave too—"

Mina smiled at the mention of Jake's cleverness and smiled again when Aunt Caroline mentioned the servants. "Alice and Hettie left as soon as they finished eatin'."

"How about Mr. Gridley?" I asked.

"Jake say he drank deep of the cider. Just to make sure, Jake offered him some rum with laudanum too." Her lips lifted. "By now, he be sleepin' like a baby."

After we'd eaten, I took the lunch tray to the silent kitchen. When I returned, Aunt Caroline was sitting at the window watching the stable. The brightness of her eyes as she nervously pleated her nightgown told me of her restlessness.

I bent and kissed her cheek. "Everyone has gone." Looking past her, I saw Jake and Ezra readying the horses and carriage.

"Now I can get dressed." Excitement lifted Aunt Caroline's voice as she unbuttoned her nightgown. "It will feel good to wear something besides nightgowns again."

In no time, she'd donned a chemise and the petticoat with coins and her jewelry sewn into the hem. Nerves made my fingers clumsy, and we giggled like girls as I cinched in the ties and helped her dress.

Retrieving my own coin-laden petticoat out of Aunt Caroline's wardrobe, I went to my room to don it and retrieve my trunk. I was conscious of the weight of the coins and the bulk of the trunk as I walked along the corridor. Mina met me, her breathing quick from rushing up the stairs.

"Jake say hurry . . . that Mr. Whitlock is here." Hardly pausing for breath, she took Aunt Caroline's trunk out of the wardrobe and carried it to the door.

"Lie down and try to rest," I told Aunt Caroline. "Jake or Gideon will come in a few minutes to help you down the stairs."

Though she nodded and settled onto the bed, I doubted she'd be able to rest.

Nerves turned my hands damp, and my stomach fluttered each time I thought of what we were doing. Since the back stairs were steep and narrow, I took the front ones. When I reached the bottom I set down my trunk and ran into the library to grab the false book containing Dr. William's coins. Urgency pushed me as I lifted the trunk, quickening my steps and shouting for me to hurry. Hurry!

I stopped to catch my breath when I reached the backyard. Mina was halfway to the gate with the larger trunk, the determined set of her wide shoulders and her firm steps encouraging me to follow.

I hadn't taken more than a few more steps when icy fingers of dread slid down my back. I'd left Aunt Caroline alone, something Gideon had warned me not to do. Seeing that Mina was going through the gate, I pushed the feeling aside and hurried faster. With each step, the feeling grew stronger. Stop! Go back!

Setting down the trunk, I lifted my heavy skirts and ran back to the house, pausing in the kitchen and again at the bottom of the stairs to listen. The only sound was my frightened breathing. Urgency impelled me up the stairs, feet flying, my heart racing.

When I reached the top, I threw a quick look down the corridor and saw that the bedroom door I'd left open was now closed. A muffled cry sent my blood pounding and my feet flying. In a trice, I was there, the heavy hammer of my heart and shaky breathing blotting out sound as I thrust the door open and saw Joseph Lind holding a pillow over his wife's face. Some part of me realized that she no longer moaned and that her shod feet moved feebly atop the coverlet.

Horror sent me running to the wash stand, where I grabbed the filled water ewer and brought it down hard on the back of Joseph's bent head. Piercing screams mingled with his startled gasp as he fell across his wife. Panic lent me strength to shove him aside and snatch the pillow from her face. Only then did I realize the screams were mine and that Aunt Caroline's eyes were closed and her face had no color.

For a moment, it was as if I was caught in a nightmare, unable to move or speak as I watched her draw in a long quivering breath, cough, then let it out and gasp hungrily for more air.

"Thank God!" I cried as color returned to her cheeks.

An unintelligible sound jerked my gaze to Mr. Lind, whose white wig had been knocked awry by my blow. Blood oozed from a cut on the back of his shaved head. As if sensing my attention, he lifted his face and looked around with an unfocused gaze. Giving a groan, his head fell back onto Aunt Caroline.

"Quick," I said, grabbing his shoulders and lifting him long enough for Aunt Caroline to free herself and slide off the bed. "Run!" I cried when he lifted his head again.

The anger and recognition in his gray eyes sent me to grab the fireplace poker. When I turned and faced him, he'd pushed himself off the bed and was standing. Although his stance was unsteady, the hatred and fierceness of his expression made me catch my breath.

"You!" he cried, the word flung at me like a vile curse.

When I raised the poker, he flung himself at me, the force of his body almost toppling me as his hands grappled to wrest the poker away from me.

"Beast!" Aunt Caroline cried. Seeming to come from nowhere, she grabbed his arms and kicked his legs. Her strength, though meager, was enough to momentarily distract him. Flinging her aside like an annoying puppy, his grip on the poker had lessened enough for me to pull it away.

I hastily swung the poker, but it glanced off his shoulder. Before I could swing it again, Joseph was at me, his hands grabbing and twisting the metal rod, the two of us locked as we grappled, his mouth a grimace and his eyes filled with hate. Hard as I tried, I could feel my hold weaken.

In the confusion, Gideon burst through the doorway. Sensing danger, Joseph let go of the poker and spun to face him, snatching a pistol from his boot and aiming.

I brought the poker down hard on his head just as the pistol cracked, the sound deafening and the smoke an acrid cloud. As Joseph crumpled to the floor, Gideon staggered and grabbed his shoulder.

The poker slid from my fingers as I stepped over Joseph and hurried to Gideon. Horror tightened my throat as blood stained his vest and seeped between his fingers.

"Gideon . . ." I ran for the chair and helped him into it. Then I snatched the towel from the washstand and pressed it hard against the growing circle of blood on his brown vest.

With my mind and heart wholly taken with Gideon, I scarcely noticed when Jake and Mina rushed into the room to find Aunt Caroline standing over Joseph with the poker in her hands. Jake went to Aunt Caroline and Joseph while Mina stayed with Gideon and me.

"Mercy," she breathed when she saw his white face and the crimson saturating his clothes.

"I'm all right," he said, but his voice had lost its vigor, and lines of pain etched the corners of his mouth.

"We gotta cut his clothes away so we kin get a better look at his wound," Mina said.

While I continued to press on his shoulder, Mina hurried to find scissors. Seeing the bloodstain grow, I pressed harder with shaking hands. If only Prudence Blood were here to stop the bleeding and tell me what to do.

When Mina cut away Gideon's shirt and vest, I saw he also bled from a wound on the back of his shoulder. My insides quivered when I saw the larger, jagged hole torn by the ball as it had exited his body.

"Good," Mina said when she saw it. "That mean he won't need no doctor to dig out the ball." She gave a worried shake of her head. "Somehow we gotta stop this bleedin'."

The minutes passed in a haze of urgency and near panic. Using the piece of shirt Mina had cut away, I pressed hard on the larger wound while continuing to put pressure on the front one. *Stop . . . please stop the bleeding!*

I bent and laid my cheek against Gideon. "You're going to be all right, my love," I whispered, knowing the words were meant as much for me as for him.

Scissors in hand, Mina cut and tore long strips of the sheet to make bandages and pads for Gideon. Using one of the bandage strips, I tied it around the thick pad Mina held to the wound on the back of Gideon's shoulder. Now that the worst of the bleeding was slacking, I began to have hope.

While I'd been busy with Gideon, strips of sheeting had been used to truss Joseph's hands and feet and tie him to the bedposts. Aunt Caroline and Mina had also dosed him with laudanum, Mina holding his nose while his wife administered it.

When I looked at Mr. Lind's pale face, he no longer seemed a menace. Eyelids covered his cold, gray eyes, and his slack expression held no trace of hatred and anger. Then, as if to prove me wrong, his head lolled to one side, and I heard him curse in a harsh voice.

Turning away, I again laid my head against Gideon's cheek. "I love you," I whispered, wishing I could take him in my arms and make him safe.

He took my hand and kissed it, his lips running across each finger in a gentle caress.

Aunt Caroline walked over to Gideon. "I'm so sorry my husband shot you. You've been so good to help."

"I wanted . . . to help," he answered in a failing voice.

Mina laid her hand on Gideon's shoulder. "While Missy look after you, I'll get some of Mr. Lind's clothes for you to wear." She studied Gideon, who looked like he should be lying on the bed instead of Joseph. "You know you gotta leave Boston with Mistress Lind and Missy, don't you? Me and Jake and Ezra gotta leave too. Ain't safe for none of us to stay here no more."

That Gideon didn't argue told me of his weakness.

Ten minutes later, after Mina and I had helped Gideon into Mr. Lind's shirt and coat, the five of us left the bedroom, Aunt Caroline leaning heavily on Mina's sturdy arm, Gideon leaning weakly on Jake and me. Urgency stalked us out to the stable yard, and we were at last leaving Boston.

Chapter Thirty-One

THE LIND CARRIAGE ROLLED OUT of the stable yard with Jake driving the horses and Ezra perched on the seat beside him. Inside, Aunt Caroline and Mina sat together on one seat while Gideon and I sat on the facing one. Tied by a rope to the carriage, Dolly followed behind.

Aunt Caroline sighed in relief when her home was no longer in sight. "Now I can begin to take control of my life again." She smiled across at me. "Though my future may be uncertain, it will be mine to do with as I please. Not as Joseph pleases . . . not as the laudanum demands."

"Yes," I agreed. Part of me rejoiced that we were finally on our way and that Gideon was going with us, but his pasty face and the pricks of moisture on his brow diminished my pleasure. More than that, we still had to get safely past the redcoats at the barricade.

My silent prayers were fervent as the carriage proceeded at a decorous Sabbath pace along Melbourne Street. Although the pass looked genuine, the number of passengers listed was three, not four. Thankfully Gideon had thought to include Jake and Ezra as driver and groom.

"I will tell the soldiers Mr. Whitlock is my nephew and that he's suddenly been stricken with . . . typhus . . . yes, typhus," Aunt Caroline said after scanning the pass. She looked with pity and concern at Gideon, who sat with closed eyes and his head lolling on the back of the uphol-stered seat. "There's no doubt he looks very unwell."

I tightened my hold on Gideon's hand. *Not only unwell*, I thought, *but clinging to life with only prayers and determination.* Dread and fear of losing him clouded my thinking, and the sights outside the carriage window were no more than half-formed images. Since it was the Sabbath, all the shops were closed and only an occasional carriage passed us. In place of pleasure, a lump of fear sat heavy in my stomach, and shivers of worry flitted through my insides.

All too soon, we were on Orange Street, and the blockade loomed just ahead. Would the guards ask us to get out so they could search the carriage? What about the coins sewn into our petticoats and the fake book between my feet? Tucking one of Aunt Caroline's shawls more firmly around Gideon and my blood-stained skirt, I lifted my shoulders. Despite Aunt Caroline's brave words, tension tightened her features. Even Mina, who sat straight and solid on the seat beside her, looked worried.

The carriage began to slow, and I heard someone order Jake to stop. Two armed redcoats approached on either side of the carriage. Although I strove for calmness, my heart jerked when the soldier on my side opened the door.

"I need to see your pass," he said in a brusque voice. His ruddy face was stern, and his gaze seemed not to miss a thing.

"Of course," Aunt Caroline replied. Where the sudden strength in her voice had come from, I didn't know, nor the steady hand that handed the guard the pass. "I hope this won't take long. As you can see, my nephew is not well."

The door on the other side of the carriage opened in time for the second soldier to hear.

The first guard's eyes flicked from the pass to Gideon. "There's no male name listed on this pass."

"That's true," Aunt Caroline acknowledged. "When I applied for the pass, I didn't know my nephew would take so violently ill."

The guard's shoulders lifted. "Just the same, if his name ain't on the pass, he can't go through."

Aunt Caroline's shoulders lifted as well. "Perhaps you don't know I am the wife of Joseph Lind, one of Boston's leading citizens. He is also a close friend of General Gage and his aides. Indeed, it was my husband who bade me take my poor nephew out of Boston post haste." She paused and gave Gideon a pitying glance. "But an hour past, our doctor diagnosed my nephew with typhus. Fearing an epidemic in Boston, the doctor ordered that he be taken into the countryside at once."

The second soldier quickly pulled his head out of the carriage and slammed the door.

The older redcoat wasn't as quick to panic. Instead, he turned his full attention to Gideon, his expression unreadable, his jaw jutting stubbornly.

My mouth went dry, and my heart drummed so hard against my ribs I feared he'd notice. Gideon sat without moving, eyes closed and beads of perspiration glistening on his sallow face. Then, without warning, his head slumped onto my shoulder, and he gave a low moan.

"No!" I cried.

My anguished cry joined that of the younger soldier. "Let 'em through, Sergeant, before we catch what he's got and die too!"

I frantically searched for a pulse and pleaded with Gideon not to die. I was only half aware when the sergeant slammed the door and yelled at Jake to move on.

As the coach lurched forward, Gideon weakly squeezed my hand. "I'm all . . . right," he said faintly.

Tears of relief slid down my cheeks as I stifled my sobs. I wanted to cry on his shoulder, but when his head continued to loll on mine, I realized how badly the loss of blood had eaten at his strength. Was he bleeding again? Should we stop when we were off the peninsula road to check?

"You sure you all right?" Mina asked.

Gideon nodded weakly.

"Thank the Lord." She sighed.

"Amen," Aunt Caroline said. The woman who'd spoken with such authority to the sergeant had wilted like a flower without water. The trauma of the past hour had taken a great toll on her as well.

My anger flared at what Joseph Lind had done to his wife and Gideon.

Jake kept the horses at a steady pace along the peninsula road, but when we reached the mainland, he urged them faster. Less than an hour later, after stopping for directions, he brought the carriage to a halt in front of George Smyth's home. Carefully easing Gideon's head off my shoulder, I hurried to the front door of the house. As I looked back, I saw Mina bending over Gideon to check for more bleeding.

Mr. Smyth was astonished by the information I gave him, hastily jotting down facts and staring in amazement when he saw the numerous coins inside the false book. Five minutes later, I excused myself to return to the carriage.

"God bless you, Mistress Abigail. What you've done is not only brave, but it will greatly aid the thousands who've gathered here to fight for freedom." He shook his head in amazement. "All that powder and balls."

"That's my hope. Did you and Father receive the letter I sent about Noddle's and Hog islands?"

"We did and steps are being taken."

"Good. Should you see Father, give him my love and tell him I'm on my way back home." I dropped him a curtsey and left.

As soon as I was inside the carriage, I asked, "How is he? Is he bleeding more?"

"Some," Mina said. Her voice told me she was worried.

"I'll ask Mistress Smyth for directions to a doctor."

Gideon's voice stopped me. "No . . . Cambridge . . . isn't safe."

"But—" I began.

His eyes opened, their look dissolving any thought of arguing. Was it pursuit by Colonel Paxman or Joseph Lind he feared? Though we took great risk with his life, we continued on.

★

The long ride to Mayfield was fraught with worry. Not only did Gideon look as if his hold on life was tenuous, but Aunt Caroline slept as if all strength had left her.

Once we left Cambridge, I repositioned myself so Gideon could rest more comfortably. My heart flinched each time the ruts in the road caused the carriage to bump and jar. Afternoon gave way to evening, and the sunset slowly faded into dusk. Jake stopped twice at taverns to water and rest the horses. After he lit the two driving lanterns on the front of the carriage, we were on our way once more.

Aunt Caroline immediately fell asleep again, and Mina's soft rumble told me she slept too. My attention was wrapped up in a nighttime vigil over Gideon. Gently resting my cheek against his forehead, I willed my strength into him. As the slow hours of the night slipped by, I remained alert to ward off the hovering menace of death.

The trip between Cambridge and Mayfield normally took the better part of a day, but to travel half of it in darkness made our journey even longer, especially when Jake was unfamiliar with the road.

Finally, after I'd given more directions, Jake turned the carriage into the lane to Stowell farm.

When we reached the barn, I eased Gideon down onto the carriage seat and climbed outside. The dark outline of house rose into the pale light of a new moon. Opening the back gate, I hurried toward the house, the dips and rise of the yard so familiar I traveled them as if it were noonday. Even so, the heaviness of my coin-laden petticoat made my steps awkward.

"Mother!" I called, pounding on the bolted kitchen door. "It's Abigail!" After knocking and calling the second time, I saw the glimmer of an approaching candle and heard her voice.

"Abigail . . . is it truly you?"

Hearing my reply, she unbolted the door and threw her arms around me. Bethy was there too, her arms wrapped around my waist, her happy cries blending with mine. Good as it felt to have them close, my thoughts remained on Gideon. "I brought Aunt Caroline and a friend with me. My friend was shot. He's bleeding and unconscious. I must take him to Mistress Blood."

"Friend . . . bleeding?"

"I must hurry. Aunt Caroline and Mina will explain."

As I returned to the carriage, I saw Ben running from the laundry house, his mother and Jane following. Minutes later, Jake and Mina had helped Aunt Caroline into the house.

After slipping off my heavy petticoat and charging Ezra to keep Gideon firmly on the carriage seat, I climbed up beside Jake to direct him to Prudence Blood's cottage.

Only Jake's skill got us there so quickly. When we reached the end of Mistress Blood's rutted lane, I called to her. Her cats came at a run to meet the carriage, and the old woman met me at the front door with a lighted candle in her hand.

"Mistress Abigail!" she exclaimed, her eyes shining bright and alert in the flickering candlelight. Did the woman never sleep?

It seemed she did, for she went on to explain that not an hour before, she'd dreamed of me. "I saw a carriage coming with a big black man driving it, and inside . . ." She paused and gave me a steady look. "Inside lay a man badly hurt and bleeding and needing my help. With him was a black boy."

I shook my head in wonder as we hurried to the carriage. Jake had the door open before Mistress Blood reached it. He bowed to her as if she were a woman of great consequence, then took her candle and helped her up into the carriage.

I ran to the other door, which Ezra had opened as he'd gotten out. I was inside and sitting on the seat across from Gideon in time to see the old woman peer down at him with the candle in her hand.

"Hmm," she said, after feeling his forehead and checking his pulse. "His heart beats too slowly, but at least it beats."

"Will he be all right?"

Rather than answer, she asked. "Where was he shot?"

"In the shoulder. The ball passed through it. Mina said 'twas a blessing."

"It is." She backed out of the carriage, candlelight casting Gideon's face into changing patterns of light and shadow. "We must get him into the house."

Jake nodded. Despite his strength, it still required Ezra and me to help lift Gideon out of the carriage and into the house. Mistress Blood hurried to light the way, shooing the cats out of our path as she opened and held the door. I wanted to cry out each time we jarred Gideon, but his only response was a low moan.

Mistress Blood led us to a room I'd never seen before. It smelled of stale air, but in the dim candlelight, the bed's blue coverlet, though worn and faded, looked clean and freshly made up as if awaiting our arrival. Hadn't she said she'd seen us in a dream?

Lighting another candle by the bed, she sent me to bring more candles from the kitchen. "We need all the candles we can get."

While Ezra and I held the extra candles, Mistress Blood and Jake gently eased Gideon's arm out of Joseph's coat and shirt. I bit down on my lip when I saw the blood-soaked shirt and bandage. Blood seemed to be everywhere.

The little woman quickly extracted scissors from her apron pocket and cut the blood-saturated bandages and pads away from the wounds. Then she took a folded towel and pressed it against the gaping wound.

Her voice partially covered Gideon's moan. "Yarrow will stop bleeding. Get yarrow leaves and the jug of turpentine from my herb room. There's hot water and linen on the fireplace fender to make poultices. Bring them and the turpentine as quick as you can."

The urgency in her usually placid voice sent me hurrying to the herb room. By the time I returned, Jake had helped her roll Gideon onto his side and was pressing with another towel against the jagged hole on his back.

Gideon lay as if dead, his face the color of chalk.

"Is he . . . ?"

"He's alive," Mistress Blood said, "but he won't last long if we don't get the bleeding stopped. Before we put on the poultices, dampen a cloth with turpentine and clean the wounds."

I tried not to look at the oozing blood, and I flinched when Gideon jerked from the stinging turpentine. I had to steel myself to do the same to the second wound, and it was with relief when I finally covered his torn skin with the warm yarrow poultices. Through it all, Ezra held two candles close, his brown eyes watchful and his round face as stoic and impassive as his father's.

Exhaustion ate at my courage, making me want to flee the room and the sight and smell of so much blood. Instead, I knelt by the bed and laid my cheek against Gideon's. "Don't leave me, Gideon." And in the next breath, "You're going to live!"

The faint sigh of Gideon's breath and the warmth of his skin brought a renewal of hope. Hope grew stronger when I opened my eyes and saw that no new blood had seeped past the poultice.

"It's working."

"Aye . . . but there's still much to do."

After Mistress Blood was sure that the bleeding had truly stopped, she instructed me to hold the wounds closed while she stitched them together with a needle and silk thread. My insides quivered, and dots swam before my eyes as I watched the needle pierce Gideon's white skin, heard his moan, and saw his face twitch in pain on the pillow. Finally, the sewing was finished. As the old woman cut the thread. I saw that her stitches were as neat as those on Mother's samplers.

By the time the first streaks of dawn had penetrated the darkness outside the little cottage, Gideon's injuries had been cleaned with turpentine again and fresh bandages had been wrapped around his shoulder.

With the worst of the crisis past, fatigue turned my thoughts to mush and my legs to butter. I turned and embraced Mistress Blood, the feel of her slight body like that of Bethy's, her smell one of herbs and old age. "Thank you," I whispered. "Thank you for all you did."

"'Tis what our Maker sent me here to do." She smiled as she pulled away. "My bed awaits you."

Somehow I found the strength to shake my head. The next thing I knew, I'd curled up on the rug beside Gideon's bed, my arm a pillow for my head, my eyes closing in sleep.

Sometime later, I roused enough to know that a quilt and pillow had been added to my improvised bed and that Mistress Blood dozed in a chair but a foot or two away. Where Jake and Ezra were I didn't know, but I was aware that Ebony was curled on the bed next to Gideon, his soft purr assuring me that all was well.

Chapter Thirty-Two

It was midmorning before I wakened. Sunlight filtered through the dense branches of a lilac bush to dapple Gideon's bed with splashes of gold. Then all that had happened tumbled through my mind in a rush—Gideon's plight, Mistress Blood, and our fight to stop the bleeding.

I scrambled to my feet. Before I could take in more than his pale face on the pillow, Prudence Blood spoke.

"Your friend rests, and if fever doesn't set in, I think he'll live."

"Thank you." Relief and gratitude brimmed in my words. As I looked at Gideon, I saw that despite his pasty skin, he breathed as if asleep rather than unconscious. I brushed his brown hair away from his forehead and trailed my fingers along his cheek. "Gideon," I whispered.

His eyelids briefly fluttered open. In his fragile condition, I thought this his way of saying he loved and was aware of me too.

Easing down carefully onto the bed, I covered his hand with mine. After a brief moment, his fingers curled around them, their pressure as light as butterfly wings. Basking in his response, I smiled.

Mistress Blood spoke into the silence. "The tea leaves didn't lie, Mistress Abigail." Seeing my puzzlement, she went on. "Didn't the leaves say you would find a great love? And that there would be great danger to both you and the one you loved?"

The memory of that day returned. "As I recall, I asked if there would be marriage, and you said such would be up to me."

The ghost of a smile hovered around her mouth. "Have you made your decision yet?"

"I have." I looked down at Gideon, hoping that in some magical way, my loving gaze would heal him. "We will wed as soon as he is strong and well."

The old woman didn't speak for a moment, her fingers busy casting coarse gray wool over her needles, her gnarled, age-spotted hands moving as quickly as a woman's half her age.

With reluctance, I dragged my next words out of the dark hole into which they'd fallen. "You spoke of fever."

She nodded. "More times than not, a fever follows hard on the heels of wounds such as this."

"Can . . ." I had to force the words out of my mouth. "Can the fever be fatal?"

"It kills many." She raised her eyes from her knitting. "Much will depend on your friend's constitution and his will to live."

My gaze flew to Gideon, who breathed with no more strength than a kitten. Her words seemed to echo through the room like a rumble of thunder. "He is strong and a fighter," I declared as if my fervor could save his life.

"Then we, with God's help, will do our best to save him."

"I will do anything you ask me."

The little woman set her knitting into a basket and got to her feet. "As I have taught you, yarrow can stop bleeding and heal wounds. Elderberry is useful for fever." Her dark eyes met mine. "I'll leave you to tend your chosen man while I prepare more herbs to help him."

As she walked away, I saw that her back was bowed, the pain no doubt caused by her long sojourn in the chair. Guilt came but was quickly quelled when she paused and spoke.

"Your friend is not the first I've spent the night sitting up with . . . nor will he be the last. Instead of wasting your time feeling guilty, think on how God has given you the gift to heal. Though you are young, I shall need your hands and skill if we are to nurse your young man back to health."

For the next few hours, I did just that, sometimes sitting with Gideon but just as often helping Mistress Blood in her herb room and kitchen. We boiled or steeped crushed leaves and ground roots in pots over the fire, the pungent, spicy aroma wafting thick through the cottage. Twice, we laid warm poultices on Gideon's wounds and spooned teas and tinctures into his mouth. Though he was mostly unresponsive, I took hope each time I laid my hand on his forehead and felt no sign of fever.

Through my thoughts and prayers for Gideon, questions about Prudence Blood filled my mind. Along with her ability to read tea leaves, she seemed to possess the uncanny talent to read my heart and mind. Rather than making me uneasy, I felt even greater assurance in her gift to heal Gideon.

Toward noon, I went out back to get a breath of fresh air. As soon as I stepped out the door, Ebony ran to greet me. As I raised my head from petting him, I saw Jake mending the door to the chicken coop and Ezra drawing a pail of water from the well. Caught up in worry about Gideon, I'd almost forgotten about them.

"Jake," I called. Walking toward him, I saw that besides Mistress Blood's horse and cow, the two carriage horses grazed in the pasture.

"How's Mr. Whitlock?" he asked when I reached him.

"He's still unconscious, but Mistress Blood says that's to be expected after losing so much blood."

"Me'n Ezra been sayin' lots of prayers for him."

"We all have."

"The old woman seems to know lots 'bout healin', but—" He paused and looked at the old barn and cowshed. "This place is too much for a woman her age to keep up. While me'n Ezra wait for Mr. Whitlock to get better, we'll fix it up a bit."

"That would be wonderful." Noticing the old straw hat on his head and the hammer he held, I thought he looked to have made himself right at home.

"Where did you and Ezra sleep last night? And where's the carriage?"

"There was hay to sleep on in the barn. And the carriage . . ." He pointed with the hammer to a grove of trees on the other side of the pasture. "Not knowin' what Mr. Lind might do when he finds we took his carriage, I thought I'd better hide it."

"I've been so worried about Gideon I haven't even thought about Mr. Lind. Do you think Briggs untied him?"

"Probly so. If that colonel fellow got the letter Mr. Whitlock sent, maybe he's in jail. Just in case—" He pointed again at the grove.

I shaded my eyes and studied the trees. "I can't see it."

"That's 'cause me'n Ezra put branches over it."

"You've thought of everything."

"I been thinkin' all right . . . 'specially 'bout Mr. Lind. He's a hard man. Sure wouldn't like to have him follow us here. Does he know where you live?"

"Yes . . . though it's been years since he visited us. He doesn't know about Mistress Blood or where she lives though." I let out a sigh. "If he isn't in jail, I'm sure Mother and Mina and Mistress Lind have a plan to keep us safe."

Just as if Mother had heard me talking, she and the little cart Dolly pulled arrived at Mistress Blood's front gate.

"Abigail," she cried when I went out to greet her. She held me tight, and when she released me, tears were in her eyes. "What an ordeal you've been through. When I heard what Joseph did to Caroline . . . to you . . ." She pulled me to her again.

"We're safely away from him now. How is Aunt Caroline?"

"Surprisingly well. She says by tomorrow she'll be herself again. But it's you I worry about . . . and your friend." She paused and studied me.

I'm sure I looked a fright in blood-stained, rumpled clothing and with my hair uncombed. "I've taken little thought for myself."

"That you're safe is what's important. And your friend? How is he? Mina—what a help she's been—and Caroline are so concerned."

"He's very weak, but the bleeding has stopped, and Mistress Blood has sewn up his wounds."

I led her into the house and to the bedroom door. After looking at Gideon, she said, "I don't recall seeing him before."

"He attended Sabbath meeting with Charles Carter last February, but I doubt you noticed him."

Mother's eyebrows rose. "He's a Tory?"

I shook my head. "He's a patriot and Father's trusted friend."

Recognizing that now wasn't the time for questions, Mother went out to retrieve a basket from the cart. "Ben killed one of your hens, and I roasted it and boiled the heart and giblets to make a strengthening broth for your friend. There's bread and fresh-churned butter, and Goody Boatrick made a pudding."

As Mother set the items on the kitchen table, Mistress Blood looked up from straining yarrow leaves from a pot of water. "All are most welcome."

"I'll bring more tomorrow," Mother said. "Mina said her husband and son are staying here."

"They are."

When the old woman turned back to the yarrow, I walked out to the cart with Mother. Dolly nudged me when I stroked her neck. "Have you any news of Father?"

"He sent a letter last week with Reverend Whipple, who came home with a bad case of summer complaint . . . though Mistress Blood said 'tis likely camp fever. Your father wrote that he and the men are doing well and are daily awaiting an attack from the redcoats." She firmed her mouth before going on. "I do my best to keep up my spirits, but I own the waiting and not knowing is difficult."

I kissed her on the cheek. "I know."

As soon as Mother took up Dolly's reins, I hurried back into the cottage. After eating, I sent Mistress Blood to her bed to sleep and I took up my watch beside Gideon.

I felt his forehead to check for fever and whispered a fervent thank-you when I found it cool. Rather than sitting on the chair, I slipped to my knees to be closer to Gideon and took his hand. "I love you," I said, raising his hand to my lips.

"Abby."

Scarce believing my ears, I lifted my head. "Gideon."

The corners of his mouth lifted in a weak smile. "My . . . Abby."

As his green eyes held mine, I knew as clearly as if an angel had whispered it that Gideon would live.

★

A fortnight later, Gideon and I sat on the settle Jake had carried out to Prudence Blood's garden. Gideon's left arm was in a sling to protect his shoulder, and after much scrubbing and hours in the sun, the bloodstains on his shirt were hardly noticeable.

It was a lovely June morning, neither too hot nor too cool, and billowy clouds made graceful patterns across the blue arch of the sky. Red roses climbed in a blanket of color on a trellis, and the lofty heads of pink and red valerian vied for beauty against a border of foxglove.

Content to be in this idyll of fragrance and color and birdsong, neither of us felt the need for conversation. Instead, with my hand clasped firmly in Gideon's and our shoulders touching, we spoke a language of our own.

Ebony intruded when he came to rub his head against my skirt, his purr like the buzzing of bees. Without invitation, he jumped onto my lap and, after twice turning around, curled up in a pillow of black fur.

"It seems I'm not your only admirer." Gideon chuckled.

"Ebony and I have long been friends," I admitted. "More than once, Mistress Blood said she knew I was coming before I arrived. When I asked how she knew, she said Ebony had wished me there and told her."

"Interesting." Gideon's tone was amused. "Is she a witch and the cat her familiar?"

"Some in the village say 'tis so, but I . . ." I glanced at him and smiled. "I think she is but a woman blessed with great insight and the gift to heal."

Gideon nodded but said nothing.

"Do you know she dreamed of the battle of Concord two nights before it happened and that she waked from a dream but an hour before we came . . . a dream of a black man driving a carriage with me and a wounded man inside?"

Gideon's brows lifted. "Did her dream show that she healed me?"

I shook my head. "Only that you were coming."

"She did heal me." He raised my hand to his lips and kissed it. "You and Mistress Blood. I owe my life to you both."

"'Twas mostly Mistress Blood. I but followed her instruction. And God, of course. I've never said so many prayers."

"I felt each of them . . . and your hand on my brow . . . your voice pleading with me to live. Your love pulling me back from yawning darkness that threatened to suck me away." His voice broke, and he firmed his lips in apology for his weakness, one I knew galled him.

"I've thanked God for every breath you've taken since," I said. "That no fever came was a miracle. Mistress Blood and I are much pleased by your daily return of strength."

"The return of my strength can't come fast enough to suit me." His voice held traces of petulance, something the old woman assured me was common in one recovering from illness or serious injury.

"I've had much time for thinking though . . . what to do now that I've left Boston and how I can best serve the patriots. But mostly about you. About us."

"Yes," I prompted, eager to hear his plans and to perhaps add some of my own. "Just what are your thoughts about us?"

"With the times so uncertain, I didn't feel 'twas fair to declare myself in Boston. But now—" His hand tightened on mine. "If you'll have me, sweet Abby, I want very much to have you for my wife."

"'Tis my greatest wish also."

His smile deepened. "And would it pleasure you for us to wed as soon as I can ask and obtain your father's blessing?"

"'Tis an excellent idea and one with which I heartily agree."

"I suspected you would . . . though two days ago a heavy cloud of guilt told me I was selfish . . . that any man who truly loved a woman wouldn't wed, then leave her alone to wait and worry while he went off to fight. For fight I will if General Ward asks me."

"And I shall fight you if such guilty and noble thoughts overtake you again," I said with spirit.

"What if I leave you with child?"

"Your child would be the most precious gift you could give me."

With his good arm, he pulled me to him. "Sweet Abby. I should far sooner spend the short time we have as husband and wife than a courting couple who must be content with holding hands and stealing an occasional kiss when no one is looking."

He glanced at Mistress Blood's door, then at the barn before getting to his feet and pulling me with him. "Come," he said, holding tightly to my hand.

We traversed the length of Prudence Blood's garden, Gideon releasing my hand to put his arm around my waist, the hem of my skirt brushing the heads of johnny-jump-ups lining the path. When we passed the rose-covered trellis, Gideon pulled me to him, the glory of the blooms shielding us from prying eyes.

For a man with but one free arm and who'd been at death's door but a fortnight before, Gideon contrived to kiss me most thoroughly—softly and tenderly at first, then with the hunger and fervor of our first kiss in the hayloft. My fingers stroked his cheeks, then moved to encircle his neck and bring his mouth more firmly against mine. Birdsong and the sweet fragrances of roses were forgotten in the pleasure of his kiss.

'Twas but a week later when Gideon and I stood in the sitting room at Stowell farm to exchange our wedding vows before Reverend Whipple. Gideon, standing tall, without a sling and wearing borrowed clothes, responded to the reverend's questions in a voice that held no trace of weakness. Mine, though solemn, held excitement and the trembling of tears.

Whether Prudence Blood or Ebony played a part in bringing Father home before Reverend Whipple returned to the army, I do not know. But I do know Father gave his consent for Gideon to marry me, and he and Mother and Bethy sat on chairs but a few feet from where we stood—Father with a pleased expression on his face, Mother and Bethy wiping tears as they smiled.

Mistress Blood sat with Aunt Caroline and Mina, while Jake and Ezra stood behind them. Goody Boatrick and Jane and Ben were there as well. Ben had confided earlier that he'd ridden Dolly to Mistress Blood's cottage every day to make sure no crows sat on her roof.

I didn't mind that only a few of our closest friends attended our wedding. It was done to protect Gideon should Colonel Paxman be looking for him.

Father had cautioned but the day before. "The fewer who know Gideon's face and name, the better it will be." I, on the other hand, knew both face and name well. Hadn't I kissed and touched his face, and didn't I take his name as we exchanged our vows?

The kiss he gave me in the sitting room was chaste, though the twinkle in his green eyes told me such wouldn't be the case when we were alone. As for our future, I, like so many, knew much would depend on how events played out between the redcoats and patriots in the months ahead.

One thing I did know was that whether Gideon was spy or soldier, I would be near him. The troth we pledged this day had tightly bound my heart to his. So it would stay forever—whether following the army or aiding Gideon in games of wits against our enemy. Abigail and Gideon Whitlock would remain together for as long as God allowed.

Fictional Afterword

NOTHING WAS SEEN OR HEARD of Joseph Lind until after the Tories and redcoats abandoned Boston aboard British warships and sailed north to Nova Scotia in April 1776. Whether he languished as a prisoner on Crown Island or was set free as a broken man was never clearly known by those at Stowell farm. But he was later seen boarding one of the British ships just before it sailed out of Boston Harbor, and word was received later that he died aboard that ship.

As one of General Gage's aides, Colonel Paxman returned to England in October 1775 without ever discovering the whereabouts of Gideon Whitlock.

Jake, Mina, and Ezra remained at Stowell farm to help Mistress Stowell and Bethy run the home and farm. They also continued to help Mistress Blood.

Caroline Lind fully recovered her health and remained at Stowell farm until a year later when she learned that Joseph had died. She then went to Philadelphia to join her daughter and new grandbaby.

Historical Facts

April 18, 1775—Battle of Lexington-Concord.

April 20, 1775—The long siege of Boston begins.

May 4, 1775—General Howe arrives in Boston with an additional 4,500 British troops.

May 27, 1775—British raid Noddle's and Hog islands for hay and food.
Colonials—3 wounded.
British—2 killed, one schooner captured.

June 17, 1775—Battle of Bunker Hill (Breeds Hill).
Colonial casualties—140 killed, 271 wounded.
British casualties—245 killed, 828 wounded.
Short on ammunition, the colonials were ordered not to fire until they saw the whites of the redcoats' eyes. They repelled the first two assaults, but after running out of ammunition and having to resort to bayonets and rocks, they lost the last assault. The redcoats won the hills of Charles Town, Massachusetts (Bunker Hill). A member of British Parliament was heard to say, "A few more such victories will surely spell ruin for the victors."

July 3, 1775—George Washington, after being appointed as general of the colonial army, arrives in Cambridge and takes command.

October 1775—General Gage is recalled to England and is replaced by General Howe.

Fall of 1775—Washington begins to move part of the Continental army south to New York, where he believes the next battle will occur.

March 17, 1776—The siege of Boston ends when the British army and Tory citizens board British warships and sail north to Nova Scotia. The army later returns to New York.

July 4, 1776—The colonists declare their independence.

About the Author

IF, LIKE A CAT, I had nine lives, I would live eight of them in the past. When I was young, I loved to dress up in long skirts and pretend I lived in olden times and had wonderful adventures. As an adult, I put my heroines in my historical novels in long skirts and take them on adventures all over the world as they are rescued by aboriginies, help a slave escape to freedom, or become a spy. My imagination still whispers tales to me, and who knows what wonderful adventures and plots I'll come up with next—maybe the fate of a young woman who is born on the night of an eerie moon eclipse!